TEN
SECONDS TO
TOTAL
EXPOSURE

L.A. CLAYTON

Ten Seconds to Total Exposure
Copyright © 2020 L.A. Clayton
Cover Art by Becky Monson

To John. I love my life with you.

CHAPTER 1

Wales
Kate

"This better be it," I said, as I looked over at Jake Lyon, who no longer looked like Jake Lyon.

We stood on a small bluff overlooking the quaint, traditional stone cottage in the middle of nowhere, Wales. The home was several shades of gray, fashioned from stones of varying sizes, in width as well as length. It had two chimneys, a simple white front door, and only a few windows. The surrounding area was verdant and lush; a large portion of the cottage itself had greenery growing up the stone walls. It looked almost as if the vines were growing out of the stones themselves. The road that ran by the house, if one could call it a road, was just two small dirt tracks that cut through the roughage. There was a herd of sheep blocking the small gate that led to the front door.

We had spent a month looking for Nigel Brown. He'd hidden himself well. We'd traipsed all over Great Britain trying to search out the man my father had told me to find just before his death. All of our efforts had led us to this cottage. After this, we were told, we would have to give up trying to find him and start elsewhere to take down the Alternate Government Initiative, or the AGI, as we most commonly referred to it. I really wanted to find Nigel, though; my dad had left important information with him, and I wanted to know what it was.

"Only one way to find out," was Jake's response.

We began our descent to the cottage, neither one of us talking. Once we made our way down the bluff, we crossed a dry riverbed. We were just steps away from the cottage gate, making our way through the bleating sheep, when the smell hit us.

"Noooooo!" Frustrated, I fisted my hands and kicked the dirt beneath my feet. Jake groaned. Whoever was inside the cottage, they were no longer breathing and hadn't been for at least a week.

After a long, hard sigh, Jake gave my shoulder a squeeze and said, "Come on, let's see if it's our guy." Jake tapped the comm in his ear, "Fin, Scarborough, whoever's inside is dead; we're going to check it out."

"Fantastic, let's get this over with," Scarborough, our mission leader, sounded in both of our ears, his tone equal parts irritated and relieved. I looked over to Jake and rolled my eyes. Scarborough had never wanted us to look for Nigel in the first place—he felt like it was a waste of time. I didn't agree at all. I felt that finding Nigel was paramount; he had information, the information that my dad had collected, which, granted, was eleven years old now. But surely Nigel had information of his own as well. Nigel was an AGI agent gone rogue, and as far as I was concerned, he was absolutely worth finding. We needed somewhere to start.

"Approaching door." We both had our guns out and were taking all precautions. It hadn't slipped my mind that this could be a setup. Which, frankly, wouldn't have been so bad; the last month had been incredibly boring.

Jake knocked on the door. "Hello? Anyone there?" No answer. He nodded to me, and I gave the door a hard kick. It slammed open, and the smell was ten times worse; the reek of decay was something I could have gone the rest of my life without ever smelling again. I could hear flies buzzing around their feast before I even caught sight of him.

"What the . . . ," Jake began, but couldn't even end his sentence. I gasped and then went into a coughing fit at the smell and taste of decay that was so prevalent in the air. "What the . . . ," Jake said again. I looked at him, and I knew that the utter shock and confusion on his face was mirrored on my own.

I was shaking my head, perplexed, while looking all around the main living area where Nigel's dead body lay. Even in his decaying state I knew that it was him; I'd studied enough pictures of him over the last month of searching to know for sure.

"What is going on?" Scarborough's voice drew us out of our trance.

I looked to Jake, hoping he would speak first. "Well . . ." He tilted his head to the side and scratched his neck, his expression revealing that he had no words for the scene spread out before us. "It's Nigel."

"And . . . ?" A few beats passed, and neither one of us responded to Scarborough's prompting. How did you tell someone what you were looking at when your brain could barely make sense of it?

I did my best anyway. "Well, um . . . uh . . . you know what? I'm going to put a camera on." I pulled out a camera from a pocket of my catsuit and turned it on; it wirelessly connected to my phone and the secure line we used for transmitting video. I held it up and slowly did a circle so they could see the entire room, as well as Nigel's body.

Scarborough did not hold back his surprise and let out some colorful language. "My thoughts exactly . . . ," Jake finally spoke again.

The room was covered floor to ceiling in black and red marker. The entirety of the walls and floor, including the spines of the books in the bookcase, had been written on. Everything was written on. There were a lot of complicated equations, and statements that were underlined and followed by several exclamation points. Some sentences made sense, while others seemed to be complete gibberish. Over and over he'd written "Search" and "DNA" and "murder" and "NOS is killing me." "NOS" was everywhere, on every surface, everywhere we looked.

"What or who the hell is NOS?" Scarborough sounded in my ear again.

I shook my head. "I don't know . . . NOS . . . I never heard anything about it at the AGI." NOS . . . I kept rolling the acronym over in my mind, though, because there was something about it that triggered my brain, but I couldn't figure out why. That was new for me; I remembered everything, especially if I'd read it. So I knew that it wasn't something I'd read, but maybe something I'd heard and not committed to memory? Still it tugged at my brain, like my subconscious knew it and was trying to bring it to the surface but couldn't.

Scarborough spoke again, "Bring me closer to the body."

I did as he asked, but Jake held me back from getting too close. "Nigel was killed by a virus of some sort. His bodily fluids are still wet and may contain some of the live virus." He looked at Nigel and couldn't help the shudder that went through his body. "That is not something we want spreading."

I nodded and walked the camera over to about a foot from some of the gore. The scene was horrific. This was not the aftermath of an AGI "heart attack." His mouth and eyes were open, and he had blood coming from every visible orifice. His bowels had emptied, and the fluid was filled with blood and clumps of what were probably his organs. His body was skin and bone, but it was hard to know whether that was from the virus or from the length of decay. It was then that I realized that we should have been in hazmat suits. We shouldn't have been anywhere near that body.

"You guys need to get out of there." This time it was Fin that spoke. "I have no idea what virus that is, but it looks a lot like a sister to Ebola, or maybe Marburg. It's hard to tell; there are clear signs of both, but also neither. Get out of there. Ebola can live for days at room temperature without a living host. His bodily fluids are all over that place whether you can see them or not. Get out now."

Jake already had his hand on my arm, ready to pull me to the door. "Hang on, we haven't touched anything, and we'll burn our shoes when we leave here, but we need to document this. I want to get pictures of both Nigel and his writings."

Fin sounded in my comm again, "Kate, those so-called *writings* are from the mind of a man dying with fever. In the end, most viruses cause psychosis. They could be, and most likely are, meaningless."

"Shouldn't we at least get a sample?"

Scarborough spoke up, "We have enough, Kate; we're recording the video feed. We will alert the British authorities regarding the illness. It's time for you to go."

I knew I needed to leave, but there was important information there; I could feel it. That information could be just what we needed to take out the AGI. It was hard for me to leave without time to study and read it all. And though I was frantically reading on the way out the door, I did eventually let Jake pull me all the way out of the cottage.

CHAPTER 2

New York City, NY
Oliver

"Oliver, you were amazing." Valentina, Oliver's "wife," whispered excitedly into his ear as they walked off the stage, her arm weaved through his. She wasn't wrong; the interview had gone off without a hitch.

"You think so?" Oliver craved Valentina's approval. She was gorgeous with her long, dark hair and blue eyes. She was poised and practically perfect in any situation; Oliver loved the times when they were in public together and got to play husband and wife. Her attention was on only him, and her touch and affection felt so good that he just wanted to be in public more often so he could get another hit.

She smiled at him and winked. "You know you were great up there. Couldn't you feel that you had the audience wrapped around your finger? The host, too, for that matter. Everyone loves you, Oliver." She gave his arm a squeeze.

"Any chance you are falling under my spell, my lovely wife?" He looked at her with his eyebrows raised and a coy smile on his face.

Normally she would give him a derisive look and tell him, in a kind way, not to get his hopes up. But that day she looked deeply into his eyes, and with a smile, said, "I just might be, Oliver."

He felt a rush of blood go through his body at her answer. Valentina had been Oliver's "wife" for two and a half years. They were married in Oliver's home state of New Hampshire in a courthouse with only a few friends in attendance soon after he was hired on at the Alternate Government Initiative. Oliver was an actor, and he was hired by the AGI as such. He'd attended the Yale School of Drama and doubled majored in political science, but acting was his real passion. Oliver also considered himself an activist, though admittedly his political opinions tended to be more of the moment and he could be easily swayed by a good argument.

Oliver was an attractive man. He was tall at 6'2", but not too tall. He had dark-brown hair streaked with gray at the temples that was always perfectly coiffed into a modern pompadour. His skin was so fair, and his hair was so dark, that no matter how close his shave, he always appeared to have a five-o'clock shadow. The AGI kept him dressed impeccably in expensive suits and shoes that weren't too showy. The goal was to have him appear down to earth but also elevated in a way that inspired emulation.

Oliver heard the women all around them talking backstage; it was always thus. He could see their eyes get bigger as he neared, their cheeks pinking, and he could hear murmurs of "it's Oliver Strands" and "so hot." He overheard one woman say, "I wouldn't mind a congress with that guy . . ." That one was rather clever, as he was the newly appointed congressman for the state of New Hampshire, and he found himself holding back a laugh. He gave the group of women one of his signature smiles and a nod. "Ladies." Valentina never seemed to be affected by the attention he received, though he wished she would be.

It was a strange predicament, being married but not really *married*. A man had needs, and his were not being met. And yet, he knew he couldn't have a whiff of scandal on him. It was part of the job that he was being paid handsomely for. A job he was loath to give up, not only because of the notoriety and instant fame but also because of the contract. The contract was intense, and frankly a little insane. He had signed his life away with that contract. There would be no messing around with anyone, regardless of his desire.

Oliver and Valentina made their way back to their dressing room, and as soon as the door was closed, he turned to Valentina and pulled her in for a tight hug. "Wired?" Valentina asked with a smile.

Oliver laughed. "How'd ya guess?" He pulled back and went to run his hands through his hair but stopped himself before he wrecked the perfectly styled strands. He instead fisted his hands at his sides to keep himself from ruining his look or touching his wife in the ways he craved. He huffed a humorless laugh and swore. "The high from a successful interview on national television is amazing; I just need a few minutes to calm myself down."

"That wasn't just a show on national television, Oliver; that was *The Late Nite Show*. You're becoming a sensation, just like I knew you would." Valentina threw herself onto the couch like she'd just finished a marathon. She probably felt like she had. She was Oliver's coach and trainer. She was the one who told him what to say and how to say it. For the last two and a half years she had groomed him into the politician that the AGI wanted him to be. They worked every hour of the day that he wasn't meeting with the congressional House and his other various committees. Before his step up to Congress, the AGI had placed Oliver as a state senator, which was a much easier job. Since he'd been appointed to the office of Congress things had been much busier and far more intense. He and Valentina spent so much time training that they barely slept these days. Oliver was exhausted. But these moments made it all worth it.

After a minute or two of calming himself down, he sat on the couch with Valentina, sitting himself close but not too close. "That was pretty amazing, being featured on the *The Late Nite Show*. I always hoped that would happen for me someday—not necessarily as a politician, but it was amazing regardless."

"Oh, Oliver, this is only the beginning." Valentina looked over at him with her big blue eyes, and he could see the determined excitement on her face.

"There's something after this?" He knew that the AGI had a plan for him, but he thought this was it. He was happy to hear that there was more because he didn't want to give up his paycheck anytime soon.

Valentina laughed. "Of course there is!" She turned so they were facing each other and grabbed the lapels of his jacket, bringing his face mere inches from hers. She looked him in the eye and said, "Oliver, didn't you know? We are going to make you the most powerful man in the free world."

CHAPTER 3

Washington, D.C.
Kate

I growled. "There is good information here, I know it." Frustrated, I got up from the computer and paced the length of the conference room; I didn't need to look at the computer to study it anyway. The images were imprinted in my mind.

"There probably is, but we would have to work through all of the asinine garbage to find it." Fin the Genius sat staring at his computer, shaking his head. "The truth is, the bulk of this is gibberish. The correct complex mathematical equations are the only thing keeping me tethered to the idea that Nigel Brown's brain was still functioning on a coherent level."

Jake and I were back in D.C., and together with our team we were studying the writings of the dying Nigel Brown. We had verified through a handwriting sample that it was indeed Nigel who had written all over the walls of his rental. The problem was they seemed more like nonsensical ramblings than anything useful. But why would he take the time to write it all down if it weren't for a purpose? He was trying to send a message; unfortunately the message made absolutely no sense.

We were all seated around a large boat-shaped, espresso-colored conference table. We met in rented office space in D.C. that changed fairly often, to keep ourselves hidden. We'd been meeting in the current space for the past week since Jake and I had returned from the UK. Aside from me, everyone was at a computer; we were all studying the writings, trying to grasp for anything at all that might help us. All twenty-two of us. I could tell that Scarborough was getting irritated. We'd spent so much time looking for Nigel and to no avail. We were still at square one.

Dr. Williams and Dr. Bakshi, the two doctors who had operated on me twice—once in an attempt to remove the Implantable Cardiac Terminator, or ICT, from my heart and the second time when they actually did remove it—were part of our group. They were good doctors and had worked for the CIA for many years. Dr. Williams was the surgeon; he was older, sixty perhaps, with white hair and bright-blue eyes. Dr. Bakshi was a diagnostic specialist; he had a slight Indian accent and appeared to be in his forties, with rich brown skin and eyes so dark brown that his pupils almost disappeared. They were frustrated as well, though they were looking at images of Nigel's body as opposed to his messages. Dr. Bakshi let out a breath that he had been holding in his cheeks. "This doesn't look exactly like anything we've seen before. Fin was right that it does look like Ebola, but it also doesn't. It has signs of Marburg, but it also doesn't. Maybe both?"

Jake cut in, "That would be the world's worst luck."

Dr. Bakshi nodded. "Indeed. Though there would have to be more than bad luck involved. There are no known cases of Ebola currently, and we haven't seen any Marburg outbreaks since two thousand five. If Nigel was infected with a combination of deadly viruses, then he was given them; he didn't catch them." He shook his head. "It's impossible to know what we are dealing with until we hear back from the Centre of Infectious Disease Surveillance and Control in London."

I snapped my fingers once and said, "Dr. Chang in Montana—he had a lab, and he's the one who creates medications that make agents sick enough to require surgery so that the AGI could implant the ICTs. Could he be making other viruses?"

Dr. Bakshi pursed his lips and cocked his head to the side while he contemplated. "He could, but that would be a rather expensive and unproductive way of killing someone. A nine millimeter round costs fewer than fifteen cents. Why spend years and outrageous amounts of money creating a deadly virus that only works if you get close enough to the person to infect them and then wait for the weeks that it takes the virus to kill them? Unless you're planning on spreading a pandemic or epidemic, what would be the point?"

"What if they are planning to spread a pandemic or epidemic? Perhaps Nigel was just the first," Megan, one of the CIA officers in our group, cut in. Megan was in her mid-thirties and had well-styled long blonde hair and blue eyes. Looking at her made me a little melancholy. I missed my blonde hair and blue eyes.

Jake responded, "That doesn't make any sense. Nigel was on the run. He was renting Airbnb after Airbnb under false names. Only staying for days sometimes. If he has any living family, they are well in hiding; he was always alone. Why attempt to spread a pandemic through a recluse?"

Megan shrugged. "They could have been testing it out."

Jake rubbed his chin. "If the AGI killed him, it would be to send a message."

Fin jumped in, as always. He couldn't help himself; he always had to prove he was the smartest person in the room. Which may have been true, but it was annoying to have it rubbed in your face all the time. "And whom would that message be for, exactly?" He rolled his eyes. "The AGI has no idea that we are looking for Nigel. They know of no connection between Edison and Nigel. They don't know that we even know that he was an agent of the AGI."

"Unless they found the thumb drive left by Edison's dad," another officer piped in.

"Kate's computer was scrubbed, and everything in it was shredded, by me. The thumb drive was destroyed. They don't know we were looking for Nigel Brown," Jake responded.

There was a chorus of noise at that point. I could make out some phrases: "That makes no sense" and "How do we know what the AGI knows?" and "We need someone on the inside." That last one made me incredibly irritated. We had people on the inside. We had Lena and Brahim and Liam, not to mention a whole group, granted I didn't know how big of a group, of AGI agents who had formed a resistance. We had people; we just needed to get to them.

I got up and left the room. I couldn't think with all of the noise and commotion in the boardroom. I worked best with quiet and solitude. I was losing my mind stuck in a room with a whole bunch of people yelling out their thoughts.

I walked into the bathroom and splashed some cool water on my face. I looked up into the mirror at the foreign reflection looking back at me. It had been almost six weeks since the CIA had changed my appearance, and it still shocked me every time I saw myself. My once naturally blonde hair had been colored brown. Not a pretty, rich dark brown, but a mousy, ashy, light brown that in fluorescent lighting looked slightly green. My once-blue eyes were covered in brown contacts: again, not caramel brown or golden brown or even dark chocolate brown—they were the most boring color of flat brown contacts available. I was given a foaming tanning lotion that I used every other day religiously. That part I did kind of like; my skin had always been incredibly pale, and with the help of the constant application of the tanning lotion my skin had a rich, golden glow that it could never attain naturally. Though my pretty, golden tan made my hair and eyes look that much mousier.

I hated looking at myself in the mirror. I hated it so much, and yet there was also a comfort in looking virtually unrecognizable. The AGI was quietly looking for me everywhere. The one benefit that I had was that since the AGI was an illegal organization, they couldn't go through legal means to find me. No one would see my picture on a most-wanted list, nor would I have an official warrant out for my arrest. They were looking for me, but they would have to find me the old-fashioned way. Yes, they could employ facial recognition software, but they would have to catch me on camera, and for all of the power the AGI had, they didn't have access to, nor could they keep watch of all the security cameras in the world. If they found me, it would be because luck was on their side, not technology. For all they knew, I could have fled the country, which is what the CIA had made it look like. Someone used my passport to buy a one-way plane ticket to São Paulo. And my credit cards were consistently being used to rent hotels and buy food in various places in Brazil.

There was a gentle knock on the bathroom door. "Just a minute," I said, just loudly enough for whoever was on the other side to hear. I just needed one more minute to gather myself together.

"Kaylee?" I heard Jake's muffled voice come through the closed door.

I couldn't help succumbing to the chuckle that bubbled up. The CIA had set both Jake and me up with new identities. According to my driver's license, passport, and bank accounts, my name was Kaylee Edwards, and Jake was now Jason Leopold. Neither of us liked our new names, and we often razzed each other by using them even when we were out of the public eye. Honestly, why Kaylee of all names? It made me sound like a Southern cheerleader, a thing I definitely was not.

I opened the door. "Leopold? Is that you?" Jake smiled and walked into the bathroom, shutting and the door behind him. As difficult as it was to get used to my new "look," I saw Jake so often that I was quickly getting used to seeing him in his new persona. Admittedly, I missed his gorgeous copper hair, but the dark brown he now wore made him no less attractive. He wore his beard full, dyed dark brown as well, but the coarse copper strands were stubborn, and in the light his beard still shone red. His gray eyes were now green, and he was also given a tanning lotion to use, but it made his skin much darker than mine did. He looked like a different ethnicity, and it was not a bad look on him. Jake Lyon could probably never look unattractive, no matter what they changed about his looks.

It felt weird and nice to be alone together for a few precious minutes. We were hardly ever alone these days. When we were traipsing through the UK, both Scarborough and Fin had been with us; we were alone only when we were out in the field looking for Nigel. And even then, they were always with us on our comms.

Jake's smiling face at my teasing changed to concern. "You okay?"

I nodded, slowly. "Mostly. It's hard for me to think clearly with the whole group. I just needed a few minutes of quiet."

"Do you want me to leave?" Jake grabbed my hand and gave it a squeeze and released it just as quickly, letting me know that he wouldn't be offended if I said yes.

"No, I'm ok. I'm just frustrated and stressed out." I took a deep breath and let it out quickly. "I hate that Lena and Liam are stuck in the AGI right now and either think that I am a traitor to my country or, worse, that I left them there to rot. I'm frustrated that we have a resistance within the AGI that we aren't using. It just seems like this is all taking such a long time and there is so much to do. We've been sitting in that office for over a week now, and we are no further along than we were when we started."

"Ha! Welcome to working for the *real* government." He winked, and we both laughed because the joke was funny and also true. "It can be really frustrating, and I know that you want to see quicker progress, but we can't just walk into the Montana AGI facility and find your friends." He rubbed my arm, and goose bumps exploded down my limbs. "We can't afford to be single minded; there is a big picture here."

I moved so that he was no longer touching me. He looked momentarily frustrated at my moving away from him, but his touch was a sweet kind of torture for me. Nothing had happened between us since I'd signed on with the CIA. I kind of expected as much, but it was difficult for me to just turn off my feelings—a lot more difficult for me than for Jake, apparently. Unless he was going to touch me with purpose, I really didn't want him touching me at all. It was too hard, and it made me weirdly angry at him. I knew in the logical part of my mind that I had no real reason to be angry with him, but I was, nonetheless. This is why companies discourage romantic relationships among employees. It's fun to work with someone you are attracted to, and even more fun when that attraction is reciprocated, but it is truly awful when the other person cuts it off and you are left working day to day with someone you still pine over.

I had to work hard to set aside my personal feelings for Jake, because the truth was, Jake Lyon was an incredible human being. He was remarkably talented and incomparably smart, and we worked very well together. I knew, deep down, that working on this with Jake and our team was the best chance I had at ridding the world of the AGI. I would not blow our working relationship over a crush.

"I'm not trying to be single-minded, Jake. Aside from being my friends, they are people who could help us from the inside. And what about the resistance?"

"I'm thrilled that there's a resistance; I can't wait to find out how big it is and what they have already accomplished. But you are only thinking about Montana, and the United States. This organization is worldwide. We don't even know how much, if anything, the AGI staff at the Montana facility know about the organization as a whole. There is a good chance that the Montana facility offers us little to nothing on the worldwide scale, whereas if we can take the AGI out at the source, then all of the people in the Montana facility will be freed automatically. And not just them, but every AGI agent in the world."

"I get that, Jake, I really do. But they are my friends and they're important to me." I felt tears prick my eyes, and I blinked them back, but my choked voice gave my emotions away anyway. "I don't even know what's happening to them. Liam didn't shoot me in the outpost when he could have, and the agent he was working with knew it. Who knows how he was punished? Lena could have been tortured for more information on me, even though she really doesn't have much. I don't know what's happening to them, and it's haunting my dreams."

Jake nodded and reached out to touch me again but thought better of it and pulled his arm back before he got too close. "I know you've been worried. And I can tell that you haven't been sleeping well, and that worries me. I am concerned for your friends and the state of the AGI facility in general without Westwood, but we can't forget that the AGI employs tens of thousands and possibly hundreds of thousands of people and that all of those people are important to someone. They are brothers and sisters, mothers and fathers, sons and daughters, and friends to people who love them. They are all important, and through the CIA, we just might help them all."

I closed my eyes and nodded. He was right, but I was still unhappy. I stiffened slightly when I felt his arms go around me and his warm breath at my ear. "I care about the things and people you care about, Kate. I can't help myself. I promise I will do all that I can to get your friends to safety."

Jake didn't let go, and I felt some of the tension that I had been carrying drain out of me; that was the promise I'd needed. Jake Lyon promised to help my friends, and he did not make promises lightly. It was as much as I could ask for. "Thank you, Jake."

"Hey, that's Leopold to you."

I smiled and rolled my eyes at the same time. He pulled away, and we walked back to the boardroom for another round of brainstorming.

CHAPTER 4

Palo Alto, CA
Vinny

Search was not a bad place to work. The facility was nothing short of amazing: the Search complex had over one and a half million square feet of office space and even more square footage dedicated to various break activities, including game rooms, swimming pools, gyms, bowling lanes, and two full-size basketball courts, to name a few. The facility boasted fifteen cafeterias that felt more like restaurants, offering as wide a variety of foods as one could imagine. The salaries were as high as the workload, and they weren't afraid to pay their employees what they were worth.

Vincent Anthony Rossi, better known as Vinny, was twenty-eight years old and had been working for Search since he'd received his master's in behavioral science at Stanford. He was a research scientist for Search, and if he could manage it, he planned on retiring with the company. Vinny was from the Bronx, and he had no intention of living through the bitterly cold New York winters ever again, despite his mother's near-constant guilt trips.

Vinny was prepping for his Tuesday morning meeting but kept getting sidetracked by the sand volleyball game going on out his office window. His coworker Tracy was out there in her short spandex shorts and sports bra, and he couldn't manage to keep his mind, nor his eyes, on his work. Tracy was the epitome of a California girl, with her bleached blonde hair and deeply tanned skin. She never wore makeup, and she was fit and funny and super laid back. She was supposed to be at the meeting, too, and she would be. In a few short minutes Tracy would run her sweaty body back to the office they shared and throw on a graphic T-shirt—perhaps with a swear word or two written on it, because Search was cool like that—and some low-slung board shorts and head straight to the first-floor conference room. Without a care in the world.

Vinny was not like Tracy. He was wearing a long-sleeved collared white work shirt and tie with suit pants and a belt that matched his well-polished shoes. His skinny tie was the only thing marking him as a millennial. He tried to get back to his work but was mentally counting down the minutes until the hurricane that was Tracy whirled her way into their office.

He could hear her running shoes on the floor outside their office door, and he looked up to see her bounding into the office in all of her golden, sweaty glory. He swallowed and tried to force his eyes to look elsewhere. "Hey, Cousin Vinny!" Tracy said in her terrible impression of a New York accent. Vinny was well used to the *My Cousin Vinny* jokes, as he was a first-generation American in a very Italian family from New York. No one from home ever made *My Cousin Vinny* references, but as soon as he moved to California for school, they came at him nonstop. He'd made it a point to watch the movie shortly after arriving. He liked it but wasn't thrilled with the constant comparisons to Joe Pesci. Their only similarities were their dark hair and their New York accents.

Tracy came over and tousled his short brown curly hair. Didn't she know that you didn't mess with curly hair once it was styled? Apparently not, because she did it every single day. And it half annoyed him and half endeared her to him every single day, just like everything else about Tracy. "Hey, Tracy, I see you've put in a lot of effort for our meeting this morning . . . as usual." He gave her a flat look. He didn't really know how to act around her; she was just so much to wrap his brain around.

She laughed as she donned her T-shirt, grains of sand falling to the floor. This one said "Strange Fur Things" and had a picture of cats dressed up like the *Stranger Things* characters. "Playing volleyball *is* me putting in effort; it clears my mind and gets me ready to get my head in the game." She winked at him.

Vinny gave her T-shirt a pointed look and said, "You do know that research shows that people work more effectively when they are in appropriate work attire." Truth was he liked Tracy's T-shirts, but he had to give her a hard time about it because that was their shtick.

She smirked—"Research, sme-search"—and headed out the door.

He grabbed his laptop as well as hers and followed a handful of steps behind her and said, "You know that we're research scientists, right? Research is literally what we do for a living."

She turned her pretty head back toward him and laughed.

Vinny found the meeting slightly disturbing, as usual. He shrugged it off, gave Tracy's muscular, tanned legs a once-over, and reminded himself that Search was not a bad place to work.

CHAPTER 5

Washington, D.C.
Kate

"The results are in." Dr. Bakshi looked even more confounded than before. He kept looking at his screen and then looking back up, opening his mouth to talk, and then he would shake his head and look back at his screen. Just when we were all about to lose our minds, he said, "It's Ebola, but different. It's contained to just Nigel and perhaps his children if they have the same genetic markers. No one else could get it. The virus was formulated for his DNA." Dr. Bakshi shook his head again. "Nigel had a virtually noncontagious strain of Ebola."

"How is that even possible?" Megan with the long blonde hair asked.

"It would take a brilliant mind and a knowledge of the DNA of the person you want to kill to do it. And not just a blood test, but a deep DNA testing. The DNA markers used to make Nigel's strain of Ebola are markers that are rarely screened in any normal sampling." He shook his head again. "But it would be expensive and take years to get it just right. Not to mention the mistakes and miscalculations, there would have to be trials, no one would get this right in the first go, probably not even the hundredth. I've never heard of people dying of a personal strain of Ebola until just now, and this is my jurisdiction within the CIA. If it was happening around the world, I would have heard of it."

"What is the UK going to do with the results?" Scarborough scratched his head and mused aloud. "Perhaps we only heard of it because we were the ones who found the body and asked for the test results? Maybe countries are keeping this quiet?"

"How could they keep something like this quiet? It's protocol to alert the World Health Organization of an Ebola outbreak," Jake chimed in.

"It's not exactly an outbreak, though." I threw my thoughts in the ring: "What if they were testing people in rural areas of third world countries? Places where they might find a dead body and just bury them instead of running tests? There are plenty of areas of the world where a dead body may even just get left around and ignored. If the virus never spread and a real outbreak never occurred, there's a good chance it would never be shared with the World Health Organization."

"Not likely," Fin the Genius spoke up. "How would they have a sample of some random person's DNA from some random place in the world? Think of the work it would take to get that information. They would have to pick the person and get out to them in someplace like rural Africa, sample their DNA, do extensive testing and make that person's strain of the virus, and then go back out to give it to them. And then they would want to test the body after to make sure it had worked like they'd planned. That would be the world's biggest waste of time. They probably have a compound."

Normally I bristled at being wrong; it was an immature reaction, but it was typically mine, nonetheless. That seemed to be happening less and less the more I was around Fin; he was often right, and I was starting to appreciate his commentary, even if he was more than a little smug about it. "Right, a compound makes sense. Where could it be?"

Mark shrugged and chimed in, "It could be any one of the usual suspects: Russia, Middle East, China?" Mark was in his thirties. He had a wife and two daughters, and it was clear that he loved them dearly. His family was the screen saver on his computer and the wallpaper on his phone. It was hard to fathom how people with spouses and children could work in this area of the CIA without wanting to build them an underground bunker and hide them away forever. It was in the CIA that you learned just how incredibly dangerous the world could be.

My family was in hiding, for their safety I had no idea where, and I worried about them every day. I wished I knew how they were handling their new identities and new hometown. I was forever curious about how my little nephew, named John after our father, was doing. I wanted to know when he started crawling and what his first words would be. I wondered how my sister, who loved romance and dating and couldn't wait to get married and have children, was faring, under her new identity. Did she have a hard time not being honest about who she was? She was an actress, and I had no doubt that her skills could extend beyond the stage, but how would that ever lead to something lasting? What if she fell in love—could she withstand the urge to tell him the truth? For her sake as well as the rest of my family's, I really hoped so. I knew, though, that my questions would have to go unanswered until the AGI was destroyed and the threat against my family was neutralized. It made me even more anxious to get the job done.

Jake weighed in, "It could be, but it could also be from anywhere; this is not just a threat against the United States, it's a threat against the world." He rubbed his forehead. "Also, we have to acknowledge the fact that this may not be connected to the AGI."

"Of course they're connected! It's Nigel Brown we're talking about—AGI agent gone rogue. They have every reason to want him dead." My voice was rising; I knew I was on the verge of yelling and I needed to calm down. This is how we talked things out in this group. Everyone threw out ideas, and it helped us come to a better conclusion than any of us could have come to on our own.

Jake threw his hands up in mock surrender. "Okay, but think about this: the AGI had no reason to suspect that you knew anything about Nigel Brown. There is almost no way to connect the two of you. We also don't know if the AGI knew he had gone rogue. Nigel worked for the AGI for a pretty long time. Who knows what he was into while working for them or what people he could have pissed off. The AGI involves themselves with many a shady character. One of them could have done this just as easily."

I stood up, angry and adamant that this was connected to the AGI. "Lyon! This is part of what the AGI does! They mess with medications. They are masters at lowering heart rates and making people believe that their appendix has ruptured. It is just a small step, and a smart one at that, for them to get into the business of personalized viruses. It was the AGI."

With his hands still in the air, he said, "Nigel wrote a lot of messages in his last days, and not once did he write AGI. Not once in all of his ramblings."

I threw myself back into my chair, defeated, because he was right. Nigel didn't mention the AGI. Why? Who else could have done this to him? I roughly rubbed my eyes with my fists and growled, "So we are no further than we were before. We are still right where we started."

I knew Jake wanted to come and talk to only me, but we were in a room with twenty other officers and he was several chairs down from me, and it would have looked weird. Even though he wasn't right next to me, his words soothed me like a caress. "Kate, all information is good information. If it wasn't the AGI who did this, then we will find out who it was, and we will trace them back to the AGI. We can use them to propel our investigation. We will find the AGI's weak spot, and we will destroy them."

"If Jake is right, we need someone on the inside," a female agent named Candace said.

That was it, I may have lost it a little bit when I yelled, "We have someone on the inside! More than one person, actually! We just need to get to them, and they could help us!"

Anthony Scarborough, our fearless leader, stood up. "Okay, everyone, let's just calm down a bit." By "everyone," he meant me. "Kate, I know there are people on the inside who can and will help us, and when the time is right, we will go to them. Dr. Murphy and Nurse Clary are at the top of my list. But when we do, their lives will be at stake"—he held up his hand to the objection on the tip of my tongue—"even more than they are right now. Asking them to help will be a big deal and risk. One I am willing to take, but not until the time is right."

"What about Lena? She is a computer wizard and could do a lot of undetectable work for us."

"We can't be sure where Lena's loyalties lie," Scarborough objected.

"Yes, we can. I worked with her for months. Lena is on our side."

Jake piped in, "I trust Edison's judgment. She hasn't led us wrong yet."

"I believe that Edison believes that Lena Johnson is clean. However, we also know that the AGI trains their employees to lie convincingly. They are scrupulous in their underhandedness." Scarborough looked around the room at the officers and made his point crystal clear. "Every person in this room has unknowingly worked with at least one AGI agent, and we are all trained to spot exactly that sort of thing. It's just too much risk."

I took a deep breath. "I understand what you're saying, but it's a risk that I think we should take. Lena is clean. She has been implanted with the ICT, for crying out loud."

Scarborough nodded. "That's just one more reason not to use her yet. If she is clean, and I do believe the probability of that is good, then we would be endangering her even more."

Fin finally spoke up, "Why don't we find her and test her? She should be out in the field now, right?" He looked to me and I nodded. "Then let's set Kate up as bait and see if Lena turns her in."

Jake stood up. "Absolutely not."

I stood up and countered, "Why? It's perfect! I can prove to you all that she's clean, and we can finally have someone on the inside." I looked around the table. "We all agree that we need someone on the inside." There were several nods. "Then let's find her."

Jake looked at me, and if looks could kill, I would have definitely died on the spot. "No. No way. It's too dangerous, and Kate is too valuable to lose. I'll do it. Lena hasn't met me, but she knows of me. I'll act like I'm looking for Kate too; she'll turn me over if she's loyal to the AGI."

"No, she won't. If she's loyal to the AGI, she'll tell them, and they will track you to me. It's me they want; I am the best person for this job. I'll do it." I looked Scarborough in the eye. "I'm ready."

Jake stood up and pointed his finger at Scarborough. "No. It's too dangerous; she could shoot Kate on the spot!" He was adamant, and his cheeks were red with anger and indignation.

I shook my head. "The AGI would never approve of that. They want me alive, I guarantee it."

I turned to Jake and said, "I can do this—this will work." It was the progress that I was craving. "I need to do this." Jake turned his head away from me and gave the smallest of shakes, letting me know that, regardless, he didn't approve.

Scarborough nodded. "It's settled. Let's find Lena."

CHAPTER 6

Minsk, Belarus
Aksana

Drs. Aksana Kozel and Johan Krause stepped down the stairwell to their medical lab in the basement of a large and rather rundown building on the outskirts of Minsk.

It was after dark, and the area of Minsk that they were in was not the safest, nor the most well lit. The concrete walls surrounding the stairwell made the door at the bottom difficult to see—the light of the moon barely cut through the inky darkness. Johan dug around in his pocket for the key and came up empty. "Did I give you the key?" the older man asked Aksana in his heavily German-accented English.

Aksana opened her purse to begin looking, when Johan held the key aloft and declared, "I found it." Aksana held in her eye roll. Johan was a genius, and that was not a term she just threw around, but the little things in life were often forgotten by him. She'd lost count of the times that he couldn't find the key to the lab or left something back at the apartment they shared.

Johan fumbled around with the key, trying to find the lock, and Aksana held back a huff. She found it was better in the long run to let men think that they were the smarter and stronger sex, so Aksana waited, not so patiently, in the freezing cold of the harsh Belarus winter, for Johan to unlock the door.

The door finally opened, and they stepped into the dark laboratory. Once the door was closed behind her, Aksana flipped on the light switch, and the room around them came to life. They stepped into the first makeshift vestibule and donned their full protective gear. First, they put scrubs on. Neither of them bothered with modesty—they stripped down to their underthings and put the sterilized clothing on. Then thick rubber boots that went to their knees. Those were followed by a bodysuit made of impermeable material, two pairs of gloves, a face mask, an impermeable hood that covered their faces and necks, and finally, goggles.

Aksana had been working with deadly viruses for so long that she hardly noticed the gear anymore. Johan had spent the bulk of his career working on the vaccination side of viruses, and had not had to wear the full personal protective equipment. He was constantly picking at and adjusting his gear, and it drove Aksana crazy; for as smart as he was, he had no sense of how easily he could be contaminated.

After getting their protective gear on, they stepped into the next vestibule one at a time to be sprayed thoroughly with bleach followed by purified water. As important as it was to keep the viruses they were working on off them, it was just as important for them to keep the rest of the world off the viruses. They had to maintain a constant state of sterilization in the lab. They didn't eat or drink anything for the hours that they worked there; the contamination risk was too high and the price too steep. Luckily the lab had very little in the way of central heating and was practically freezing, so they didn't sweat out too many electrolytes during their long hours of work.

Aksana made her way from the sterilization vestibule into the lab. "Are you working on eleven twenty-four?" She wanted to make sure that Johan stayed on task. His mind was a unicorn, but he could be easily distracted by his findings and take them down a path that was, while often interesting, unnecessary and unhelpful for their cause.

Johan took his seat across from her, and through the jumble of equipment, he looked at her and said, "Eleven twenty-four, ja, ja."

She nodded back to the older man, and they got to work. Both Aksana and Johan worked on making personal strains of the virus for the test subjects. Together they'd made incredible strides in personalized viruses. It used to take months, and in the beginning, years, to make a personal strain of their deadly virus of choice. Now they could do it in hours. Thanks to Johan, they'd had a breakthrough in genetic testing and found that they could make the virus bio-available to only specific single nucleotide polymorphisms, and therefore it would have the ability to work only for individuals with specific DNA markers. It was so perfect that they could make it fit for one person only, or that person and their posterity. Using specific genetic markers, they could even go so far as it infecting the large majority of entire nationalities. Currently, they were working on only personalized viruses, but the other variations were easy enough to apply.

Johan, who was sixty-five if he was a day, looked up from under his white hair at Aksana, his blue eyes with heavy bags underneath, and for the thousandth time asked, "What do you think the NOS is going to use this science for?"

As usual, Aksana held in her eye roll. Why must he always ask such stupid questions? "I work for the NOS, I do not run it." Her English was good, but her Russian accent was heavy, and at times they struggled to understand each other, so she kept her chatter with Johan at a minimum and her words succinct. She had no desire or time to constantly repeat herself. He knew what they were going to use the viruses for; he had seen the way they affected their test subjects. They were meant to kill people, and they did an excellent job of it. Aksana and Johan worked for hours in companionable silence.

Aksana looked up from her work and stretched her neck. They were going to have to foray into the other half of the basement soon to see their current subjects. She hoped that none of them remained alive this time. There was a teenaged girl, number 1017, who had remained alive and mostly unaffected by the virus. No matter how many times Aksana retested her DNA and reformulated the virus for a different single nucleotide polymorphism, she continued to beat the virus. Subject 1017 got sick, just not sick enough to die, and that was unacceptable. Aksana was doing everything she could think of to thoroughly infect the young girl with the virus, but thus far it had been to no avail.

Whenever a virus made its way through a population, there were always individuals who were immune to that particular virus due to their genetic makeup. That couldn't be the case with 1017, though, because the virus had been formulated for her exact DNA. In the last year they had tested well over a thousand people, and every single one of them had died. Every single one except 1017.

Aksana got up to stretch out her back—the chair she worked in was less than ideal, and after hours upon hours a day in it, it became a strain. "Let's go check on the subjects."

"We could use the camera feed, you know." She knew that it was Johan's least favorite part of the day. He didn't like seeing the people that he killed. His biggest problem was that he saw them as people. To Aksana, they were little more than lab rats. They were people who were found homeless and living on the streets. They didn't have lives anyway, nor people who loved them or cared to know why they disappeared. They were the perfect test subjects.

"No, it is better to see with my own eyes." Johan huffed but moved to get up anyway.

They kept ten subjects at a time and personalized the virus for each of the ten. They made notes of how they reacted all through the infection process. How high was their fever? Were they tired, weak? How was their appetite? Were they suffering from muscle pain, joint pain, headache, confusion, rashes, open sores, bleeding from unusual places, or any other symptoms? The NOS wanted any and all information they could get from the subjects regarding the viruses they were injected with. So that is what Aksana and Johan did. They infected and tested.

Johan grunted as he got up from his chair and made his way to the back of the lab. Aksana opened the door, and they walked into the dimly lit hallway. A company had leased the building years ago and built out offices in the basement, and those offices were now used for the test subjects. There were five doors on each side of the hallway, each room locked and each one deadly silent. There was no moaning or screaming as there had been the past couple of weeks, just complete silence, and Aksana found herself on edge as they neared 1017's room. They looked in the window on each door to see the progress of their subjects. Each one dead or very close to it. Test subject 1017 was at the end of the hallway, and as Aksana neared, she found herself hoping that she'd finally infected 1017 with the correct form of the virus. Johan made his way to 1017's window first, and he looked in and turned back to Aksana and shook his head.

"What? It can't be! How is she still alive? Is she a machine? An alien?" Aksana pushed Johan out of the way and looked in the window and swore. The girl was sleeping soundly on her cot. She didn't seem to be affected at all by the new strain of virus that Aksana had made for her. "How can that be?" Aksana hit the door with her fist, and 1017 startled awake. She saw them in the window and quickly moved back into the corner of her cot. Her arms wrapped around her legs, she was visibly shaking from fear.

Number 1017 was a young girl of seventeen. She was an American, and she was pretty with her long, dark hair and fair skin. Aksana wondered, not for the first time, how 1017 had found herself in the hands of the NOS.

Johan just shook his head and shrugged. "We try again." He turned on his heel and walked back to the lab. But Aksana knew that there was no "we" about it; subject 1017 was her responsibility, and she was the one who'd continually failed to do her job. They could hide this from their superiors for only so long. Aksana just stood there at the door and stared through the window at the girl who kept living.

CHAPTER 7

Baltimore, MD
Kate

We'd located Lena, and today was finally the day I would make contact. She was working out of the Baltimore AGI office building, the same one where I'd had my initial meeting with the AGI. We caught her on security cameras around the vicinity and then watched the door for her comings and goings. She was sleeping there, so whatever assignment she was on, it was temporary. She frequented the same coffee shop every morning like clockwork; Lena never could get going without her coffee, it was nice to know that some things never changed.

She looked good, healthy. Whatever they'd put her through at the AGI, she looked like she had come out on top. It had been fewer than three months since I'd left her behind in Montana, and seeing her face in real life, from our surveillance van, her curly red hair blowing in the breeze, made my heart beat faster and my anxiety to see her grow by the second. I was itching to make this happen, but the CIA, as usual, was as slow as molasses. That was perhaps the one thing I missed about the AGI—they had no red tape. When they wanted something done, they didn't wait for a second window, they did it immediately. Jake assured me the AGI acted that way because they didn't care about the lives they lost and that the CIA didn't throw officers into a situation that they hadn't fully vetted. The CIA did nothing without a plan, and that plan was discussed and then discussed some more and then reworked until I wanted to pull my hair out. I wasn't obtuse enough not to see Jake's point, but I still thought the CIA overdid it a little.

I was finally allowed to make contact. I got to the coffee shop about twenty minutes before Lena typically arrived. They didn't want me going in too early, but there was always the chance that she decided that she wanted her coffee earlier than usual. The logistics were hemmed and hawed over, and twenty minutes was finally agreed upon.

I was there with a book, but of course I was paying no attention to it. I'd read the same sentence no less than thirty times. I was trying to look like I was enjoying a leisurely latte while reading my novel, when in reality I was trying to save my friend from the most corrupt organization in the world. Acting casual was difficult. Add to that the fact that I was always somewhat nervous to be in public for any length of time. No matter how often I reminded myself how unlikely it would be for the AGI to find me, it still freaked me out. I had been having my fair share of nightmares that I was still chained to the wall in the torture room within the Montana headquarters of the AGI. I kept those dreams to myself, not because I thought it showed weakness, but because I didn't want to talk about it out loud and give it more head space than it deserved.

It was only a few minutes until Lena's regularly scheduled coffee break. Every time the bell over the door rang, a zing of anxiety pulsed through me. I calmed myself by taking a deep breath of the coffee-scented air. The coffee shop was everything I loved in an owner-run, local shop. It was eclectic in the best way, with the mismatched tables and chairs. The table I was sitting at was small, round, and robin's-egg blue, and the three chairs that surrounded it were all different, as if they had bought each chair from a different garage sale.

I heard Jake say in my ear, "She's about to walk in." I busied myself with my book and read the same sentence again while also watching for Lena out of the corner of my eye. She always got her coffee and sat down for fifteen minutes or so to drink it. The plan was for me to move to her table when she sat down. I would be lying if I said that I wasn't slightly nervous that Lena was loyal to the AGI and this would all backfire. But in my heart of hearts, I truly believed that Lena was on the right side. She had already started to suspect the AGI back when we were there together.

Lena walked in, and I could feel the energy in the room shift. The barista practically jumped to the counter to serve her. I chuckled to myself; that right there was probably half the reason she came to this shop at the same time every day. Lena reveled in attention, and she thought the barista was cute. Cute enough to tease and flirt with him like the Southern girl she was. I saw her lean over and with a smile and a wink share something conspiratorially with the worker. He smiled and blushed, and I shook my head. She had that barista in the palm of her hand. I'd even bet that she got her coffee fix for free.

Then, to my utter frustration, she got her coffee to go, and she walked right out of the shop without so much as a look in my direction. I growled and, quietly enough for only Jake to hear, said, "She took it to go today."

I leaned back in my seat, irritated that my meet and greet with Lena would have to wait for another day, when I saw the barista approach. He set a folded napkin down on the table and awkwardly said, "Sorry I forgot to give you a napkin earlier." I looked at him, confused, because he had given me a napkin earlier. He silently shrugged and walked back behind the counter.

I unfolded the napkin and saw Lena's scrawl. I took a quick breath in, and with my heart pounding, I read the note.

I am bugged, both audio and video. RUN.

I swore under my breath. "Are you seeing this?" I asked quietly. This was not an outcome we'd planned for. I felt incredibly stupid for not seeing it coming. This was so typical AGI. They had been trying to draw me out, and they were using Lena as bait. Well played. I put the note in the pocket of my pants and took out my phone, holding it up to my ear so that I could speak to the group in my comm without looking like I was a schizophrenic.

Over the comm, I could hear a plan being made, and argued over, to get me out safely. I wanted to scream, "Someone make a freaking decision!" Instead, I said as calmly as possible, "What do you want me to do?"

Scarborough came though and said, "We have no reason to believe that they spotted you. Johnson did not turn her body to you even once; she did a good job hiding you from AGI eyes. I think it's safe to send one of the guys in to meet you, and you two can walk out together."

I began to shake my head before I realized that they couldn't see me. "No, there is no walking out of here. I'm probably surrounded; the AGI bugged her. She knew that she had audio and visual on the front of her coat, but she is smart enough to know that it was probably on the back as well. The AGI is nothing if not thorough. If she suspects that they saw me, she's probably right." I heard a slew of swear words.

"Why haven't they stormed the place, then?"

I was still acting as if I were just casually talking on my phone, when in reality I was trying to calm my raging heart and talk sense to the CIA at the same time. I kept my book up so that it covered my mouth in attempt to keep my conversation private. Now was not the time for a lesson in AGI practices, but I had no choice but to explain a few things. "It's not their style. They are still a private organization, and they take that seriously. They won't do anything that could be traced back to them. They won't storm the place; they will be much stealthier." It went unsaid, but we all knew in that moment how absolutely stupid it had been to try to meet Lena right next to the Baltimore offices. The AGI had tons of agents half a block down the street. How could we have been so arrogant? "Besides, they want me alive. They want to know where I've been the last three months. Whom I've told and if I've been believed."

"So what do you think we should do, then? We sure as hell aren't going to let them take you. They might not want to storm the place, but we don't have a problem storming in to get you out," Jake practically growled into my ear. He was mad, probably at me; I had gone against his wishes by meeting Lena.

"Jake, that blows my cover. We, in no way, want the AGI aware that I am working with the CIA."

"You aren't working *with* us, you are *one* of us. We are not the AGI, we take care of our own," he yelled into my comm.

It was difficult to keep my voice down. "Right, and how are you going to protect me from the CIA agents who work for the AGI?"

More arguing over the line. I could hear Scarborough say, "She's right, Jake. We have to keep our cover at all costs."

Then Jake practically raged, "Even if the cost is her life?" Then radio silence, which was answer enough for me.

I shook my head, trying to clear it enough to have a good idea about how to proceed, and I blew out a breath as inspiration finally came. "Get Charlie in a car, preferably a Lyft or an Uber. Have him pick me up at the door. They will follow, and Charlie can work his magic and lose them. It's the best option I can think of."

More silence, then Jake piped up, and I could hear the relief in his voice when he said, "That just might work. Mark, call an Uber; Megan, call a Lyft; whoever gets here first is our lucky winner. Mark, you and Candace get the driver out of the car and into our van; we'll explain to them that their vehicle has been commandeered. Charlie, get ready to jump in as soon as the car is vacated."

It wasn't more than two minutes before I heard Scarborough say, "We have a car. It's a silver Honda Civic. It's coming around the corner now. Be ready to move out of the coffee shop and into the car. Be on the lookout; I doubt they would try to take you in the middle of the day in public, but we can't be sure they won't."

I nodded my head. "Got it." I saw the Honda with Charlie in the driver's seat, and I quickly got up from my table to leave. Out of the corner of my eye, I saw several people move at once. There was a man who was having coffee and reading the paper at a table two over from mine; he got up as soon as I did and looked at his watch, acting like he was paying me no attention. There was a woman in the front of the store, standing next to the door, who moved to stand in front of it as I approached. She was acting like she was searching her bag to make sure she had everything that belonged in it before leaving. There were two men in the back, dressed in suits, who stood up and blocked the back exit by having a conversation in front of the door. It was all impressively subtle.

With both exits blocked, I decided to go for the front; it was a woman, after all, and I figured she would be my easiest opponent. It didn't escape my attention that Newspaper Guy would probably come to her aid. I had to be quick. I acted like I didn't even notice that I was surrounded, as if I were the dumbest person the AGI had ever hired, and walked right up to the front door. The woman smiled at me, and as I got near enough to her, she grabbed my arm and held it firm. She pulled me closer to her, and with her sweet smile still in place she said, "We have some questions for you, Kate Edison."

I looked at her, matching her smile. "I'm sure you do. Unfortunately for you, you aren't going to get to ask me those questions today." I stepped even closer to her, putting one of my feet in front of hers, and then I twisted my arm so that it was vertical and yanked it out of her grasp. I almost laughed at the ease of getting away from her; I'd learned that trick in martial arts class when I was eight. Then I slammed my straight hand into her carotid artery, at the base of her neck, and swept my foot right through hers, and she was down. I went to step over her and open the door when I found it locked. Which gave Newspaper Guy just enough time to get his arm around my neck from behind.

There are several ways to get out of a choke hold, but all of them require a person to be able to move their feet, and with the passed-out woman in a lump in front of me and Newspaper Guy directly behind me, I couldn't get enough room. I could feel my airway restricting, and I knew that I had only seconds to act before I would pass out and be in the AGI's hands again. I'd rather have died than let that happen. I grabbed onto his hips; with him behind me this was most definitely an awkward angle, but as soon as I got purchase, I lifted my knees and then slammed my feet backward into his knees. I heard a crunch and a grunt, and his arm loosened enough for me to get out of his hold. I took his arm and twisted until I heard another satisfying crunch. He wailed, and only then could I hear the commotion in the background.

The barista was freaking out with what had to be 911 on the line, and I heard heavy footsteps running toward me, and with one look back I could see it was the two guys from the back door. They were holding out badges, and the barista sagged with relief. I really didn't want to try to fight off two men with a coffee shop full of people thinking that I was fighting off cops. I flipped the lock on the door and jumped over the woman, sprinting for the Honda only five feet in front of me.

The door was open; I threw myself in, and the car took off before I had time to shut the door. I grunted as I grabbed for it, and Charlie jerked the car to the right, assisting me in getting it closed.

Charlie looked at me in the review mirror for a millisecond and smiled widely. "Heeey, girrrrl." He handed me back a bug detector that had been sitting in the passenger seat, and I started to run it over my clothes. I was glad that Charlie had thought of that; my mind was somewhat jumbled from the confrontation with the AGI agents, and the possibility of being bugged hadn't even crossed my mind. It should have though, bugging the unsuspecting was an AGI specialty. The detector buzzed twice—I had one bug on my arm and one on my back. I peeled them off and threw them out the window.

I took a deep breath and let out a huff of relief. "Hey, Charlie." Charlie had short dreadlocks and deep-brown skin. He had kind eyes and a quick, big smile. I'd driven with Charlie before. The first time was months earlier when Jake first kissed me, after the failed surgery to remove my ICT. Talk about a day of highs and lows. I remembered that Jake had told me then that Charlie was the best tactical driver he knew, and I was seeing that now. The man could *drive*.

We raced through streets and alleys, and Charlie was all smiles. "This car is saweeet! Brother who owned this thing jacked it uuuup! The man liked some speed!" He hooted and slapped the steering wheel, laughing. I couldn't help but laugh with him; Charlie's personality was contagious. He was always happy, but in his element, he was on fire.

I'd never felt so safe driving so fast. I watched the world whiz past while my heart rate returned to normal. Charlie's ease with the automobile was impressive to say the least. Tactical driving wasn't Charlie's only talent either. He could fly almost any plane or helicopter, he could captain any boat, yacht, or catamaran, and he could even run a bullet train. The last was a thing of legend; I had been with the CIA for only a matter of months, and I'd heard the story of Charlie with the bullet train no fewer than ten times. He was a genius, in a completely different way than anyone I'd ever met, and it made him very intriguing to me.

"Have we lost them?"

"Ha! They never had us. Those two buffoons with the badges were still getting in the car when we took off. I haven't seen anyone on our tail."

"Then why are you driving like there's someone on our tail?"

"Because it's the only way worth driving." He winked at me in the mirror.

I laughed and blew out a hard breath, lying back against the headrest. "Thanks for your help, Charlie; there is no way I could've gotten out of that mess without you."

"You were bomb back there. I was about to get out and assist you when that guy had you in the choke hold, then I saw you hyper-extend his knees and I thought, 'She got this.'"

I laughed again. "I was pretty good back there, wasn't I?" I was still laughing, mostly at myself, because while the ending had turned out okay, the mission was a mess. I decided to think about that later. "I have to admit, this feels so good. I haven't done anything life threatening in a while—I almost forgot about the high."

"Be careful, that high is as addictive as a chemical one." He raised his eyebrows at me. "Take it from someone who knows. You don't get the reputation I have without enjoying your work a little too much."

Charlie hit his comm. "Looks like we are in the clear. Where do you all want to meet?"

CHAPTER 8

Cambridge, MA
Arthur

Arthur Whitehall set his water glass down with a trembling hand and got up to speak to the press. He gave himself a couple of calming breaths before he started. "We at DNA Global are proud to announce that we have been the only DNA testing company that has been approved by the FDA for genome testing to prevent the possibility of future disease in regard to genetics. We now test DNA for the probability of fifty different diseases, from Alzheimer's to colon cancer. If you have had your DNA tested with DNA Global before, you do not need to retest. You can simply request your results for possible genetic diseases right on our website for free. We are proud to be leading the way in the prevention of disease and hope to make the world a healthier place for individuals all around the world. One person at a time."

"Mr. Whitehall will take five questions," the PR guy to Arthur's right said to the crowd.

Arthur nodded to the first hand that shot up. "What are some of the diseases DNA Global is now testing for? What is the likelihood that a person who tests genetically positive for one or more of these diseases ends up getting it?"

Arthur smiled. "I won't bore you by naming each disease that we test for right now." The audience of journalists laughed. "They are posted on our website; we encourage everyone to look them up.

When you get your genome testing results with DNA Global, you will receive a percentage of probability that you will end up with a particular disease. I have seen numbers as high as ninety-nine percent and as low as one percent. Along with our findings, we also give you ways that you can outsmart your genetics and try to avoid these life-altering diseases."

Arthur nodded to a pretty woman in the back. "Isn't it dangerous to know diseases you might get? Not everything in our genetics can be 'outsmarted.' We all have to die someday."

In that moment Arthur wished that he hadn't been so charmed by a pretty face. He hated this question, and he felt like he'd answered it at least five thousand times to date. Probably more. He pasted a smile on his face anyway. He wasn't the CEO of a Fortune 500 company for nothing. "Thank you for that question. Knowing what diseases you are genetically prone to getting is the opposite of harmful. It can be extremely helpful; you can take precautions that you otherwise may not have taken. One genetically prone to colon cancer, for instance, may choose to follow the protocol DNA Global suggests by cutting processed meats from their diet and getting yearly colonoscopies. Knowing what the future holds can keep you free of painful and deadly diseases, and it is a gift of modern technology and science."

Arthur picked the worst-looking male to ask the next question, going against his natural tendencies and hoping to get one that painted DNA Global in a more positive light. "Have you done the testing yourself, Mr. Whitehall?"

Yes, just what he'd hoped for, thank you, Ugly Man in the back. "I have, and I found that I am genetically prone to Alzheimer's disease. I take all of the precautions research suggests to prevent myself from getting it. It's not that difficult of a protocol but something I probably wouldn't have thought to do if I had never gotten the testing." Arthur loved that question, and he knew from past experience that DNA Global would sell tens of thousands of genome testing kits from that answer alone. There was nothing quite as powerful as a personal testimony.

Two questions to go. Arthur hated press conferences. He had never been a huge fan of public speaking, and he hated answering questions off the cuff. He liked time to think. He much preferred interviews where he got the questions in advance. Being the CEO came with its highs and lows, and this was definitely a low for Arthur.

The PR guy, who Arthur always referred to as "PR Guy," because Arthur couldn't be bothered to remember his name, picked the next member of the press to ask a question. "How long does it take to get your testing results back?"

Maybe Arthur should remember PR Guy's name; he'd just done him a solid. "We always say that testing takes four to six weeks, but we get the testing done as fast as we can and most often beat our timeline. Our goal has always been to under promise and over deliver."

With a smile, he picked out the last person to ask a question. It was a woman in the back corner, and right after he nodded to her that he would take her question, he noticed that she didn't seem to have anything there to record his answer—no cameras, not so much as a handheld recorder. "Mr. Whitehall, what do you do with the results you get from the people who trust you with their DNA? Is there a massive database in which all individual testing is filed away? Are the results sold to the government? Who has access to these results? Anyone at DNA Global? How about your parent company? Do they have access? What about—"

PR Guy cut her off, "If you don't mind, we only have one minute left in this conference." PR Guy gave the woman a flat smile. "I think it would be good to stop the questioning there so we can let Mr. Whitehall have the remainder of the time to answer your questions."

The woman looked less than happy, which made Arthur happy. They had dealt with her type before; she didn't really want answers, she wanted to make them look bad. There were many conspiracy theories regarding genome testing, and the naysayers were ecstatic to make themselves known.

"There is a complete report of our privacy policy available on our website. Each individual who tests with DNA Global is required to sign that they have read our privacy policy and they agree to our terms. I will do my best to explain a few of our policies with the minimal time we have left. The test results are completely private. We will only share them with the individual tested. What they do with those results is their own business. Many share them with their spouses, families, and doctors, but they have every right to keep the results to themselves. We do keep a database of the results, in case an individual misplaces their results and needs another copy. I encourage everyone who has any concerns to read the privacy policy on our website. Thank you."

As Arthur walked away, he could hear the woman in the back screaming out more questions. These people couldn't help themselves. How had she gotten into the press conference? She was probably from some newsletter called *Conspiracy Theorists Unite* that had all of five readers.

Arthur rolled his shoulders, attempting to relax them now that the press conference was over, but they remained tense. Truth be told, that woman wasn't all that crazy; she was right to be concerned about their privacy practices. Arthur sighed. He hated press conferences.

CHAPTER 9

Washington, D.C.
Kate

"Well, that was a disaster. Not only did we not meet with our desired contact, but we almost lost our mission's most valuable asset." Fin started us off on that high note.

We were gathered around the boardroom back in D.C. only a few hours after our failed mission to meet with Lena. I was feeling slightly sheepish, as the meetup had been my bright idea. The mission hadn't just failed—it had failed spectacularly. I knew I wasn't the only one at fault: Scarborough, our director, had been on board, too. But I had been with the AGI, I knew that we were just down the street from their Baltimore office, and it hadn't even crossed my mind that they would even recognize me, let alone have the manpower and the stealth to act as they did. It would have been rather impressive if the reason they'd done it weren't so glaringly obvious.

"They were surveilling Lena in the hopes that I would reach out to her." Everyone stopped talking and looked at me. I sighed, irritated with myself. "Lena was getting coffee from the same shop at the same time every day that we surveilled her. Lena doesn't have habits like that. She is a fly-by-the-seat-of-her-pants kind of girl. She does drink coffee every day, but she wouldn't leave the comfort of her apartment to get coffee, and most certainly not at the same time every day. It was a setup."

"It was definitely a setup, but how could you be so sure how Johnson would act in this circumstance? You and Lena only worked together a short time in Montana. I'm not sure it's possible that you could know how she would behave under normal circumstances." Scarborough was giving me an out; I wasn't sure if it was for me or himself, though, given that we had been the ones pushing the meetup.

I flashed him a grateful smile and shook my head. "No, she was wearing workout clothes. Lena abhors exercise. She was tossing me a clue, and I was too excited to see her to make the catch." I steepled my hands and rested my chin on my forefingers. "She knew that the AGI agents were there, and if she hadn't sent the barista with the note, I would likely be back in AGI custody." I shook my head again. "I'd wrongfully deduced the reason that she went to that coffee shop at the same time every day was because she thought the barista was attractive, but in actuality she was befriending the barista just in case she needed a favor, like passing a message along." I wanted to pound my fist on the table because I was so angry, but I managed to fold my arms across my chest instead.

Megan piped up, "That Lena is resourceful. It's too bad we didn't get to talk to her—I'm guessing we could really use her."

Jake looked thoughtful. "We aren't giving up on that meetup yet." My head snapped in his direction. He looked at me, and I could see the sincerity in his eyes. "I wasn't against getting in touch with Lena; I was against using you as bait."

Just when you're trying to get over someone, they have to go and say something sweet. I nodded, conceding his point. I shouldn't have been the one to meet with her—it was too obvious, and I played right into their hands. I would not do that again. I vowed to get my head on straight. I also vowed to stop ignoring Jake's arguments; he had very good points and ideas, and I needed to give them room.

I smiled as I thought of one good outcome from this disaster of a mission. "Now that they've seen through my disguise, does that mean I can have my old hair and eye color back?"

They all laughed; they knew how much I hated my hair color. "How about red?" Mark Hampton chimed in.

"Black?" That suggestion was from Candace.

"Wasn't the idea to give me something that was less noticeable? Everyone notices redheads,"—I sure did at any rate—"and black hair with my skin tone would make me stand out as well. Blondes are overlooked all the time. Clearly, I'm not fooling the AGI anyway. If I'm out in public, maybe it would be better to use wigs, glasses, and hats that change all the time."

Megan with the long, blonde hair spoke up, "I can help you color your hair back."

Fin looked up from his screen and said, "Megan knows her way around hair color; not sure I'd trust her to do something natural, though." Then he went right back to whatever was on his computer screen.

Megan looked mock offended and then laughed. Looking at me, she said, "You haven't known me very long, but I like to get creative with my hair color. This is the most natural it's looked in years." She pointed to her blonde hair and shrugged. "My sister's a hairstylist, and she's taught me a thing or two. I could help you." She looked pointedly at my hair. "I would love to get rid of it for you—that color is truly hideous." She shivered, as if I were hard to look at. I didn't even bother to act offended; hideous was an understatement.

Fin chuckled, and under his breath he said, "My dad's an orthodontist, but that doesn't mean you should trust me to adjust your braces . . ."

Megan good-naturedly rolled her eyes.

I needed all the help I could get. "Thanks, Megan, that would be great."

Scarborough looked as though he was contemplating the idea, and then he looked to Lyon. "Thoughts?"

Jake looked at me and winked. "I think at this point wigs and such may work better, but perhaps we should keep the mud-green brown, just in case."

I laughed and threw my head back. "Nooooooo!"

Everyone laughed, and Scarborough said, "It's final, then; Edison can have her hair color back."

I held up a finger. "And eye color?"

He smirked. "And eye color, too."

My hands shot up. "Yes!" I started laughing, excited about the win. I looked to Jake to do a little jazz hands to show my excitement. But he wasn't looking at me. He was staring at his computer screen, his expression confounded. He started typing and hitting buttons, shaking his head. Then he got up close to his screen and hit more keys. "Jake?"

He picked up his laptop and looked underneath and at the power button. "What the . . ." He looked at the screen again, and his eyes got wide, and he looked at me and said, "It's Lena . . . she's broken into my computer."

I jumped up from my chair and went to stand behind him. His screen was blacked out, but words were starting to appear in green at the top.

Lyon, it's Lena Johnson. I need to talk to Kate. Is she with you, or do you know where she is?

I gasped. Jake turned to me, his eyebrows up to his hairline. "Do you know how many layers of protection I have on this computer?"

I almost laughed. "You're good, Lyon, but you are no match for Lena Johnson. She broke into the NSA's computer system while she was a recruit with them. They were not very happy."

His expression showed his surprise. Under his breath he said, "Well, I'll be damned."

Scarborough was right there next to me looking at Jake's screen. I looked up and around the table and relayed what Lena's message said to the rest of the group, who were clearly anticipating an explanation.

Kate! Is that you? Oh, thank goodness!

"Can she hear me?"

She sent a rolling eye emoji, and then we watched as she typed out, *Of course I can hear you, I've accessed Lyon's microphone. His camera is turned off, otherwise I would be able to see you, too.*

Fin got up from his chair and stood at my other side; he whistled in appreciation. I think he may have been a little turned on—he'd already seen Lena, who was stunning, and now he was seeing just what she was capable of. There wasn't a smart guy in the world who could resist falling under her spell. She was the girl who beat all of the guys in Dungeons & Dragons. The girl who could speak Elvish and got dressed up to go to the *The Lord of the Rings* premiere with a group of online friends who were all speechless when they found out that not only was their friend a girl, but she was a pretty girl.

Candace spoke up, "How do we know she's not doing the AGI's bidding, or at least that she isn't being watched?"

It was a good point. A troubling one, perhaps one we wouldn't be able to verify until it was too late.

Give me a little credit. The AGI only knows a fraction of what I am capable of. Trust me, this is secure and untraceable. I am not in the AGI building. I'm at a library, and the only person who saw me come in is a one-hundred-year-old lady who is currently asleep up at the front desk.

I guffawed, incredulous. I'd missed her so much. I was unspeakably grateful that whatever she'd endured at the AGI, it wasn't nearly as bad as my nightmares made it out to be. She'd looked healthy when I saw her earlier that day, and she seemed every bit her authentic self now.

I looked to Scarborough and Jake with my eyebrows raised, silently asking if I could talk to her. Jake gave a half shrug, still in shock that she was able to break into his computer. Scarborough lifted his hands in that "I suppose we really don't have any other choice" kind of way.

The red light at the top of Jake's laptop blinked a couple of times and then gave one long blink, and then we read Lena's next message.

There you are!! I've missed your face so much!! That hair, though, yikes. It's awful. I mean really awful and doesn't hide you for a second. I knew who you were the minute I walked into the coffee shop this morning. Of course, the AGI did too; I saw all kinds of scuttling around as I was leaving to get "my daily coffee" that I'm forced to get at the same time every day. I knew something im-

portant had happened—you could feel the excitement in the air in the AGI facility. They don't trust me anymore, so no one told me what the craze was about, but I noticed a few of the guys that I've been working with in the coffee shop when I walked in. I'd hoped it was you! I mean it was really dumb to come there, but I knew you would come for me eventually!

Jake was incredulous. "She turned on my camera?"

Didn't your mama teach you that it's rude to talk about someone who's in the same room as you? Of course I turned on your camera, it just took me a minute.

I snickered. "Did you get in trouble for leaving the coffee shop early? Aren't you supposed to stay and drink it there?"

Hahaha, I told them that I had girl problems, the kind that needed urgent attention.

I laughed. I couldn't help it. It was just so Lena. "I've seriously missed you."

Yeah, yeah, blah, blah. Let's get to the good stuff. When are you springing me from this hellhole?

I looked at Scarborough; he just lifted his eyebrows. She could see and hear us, so it was impossible to have a real conversation about her. But if Scarborough was thinking what I was pretty sure he was thinking, then we had no plans to spring Lena. She was going to be the new mole.

I pursed my lips and looked at Jake; he wore the same expression as me. He was worried that I wasn't going to be happy that we were keeping Lena in the AGI. He was both right and wrong. I would have loved nothing more than to get Lena out of there. But I also knew how talented she was; it was impossible not to imagine all the information she could get us on the inside. It made no sense to get her out—if we wanted to take the AGI down, then we needed Lena's help from the inside.

I nodded to Jake to let him know that I understood. However, there were two main problems. I had never been all that forthcoming with Lena in regard to what I had discovered. I didn't think that she knew the depth of evil that was the AGI. I didn't know if she knew that Nick was dead. Or that Claire had been tortured to death. I was fairly certain that she didn't know that she wore the ICT. That was something I wanted to keep from her. Knowing about the ICT, and that I had one, had been probably one of the most difficult experiences of my life to date. That reality was horrific, and I wasn't at all sure we should put Lena through that. Especially given the fact that at the moment nothing could be done to destroy her detonator.

"Lena, I'm sure you don't want to hear this, but we need you on the inside. We want to get you out, and we will, but we need some help, and your talents make you a perfect person. That is part of the reason I was trying to see you today. The other part was to make sure you were okay. I wasn't sure what the AGI was going to do to you after I left. I have been freaking out, worried what they might have put you through."

Oh no. No, no, no, no, no. I'm not staying here. Listen to me, I won't be able to be any help to you—they are watching me like a hawk. I'm not even allowed access to a computer within the AGI buildings unless someone is there monitoring my every move. Speaking of which, I don't have much time here. I'm supposed to be getting lunch, but if I'm not back soon, someone will come looking for me. I have a GPS tracker on, and I've managed to make it look like I'm in the Thai restaurant next door, but if they send someone to the restaurant and I'm not there, I will be in a world of trouble. I can tell you this: you probably already know, but you are being searched for everywhere. For a while they thought that you were in Brazil, but another agent thought they spotted you with brown hair in D.C. a couple of weeks ago. That was when my coffee trips started. Among other things, you are being accused of killing Westwood. I assured them that you would never do that, but my defense of you seems to go in one ear and out the other. They're using me to get to you, and I'm worried that they'll have little use for me if they ever do get to you. The AGI is messed up. I suspected foul play for a while, but I've been seeing things lately that send chills down my spine. Brahim knows, too, but he won't say a word about it. He's made it clear to me that there are ears everywhere and there is no safe place to have that conversation. Not that we are allowed to talk to each other. The only way that we get to communicate is here in the library, and even that is very stilted. They have me separated from everyone that we trained with. I'm surrounded with people who don't trust me and think that I'm a ticking time bomb. I'm always on edge, and I'm scared as hell, Kate. I have to get out of here.

Scarborough spoke to her next, "Johnson, when can you get in touch with us next?"

Hard to know, but it'll probably be at least a few days.

"Okay, we'll be ready. We will discuss our next steps then."

Okay, I'll come through Lyon's computer again. It's been real.

She signed off, and we all looked at each other with wide eyes. I think it was safe to assume that we all had mixed feelings. Fin spoke first: "I can't believe she was able to do that." He was still starry eyed.

If I hadn't been so concerned about her, I would have laughed. "She's amazingly talented. But I can tell you all firsthand that Lena doesn't do conflict well. She freaks out. You should have seen her when she was telling me about the AGI surveilling me through her—she was crying and practically having a panic attack about the possibility of torture." I shook my head. "I know I said that she would be a great person to have on the inside, but I think I'm changing my mind. She will crack, and I'm concerned the splintering has already started." I rubbed my hands over my face. "She doesn't even know about the ICT. She doesn't know the half of what the AGI really is."

Jake's head snapped up, and then he looked at me as though he knew that the next thing he said was going to hurt, "She has the ICT," he confirmed.

I nodded my head.

He winced. "We can't get her out; they know what she's capable of, how valuable she is. They will kill her immediately."

I gasped, and my hands came to my head, my mouth dropping open. How had I not thought of that? I swore. "You're right. She's stuck in there until she's no longer useful, and then she'll die." I closed my eyes and swore again. "Lena's as good as dead."

CHAPTER 10

Manchester, New Hampshire
Oliver

Valentina palmed Oliver's cheek, and her thumb caressed his lips. He could feel his insides melt and rev up at the same time. She looked into his eyes and said, "Are you ready?"

How could he possibly be ready for this? He told her as much.

She smiled her dazzling smile at him, all big white teeth and red lips. "I will be here with you every step of the way." Her other arm rubbed up and down his. He knew that he was being manipulated, but he just couldn't bring himself to care. "Hit Enter."

His eyebrows came up. "Isn't that your job?"

She laughed softly. "Normally, yes, but I want you to be in this as much as I am." She took both of his hands in hers. "Things will get crazy after you hit that button, Oliver. I want to know that we will be in this together."

"You're my boss, Valentina. I took this job, and I will see it through to the end." This was so much more than he'd bargained for when he took the job with the AGI that it was laughable. His whole life all he'd ever wanted to do was act. He wanted to be in films that made a difference in the world. He wanted to give his opinion on politics and anything else he felt moved by and have it matter. He was getting all of that through the AGI but on a far larger scale than he'd ever imagined.

Valentina squeezed his hands, and in her soft Colombian accent, said, "That is something else we must discuss. Up until now, we have spoken plainly in private. After we hit Enter, we can no longer afford to do that. True privacy will be a thing of the past. You must never speak of me being your boss or you getting a paycheck, and most importantly, you must never speak the name of the AGI again."

"This was all in my contract, Valentina."

She squeezed his hands harder this time. "I know, but now I need you to get serious about it all of the time. You are on the job twenty-four seven after this moment. I am your wife, and I will never leave your side from here on out." Valentina had a large job within the AGI; she was often jetting off to different places for work.

"You are my wife and will be by my side from here on out?" Oliver's eyebrows rose, and his head cocked to the side. "What exactly do you mean by that?" Was he getting a full-time babysitter, or was Valentina going to act like a wife . . . behind closed doors as well as in public?

"When you hit Enter, there will be no more 'work' between you and me. You will be my husband, and I will be your wife, in every way."

Oliver took no more time to think it over. He hit Enter.

Then he took his wife by the hand and led her to the bedroom that would be *theirs* from that moment on.

CHAPTER 11

Richmond, VA
Kate

The CIA had rented two houses that we would be staying in for the next week or so, though I was hoping for longer. Our group was split in half, eleven at one house and eleven at the neighboring house. It was a nice break from all of the hotels we'd been staying in. I had never been much for cooking, but I found that I practically ached to cook in the house's gorgeous kitchen. It had been what felt like ages since I'd had a real home-cooked meal. I wanted to get out a pan and turn on the gas stove and chop vegetables and make something, anything, really. I knew that it wasn't going to happen, though; we had no time for luxuries like cooking. Certainly not when I had to figure out how to tell Lena about the ICT.

I ate a late dinner of takeout with the group and went up to my room for some much-needed alone time. I lucked out getting my own room this time, and this room had an en suite bathroom. I felt like I had won the lottery. Typically, I had to share with another female officer. As much as I wished to have my own room all of the time, I could appreciate the care the CIA took with taxpayer dollars. When I did get some space of my own, I relished it. At that moment I wanted nothing more than to take a long bath and think about the best way to talk to Lena.

She hadn't gotten back in touch with us since she'd taken over Lyon's computer two days earlier. And since I realized that we couldn't get her out, I had been fretting over what to do. I finally decided that we needed to tell her about the device. She deserved to know, but also, selfishly, I wanted her to know the real reason why we couldn't get her out. I didn't want her to think I didn't care about leaving her there. I would have done anything in my power to get her out, but it would have killed her, and I wouldn't do that. I wanted her to know that it was very much a life-and-death situation.

I started running the bathwater and added some of the lavender-scented bubble bath that was on the counter, because why not? I hadn't had a bubble bath since I was a child, but I craved indulgence, even if it was just for a moment or two.

I slid into the hot water and let my head fall back against the wall and released a sigh. There was nothing like that first minute in a bath, when you are practically weightless and the water is almost scalding. If felt so good that I almost felt like I was doing something wrong.

After a few minutes of luxurious relaxation, I picked up my phone. It was registered to my Southern cheerleader pseudonym, Kaylee Edwards, and I was so grateful to have it that the name didn't chafe as much when I saw it come up on the screen. I scrolled through the news, and in an instant I felt my blood run cold, even in the hot water. The picture and headline I saw had me jumping out of the bath sopping wet, almost slipping on the tile floor. I threw on a robe and practically ran out of my bedroom.

"Lyon?" I yelled down the hall. I wasn't sure which room was his, so I called for him again, this time with a bit more panic in my voice. "Lyon!"

A door opened a few down from mine, and a soaking wet Jake Lyon ran out into the hall. Apparently great minds think alike. He wasn't wearing a robe, though; he was wearing a hastily thrown-on T-shirt and basketball shorts. His casual clothes combined with his wet hair and skin made my mouth water. His eyebrows shot up when he saw me, and his cheeks pinked a little. "Edison?" I realized then how I probably looked, soaking wet with a thin, silky robe sticking to my skin.

I cringed a little and said, "Sorry, but we have a problem."

He visibly swallowed and tried to keep his gaze locked on my face; hard as he tried, his eyes eventually wandered. When his eyes met mine again, he cleared his throat, and his voice was strained when he asked, "What's going on?"

"There's something I didn't tell you . . . from before . . . when I was with the AGI."

He looked to the side and said, "Okay . . ."

"Yeah, I realize that I could have gotten dressed before coming to find you. Um . . ." I looked back into my room and then back at him and held up one finger. "Just give me one minute. Okay? It's important."

He nodded his head, with his eyes again trained on mine.

I went into my room, shut the door, and took a deep breath. Gah, I hated making a fool of myself. Darn Lyon for being so attractive. I picked up a pair of yoga pants and a T-shirt and went into the bathroom to change. I threw the clothes on and peeked in the mirror and smiled at the sight of me with my blonde hair back. It wasn't exactly my original color, but it was a thousand times better than the puke-green brown. I loved it. I also noticed that I'd forgotten to put on a bra. I was grateful that I'd realized my mistake before I invited Lyon into my room—I didn't want it to look like I was trying to seduce him. I quickly donned the undergarment, left the bathroom, and opened the door to find Lyon waiting on the other side.

I ushered him in and sat on the bed. He went to grab the only chair in the room from where it sat in front of the small desk and rolled it over to where I was. He sat down, rested his elbows on his knees, and looked at me expectantly.

"Right, okay. Sorry about earlier, it's just that I read a disturbing headline and I realized that there was something important that I never told you before. It just got lost in the craziness of the fray."

He nodded again. I cleared my throat and dove in. "My very first job with the AGI was to surveil Congresswoman Barbara Randall's house in New Hampshire."

"The one arrested for child sex trafficking?"

I nodded once. "That one, yes. We surveilled her for a week, a few weeks before the scandal came out. We combed through everything on her computers and social media. We listened to every phone call, read every email, and we never found a shred of evidence of wrongdoing." Jake's brow furrowed, and I held up my hand. "I know. A week later, little more than a week before the Randall sex trade scandal broke the internet, I was sent on my second mission. It was to surveil Jay Conner's apartment. Jay was an FBI agent as well as an AGI agent. Although, I didn't know that he worked for the AGI until I pulled his file back in Montana."

Lyon shook his head. "I don't remember a file on Jay Conner. Wasn't he the guy who worked with Randall in the sex trade? He worked for the AGI?"

"Right, yes, the same guy, but hang on, it's not what you think. The reason you don't remember the file on Jay Conner was because I didn't send it to you. I hadn't told you the whole story yet, so the file wouldn't have meant anything to you. I only pulled it because I was so shocked to have found a file on him within the AGI, because until I read his file, I was led to believe that he was nothing more than a crooked FBI agent."

"So, what was he really?"

"Hang on, I'm getting there. I was tasked with installing the surveillance equipment at Conner's apartment. It was easy to deduce what was happening there, once I was inside. The apartment was atrociously disgusting, and there were mattresses with handcuffs attached to the piping through punched-out drywall." Just thinking about it made my stomach roil. "During the install, I was informed that Conner was much closer than we had realized, as in he was walking from his vehicle to his apartment. I had less than thirty seconds to learn the role of Viktoriya." Jake's eyes widened—perhaps he was thinking of my lackluster roleplaying skills when I'd first been recruited by the CIA. "Jay arrived with four children in tow. It all went well, until the end. Lieutenant Officer Cave was watching via the surveillance cameras I'd installed, and he was playing the part of Vlad, Viktoriya's boss-slash-boyfriend, over the phone. In the end I almost got myself killed by not knowing the proper procedure one uses when selling children. A bullet grazed my cheek, and I managed to shoot Conner in both of his wrists so he dropped his weapon."

Jake sat up straight. "That's when I ran into you outside that coffee shop—your cheek was bandaged. I wondered what had happened to you, but there were always more pressing matters when we were communicating that I never got around to asking about it."

"Yes, I ran into you only hours after the Jay Conner debacle. Anyway, I learned from reading Jay's file that he was shot and killed by Cave. I heard the bullet when I was in the parking lot of the apartment building with the kids. I thought Conner had somehow managed to use his gun on himself. So fast forward to a couple of weeks later. I was coming home from Los Angeles after my third, and most harrowing, mission with the AGI. I was in the airport when I saw a report that Barbara Randall was being accused of sex trafficking, and they cited Jay Conner as her cohort. You can imagine my surprise, as I had searched everything on Randall and there was absolutely no connection to Conner. This was not the first time that I'd questioned the validity of the AGI, but it was the first time that my suspicions had gained traction. I got back to the Montana facility and got Lena to research what was going on. She found that the connection had been planted and that Oliver Strands, an AGI agent that we had seen at our induction dinner, had been appointed in Randall's place."

Jake's eyes widened in surprise, and then his jaw dropped open. "Oliver Strands?" I nodded. "The one who just announced his run for president?"

"The very one."

He stood up, and his hands went to his hair, threading through and fisting it, making the strands stick up at odd angles. "We need to get everyone together; you need to tell them what you've just told me."

"Now?" It was late, and most everyone was in bed.

"Right now."

CHAPTER 12

Richmond, VA
Kate

We met in the large living area that opened up to the ample kitchen of the house. Those who didn't get there in time to get a seat on a couch or chair sat on the floor. Everyone was in some form of lounge clothes or pajamas. They may have been CIA agents who were trained to run on little sleep, but that didn't mean that they liked getting up in the middle of the night any more than the average civilian. Fin looked as irritated as ever, with his eyes narrowed at Jake and me when he said, "This better be good."

Jake sent him a flat look that said, *Do you really think we want to see you more than we have to? Of course it's good.* To the group he said, "Sorry to wake you all up, but some very important information about the AGI has just come to my attention, and you all need to hear it." He motioned to me. "Kate is going to tell you all the story she just told me."

I took a deep breath and jumped in. I told them the whole thing with as much detail as I could. When I dropped the bomb that Oliver Strands was an AGI agent, the room erupted. Everyone was freaking out in their own way.

Scarborough jumped out of his seat and turned to me. "Why are we just hearing about this now?" His voice boomed over all the others, and everyone quieted down to hear my explanation.

My face was on fire, and I knew that I looked as embarrassed on the outside as I felt on the inside. My first instinct was to apologize, but then I thought better of it, realizing that I had nothing to apologize for, and just gave the only explanation that I had. "Things were insane back then. All at the same time,"—I used my fingers to tick off the items on my list—"I learned about the depravity of the AGI, what they did to my father, that I had been implanted with their killing device, that they had killed my one friend and tortured another, and endless other horrific things. Oliver Strands took a back burner; his name hadn't crossed my mind in months until just over an hour ago when I saw that he was running for president."

Scarborough was seething; with his hands on his hips, he yelled, "Edison, you are our only link to knowing what the AGI is up to. We need to be able to count on you for every detail. Every. Detail."

Jake stood up then. His face was also red, but not with embarrassment. His voice was the kind of calm that made the hair on the back of your neck stand up. "Officer Scarborough,"—he was good and angry; he never used anyone's title—"Kate thought that she was going to die any second. You know as well as I do that survival always takes precedence over anything and everything else. Always."

Scarborough's expression softened slightly when he looked at me and said, "Is there anything else we need to know about this situation, Edison?"

I swallowed, dropping the other piece of information like a bomb. "Well, you should probably know that Valentina, Oliver's wife, also works for the AGI. She has a fairly high position. I met her in my initial interview as she was their attorney. I had no idea she was married, and I have no idea if she is an actual attorney. But she has freedom to move about the facility as she pleases, and she is aware of many of the dealings within the AGI. Through my research into the AGI, it became clear to me that Valentina is aware of what the AGI really is and how they make money and that she supports their mission of a New World Order. I am certain, or almost certain, that their marriage is a sham."

That revelation made everyone, including Jake, sit back down with shock. Fin ran his hands through his hair and swore, long and loud.

"I will do my best to fill you all in on my time with the AGI. So much happened in such a short period of time, and I am realizing now that there are many things that I need to inform you all of. Who knows what connections we can make when everything I know is on the table."

Scarborough sighed, and his eyes looked like they'd hit a new level of tired. I think he knew that sleep, for him anyway, was a long way off. "Well, there's nothing we can do right now." He looked around the room. "Let's all go back to bed."

Jake and I went upstairs last. When we got to my door, I went to turn the knob, and he stopped my hand with his. I turned to look at him, and he was leaning close—his arm on the doorframe was the only thing holding him back from leaning his entire body against mine. "Are you okay?"

His question both appeased and chafed. I was a big girl, and I had proven that I could handle difficult situations; Scarborough's temper didn't scare me. Yes, I was embarrassed, and yes, my voice may have wobbled a little when I gave my explanations, but I could do hard things. I needed Jake to know that I could do hard things and that I didn't need rescuing. I wasn't a stray dog. I huffed out a breath. "Jake, I'm okay. I appreciate your concern, but I can handle myself just fine. I deserved Scarborough's ire; you all *do* need to be filled in on everything that I did and learned while I was at the AGI."

Jake lifted my chin until I was looking into his eyes; eyes that were very close in proximity to my own. "Kate, I have never, not for even one second, thought that you were incapable of anything. I know that you can handle yourself. I know that you are strong and smart and logical and practical. I would have stood up for anyone in that situation. The way that Scarborough was treating you was unfair." He rubbed along my jawline with his thumb, and I could feel his warm breath on my face. "But I can't seem to stop myself from getting angry with anyone who's angry with you. I have a serious blind spot when it comes to you; it's why I've taken a step away from a physical relationship. Well, that and that we work together now. But it's not easy. It's actually really, really hard. I have feelings for you that I've tried to put on the back burner for the sake of the mission. I know how badly you want to take down the AGI, and I don't want personal feelings messing with our work and concentration." He closed his eyes briefly and let out a humorless chuckle. "Though, regardless of my intentions, I always seem to focus on you. I can't stop thinking about you and watching you"—he swallowed and lowered his voice—"and dreaming of you." He let his forehead rest against mine and closed his eyes.

I could hear my pulse pounding in my ears, and my voice came out huskier than I'd intended when I said, "So what are we going to do?"

After a few beats, he pushed himself back off the doorframe and smiled slightly. "I've been trying to figure that out for months. Let me know if you come up with a better working plan than I have." And with that, he turned around and walked to his room, closing the door behind him.

CHAPTER 13

Minsk, Belarus
Aksana

Aksana opened 1017's door. The girl was huddled in the corner of her cot like a scared kitten. The only signs that she wasn't a perfectly healthy teenager were the dark circles under her eyes and the fact that she was little more than skin and bones. She knew that Johan brought her food occasionally, always with the excuse that she couldn't die of starvation, they needed the virus to kill her. He was right, but Aksana was so tired of seeing the pretty girl alive that she didn't care what killed her. It had been months of new viruses for 1017 and to no avail. Her body kept fighting them—she kept living through what were literally impossible odds. Every time Aksana gave her a new and improved version of the virus, she was certain that that would be the one to finally get this girl off her hands. If she were honest with herself, she would see that it wasn't the girl she had the problem with, but that the girl represented her failure as a scientist. She couldn't tell her superior about 1017—it would make her look weak, and inevitably he would try and tell her how to do her job. He claimed to be a scientist, but compared to Aksana he was little more than a middle school biology teacher with a big ego. No, she couldn't let him know that 1017 wasn't dying; that would be unacceptable.

The room had old office carpet that had been stained several shades of red, yellow, and green from the bodily fluids of the previous test subjects. It was disgusting, and if Aksana had been 1017, she would have wanted to die just from having to stay in that room.

Dressed in her hazmat suit, she walked up to 1017. The girl gave a weak, "No, please, no more." But Aksana had learned to tune out the cries of the test subjects long ago. She pulled 1017's arm away from her body and punched the needle into the flesh of her upper arm, making sure to deliver every last drop of the virus.

The girl started to cry, but Aksana just stared at her for a moment, hoping beyond hope to see the effects of the virus taking hold quickly. After a few minutes, Aksana turned on her heel and walked out of the room.

CHAPTER 14

Richmond, VA
Kate

Aside from assassination, which wasn't out of the question, we had yet to figure out a way to deal with the Oliver Strands situation. We were seated around the living room and kitchen of one of the rental houses, doing what we did best, yelling out ideas and getting nowhere. We were all tired and frustrated and felt like we were just spinning our wheels when the contact came.

"She's live," Jake called to the room. I was sitting by him on the floor and moved over until my side was flush with his to get a closer look at his screen. I felt a jolt of excitement mixed with absolute dread that Lena had finally gotten in touch with us again. This was it—I was going to have to tell her about the ICT. I saw the red camera light flash, and I knew that Lena could both see and hear us.

Kate! You're back to blonde! You look soooooooo much better!! From one friend to another, never change your hair color again. Lyon, I see you too have gone back to your roots. Nice choice, Kate prefers redheads. <wink>.

Lyon looked over at me, and with a smirk, raised one eyebrow. I smiled and rolled my eyes.

Scarborough motioned to Jake, and with a couple of taps on his keyboard, his screen connected to a projector and flashed on the wall. We'd set it up so that when Lena got in touch again everyone could see the conversation.

Gah! You two are so cute. Kate, I hope this means you've done something about that massive crush you've had on him by now.

I felt my face flush a hot deep scarlet. Fin looked up from his screen, his face smug. "Called it." Everyone else in the group felt badly enough for me that they kept their mouths closed, which almost made it more embarrassing. All of a sudden, I didn't feel so badly about leaving Lena in the AGI.

"Okay, let's get to the point here, Lena." I swallowed, unsure of how to phrase what I had to say next. "There is something I need to tell you." I ran my hands through my hair. "It's important."

Okaaaay.

I closed my eyes for a moment. "First, let me say that it is a big deal, and it's going to feel like the end of the world, but it's not the end of the world."

You're trying to leave me here, aren't you? You CAN'T leave me here, Kate.

I shook my head. "We're not trying to leave you there; we *have* to leave you there."

No, no, no, no, no. Kate, no.

"Lena, stop for a second. Let me explain." I took a breath and went for it. "Lena, remember during training, when I had to get a pacemaker? And you had to have your appendix taken out, and Nick had to have gallbladder surgery?"

Yeeeess . . .

I took a second to think of how to phrase it—how do you tell someone this kind of news? "Well, none of us needed those surgeries. We were drugged, and those drugs caused our bodies to behave in a way that made the surgeries seem necessary."

I'm sorry, come again???

"Lena, you didn't need your appendix removed, though they likely removed it anyway, just to cover their tracks. They needed to get you into surgery so that they could implant you with a device. It's called an Implantable Cardiac Terminator, or an ICT. It's implanted in your heart and connected to a remote. If the remote is detonated then you will die in ten seconds." I took a deep breath, willing myself not to cry. It didn't work. With a choked voice, I continued, "Lena, if we take you out of there, they will kill you. You are too valuable to lose—it's why they implanted you in the first place. They don't have to know where you are, they can kill you at any time. It's how they control us." I sniffed and wiped a tear from my face.

No offense, Kate, but that seems pretty farfetched. Also, it seems like an awful lot of trouble for the AGI to go through. There are easier ways to wield control.

"Does it not seem farfetched that three of us, out of twenty, had health issues that needed surgery all within a couple months of each other?"

That seems a lot more believable than an ICT . . .

I nodded. "You're right. It sounds, and is, crazy. But that doesn't mean it's not true. You know that my dad worked for the AGI. You know that I watched him die of a heart attack right in front of me. You know the eagle pendant I wear every day?"

Yes.

"My dad gave that to me just days before he died. I didn't know until a few months ago that the pendant opened, and there was a thumb drive inside." I looked to Lyon, and he nodded back at me. "I am going to send you the video that was on the thumb drive. We will wait while you watch it."

Lyon had the file on his computer, and within seconds it was sent to Lena. I wrung my hands while we waited. I knew how terrible this revelation was, to know that at any moment you were a mere ten seconds from death. I'm not even sure that it was possible to really wrap your brain around it. Humans aren't built that way.

Lena finally began typing again.

If you were implanted with the ICT, how did you get out?

I paused for a beat. "It's such a long and convoluted story, and I will tell you every single part of it as soon as we get you safe, but suffice it to say that I broke into the detonator room in the Montana AGI facility and ruined my machine. I had had an exploratory surgery through the CIA that showed the ICT to be fairly rudimentary and that all I had to do was turn the machine off and the ICT could be safely removed."

And you didn't think to turn my or anyone else's machines off???

"I did, and I wanted to, but we didn't know at the time exactly what was going to happen when we turned one off. Our resident genius was the one who said I could turn it off safely, but we didn't know for sure until the moment I did it. I had planned to go back for yours, but Westwood caught me in the room. He beat me up badly and tortured me. I barely got out with my life."

So . . . you DID Kill Westwood??

I nodded. "I did."

And Nick and I are just left for dead.

"Lena, Nick is already dead." My tears started in earnest now.

What????? What?!!!!!

I closed my eyes and nodded my head. "There is a medical lab in the Montana facility, and it has refrigerated body drawers. During one of my nighttime searches of the facility, I opened up one of the drawers, and I found Claire's body. She had been tortured, badly. There were several other drawers, and I opened up every one. At the time I was worried about Brahim—it seemed unlikely that he had ghosted you, and I was worried that he might be another casualty of the AGI. But instead of Brahim's body, I found Nick's." I swallowed. "I found out later that the drug they had used to make him require gallbladder surgery hadn't been tested enough. He went into organ failure."

Oh, my gosh. Nick is dead? Nick is dead. And I'm next.

"No, Lena, that is only true if we take you out of there right now, as things are. All you need to do is stay out of trouble and hold tight. We are going to figure this out and get you out of there."

Kate! Me staying out of trouble is more likely to get me flagged than me getting into trouble! You don't know what you're asking! I can't act like nothing is going on, like I didn't just learn that I'm on the verge of death!

I raked my hands through my hair and looked to Jake; he put his hand on my knee and said some familiar words. "Lena, listen to me, you are not going to die. You are not going to die. Believing that you are going to die will make you reckless. What you need right now is to keep your head on straight. Our mission is to take down the AGI. The whole thing. We plan on freeing you as well as all of the other AGI employees. Lena, I want you to know that you are Kate's top priority and therefore have become one of mine. I am giving you my word that we are doing everything in our power to protect you."

Let me get this straight. You guys think that you can take the AGI down? Your little CIA group? And that is supposed to keep me CALM??

Let me tell you something, they are not just one step ahead of you, they are ten steps ahead of you. Westwood's death has done nothing to thwart the AGI in the least. You have no idea of their reach or their capability. And you never will without me. You NEED to get me out, because I can hack ANYTHING. You want to take them down, then you figure out a way to get me out of here alive and I will work with you until it's done.

She wasn't wrong. We could really use her talents. I looked up at the group of CIA officers, and Fin was holding up a piece of paper that said, *We need her.* Other agents were nodding their heads.

Scarborough was rubbing his chin, his tell that he was problem-solving. He came and sat on Lyon's other side so that Lena could see him. "Lena, I'm Officer Scarborough, the leader of this mission. I think you might be right that we need you. Give us a few days, and we will come up with a plan. We will be ready when you get back in touch."

My heart soared at his words and then plummeted just as fast when Lena wrote back.

I don't have a few days, Officer. I found out this morning that they're sending me back to Montana tomorrow.

Jake's head snapped to the screen, "You're going to the Montana facility? Tomorrow?"

Yes.

He smiled. "I have an idea."

CHAPTER 15

Palo Alto, CA
Vinny

It sounded like Tracy was hitting her keyboard with a hammer, and she was huffing out breaths like she'd run ten miles. Vinny looked over to her and with raised eyebrows, asked, "You okay over there?"

Tracy took a sharp breath and bit her lip, her eyes still focused on her computer screen. "Not really."

"Anything I can help with?"

Tracy stopped typing and put an elbow up on her desk, resting her cheek on her fist. She strummed her desk with the other hand. Vinny could tell that she was on the verge of spilling her guts, and if he just pushed a little more, she would open up. "It certainly seems like—"

She cut him off, "Doesn't this seem wrong to you?"

"What?"

She motioned toward her screen. "This! The work we're doing on Oliver Strands. Does it not seem wrong to you?"

He shrugged. "What's wrong with it?"

She gave him a wide-eyed look that implied he was an idiot if he didn't already know. "Vinny! We're pushing a politician in a search engine. A search engine that's supposed to be organic."

He shrugged again. "We're a private company."

She huffed, incredulous. "Vinny! Search is the most used search engine in the world! People rely on us to be the place to find honest information. But now, when they Search any politician, Oliver Strands comes up first. When they Search 'Who is the most honest politician?' Oliver Strands comes up. When people Search 'Who should I vote for?' Oliver Strands comes up! When people Search 'Which toilet paper is the softest?' Oliver freaking Strands comes up! It's *wrong*."

He pointed at her. "Hey, that last one is legit; he talked for two minutes on *The Late Nite Show* about his favorite toilet paper."

She was fully turned toward him now, with all of her tanned, beautiful glory staring right at him; it made it hard to concentrate. It was clear enough that she was having a bit of a crisis that he thought better of teasing her, like he normally would. There was just something so satisfying about giving Tracy a hard time. Vinny really just had one question for her: "Why now? We've been doing stuff like this for years. I never heard you complain when we made GreatStart the biggest name in breakfast foods, or when we made Dr. Paul the go-to guy for all things medical advice, not even when we worked like crazy people to make DNA Global into the biggest DNA testing company in the world. Why now?" He was genuinely curious. He had always had reservations with these kinds of projects, but Tracy had never seemed affected.

She bit her lip, which did nothing to help his concentration, and said more softly, "I don't know. I guess I thought those other things were benign enough that it didn't really matter. But this"—she motioned to her monitor, shaking her head—"it's too much."

"So Search finally jumped the shark?"

Tracy tilted her head and squinted her eyes. "Jumped the shaaak?"

He couldn't help the smile that spread across his mouth at her terrible impression of his accent. "First of all, that's a Boston accent, but yeah, jumped the shark. It's from an episode of *Happy Days* when the Fonz literally jumps over a shark while on water skis. The show started to tank after that episode because they went too far. So

Search jumped the shark for you with this whole Oliver Strands thing."

She laughed, and he couldn't help but notice the crinkle of her eyes. "A simple 'They went too far' would have worked." She laughed again. "But, yeah, I guess they did jump the shaaak this time." Her expression got a little sad. "I guess what I'm really saying is that I'm not sure I can be a part of this anymore." She slumped back in her chair.

Vinny panicked a little. Tracy couldn't quit. Who would he have to share an office with if she left? Some rando? No, thank you. "Hey, don't say that." He leaned close enough to squeeze her knee. "If I'm being honest, I've always had issues with this part of our work. I think it's shady. But we work for Search, and they are a private company who can do what they want. Truth be told, I think it's hurting our brand. The public trusts us less than they used to. There are websites dedicated to proving that Search is biased. Yes, our searches are supposed to be organic, but any Joe Schmo can optimize a company or brand in a search engine. Most companies have an employee who does just that all day long. How much of Search is truly 'organic'?" He shrugged. "Probably not much."

Tracy nodded. "I get that, I really do. But this is the presidency we're talking about, not breakfast foods. It wasn't until we pushed GreatStart and DNA Global that I realized how truly huge Search's impact is. This is a big deal, and unfortunately there are too many Americans who get their news from social media and Search. How can we just stand by and let this happen?"

CHAPTER 16

Kalispell, Montana
Kate

I would have had a whole lot more confidence in Jake's plan had Lena not been the one who had to carry it out. She was an unmatched talent in computers, but stealth and scheming were not her strong points. She was too easily spooked, and she was terrified of getting caught, which made any agent far more likely to get caught.

I paced our hotel room, burning a trail in the short carpet. When Jake told Lena what she was going to have to do in order to pull this off, she'd jumped right on board. I had reservations, though; the job was a huge risk, and I was not at all convinced that Lena could pull it off. She was scheduled to have arrived at the Glacier Park facility two days ago, and in the last two days she'd had several tasks that needed to be done for us in order for this to work. One of those tasks was to was make a bomb.

Lena had never made an explosive device, but Fin's instructions were exact and airtight. I wished more than once that we could have met up with her to give her the supplies that she needed and a comm, or that she still had the computer set up in her old room in the barracks. But there was a new training class that was staying in the barracks now, and the AGI was smart enough to make sure she didn't have any unsupervised computer access. So we were stuck in a Kalispell hotel hoping beyond hope that she could pull this off, with no way of knowing if she did until we were at the meetup spot.

"Kate." Jake patted the bed next to him. "You're going to ruin the floor."

I stopped pacing for a second and smirked at Jake. Then I started up again. "But what if she gets caught? What if she never got into the medical supply room to get the materials she needed? Or what if it all took her extra time and she can't get in touch with us to change the meetup time? What if things didn't go quite as planned and she needs one more day? There are a million things that could go wrong, and we are counting on Lena to pull this off. She has zero experience in espionage. Zero." I fisted my hair and gave it a tug out of frustration while I continued to pace. Over the last two days, Lena had had to break into the facility's lab for supplies and make three explosive devices—one that would implode the door to the detonator room and two that could blow the room, and all of its contents, to smithereens. And, in just a few hours, she was going to have to use those homemade bombs, and then she was going to take advantage of all the uproar to get out of the facility and make it to the meetup spot.

Jake nodded. "We can see from the security footage that things are going as well as they can be. But yes, there are a million things that could go wrong; but, Kate, things could go right, too. And as hard as it is for you to accept, you have no control here." He patted the spot on the bed next to him again. "Come on,"—he shot me a soft smile that had a definite edge of concern—"sit by me for a minute."

I took a deep breath and sat down. But sitting did nothing to calm my anxiety. I bit my lip and drummed my fingers on my knees. Jake tucked a few strands of hair behind my ear, and I turned toward him. "Kate, I know how hard this is." His eyes bored into mine. "Imagine for a minute how I felt when it was *you* in there." He swallowed and shook his head. I was all ears; this was something we'd never talked about, and while I could infer how he felt when I was caught by Westwood, Jake had never actually spoken to me about it. Unfortunately, he didn't say anything more.

"I, at least, had a comm. We have no way of communicating with her. What if she already got caught? What if they're pulling her teeth out as we speak?" My hand went to my jaw—I could feel a shadow of the pain of having my molar yanked out of my mouth at just the thought.

At that, Jake was up pacing, running his hands through his hair. "We can't talk about that." He shook his head. "I went crazy that night."

I stood up and stopped his pacing by grabbing him by the shoulders. "Jake, it all worked out, and I'm fine." I motioned to my mouth and down my body. "Thanks to you."

He had a haunted look in his eyes. "When you were screaming in pain, when Westwood was hurting you, when he had his hands on you . . ." Jake shook his head as if he were trying to clear the memory. He cupped my face with his hands, his voice little more than a whisper. "Kate, I have *never* felt that kind of fear or rage, and I've been doing this for a long time." His thumbs caressed my cheeks, and I breathed in his scent, that mix of sandalwood and masculinity. "The strength of my feelings scared me; it still scares me. I never want to go through that again."

I put my hands over his. "I wish I could tell you that you never will." I gave him an apologetic look. "But we're trying to take down the most corrupt organization the world has ever seen. The work we do is dangerous, and I need to know that you're going to let me do what has to be done. Even when it puts me in danger."

He stepped away from me and roughly ran his hands through his hair. "Kate, I'm trying. I'm trying. Being here in this hotel"—he shook his head—"it's taking my mind to dark places."

That much I understood. This was the hotel they'd stayed in the night I broke into the detonator room; it was where they were when I was being tortured by Westwood.

Jake looked at me. "Imagine if the tables were turned and I was the one being tortured, someone had me chained to a wall and was pulling out my teeth, I was screaming in pain, and you had to listen to it, powerless to help me."

My stomach dropped and spun. The idea of hearing someone make Jake scream in pain, and me being powerless to help had me seeing red. I put my hand up. "Okay, I get it." I swallowed back the burn in my throat.

He stepped up to me and cupped my face with his hands again. "That's why this is so hard for me. You're just imagining it; I had to *experience* it. It's part of the reason I had to take a step back from us." He shook his head. "I'm too caught up in you, I'm too afraid of something happening to you."

"And is taking a step back helping you become less worried about me?" I took a chance and leaned in slightly, until I could feel his warm breath on my face.

His eyes burned into mine. "Not even a little." His thumbs stroked my face again, and he blinked several times. He licked his lips and leaned the rest of the way in. His lips had just barely brushed mine when the door to the room started to open.

We jumped apart like two teenagers caught by their parents. Scarborough, Fin, and Mark either didn't notice the tension between us or decided to ignore it as they carried in the food they'd picked up.

I stole a glance at Jake, who had his hands on his hips and his brows furrowed. I was glad that I wasn't alone in my irritation at being interrupted. At least I hoped that he was frustrated at being interrupted and not because he had let down his guard with me. Jake had been about to kiss me but never got the chance. I hoped that didn't set us back.

"We got the very best Kalispell had to offer—Quarter Pounders and fries for everyone." Mark held the bags of fast food aloft like they were a trophy, and as hungry as we all were, it was most definitely a prize.

Scarborough put his hand on my shoulder. "You hanging in there, Edison?"

I cringed a little. "Kind of?"

He nodded. "It's the hardest part of the job." He let his hand drop. "Officers mistakenly think that the work, being undercover—especially when the margin of error is practically nonexistent—is the hardest part of the job." He shook his head. "They are wrong. This—"he brought a hand up and moved it in a circular motion, to showcase us all waiting for Lena—"This is the hardest part. The not knowing, the waiting and hoping and praying that the people you work with are safe and that the very important work they are doing is getting done."

I nodded, knowing that he was right. Being tortured is not nearly as bad as listening to a loved one being tortured. I so badly wished that I could trade places with Lena. I knew how to do the job that she was doing; I had full confidence that I could get it done without a hitch. I craved being the one in control. The waiting was an anxiety-inducing nightmare. "I'm just so stressed. This kind of work has never been Lena's strong suit, and if they catch her, it's over. The bullet they will not hesitate to shoot her with will kill her even faster than the ICT."

Scarborough nodded. "Don't underestimate the power of determination. When a person's life is on the line, they can accomplish incredible things. Lena knew the risks and she didn't hesitate. This is how she's taking her power back after learning about the ICT. She has a score to settle, and I won't be surprised in the least when she walks up to the meeting point."

I smiled for the first time in days. That, right there, was why Scarborough was the mission leader. "Thank you, I needed to hear that."

He nodded once, quickly. "Good, now go get some food before those Neanderthals eat it all."

CHAPTER 17

Glacier National Park
Kate

The late-night March air was cold, and the wind whipped all around us, blowing snow in our faces and freezing us to the bone. We were in a copse of trees one kilometer southwest of the AGI facility, waiting for Lena. She had the coordinates so she knew where to find us. Our plane was another ten miles away through treacherous territory. We had used the closest Glacier Park ranger station that had a landing strip, then had to borrow snowmobiles from the rangers to get the rest of the way.

Lena was supposed to have been there an hour ago. And every minute that ticked by had the knots in my stomach cinching tighter. Jake's gloved hand discreetly held mine. He knew how nervous I was.

"How long are we going to give her?" Mark asked.

I shot him the dirtiest look I could muster. I knew he was freezing—we all were—but we were not leaving until either Lena showed up or the light of day required us to retreat. And if the latter happened, we would be doing the same thing the next night and the night after that.

Fortunately for Mark, Scarborough answered instead of me; he was much nicer. "As long as it takes."

Fin's voice sounded in our comms: "I can't leave these cameras looped all night. Someone is going to notice." He was staying at the hotel to take care of the AGI security feed.

"Let's give her as much time as we can, Fin," Scarborough responded.

"Whatever you say, boss. Just know that I don't recommend it."

Scarborough, stoic as ever, replied, "Noted."

Another miserable hour passed, and we were all huddled together in an attempt to stay warm, when we heard the rumble. It sounded like a long clap of thunder, and the ground underneath us trembled slightly. Relief flooded me, and excitement seemed to heat my body a few precious degrees. Jake squeezed my hand and said to the group, "That was it, she did it."

"About time," Fin said into our comms.

Then the chaos started. Screaming and shouting. I smiled again. The pandemonium had begun.

"Okay, officers, she should be here within ten minutes; let's make sure we are ready to head out as soon as she arrives."

I couldn't help the snort that escaped. "We are over half a mile from headquarters, and the way is dark, cold, and blanketed in deep snow. There is no way Lena will get here in ten minutes; multiply that by three—at least."

They all turned to me. I laughed, and it felt so good. "Imagine that Fin was Lena in this situation . . ."

Mark threw his head back. "Oh, great."

I smirked. "Exactly."

Fin spoke up in our ears, "I can hear you."

Mark and I said, "We know" at the same time and then we erupted into laughter.

Jake's mood wasn't nearly as buoyant as ours. I looked at him and raised my eyebrows in question. He said, "I don't like to celebrate until the job is complete." Party pooper.

But as the minutes ticked by, I realized that Jake was right. A job wasn't done until it was done; Lena still wasn't there. After thirty minutes, we started giving each other concerned glances. At forty minutes, I started worrying my bottom lip and hands. At fifty minutes, Scarborough looked at me. "Kate, should we be concerned?"

My eyes started to sting with tears, and I nodded my head. With my teeth chattering, I said, "What are our options? Would you be opposed to us making our way toward the facility, just to be sure?"

Mark started to shake his head, but Scarborough took me by surprise when he said, "That seems as good an idea as any."

The wind whipped at our faces as we started in the direction of headquarters, my heart heavy. Lena had been caught. That was the only explanation. She was either dead or being tortured for information, and Lena didn't do torture. "She'll tell them everything." I shook my head from both fear and concern in quick succession. "Lena told me once that she would sing like a bird if she were threatened with pain."

Jake squeezed my hand. "Don't forget that she has a score to settle. She may not fold so easily."

I wished that I could feel relief at his words; he may have been right, but he didn't know Lena like I did, and I wasn't convinced. And if she had indeed gotten caught, what did that mean for the rest of our mission? Had I blown everything because I wanted to save my friend? How many lives had I put at risk for one person? All of this work and she was lost anyway. I knew the men around me had lost partners and friends. They did it for the greater good, they made the hard decisions, they did what was right. I wasn't one of them yet, but I needed to be. We needed to go back before we were found by the AGI and this entire thing blew up in smoke. There was too much at stake here.

Decision made, I stopped walking. "Wait." They all stopped and turned toward me, and I closed my eyes for a second to gather some courage, when I heard her. My eyes flashed open. "Did you hear that?" They shook their heads, and I held up my hands. "Shh-hhh—listen."

"Shut up!" That was Lena—I was positive. I heard male laughter and my head shot up, brows furrowed. "I'm serious, y'all! These are CIA officers we're meetin' in the dark, and they don't know you two buffoons are taggin' along." My relief was a palpable thing, something so strong I could touch it, but relief wasn't the only thing I felt. Panic was rising inside me. She'd brought people with her?

Mark, Jake, and Scarborough had their guns out the second they heard that Lena wasn't alone. I held my hands out and motioned for them to hold their fire; I wanted to find out who was with her. Clearly it wasn't a threat—otherwise she wouldn't have been talking to them the way that she was. Regardless, though, what was she thinking? The CIA did not welcome surprises; they killed surprises. And these three officers that I was with would, without a doubt, shoot first and ask questions later.

"Lena?" I quietly called.

"Kate? Is that you? Why aren't you guys at the meetup spot?" Lena's voice sounded from about twenty feet away, and I could hear the concern in her tone. I'm not sure how she had been planning on breaking the news that she had tagalongs with her, but I could tell that this wasn't it. Regardless, it was happening now. Lena and her entourage were close, and I could feel the tension rolling off Scarborough, Jake, and Mark.

"It's us, Lena. You had taken so long that we were starting a search party."

She had moved even closer when she said, "Y'all,"—she cleared her throat—"um . . . I'm not alone . . . Brahim and Liam are with me."

I gasped and ran for the sound of her voice, but Jake grabbed my arm, holding me back. I turned back to him, and he was looking at me like I had lost my mind. I understood where he was coming from; he didn't know Liam and Brahim like I did. So I smiled and said, "It's okay—it's more than okay, actually."

He didn't smile back at me. "It is definitely *not* okay. And you are definitely *not* running out there to greet people we don't know, people who haven't been vetted for our inner circle."

I took a deep breath and tried to see from his perspective: there were two men trying to join our group that he didn't know, and they were current AGI agents. I understood that there could have been so many problems with that. They could be acting like Lena's friends but really be here to take me or kill me, they could be AGI informants, or bugged, or tracked, or just dead weight that our group couldn't afford to take on.

But this wasn't just anybody, it was Brahim and Liam. I may not have specialized in reading people like Jake had, but I knew in my soul that these were good people. "Jake, Liam was the reason I made it out of the AGI facility alive. If it had been anyone else in that outpost stand, I wouldn't be here right now. Nick was his friend, too, and he knows that he's dead. I had him convinced enough that the AGI was corrupt that he risked his life to save me." His hold on my arm seemed to soften somewhat. "And Brahim is as talented as Lena,"—I paused—"well, almost as talented as Lena."

Brahim sounded loud and clear from just outside our little circle. "Hey! I heard that! Do not underestimate the Bramister!"

Then Lena said, "Shut up! I'm serious! Now is not the time, Brahim."

I tried to hold in my chuckle, but it came out anyway in a sort of cough/laugh mashup. "Listen, Brahim has been with the AGI for the longest; he could be very valuable to us"—Jake opened his mouth to speak, but I cut him off—"*after* he has been vetted. After they both have been vetted."

Scarborough spoke up. His gun was down, and it seemed that he knew that whatever they decided to do about our tagalongs, he wasn't going to kill them. "And how do you propose we vet them? I'm not letting them anywhere near you, and the only way out of here is by plane, and ours is currently ten miles away. We don't even have enough room on our snowmobiles for two extra men."

Liam spoke up, "We can squish!"

I laugh/coughed again. The poor soul who had to squish with Liam the giant. I was giddy with excitement that they were all there. I wasn't oblivious to the fact that Mark, Jake, and Scarborough were not happy and did not find this situation to be favorable at all. But my heart was so happy, even their tension and alarm couldn't squash it.

With all three of them still hidden in the trees, Brahim spoke: "I know you all have your reservations about us, and for good reason. I stayed blind to the AGI's practices for far too long. I believed they were who they said they were." He was being uncharacteristically serious, which I hoped might go a long way in placating the

CIA officers. "But I was sent on an assignment a few months ago, and it changed everything. The work I was tasked with opened my eyes, and I am scared to death. I am willing to tell the CIA everything I know, and I know something that is huge."

Scarborough, Mark, and Jake looked at each other, silently making decisions. We all knew that ultimately it all came down to Scarborough, but he was a good leader, and good leaders consulted with their inferiors and considered their opinions. I could tell that, at the very least, they all wanted to know what Brahim had to say, but they also didn't have any reason to trust him or Liam. It would have been reckless for them to just allow Brahim and Liam to come with us, but they had good intel, and we really needed good intel.

Scarborough scrubbed his gloved hand down his face. He said loudly enough for only our group to hear, "If they were here to kill Kate, she would have already been shot at. I'm not comfortable bringing them with us, but I'm less comfortable leaving them here." With a resigned look, he motioned for Mark to follow him into the trees.

"We're coming your way; make sure any and all weapons are on the ground. If you have a weapon on you, we will shoot, and we don't miss." Mark pulled out the bug scanner we had brought for Lena just in case.

They must have scanned Lena first, because the next thing I knew she was running through the trees, arms wide, her curly red hair bouncing all around. A huge smile broke out on my face, and she slammed her body against mine in a tight hug. "Oh, my gosh, I can't believe we did it." I heard a sniffle, and her voice was choked when she said, "Thank you, Kate. Thank you so much." I pulled back, and she had tears streaming down her face, which made my eyes instantly tear up. I knew what it felt like to be free of the ICT— it was no small thing. Her machine had been ruined in the blast, but the device was still in her, and I wouldn't rest until she was truly free.

"Lena, I missed you so much. I'm so relieved that you're here."

Lena started to laugh through her tears. "You didn't think I could pull it off, did you?"

"I knew you could pull it off." Jake snorted at that, and Lena gave me a skeptical look. "Okay, I was little worried."

"Like burned a hole in the hotel floor from pacing, worried," Jake piped in.

"Well, you had every reason to be. I talk a big game, but there is no way I could have pulled that off by myself. Brahim and Liam recognized that I was acting shady right away. They cornered me and told me that they knew that the AGI was corrupt and that if I had a plan to get us out, they wanted in. We did this together. In fact, Liam was the one who gathered all of the supplies and made the bombs." My eyes widened in surprise. "I know, right? Who would have thought? Honestly, Liam was pretty freakin' awesome." She paused while I let that information sink in. "Also, Brahim has the ICT, too. Back when I had my appendectomy,"—she used air quotes when she said *appendectomy*—"Brahim was with me, and he told me that he'd had appendicitis too when he started with the AGI and that the doctors were great." She rolled her eyes. And I wondered, not for the first time, how the AGI had gotten away with this for so long. "I told him about the ICT, about the message from your dad, everything. I felt like he deserved to know. He hasn't been himself lately. But escaping from the AGI and joining with the CIA—just the idea of it has brought some of the light back into his eyes."

"We're going to need that whole story in detail, very soon," Jake said.

Lena looked to him and smiled widely. "Jake Lyon, in the flesh." She turned and wrapped him in one of her borderline-painful hugs. Jake's eyes bulged, and his eyebrows shot to his hairline. I snickered. "Thank you for getting me out of there."

She pulled back, and Jake's smile was sincere. "Just doing my job."

We turned toward the movement coming from the forest and saw Scarborough and Mark come through the trees with Liam and Brahim. I was surprised that their hands weren't zip-tied together, but I supposed they would need to be able to use them while we were on the snowmobiles.

I ran over and gave them both hugs, my eyes stinging with tears at seeing them both whole and well. I had been worried about Liam the most; he had let me escape the AGI, and the other officer that he was with well knew it. I was worried about what the AGI had done to him in retaliation. Lena, Brahim, and Liam knew so very little about what the AGI really was. I had a feeling that when we got back to Kalispell, we were going to have a very long night.

Before I could say a word to them, Scarborough cleared his throat. "We will be taking both Mr. Awan and Mr. David," he held out Liam's last name for a beat longer than normal and then paused, for what seemed like dramatic effect. Funny thing was that I had never heard Liam's last name before; within the AGI, many of us were called by our last names, but never Liam. Scarborough cleared his throat again, "back with us for questioning. They have no weapons and are not bugged. We are going to have to double up." He made a pointed look at Lena, Jake, and me. "You three are going to have to triple up." He looked back at Brahim. "Mr. Awan, you are with me."

Mark threw his hands up in the air. "What? I have to take the Incredible Hulk?"

Scarborough flashed a smile. "It pays to be the boss."

Scarborough had just barely finished his sentence when shots rang out. Scarborough, Mark, Lyon, and I had our guns out in an instant. I started firing back but stopped when I realized I was the only one. Scarborough, Lyon, and Jake had their guns trained on Brahim, Liam, and Lena. They had their hands up, and Liam spoke first, "I know how this looks, but we have nothing to do with that." He pointed into the woods, where the firing had momentarily ceased when I'd shot back.

Brahim spoke next, "They're after me for what I know." He swallowed. "I think they followed our footprints."

Scarborough looked to Jake for confirmation—he was the human lie detector of the group. He nodded once and then, almost instantly, his eyes widened, and he fell forward in the snow. He'd been shot. Bullets started whizzing through the trees. I fell to my knees at Jake's side, and Mark tossed guns to Brahim, Liam, and

Lena. The only one who really knew how to use it well was Liam, having been a former Ranger. He took shots, and we heard grunts from beyond the trees, signifying that people had been hit.

I felt all around Jake, trying to find where the bullet had hit. I could not allow my emotions to take over. The thought of Jake injured or worse was unthinkable, and it would paralyze me. My hands were in his hair, down his arms, legs, and back when it finally dawned on me: there was no blood. There was no blood. I sat back on my knees and blinked to clear my eyes. The shot must have hit his bulletproof vest. Still, a bullet to the back over a vest was no joke—it had knocked him out cold. Just as I looked up to tell the guys, Liam bent down, picked Jake up with one arm, threw him on his back, and ran in the direction our footprints indicated we'd come from.

I registered that I was being tugged to my feet and practically thrown in the direction of Liam and Jake. Lena, Brahim, and I ran toward the clearing with Scarborough and Mark on our tails, continuing to shoot behind them as we went.

As we made our way to the snowmobiles, Jake had come to but was still pretty out of it. We hopped on, with me driving with Jake sandwiched in between me and Lena. He had enough strength to hold on, so I wasted no time and took off following Mark and Liam, who were the first to leave. As we followed, I saw a trail of blood in the white snow.

CHAPTER 18

Glacier National Park

The two park rangers looked at each other when the second group of gun-wielding men came into their outpost. This was more excitement than they'd seen in . . . well . . . ever. The one in charge was a tall man who appeared to be in his forties, mid-forties maybe. He had blond hair, and those with him referred to him as CO Smith.

Smith's voice was ice: "Did you let a group of people borrow snowmobiles?"

One of the rangers answered, "We did."

Smith spoke again, "Who were they? How many? Were any of them gravely injured, and if so, I want a full description." He bit out every word, like it was painful talking to mere park rangers.

The second ranger bristled at his tone. "They were CIA, sir. They had badges, and that's all we are going to tell you."

Smith help up his gun, and the people with him did the same. "Answer my questions."

The first ranger didn't want any trouble. "There were four who arrived by Cessna, three men and one woman. But seven came back. One, a large man, was bleeding but still walking. They left in the same plane."

"The small one, the Middle Eastern man, was he with them?"

"Yes, he left with them."

Smith swore and shot the rangers in the head and turned on his heel and left, telling his minions to dispose of the bodies.

No one took notice of the small camera in the upper corner of the outpost.

CHAPTER 19

Cambridge, MA
Arthur

Arthur walked along the Charles; the weather was bitterly cold, but he enjoyed the scenic route to work anyway. As he was approaching the DNA Global building, he took a minute to enjoy the last bit of fresh air he would get before night fell and he finally got to leave the office. The sun was shining on his face, and he hoped that was a foreshadowing of his day.

He waved to the doorman and made his way to the elevators and up to his office suite on the top floor of the building. His expansive corner office was all windows, and he could see half of Boston from his vantage point. The day he moved into this office, Arthur knew he had made it. His extensive, not to mention expensive, education and hard work had paid off. He sat down at his desk and adjusted the picture of his wife, Alice, and their two daughters. He smiled at the giggling girls in the photo. They were little more than toddlers when the picture was taken, and now they were teenagers; Arthur really missed those younger years.

He opened up his email, and all of his happy thoughts vanished in a flash. The sunshine was not a foreshadowing after all. If the skies had opened up and pelted freezing rain on him, it would have been far more fitting. He stared at the message, trying to calm his racing heart enough to read it properly.

Arthur may have been the CEO, but he did not have complete managing responsibility. No, that responsibility belonged to the parent company, and when they wanted something, he was powerless to refuse. Months ago, they had told Arthur that they wanted access to all of the DNA samples they had ever tested as well as the personal information of the sample owners. It wasn't the first time that they had requested DNA information, but they had never asked for complete and unfiltered access. They knew that all of that information was stored in a locked room in the basement of the building and was protected from infiltration; the room itself was a large Faraday cage, blocking any and all electromagnetic communication. They told him not to worry about that, just to give them access and they would take care of the rest. They said that they wanted feedback from the customers who had received their genetic disease test results. But Arthur had yet to see any surveys go out. He wasn't stupid, he knew their request wasn't for feedback, but he didn't know what it was really for. He wasn't entirely sure he wanted to know.

The request wasn't a breach of the privacy agreement, but it wasn't exactly on the up-and-up either. DNA Global did keep the results of all of their customers, as was stated in the privacy policy, but they were never to be shared. Technically, they hadn't been shared with anyone outside the company, as it was the parent company that wanted the results. But if anyone found out, it would not look good for DNA Global. They had hundreds of millions of customers, and they were the most trusted name in the business. Arthur didn't want that reputation to change.

He liked his job; he'd worked hard for this position and the celebrity that came with it. If he'd refused to hand over the information when they'd asked, they would simply have fired him and gotten someone new to take his place. They'd made that clear in no uncertain terms when he'd questioned why they wanted the results in the first place.

The email he'd received made him begin to sweat and hyperventilate. He shook his head and read it again.

Mr. Whitehall,

We have a possible problem on our hands. One of our employees has gone missing. This particular employee has a gifted mind and is considered a genius by any estimation. He was the one tasked with making the test results of the customers of DNA Global available to us. Even though he was doing the work from a secure location, we have reason to believe that he may be able to access the results remotely. We don't need to tell you the implications this has for DNA Global. We have a search going for him now and will bring in the authorities if needed.

Stand by—we may need you to do a press conference if this goes public.

Arthur's hands were shaking so hard that it took him several tries to hit the button to close his email. They had screwed up. And they were going to pin it on him.

CHAPTER 20

Baltimore, MD
Kate

"How are you feeling?" Liam and I were walking to the living room of the house that our group of officers were meeting in.

He looked over at me and raised one eyebrow. I was mildly envious of people who could do that. "Are you inquiring about my arm or my mental state?"

When we got back to Kalispell, we'd gone directly to the airport. Fin was already there with all of our stuff. We hopped on the small plane while the airport attendants filled it with gas, and we were in the air in no time flat. As soon as we were off, we all let out the deep breath we'd been holding. Brahim was the first to speak: "Soooo, I guess we should have considered the trail our footprints were leaving in the snow."

Jake, who was bruised and sore, shrugged and then winced, the movement causing him pain. "There really isn't much you can do about that."

Fin scoffed. "They could have led them on a wild-goose chase through the woods. Instead they led them straight to you guys." He rolled his eyes, making it clear that he thought they were complete amateurs.

Mark shook his head. "It took them too long to get to the meeting point as it was; we would have assumed the worst and left if they had taken much longer." That was the truth—I had been planning on ending the search the second before I heard Lena.

"Hey, don't worry about the possibility of me bleeding out or anything," Liam grunted.

"We won't," Fin deadpanned.

Liam had been shot in the arm and had still managed to pick up Lyon, who was dead weight, and carry him on his back to the snowmobile. Earlier, when I'd asked him how he did that, he'd said, "I'm an Army Ranger, it's what we do."

Lena had gotten up. "Is there a first aid kit on this thing?"

"Oh. I wasn't aware that you were a doctor," Fin said, being ever so helpful.

"Well, since none of you seem to be jumping up to help my friend, I figured I'd better be the one to do it," Lena snapped back.

"Well, if you had any medical knowledge at all, you would know that because Liam isn't bleeding profusely from his would, it is much safer to leave the bullet in and wait for a trained medical professional," Fin shot out.

"I wasn't planning to remove the bullet, you moron. I was going to wrap his arm and give him some painkillers." Lena's brow was furrowed and her words sharp.

Fin flashed a ghost of a smile. "It's in the cabinet in the bathroom."

After that, we had a frank conversation about the AGI. Brahim didn't really seem all that surprised, but Liam and Lena were somewhat blindsided. They had thought that the AGI was still legit but that it was run by some corrupt leadership. But even Brahim hadn't suspected that the AGI had started at the founding of our country, was worldwide, and that their ultimate goal was a New World Order. We also discussed the ICT, and Brahim told us that Lena had told him about it already and that he believed he had one as well. Good thing they'd blown up the entire detonator room. Liam, thank goodness, hadn't had any surgeries since joining the AGI.

In light of all that had happened, I was interested in how Liam's arm was faring as well as his mental state. The truth of the AGI was a lot to take in. I shot him a tight but sincere smile. "How is your arm, as well as your current state of mind?"

"Eh, my arm is fine." He shrugged. "It's not the first time I've been shot. As for everything else, I think I'm kind of in shock. I still can't seem to process it all. I mean, it's not that I don't believe that the AGI is what you say they are—I've seen some messed-up stuff with my own eyes. But how could they have pulled this off for so many years? That part is hard to believe. I guess I'm still wrapping my head around it all."

I nodded. "Yeah, I get that. We weren't the first people to discover the issues with the AGI, though; otherwise the ICT would never have been invented. They needed a way to keep people in line, and it worked for a long time. I do think, however, that they have never seen a threat like us. They don't know the extent of our connection to the CIA—we aren't just a group of rogue ex-agents, we are a force to be reckoned with."

Liam placed his hand on my arm. "Kate, I want you to know that I'm on board. I'm all in. I'll do whatever it takes to be a part of this group and take down the AGI."

"I know, Liam. They're going to see that too—just give it a little time." I paused for a second, cleared my throat, and said, "Also, I haven't had the chance to formally thank you for saving my life when I was escaping the AGI back in December." I shook my head and let out a humorless laugh. "A thank-you is so incredibly inadequate. But thank you, so much." I got on my tiptoes and gave the giant man a hug.

I pulled back, and he was sincere when he said, "I've been an Army Ranger for a long time. I've seen and killed enemies of all kinds. When you were talking to me that night, I knew in my bones that you were not the enemy."

I had to ask the question, even if I wasn't sure I really wanted to know the answer: "Did they retaliate against you for letting me go?"

"They pulled me and the other agents who were in the outpost that night into Smith's office. He told us that Westwood had been killed and that he was the new chief officer."

It wasn't the first time I'd heard that news, but it sent chills down my spine nonetheless. Why Smith? Why not Cave or Yu? I couldn't imagine a more vicious man to run the AGI.

"He questioned us at length, and it became clear that I was the guilty party. He let the other guys go. I told him that you and I had become friends and that when the time came, I just couldn't kill you. We had a long conversation in which I was threatened and threatened some more. He told me that they had found out that you had gotten yourself into a lot of trouble and had done unspeakable things, like sold children on the black market." My heart stuttered. "He said that if you ever got in touch with me, I was to tell him immediately. And then he let me go. I was on constant watch after that. I think he hoped that we were close enough friends that you would come back for me." He looked a little downtrodden that I hadn't ever come looking for him.

My mind was whirling; there were a lot of things Liam had just told me that needed serious attention, but I knew that the first order of business was to be honest with my friend. I took his hand and squeezed it. "Liam, I'm so sorry. I'm sure that you felt abandoned by me, but I promise you that you and Lena and Brahim were always on my mind. I wanted to get you out, but frankly, I have very little pull with the CIA, pretty much no pull at all. Working with them is both a dream and an exercise in absolute frustration. Even the simplest of jobs has five rows of red tape. We may have developed an escape plan for Lena first, but I never forgot about you." I took a deep breath. "Liam, I've been worried sick imagining what they might have done to you the night that I left. It's kept me up at night, and when I'd finally fall asleep, I'd have nightmares about it. I'm so grateful that things turned out the way they did and that I have all three of you back." I worried my lip. "Now we're just going to have to convince the rest of the group of that."

"Yeeeaaah, I don't think that is going to be very easy . . ."

I squeezed his hand one more time and let it drop. We walked into the living room, and the whole group was there waiting for us. We grabbed a couple of muffins that had been set out for breakfast and sat down next to Lena and Brahim on the floor, as all of the couches and comfy chairs had been taken. Our little band of re-formed AGI agents.

Scarborough jumped right in. "We have a lot going on today that we need to discuss." *We certainly did.* "But first things first. Everyone meet Brahim Awan, Liam David, and Lena Johnson, all former AGI agents." Liam and Brahim smiled tightly, and Lena put her hand up in an awkward wave; they all seemed a bit intimidated by the CIA agents. "As I'm sure you all have heard, we picked up more than we bargained for last night." It was hard to believe that just a handful of hours ago we had all been on a flight back from Montana.

As soon as we got back, Dr. Williams and Dr. Bakshi had been there to deal with Liam's bullet wound as well as to check out Lyon. Lyon had a fractured rib. The bullet in Liam's arm was easily removed and his flesh was stitched back together. All in all, we got out with very few injuries.

"Have any of them had background checks?" Megan, who now had pink highlights, asked.

Scarborough, seeming to hold back a smile, nodded. "Awan and Johnson were pulled into the AGI via the NSA, and they had background checks before going through the recruitment process. Liam David was pulled from military intelligence, and he has a level-five clearance."

Jake's eyebrows rose, and I heard a whistle from someone else in the room. Level five was as high as it got. That was top secret. I looked over to Liam in disbelief.

"What, you all thought I was just a pretty face?" Liam looked mock offended.

Lena laughed. "No, we all thought you were a dumb jock." She was looking at Liam like he had two heads.

Brahim coughed/said, "Totally."

Liam's offense was no longer mocking when he said, "What? Seriously? How do you think I was recruited into the AGI in the first place, you jerks?" He threw his hands up but then winced because it hurt his bullet wound.

I patted his arm. "We all thought you were smart, didn't we, guys?"

"No! We all just thought you were a massive perv! I had no idea what you did to get into the AGI, but I did wonder about it from time to time." Lena pointed her finger at him as she continued to talk, "Also, you always said that you were an Army Ranger."

"I was an Army Ranger . . . until a couple of years ago, when I was pulled into military intelligence and moved up in the ranks at alarming speed." He winked at us and smiled. "Part of my assignment with the AGI was to mask my real talents. Apparently, I did a good job."

"So, what are your real talents?" Megan piped up.

Liam's smile was slow when he turned to her and said, "Wouldn't you like to know?"

Megan giggled, actually *giggled*. Lena and I rolled our eyes at the same time.

Scarborough was excited, and he was *smiling*. It looked foreign on his face—I'd only ever seen him serious and calculating. He cleared his throat. "Mr. David was a sniper. One of the best." Whaaaaat?

Liam scoffed, "Ha! *The* best."

Scarborough was smiling fully then, and nodding, and if I didn't know better, I would've said that he was internally fangirling. "He is arguably the best sniper in existence. Mr. David went on to lead missions for military intelligence. He planned and personally executed those missions. I've heard of him many times in my work for the CIA." I looked over to Lena and Brahim, the shock as widespread on their faces as I was sure it was on my own. How could we have not known any of this?

It was like a light went on for Jake; he snapped his fingers and said, "Wait a second, you're *William David*?"

Liam was trying to hide his smile. "I go by Liam."

Jake was across the room, openly gaping, and I was tempted to walk over and close his mouth. He was definitely fangirling.

"Are you kidding me?" Jake ran his hands through his hair, and his smile was beaming. "We inadvertently saved *William David* from the hands of the AGI?" He threw his hands up in the air and hollered, "We just got the best stroke of luck we've ever had!"

I was mildly offended. I looked over to Lena and Brahim, and I could tell that they were offended, too. Their expressions made me laugh out loud.

Jake turned to Scarborough. "How long have you known?"

Scarborough was smiling widely. "I suspected back in Montana. I had seen his picture before, and when he told me his last name, it clicked. Then when we were being fired at, I knew for sure. I threw him a gun, and he turned in the direction that the shots were coming from and started taking out men left and right. I couldn't even make out shadows, much less land a shot." He turned toward Liam. "So it's true, then. You don't even need to see an enemy to take them out?"

Liam looked like he was going to shrug, but thought better of it with his wound so fresh. "Kind of. That has been played up over the years. I'm able to immediately analyze where a bullet has been shot from by the type of rounds used, direction, and the force of the hit. It's not an exact science, but I'm fairly accurate, even when I can't see the shooter."

"How did you know what type of rounds they were shooting?"

Liam cleared his throat, trying to hide a smirk. "I don't need to see the bullets; I can differentiate them by sound."

Jake's and Scarborough's smiles grew even wider; if they'd gotten any bigger, I was afraid that their faces might have split right open. They were worse than teenage girls.

There was so much excitement in the room that the air itself almost seemed to crackle. It felt like we had a megastar in our midst. Liam was more than just an endearing, helpful, and moderately pervy guy. I had a lot to learn about who Liam really was, apparently.

Mark asked the same question that he often asked me and that had always seemed to perplex him: "Why did you ever take a position with the AGI?" Even as he was asking, the fact that he thought we were all idiots for ever thinking that the AGI was legit was very evident on his face.

"Same reason everyone else did, man." Liam shook his head, irritated that he, too, had been conned. "They're a lot more convincing than you think."

Candace, always one to stay on task, chimed in, "Okay, I'm glad we saved the sharpshooter, but let's not forget that we don't know anything about these three people. Any, or all, of them may still be loyal to the AGI." Lena, Brahim, and Liam reared back in shock. She shook her head. "They need to be debriefed regarding their time there, and they shouldn't be a part of any of our meetings until we are absolutely sure they are who they claim to be." Candace had clearly not fallen under Liam's spell.

I turned to her. "If they aren't a part of our meetings, what exactly do you think we should do with them?"

"I don't know. We aren't an orphanage for ex-AGI agents. We are the CIA, and we have a job to do. And the way I see it, that job is not getting done." Candace Beaujour was your classic pull-no-punches badass. She had a confidence about her that made her hard to disagree with. She was not only a great officer, she was gorgeous. Tall, with perfectly shaped muscles for days and huge brown eyes, framed with thick lashes. She had rich mahogany skin and awesomely big curly hair; her looks alone were a force to be reckoned with. But when you added her strong personality, she was as intimidating as they came.

Candace was not a person I wanted to go up against, but I had to disagree with her on a few points. "I see your point, of course I do. But these guys escaped; they ran from and were shot at by the AGI, not to mention that Liam killed several of their pursuers." I held up my hand, knowing that she wanted to cut me off. "Could this be a big master plan by the AGI? Perhaps, but given the circumstances, I think that is very unlikely. The AGI recruits very well, and the people they hire are very good. We all just learned about Liam and his talents, but Lena and Brahim have a ton to offer our group as well. I think we are much stronger with them than we would be without them."

Candace sighed. "Kate, none of that matters. We can't guarantee that they are on our side. We can't just pull any smart person off the street and put them on the job. We have a process for this; we are trained in a way that civilians aren't. Adding them to our team is so far away from CIA policy that it's off the map."

Jake, finally down from his Liam high, said, "We can't add them to our team, but they can be used as informants."

Candace nodded. "Yes, as informants, but they shouldn't be privy to our plans. Listen, I'm not trying to ruffle any feathers; ultimately, it's up to Scarborough." She turned to look at our team leader. "I just want you to know that some of us are opposed to just bringing these guys on. We need more information on them, and we don't have the time to waste to get it."

Scarborough nodded once. "Thank you, Beaujour. I haven't made a final decision regarding how we're going to utilize our new informants. For now, we have other things to discuss, things that they might be able to help with."

Candace nodded, and he went on, "It has come to our attention that the AGI seems to be most concerned with Brahim Awan." Scarborough picked up the remote and turned on the large flat-screen TV behind him. Jake came and sat next to me, seemingly to get a better view, but I was momentarily distracted by his woodsy scent and the way his pinky finger grazed mine.

Too quickly, though, we had a huge bucket of water dropped on us. Scarborough pressed Play, and we all watched the security feed from the outpost in Glacier National Park that we had borrowed snowmobiles from. It was the feed from the camera that Scarborough had asked me to install in the outpost while the park rangers were busy "teaching" Mark, Jake, and Scarborough how to use the snowmobiles. We watched as CO Smith and three other AGI agents I didn't recognize entered the outpost, guns raised. We watched Smith question the rangers about our group and specifically about Brahim. Then, when the information was less than satisfactory, we watched Smith shoot and kill the park rangers, brain matter splattering the wall behind them. The air left my lungs.

Scarborough turned to Brahim. "It seems like they either want you back or want you dead."

Brahim, looking haunted, cleared his throat. "I think I know why." His jaw ticked a little, and he was so serious, verging on scared. He had been this way since we left Glacier National Park, and it was so out of character for him. We were on the edge of our seats, awaiting his explanation. "A few months ago, the AGI pulled me from training the new recruits and sent me on a job to work for DNA Global."

A quick scan of the room revealed that everyone was as confused as I was. Jake spoke first. "Why would they do that?"

Brahim looked up and, as serious as I've ever seen him, said, "Because they own DNA Global."

CHAPTER 21

Baltimore, MD
Kate

The room absolutely erupted. The implications were too much, too huge, absolutely, catastrophically massive. DNA Global held the DNA of hundreds of millions of people. They had cornered the market almost completely, not only by being the biggest DNA company and therefore able to offer the lowest price, but also by buying up the smaller companies and therefore collecting more and more DNA.

They were advertising geniuses and had sold the world on how important it is "to know where you came from." DNA Global ran Christmas specials as well as Mother's and Father's Day specials: "This year, give Mom and Dad their own origin story." One could have their DNA tested for the low price of $49.95—all they needed was a bit of saliva, and they could know what part of the world their particular DNA originated from. Not only that, but they tested for genetic markers for many diseases. Who didn't want to know where they came from and what that meant? Who didn't want to know if there was something they could do to safeguard themselves from disease for less than fifty bucks? Everyone was doing it. *I had done it.*

I watched the people in the room around me in slow motion. Some of them were sitting at their open laptops Searching DNA Global and trying to prove Brahim wrong. Some of them were yelling at each other as they argued over the possible outcomes of this bomb that had been dropped on us. Some of them were pacing with their hands in their hair, trying to come up with ways that we could use this information. But the smart ones, the few, including me, were stunned into silence because we had already pieced it together.

Jake made eye contact with me from across the room; I knew what he was asking, and I closed my eyes and nodded yes. He stood up and shouted, "STOP! QUIET! Everyone, calm down." The room silenced immediately. Jake closed his eyes briefly and swallowed. "Brahim, the parent company of DNA Global is NexGen Organized Solutions, is that correct?"

Brahim nodded.

Fin looked up, huffed, and shook his head. "NOS for short, then." He threw the papers he was holding down like a gauntlet. He looked like he was about to be sick, if the shade of green his face had turned was any indication.

Scarborough had his eyes closed. Dr. Bakshi was as white as a sheet. We knew then. We all knew that the AGI was in the business of personalized viruses, and they had the DNA of hundreds of millions of people.

From my seat on the floor, I slumped until my back met with the arm of the couch. I looked up at everyone. "Remember the good ol' days when we thought the ICT was bad?"

Scarborough nodded slowly, solemnly. He scrubbed his hands over his already-red face. "Clearly, we are going to need to go over the writings of Nigel Brown again before we travel further down this road. But the outpost video feed wasn't the only reason I called this meeting. We have some other imminent things that we need to discuss."

In my mind there was nothing that was more important than finally having found the link between NOS and the AGI. And it all made perfect sense too—the writing all over Nigel's walls and floors. He was sending us a message, and I didn't need to see the pictures to remember it. My mind took pictures of everything, and all I had to do was recall it. I could see myself walking into that damp, cold cottage in Wales, looking around at all the writing. It covered the book spines and shelves, the hardwood of the floor and every place on the walls that he could reach without a ladder. I zoomed in on a section of writing by the bookshelf that was directly in front of me. I disregarded the numbers and focused on the messages. *The NOS did this. They will do it to you, to the world. Women and children, all who oppose will die. They must be stopped. Too late, we are too late. Gone too far, power unchecked, power. Search NOS Socials—find them, it's all for power.*

I internally growled; there was no doubt that his brain had hit the hallucination stage by that point. Who writes on walls and the spines of books? Why not paper, or email? Only a crazy person takes the time to write on every square inch of a room. And yet, not everything he wrote was crazy ramblings; now that we knew that the AGI and NOS were connected, it made more sense. Still, though, something tugged at the back of my mind regarding the NOS. A memory. It was there, but also not there; it was an awful feeling for me, not to be able to recall something. I worried my lip, willing the connection I knew I had to the NOS to come to me, but it wouldn't. I understood that the AGI owned NexGen Organized Solutions, but that didn't trigger what I knew about the acronym NOS. There was something else there, something important.

I forced myself to set that aside and focus on what Scarborough was saying. "Ms. Johnson and Mr. Awan, if you would go with Drs. Bakshi and Williams. Charlie is going to drive you to a small local surgical center where they will laparoscopically remove your ICTs."

Lena blew out a breath, and with watering eyes she looked up to the ceiling. "Thank goodness. I want this thing outta me."

As they got up to go, Jake said, "Brahim, as soon as you get back, we're going to need a full debrief on what happened while you were assigned to work for DNA Global." Brahim nodded. As soon as they'd gone, Jake left Scarborough's side and took Lena's vacated seat next to me.

Scarborough picked right back up as soon as they left. "Mr. David, you may stay for the duration of this meeting." Candace scoffed, and Scarborough lifted his hand to stave off her forthcoming objection. "His top secret clearance is still active. Liam has many talents, and one of them is strategy. We are going to use him, and just as soon as this is all over, I'll be doing everything in my power to bring Mr. David into the CIA." He looked at Liam. "Or back into military intelligence, if that is what you wish."

Liam's cheeks pinked at the praise and outright flattery, but I could also see his respect for Scarborough grow. I could tell that he appreciated having a say in his future. That freedom to choose our own destiny, was something all of us ex-AGI agents had had taken away from us for too long. Liam nodded, accepting Scarborough's request for him to stay.

"Good. Then first I would like to discuss the fact that Search is pushing Oliver Strands for president. In a huge way." People picked up their laptops and starting Searching. I didn't have mine with me, so I waited not so patiently for someone to announce their findings.

I heard a few whistles, one of which came from Fin as he rapidly tapped at his keyboard. "Do you have any idea what this would cost? Millions, probably more, per day." He pecked at his keyboard, looked momentarily stunned at what he found, and then typed something else into the Search box. He sat back in his chair, eyes wide. "Are you kidding me? Strands isn't just being pushed for political searches, but *every* search. I just Searched the Yankees, and an image of Oliver Strands at a baseball game came up first." He tapped his keyboard again and then gave a half laugh, half guffaw, shaking his head. "This is insane."

"Exactly," Scarborough said, "I've never seen anything like it. Search has an extreme amount of power. They can make or break almost any business. They can bury news, companies, and anything else. But when they promote, it's impossible not to be swayed. They are a monopoly. They are a monopoly in information and in information advertising. They know who you are, where you are, what you just bought, and what you want to buy. They know how old you are, what you drive, and what you talked to your friends about over the weekend. They know you better than you know you." He paused and shook his head. "They know that the thirty-year-old who just had a baby and can't afford for her healthcare costs to go up will vote for a president who is worried about what she is worried about.

Search knows her, and they can spoon-feed her all of the news she needs to hear in just the way she needs to hear it. If we don't put a stop to this, Oliver Strands *will* be our next president."

Matt Sanders, one of the two people that made up our legal team, piped up, "We can't stop them, not by legal means; they're a private corporation."

Scarborough nodded. "That's true, but can we at least slow them down? An injunction for them to put out equal news? Even if it will ultimately fail, is there something we could do to pause this until the election?"

That made my skin a little itchy. Did I want Search to push Strands so hard? Absolutely not. But they were a private corporation, and they were designed to make money, and as there was no doubt that this was bringing in an absolute ton of money, they wouldn't be stopped easily. Not to mention, I was uneasy with the idea of using the judicial system to block a private company from doing what they were legally allowed to do.

Matt Sanders and his co-council Amy Richards stood. Sanders said, "We'll look into it" and went to leave, presumably to find a quiet space to work.

But before they could get too far, I spoke up. "I'm not sure that's such a good idea. The CIA has no place in elections; if we want to piss off the American public, this is the perfect way to do it. It's possible that any attempts we make to silence Search will make us look like the bad guy."

Scarborough turned to me. Incredulous, he asked, "So do you think we should just do nothing? Allow Search to pick our next president? Allow the AGI to run our country?"

I was on dangerous ground here. "No, I don't think we should do nothing. But I don't think that we should attempt to outright stop Search either. I mean, listen to yourself: 'should and shouldn't'? The government is not the morality police."

"But you are?" Scarborough's brows were furrowed, and I could feel not mere irritation waving off him, but hot anger.

I was on a knife's edge. "Of course what Search is doing is wrong. They're influencing an election for money. But let's let the

American people decide. Allow them to get mad at Search. Can't we find a way to reveal what Search is doing? Instead of making the public distrust us, let's make them distrust Search."

"And where exactly are we going to share that information, Edison?" Scarborough threw his hands up and bellowed, "Search will BURY IT!"

Jake put his hand over mine and put a little pressure on it. I wasn't sure whether he was telling me to drop it or not to back down. Either way, I would choose my battles myself, and I was all in on this one. I didn't look over at Jake and instead barreled ahead. "Then we go around Search. We go to social media sites and cable news networks. We hashtag it with something catchy and clever. We promote bloggers who are against Search's monopoly and tweet their web addresses. We get the president to hold a press conference regarding what Search is doing. We take it to the people."

I felt another squeeze from Jake and knew then that he was on my side. Scarborough huffed out the breath he had been holding. "That just might work." I sagged back to lean against the couch, willing my adrenaline-filled, trembling body to still. He turned to our legal duo: "I still want you to work the legal angle, as a backup." I wasn't happy that using the judicial system was still on the table, but I supposed it was the best I was going to get.

"Okay, we need a team of people to work on making what Search is doing known to the public." A group of agents raised their hands, and Scarborough nodded. They were making to get up, but before they could get too far, I cleared my throat. Scarborough sighed. "What now, Edison?"

I cringed a little, but this couldn't wait. "The AGI told Liam that I was involved in sex trafficking. They have me on video in Jay Conner's apartment buying children and then again when I was buying children from Agent Grup, right before I met with you all for the first time. I think that they're going to use that angle to get the Feds to come after me legally."

Liam's head whipped to me, eyes wide and mouth gaped, freaked out that I had been in the business of buying children and was now talking about it so casually. Under my breath, I told him, "It was part of my work with the AGI; I'll explain later."

Fin cursed. One of the other officers asked, "How are they going to explain how they got the footage?"

Jake spoke up, "They won't have to. They'll just pass it on to the FBI through one of their double agents." He took a deep breath through his nose, and I could tell that he was seething.

Scarborough, his voice deflated, asked, "Is there anything we can do to head this off at the pass?"

"We can go to the FBI, tell them she works for us," someone from the back of the room offered.

I shook my head. "Too risky; we have no way of knowing whether or not our contact at the FBI is part of the AGI."

Scarborough thought for a minute. "Well, then I guess we monitor the situation and figure it out as we go. From here on out, Edison is never alone in public." I nodded. "If there isn't anything else, then let's get to work. Liam, Edison, Lyon, Hampton, and Fin, come with me. Let's go over the footage from Wales."

CHAPTER 22

Minsk, Belarus
Liv

Liv Barker begged her teeth to stop chattering and her body to stop shivering. Her teeth didn't heed her will as they knocked together so hard that she was sure they would start to chip. Her body ached so badly that she couldn't move, but she also couldn't sit still. Every movement shot agonizing pain through her limbs. At even the smallest of movements, her brain felt like it was clanging against her skull, the pain a jarring bell's toll.

She was lying down on the cot in corner of her cell, but lying down wasn't helping her suffering. Nothing helped her suffering. She looked around her, wishing for the millionth time that she had a blanket. Anything to offer her warmth. When they took her, she had been a happy, healthy seventeen-year-old girl, visiting Barcelona, Spain, with her family. Liv grew up in sunny Phoenix, Arizona, and while she had always loved the feel of the sun on her skin, she had never wished for it more desperately than she did in that cell.

It wasn't a cell exactly, though; it was more a dilapidated office, but it was a prison to her. Worse than a prison really—at least in prison they fed you on a regular basis. And had toilets. The room she was locked in had no windows, and she had long since lost any sense of time, never knowing whether it was day or night. The only indication that time even passed at all were the moments when the people in the hazmat suits walked through the hall outside her door, sometimes with a dead body, sometimes a live one. With no apparent regularity, the man dressed in a hazmat suit occasionally opened the door to her room and threw in food and a gallon of water. It was always something random, like a packet of tuna or a jar of peanut butter, but Liv ate it like she was never going to eat again. She never even tasted the food, just shoved it down her throat as fast as she could, licking the inside of the container until every last drop of nutrition was consumed.

On occasion, she could hear the other prisoners in the rooms adjacent to her, scratching at the walls and banging on their doors. But their cries never lasted very long before they succumbed to whatever substance they were all constantly injected with. Liv had long since stopped trying to escape; it was pointless, and she barely had the energy required to sustain life, much less fight against her captors.

She didn't know why, had no idea who these people were, or why they had taken her, but it was clear that she had become some sort of test subject.

Liv found herself reliving, yet again, that fateful day.

She had been shopping with her parents and two little sisters, Sarah and Brenna, in Rambla de Catalunya. They were in a small shoe store, and the rich smell of leather filled the room from floor to ceiling. Spain had the kind of shoes that would make any red-blooded woman drool. They were creative and different, colorful and beautiful; Liv had been mesmerized. However, her sisters were not. Being nine and eleven, they didn't have nearly the interest in shoes that Liv did. Her parents, tired of her sisters' whining, told her that they were going to the shop across the street, and she could meet them there when she was done. She waved them off with a smile, relishing the few minutes alone to look and try on as she pleased.

The Spanish teenaged boy that approached her had been cute, almost shy, with dark, curly hair, a quick smile, and deep dimples. She wished, not for the first time, to go back to that moment and to scream at herself to run, to hide, to find her dad, anything to get herself to leave. But her mind continued to relive the moment as it had happened.

She could see herself laugh as the boy smiled, ran a hand through his thick hair, and made a self-deprecating joke in Spanish, a joke that she understood little of but laughed at anyway.

She watched, an outsider in her own mind, as the boy crooked his finger and said he wanted to show her something, indicating that it was in the store next door. She smiled and tucked a piece of her dark hair behind her ear, shaking her head and saying that she should get back to her family. He nodded, indicating that he understood, but held up a finger and said, "Por favor, solo un minuto."

She laughed and, not wanting to leave him just yet, said, "Okay, just one minute, then I have to go." He smiled and took her hand. She felt goose bumps rise on her skin at his touch, and she bit her bottom lip as her smile widened.

She followed him, out the door and into the sunny early-fall day, to the shop next door, but as they passed a narrow alley between the stores, a hand shot out, grabbed her, and covered her mouth so thoroughly that no one could hear her screams of protest. Disoriented and panicked, she allowed herself to be pulled back several feet into the dark alley. She saw one of her captors hand the Spanish boy a wad of money, and the boy had the decency to look horrified at what he'd done and terrified for her. He started to protest at the turn of events but only earned himself a bullet in the head with a silenced gun. He dropped to the floor of the alley, dead, his brown eyes wide open.

Liv screamed in terror anew and thrashed and flung her body, trying desperately to either get the attention of another shopper or to get the man that held her to loosen his tight grip. She tried to bite his hand and shake her head out of his hold, growling and screaming like a feral beast, sounds she had never before heard herself make. She tried to pull his fingers back from her mouth one by one so that she could get out a scream that wasn't muffled, a scream that was sharp and loud and clear. The only thing she earned was a laugh and a filthy comment implying how feisty she might be in bed. The man had a Russian accent but spoke English to her as well as to his cohort. She continued to fight and thrash, terrified of what might happen to her once they got her wherever they were taking her. But she might as well have been a rag doll. The man didn't loosen his hold in the least, and no one passing by so much as looked in her direction. The man who held her told his partner to take the money back from the boy and to get rid of the body, and he started to drag her deeper into the narrow, dark passageway.

Her panic and fear rose to heights yet unknown to her when she heard her eleven-year-old sister, Sarah, casually calling her name from the street. Time stood still as she watched Sarah cross the alley, a mere twenty feet away, still calling her name. She knew that if her sister saw her, Sarah wouldn't hesitate to come for her, to try to save her, and that her captors would either kill her sister or take her, too. So she stopped fighting and let the man drag her backward. Liv's tears flowed freely as she knew, deep in her soul, that she was seeing her sister for the last time.

As soon as the man dragged her to the end of the alley, he gagged her and threw her in the back of a dark cargo van. The last thing she remembered was the sweet, cloying smell of chloroform.

As always happened when she revisited that moment in her mind, that moment when her life changed so irrevocably, and willed it, with all of the fervor of her soul to be different, she inevitably opened her eyes to her cell, the fluorescent lights that were on day and night burning her eyes. The smell of vomit and rot assaulting her nose. Fully back in reality, tears coursed down her face while her body continued to violently tremor.

Her lungs were on fire, so she rolled her sick body onto her side to cough, and blood splattered the carpet next to her face. Her body continued to shake and shake in a growing pool of sweat and bodily fluids. She was still in the clothes that she had been kidnapped in so many months ago, and they had been long since soiled, the fabric thick and stiff with vomit and illness, in her constant fight to stay alive.

But Liv was tired of fighting. Her body was so deeply tired, the kind of tired that pulled you under and kept you there. She didn't fight the deep sleep, the kind of sleep that one never woke from. She welcomed it.

CHAPTER 23

Baltimore, MD
Kate

Scarborough looked at Brahim. "Tell us everything, from the beginning."

Lena and Brahim were back from surgery, trying to recover. They were quickly learning that the CIA didn't allow for recovery time. Though they were allowed to have the comfy seats in the living room, much to Fin's chagrin. It was just the seven of us: Jake, Fin, Scarborough, Brahim, Lena, Liam, and me.

Brahim swallowed, and I could tell that he was struggling with what he now knew about the AGI, trying to reconcile that with what he thought, and had been taught, for so long. "Well, CO Westwood pulled me from my work as a trainer back in November, right after the Hector Gonzalez job." Just hearing Westwood's name sent a shiver down my spine. "He told me that I would be taking a break from training the recruits to do something important, something only I could do. I was being sent to DNA Global's head office in Cambridge, Massachusetts, to do some programming work for their filing system." He paused, rubbing the back of his neck.

Scarborough nodded, "Go on."

"I was irritated because I liked training the new recruits, and programming was a job, literally, millions of other people could do." He shrugged. "But you didn't say no to CO Westwood, so I packed my bags and took the next flight to Boston, along with Westwood, who was going to get me started on the project. When we got to the DNA Global building, I was introduced to a few executives, and Westwood told everyone that we were from NexGen Organized Solutions and we were there to do some work on the DNA filing system. He assured them all that we weren't there to tell them how to do their jobs, that I would be as quiet as a mouse as I fixed some bugs in their system, and then I would be on my way. I was starting to internally freak out. I knew that NexGen was the parent company of DNA Global, and I was starting to think that I had been sent on a spy mission without proper spy training. I'm a behind-the-scenes kind of guy—I don't do covert ops. Westwood slapped a hand on my shoulder, discreetly told me to calm down, and led me deep into the basement of the building. At the end of a long hallway, there were two office doors. Both had security locks on them, though one lock was much more substantial than the other. Westwood told me I would be working from both offices.

"He unlocked the door on the right, the one with lower security measures first. The lock required a fingerprint scan and a retina scan, much like many of the security locks we use in the AGI.

"When we got inside and the door was shut, Westwood informed me that the AGI ran NexGen Organized Solutions. He let that sink in for a minute and then informed me that the door had been coded for my fingerprint and retinas. He also informed me that the other door had a much higher level of security, but both had been set up for my use.

"Inside the office there was a desk with a computer and three monitors. One thing that I noticed right away were the shelves of hard drives that lined the walls—thousands of them in perfect alphabetical order. The next thing was that the computers were plugged directly into the wall—that's it. There was no modem, no internet connection in the room, not even a phone line. Nothing. It was as quiet as a tomb inside. I pulled out my phone and grimaced at it because there was no connection in the room, absolutely no service. Westwood laughed, and he told me that the room was a Faraday cage incased in steel."

Lena looked horrified. "No internet?"

Brahim shook his head. "Nothing. It was like I had walked into nineteen sixty; the hardware was new, but the capabilities were so limited." He shrugged and pointed to himself. "I'm twenty-nine years old. I have never worked with computers without all of the information in the world at my fingertips. It's a totally different language, one I've never learned. I felt like my hands were tied behind my back. I told Westwood as much, and he laughed and said that he was confident that I would figure it out. He handed me some new hard drives and said that my first job was to load specific DNA files on to them. He gave me a list of names whose files he wanted. The DNA files were loaded onto the hard drives." He paused, clearing his throat. "My second job was to design a way to get information from that room to another secure location across the world."

Lena cocked her head to the side, perplexed. "Without the internet?"

"That's what I said, but then Westwood told me that they would be able to get a connection in there if I could prove that it could be done the way they wanted it done. I was to use the other office for the bulk of my work, and only when I had proved my program to be the caliber they wanted, would I be permitted to run the internet into that office. I told him I could write a program to send information securely in my sleep, but he wanted something far more secure than anything else we had used at the AGI." Lena and Fin both shrugged, and Brahim held his hand up. "I'm not done. That's when he took me into the office on the left."

"He unlocked the door, the one with the higher security measures, using his full handprint and a retina scanner, scanning both of his eyes. When he cleared that, a keypad was revealed and he punched in a code, several digits long, waited for a beep, and punched in another code. The door finally opened. It was higher security than I'd seen used in any other AGI facility."

Fin, laptop in front of him, clacking away, stopped and looked up. "How many keys were pressed for each code?"

Brahim shook his head, eyes wide. "I'm not like Kate, I can't remember things like that."

Fin sighed and rolled his eyes. "Was it more than ten or less than ten?"

"More. Each code was more than ten digits long."

Fin pursed his lips and swore. "It's a Zimmermann." Jake lifted a brow. Fin rolled his eyes. "A Zimmermann lock. They are impossible to crack."

Jake's brows lifted even higher. "Even for you?" It was so unlike Fin to admit any weakness.

Fin scowled. "I've never tried, but to my vast knowledge, *no one* has successfully broken into a Zimmermann."

Scarborough, nonplussed, looked back to Brahim. "Go on."

Brahim swallowed, clearly uncomfortable, but went on anyway. "The first thing I saw in the other room was a dilution refrigerator."

Fin's head snapped up, and Lena gasped. I was lost. "What's a dilution refrigerator?"

Brahim answered, "It's a cooling system used for quantum computing."

I'd read about quantum computing before, but the last I knew it hadn't ever been developed enough to be applied in any real usable way. It was nothing more than theory and experiment. I said as much.

Brahim said, "Right, everyone has been racing to get the technology first, but until now, no one has been able to figure it out."

Fin's voice wasn't loud, but the intensity felt like it could level a house. "What do you mean, *until now*?"

Brahim looked up from his lap. "Quantum computing has been a focus within the AGI for decades. That was the work I did, in Florida, the only work I did before I began training recruits last July. I only started training because my brain needed a break. The computer engineers and scientists that work for the Orlando AGI group work on quantum computing full time."

Lena whistled.

Brahim continued, "Until recently, we have had some breakthroughs, but not *the* breakthrough. Superposition, entanglement, and interference are the main properties of quantum computing. Classical computers run out of memory and therefore don't have the capability to solve many problems. Quantum computers don't have those limits. Basically, quantum computing creates new possibilities and new ways to approach problems that classical computers have difficulty doing."

Jake asked, "So what did Westwood want you to do with the quantum computer, and how does that connect to DNA Global?"

"He wanted me to advance a breakthrough that the Orlando facility had made in my absence. They had created a new algorithm, something we had been working on for a long time but had never fully been able to complete. I was to use that algorithm to send information securely from DNA Global to another secure location."

Fin's eyes bored into Brahim's when he quietly asked, "Did it work?"

Brahim took a deep breath. "Yes."

Fin, his voice even quieter, his mouth gaped, brow furrowed, asked, "What else does that algorithm allow?"

Brahim quietly took a breath. "It allows for quantum cryptography." I furrowed my brow, not for the first time during this conversation. Was he saying that it could break encryptions?

Fin, as still as a lion stalking its prey, said, "In theory."

Brahim slowly shook his head. "In practice."

Fin sucked in a breath. "What level of encryption?"

"Triple Data Encryption Standard."

"So Three DES but not AES?" This time Lena asked the question.

Brahim shook his head. "No. But I'm close. With the algorithm, I was able to utilize hundreds of thousands of qubits, or quantum bits; for Advanced Encryption Standard we would need to utilize millions of qubits."

Fin frowned. "Could you recreate it now? Given the tools?"

Brahim nodded. "Yes. It would take me some time, but yes."

Fin sat back in his chair, eyes wide. "The ramifications . . ."

Brahim cut him off. "I know. At this point I knew that things weren't right at the AGI, but I didn't know nearly how wrong things were. I thought that they were run by corrupt leadership, not that the entire entity was corrupt. Knowing that the new technology was hugely important and potentially catastrophic, I tied it to a virus. The virus overrides the offending computer so thoroughly that it renders the machine unusable, even going so far as to damage the hardware. I put my signature on the technology, and no one will be able to access it without me. It's tied only to that quantum computer. It's not transferable, not without an incredible knowledge of computers and me personally."

Fin cupped his mouth with his hand, eyes wide. "You handed that kind of knowledge and power over to the AGI?"

Brahim swallowed. "I did. But not unchecked. No one in the AGI should be able to break or copy the code."

Fin threw his hands in the air. "But *you* did! You did it, which means that other people could do it, too, and you just handed that kind of discovery over to the AGI? The AGI, who is probably the greatest threat the world has ever known."

This. This must have been why Brahim had been so quiet and unlike himself since we'd rescued him. He knew what he had done and the implications of it being in the wrong hands. The very hands he'd handed the information over to. He looked like he was going to throw up. "I didn't know . . . I didn't know who they really were. We were told that we worked for the government. The entire world is racing to advance quantum computing—we were told the importance of the United States getting it first. We worked night and day for that technology—that power."

Fin jumped out of his seat, his laptop slamming to the floor; he didn't even flinch, which revealed how panicked and angry he truly was. "You didn't know? That's not good enough!" he yelled, and other officers were starting to peek into the living room to see if they could catch what was going on. I'd never seen Fin lose it, and his temper was something to behold.

Scarborough, for his part, seemed to be almost in a trance, like his brain was on information overload. He finally came to. "Okay, what's done is done."

Fin snapped, "Exactly, what's done is done, and we are all screwed." He looked at all of us, and the other officers that were now on the outskirts of the room. "Don't you get it? What Brahim has discovered is dangerous enough, but his work is mere steps away from world domination! All you would need to do is uncover Brahim's work, add to it, and you would have the world at your fingertips. Everything in this world runs on computers. Everything. That kind of technology can break any code, undo any encryption. The AGI could drain every bank account, turn off the heat in your home, direct drones, make planes fall from the sky, start one-thousand-car pileups on the highway, open prisons, START WARS!" He quieted, his voice somewhat deflated. "They could rule the world with this. We are completely and thoroughly screwed." My blood ran cold.

Brahim sat forward in his chair. "That's only true *if* they can copy my work."

Jake looked up from his seat. "How can we make sure that doesn't happen?"

Brahim looked Jake in the eye and swallowed. "We have to break into that room."

CHAPTER 24

Baltimore, MD
Kate

"I don't understand, how do we know that the technology is still only contained to that quantum computer?" I asked. My lack of knowledge in this area made me hesitant to join the conversation, but no one had asked this yet. Liam nodded his head, wanting this question answered as well.

Lena looked to Brahim, and he nodded in answer to her silent question. She spoke first, "The program is tethered to that specific computer—it's not something that you can throw on a hard drive and use somewhere else. Someone would have had to study Brahim's work from that computer to figure it out. How do we know whether that has happened already? We don't. The only way to know is to get into the program and check." She looked to Brahim. "And I'm guessing that there is no way to do that remotely, otherwise you would have suggested that first."

He nodded. "I set it up so that if someone successfully breaks into the program, the original computer will contract the virus."

I furrowed my brow. "Well then, we're good, right? Why break into DNA Global if we don't have to?"

Lena and Fin both shook their heads, but it was Lena who spoke first. "Given enough time, I could figure it out. I could work around the fail-safe. Anyone with a high level of computer knowledge would check to see if there is a trigger first. The first people they would've sent in to crack Brahim's work would be the people he worked with for the past five years. They will know him and how he works."

Scarborough spoke next, "How long have they had the program?" As in how long had the AGI had to crack Brahim's code.

"I finished my work at DNA Global in the middle of December."

I snapped my fingers. "It was the night that I escaped, the night that I broke into the detonator room. I saw you and Lena walking down the hall."

Brahim nodded. "The night Westwood was killed, yes."

Jake closed his eyes for a moment too long. "That was three months ago."

The room was silent as we all let that sink in. It had taken Brahim six weeks to put the new algorithm to use, and the AGI had had three months to crack it.

Fin sat back in his seat. "I don't think that's long enough for the AGI to get in. If they looked for the trigger, they are going to go very slowly. Especially now that they don't have Brahim, they won't take any risks."

Brahim nodded. "It would be very hard, verging on impossible, to crack it without triggering the fail-safe. I'm confident that no one has been able to do it yet."

"How can you be so sure?" Scarborough asked.

"Because just days before Lena came back and we escaped, CO Smith and LC Yu were questioning me about it." He looked around the room. "I led them the wrong way—by then I was positive that there was something wrong with the AGI, and it was enough for me not to give them the information they wanted."

Liam spoke up, "I don't understand why they wouldn't just demand that you give them the information, and if you didn't, it seems likely that they would have tortured you for it."

Brahim shook his head. "That's not how it works. It's not something that I can just explain on paper, I mean I could, but it would take books. They could have dragged me to DNA Global and made me do it there, but they still wouldn't have been able to simply watch and learn what I was doing, it's far more complicated than that."

Scarborough nodded. "It's settled, then. We find a way into that office at DNA Global."

Fin huffed out a humorless laugh. "We just have to break into a room that's locked with a Zimmermann. You do remember that I said that no one has ever successfully cracked a Zimmermann, right?"

I looked over at Fin. "You also said that you've never tried. You're not just *anyone*, Fin." Stroking Fin's ego was a level of annoying that I rarely stooped to, but at this point I was willing to try anything. We had to destroy that technology.

The living room was full then—everyone had come in from the outskirts of the room and were now seated around us. All other work dropped.

Jake was stoic, his mind whirling. "Brahim, what was it exactly that made you question the AGI's motives?"

Brahim's eyes glassed over, and he paused for a few beats before he began speaking. "When I was eighteen, my fifteen-year-old sister was abducted. She had been groomed online and fooled into meeting a boy she thought was her age, but it turned out that he was a much older man, a predator, who brutally raped and murdered her." Lena gasped, reaching out her hand to offer Brahim comfort, but he shrugged her off. Tears lined his eyes, and his voice wobbled as he continued to speak, "Knowing that will help you understand the rest of my story." He took a deep breath to help get his emotions under control. "The IP address, the one that I was making a secure line to, I tracked it to the Republic of Belarus. That's where the AGI is sending the DNA information." That had Jake, Scarborough, and me sitting up straighter. "The names on the list that Westwood gave me, the DNA files I was to download on the hard drives and that would eventually make their way to Belarus, that list included the names Sarah and Brenna Barker. They're the sisters of Liv Barker, the girl who was kidnapped in Barcelona last September. In addition to my work training the new recruits, I had been tasked with following that story within the AGI; they said that the Barker family was of interest to them and they wanted to know right away if the girl was found. The US operatives that were searching for her lost track of her in Belarus." He sniffed. "But I couldn't stop following the story. I couldn't just let it go when she was never found. I had followed Liv's story for months, had seen every interview, every tear her parents and sisters had shed." Brahim took a second to wipe his face, and I did the same. There were several wet faces in the room—it was impossible not to be emotional for Brahim, his pain was so raw. His voice came out as little more than a whisper when he said, "It's just—I know that pain." He cleared his throat and took another deep breath. "I was personally invested in that case, too invested. When I saw Liv's sisters' names on that list, I knew that something wasn't right.

"Westwood didn't leave until he had the hard drive in hand. He stood there and watched me download each file. After that, he went back to Montana, and I only gave him updates by burner phone of my progress on employing the algorithm.

"As soon as Westwood left, I started looking through the file records to find Liv's information, because if DNA Global had her sisters' information, I knew they had hers, too. I located her file and found that her DNA records had been downloaded to a hard drive on September thirteenth, just a few days prior to her abduction. While there are a few pieces to the puzzle that were, and are, still missing, I knew in that moment that the AGI wasn't ever trying to rescue Liv Barker—they were making sure that she wasn't rescued."

The room was silent, all of us stuck in our heads, trying to make sense of it all. Too much. Too much information to wade through. That was when Brahim decided to drop another bomb on us. Not as big as quantum computing, but almost as destructive.

"There is one other thing." We all looked over to Brahim. "Just days before I returned to Montana, I was given another list of names whose files Westwood wanted sent directly to the specified IP address. It was to be my first official run of the new program." He looked up. "Most everyone in this group was included on that list."

Jake's head snapped up, and when he spoke, his voice was pure ice. "No one speak another word." I didn't want to stay silent, though—I wanted to roar. I watched as Jake looked around at everyone, every single face in the room. His eyes were as fierce as I had ever seen them, and I knew he was doing what he did best: reading people. There was only one real possibility, and it solidified my ire and absolute terror when he said the words that I was thinking. "We have a mole."

CHAPTER 25

New York City, NY
Oliver

Valentina shut the door of their shared hotel suite and lost it. She violently threw the papers she was carrying, the printed white sheets flying all over the room like gigantic snowflakes. "How? How could you be so stupid?"

Oliver turned himself away from his wife, trying to tame his roiling thoughts to come up with an answer that would pacify her. He'd screwed up, and it was on camera and would be thrown in his face for a long time to come. He turned back around to face the music and said the only thing he really could say: "I'm sorry."

Valentina threw up her hands, her face contorted in rage. "You're sorry? Sorry?"

Oliver sighed. "Yes, Valentina, I'm sorry. I went off script—the reporter's question threw me for a loop. I messed up. It happens, and it will probably happen again." That was the truth, whether Valentina wanted to face it or not.

She raised an eyebrow. "The reporter's *question* threw you for a loop, is that the story you're going with?"

That caught him by surprise—she never noticed or seemed bothered when other women ogled him. He tried again, "I'm sorry, Valentina."

His apology bounced right off her, the fire in her eyes not dimming in the slightest, and with her voice like a blade, she said, "Let me be clear: you do not have the luxury of mistakes. You don't have the political proficiency to go *off script.*"

That chafed. He'd graduated from Yale with a degree in political science, after all. "Valentina, I have a top-of-the-line education. From a school that was ranked higher than yours, might I add. I am able to hold my own just fine. I am not the first person running for president who has made a slip up. I am a human being, not a puppet."

She walked a few steps closer and lifted a finger, poking at him in the chest. "That is where you are wrong, Oliver. A puppet is exactly what you are. You are a puppet. You are *my* puppet. And when my puppet decides to come alive and make his own decisions, he makes us both look like idiots. I do not take kindly to looking like an idiot, Oliver." She stepped even closer to him and dropped her voice, her tone no less hostile. "Many a fool have come out of excellent universities." She dropped her hand and brought her face mere inches from his and spat, "Now you just look like another one."

"Good grief, Valentina, I made a blunder. I didn't say that I was looking to start world war three. You are blowing this way out of proportion."

"Am I?" She picked her phone up from their dining room table and pressed Play.

He watched the screen, his face flaming.

The blonde and very pretty reporter smiled at him and leaned forward, exposing just enough of what was underneath her shirt to snag his attention. Her smile turned predatory when she noticed where his eyes had wandered. It was an offer, loud and clear, and when she asked her next question, his mind had gone to places that it shouldn't have. "Congressman Strands, we know that you speak a few foreign languages—would you be willing to enlighten the public with which languages those are?"

He smiled, still enamored with her cleavage, and said, "Yes, I speak Spanish, French, and Brazilian."

She winked and said, "Do you mean Portuguese?"

What you couldn't see behind the scenes was the reporter working her high-heeled foot up Oliver's leg under the small table that separated them. His mind was not on the words she was saying but rather what she was saying with her body. When he looked at her expectant face, he knew that he should ask her to repeat the question, but he was concerned that the reason he was lost in his thoughts would appear on screen, and he didn't want the public to see that, so instead he rushed to answer. Which was a mistake. He cringed when he listened to his response. "No, unfortunately, I don't speak that language; maybe I should learn that one next."

Valentina threw her phone back down on the table. "Oliver, you listed 'Brazilian' as one of the languages you speak fluently. The reporter *corrected* you, and you doubled down." She flung her arms in the air, her face a deep shade of red. "I can't make a president out of a complete idiot!"

He flinched; he was embarrassed, mortified even. Of course he knew that they spoke Portuguese in Brazil. He spoke Portuguese, but his mind had been fuddled. Regardless, there was nothing for it now. "Valentina, I would give anything to go back and change what I said. But it was a gaffe, a mistake. I have several interviews every day. I was bound to make a mistake sometime. I'll joke it off, charm my way out of it." He nudged her in the side, trying to see if his charm would work on her.

She swallowed. "And what about the way you looked at that journalist, would you change that if you could?"

Oliver's brow lifted in surprise. So that's what this was about? He grabbed Valentina by the shoulders, regret etched in his face. "Valentina, I'm sorry. I didn't mean for my eyes to wander, and I would never have acted on her silent offer. Never. I have made a commitment to you and to the people I work for; I will see it through to the end."

She reared back and slapped him across the face hard enough that his head whipped to the side. He gaped at her, completely blindsided. She went in for a second strike and he grabbed her arm. It didn't prevent the words that came out of her mouth like venom. "You complete idiot. I don't care who you look at. You want another woman? I'll set it up for you." He balked at that. "But if you ever, *ever*, embarrass me or the AGI like that again, I will make your life utter hell. Is that clear?"

He blinked, his brow furrowed. "Crystal." He rubbed his cheek while she turned on her heel, stalked to their bedroom, and slammed the door behind her.

It wasn't crystal clear at all, though. He'd never seen that side of Valentina before, never seen her truly lose her cool. He'd seen Valentina angry before, but it had always been her Colombian temper coming through, and Oliver found it quite attractive. This wasn't cute. It wasn't just anger and a flared temper he saw roiling in her eyes, but something more. Something darker.

CHAPTER 26

Baltimore, MD
Kate

Jake paced in my room. After discovering that we had a mole, the absolutely livid Scarborough sent us all to our rooms, saying that he would be speaking with each one of us privately. Jake refused to leave my side, he was worried that now that the mole had been outed there might be a play on my life. Scarborough conceded that I shouldn't be left alone, so Jake and I went to wait in my room together. I was hoping that we could talk and strategize about everything we'd learned. But Jake was too angry to talk. So instead, he paced.

Back and forth, his hands fisted, knuckles white. I was fairly certain that his pacing was more intense than mine had been when I was waiting for Lena to escape the Montana AGI facility. On occasion he would look over at me. His expression was a mix of hot anger and deep guilt—it was hard to decipher which emotion he was feeling more. I was angry, too. Anger was far too bland a word for what I was really feeling, but regardless, I did better talking it out with someone. I didn't like to stew. I liked to plan, to fix. Jake and I were different in this regard—he was stewing over his role in this mess, and he didn't want to talk about it. I sighed and said, not for the first time, "Jake, you couldn't have prevented this."

He didn't so much as look at me when he replied, "I could have, and I should have. I read people, it's my job, my specialty." He continued to pace, shaking his head and arguing with himself under his breath. Intermittently, he would share his inner ramblings aloud. "I haven't been paying enough attention." Pace. "No, couldn't be her." Turn. "If it's him, he is dead." Growl. Pace. "How could I be so distracted?" Pace. Pace. Pace.

I finally got up from my seat on the bed and headed off his next turn. He rammed into me, not realizing that I was in his way, and I started to fall backward. He grabbed me by the shoulders and hefted me back up, bringing my body flush with his. And for a beat we looked into each other's eyes; for a beat our breaths mingled, and my heart hammered. In a blink Jake was looking at my eyes, my lips, with a longing so deep it startled me. He swallowed, slowly, and rasped, "This." He brought up the hand that wasn't holding me tightly to his body and wagged a finger between the two of us. "This is why my mind isn't where it should be." He shook his head, minutely. "And I can't even bring myself to regret it like I should." He slammed his mouth on mine, this kiss far from the gentle ones we'd shared in the past. The insistence of his lips and the rake of his beard had me opening my mouth to his. His tongue ransacked my mouth, rolling across the roof of it, over my teeth and every other location within his reach. His hand on my back hauled me even tighter to him, and I could feel the pounding in his chest, the tremor in his body.

So many thoughts went through my mind, but none more so than the thought that insisted that this wasn't right. It wasn't the right time, it wasn't the right circumstance, and most importantly, Jake wasn't in the right frame of mind. I wanted him, badly, but not like this. Not when he was angry and full of regret and indecision.

I wrenched my mouth away from his, and he immediately let me go. I took a step back and held up a finger, signaling for him to give me a minute, while I caught my breath. His eyes were wide and his body still, like a deer in the headlights, and in between his heaves for air, he said, "Kate, I'm sorry. That was too much."

I nodded, acknowledging that I'd heard what he was really saying; this wasn't how he wanted things to go between us either. As soon as my breathing calmed slightly, I stepped back to Jake and put my hands on his shoulders, and when he allowed me to do that, I twined them around his neck and pulled him close. In my ear he whispered, "I'm so sorry. I was so angry about the AGI knowing about us, and not knowing how they have been getting their information, that I just kind of lost my mind a little." He blew out a breath and pulled back slightly. "Kate, my feelings for you are running deeper every day, and my mind was whirling, and then all of a sudden, you were there, in my arms, your body pressed against mine." He huffed and looked to the ceiling. "And . . . and I couldn't hold myself back."

I said, "I know." And I did know. I stopped him in the middle of his thoughts—he was angry in a way that I had never seen and, though my desire was to calm him down and get him to talk to me rationally, I'd walked right into his space when his rationality was nonexistent. "It wasn't just you; I was a . . . ," I cleared my throat, "very willing participant." I pulled back a little so that I could look at him. "Jake, it's not a secret that I have feelings for you." Especially since Lena had outed me to the entire group. "They run deeper than I have let on."

A small smile spread across his face. "I'm a human lie detector, Kate. I read people for a living." His smile turned into a half-apologetic smirk. "Your feelings have never been a secret from me."

I gaped, incredulous, and sputtered, my mind trying to form an appropriate response. But there really wasn't one, so I laughed instead. "How long have you known?"

Though he tried to reign it in, his smile was growing, his eyes shining. "From the first moment I saw you in that office in St. Louis." I guffawed, and he laughed. "Your eyes widened and your pupils dilated, which could mean attraction or disgust, but when your cheeks pinked, I knew that it was attraction you felt."

I pushed him playfully. "Jake! That's so unfair! I had no idea what you felt for me. Not until the car, after my exploratory surgery, at least. And even then, when you just cut things off so easily, I thought that maybe I was just fun to you, a dalliance." I shrugged.

Jake's smile faltered, the light in his eyes dimming. "Kate,"—he cupped my face in his hands—"nothing could be further from the truth." His thumbs started to rub along my jaw. "I suspected you might have gotten the wrong impression, and I hated it. But I didn't want to correct you because I didn't want our feelings to get in the way of our work. I tried to tell myself that if I just kept myself from acting on my impulses, we could put this, what was happening between us, on hold until our work was finished." One side of his mouth lifted. "Which was obviously not the best choice. This is a completely foreign thing to me. I have never worked with someone I wanted so deeply, so desperately."

I smiled. "You want me desperately?"

His smile reappeared. "Yes." Such an honest and vulnerable answer. "I haven't told you how I feel about you because my feelings run deeper than yours, and I don't want to scare you away."

I smirked. "You may fancy yourself a mind reader, Jake, but you don't know everything I'm thinking."

His smile softened. "I may not know everything you're thinking, but I know how I feel about you, and I can tell that you are not there yet. I am hoping maybe someday you will be."

I cocked my head to the side; was he saying what it sounded like he was saying? I didn't get to ask because the door swung open and Scarborough walked in.

We separated as fast as teenagers caught by the police in their car on make-out hill. But in a split second it seemed that Jake thought better of it and grabbed my hand, holding it, making a statement that I wasn't entirely sure I was ready to make.

Scarborough raised an eyebrow. "Fantastic. We get to discuss the fact that we have a mole"—he gestured to us—"and the elephant in the room."

Scarborough was in a mood, and I couldn't blame him. I was sure that this thing between Jake and me was far down the current list of potential disasters that Scarborough was dealing with. And that list was long. He huffed a breath and roughly rubbed his temples, then motioned for the bed, the only place to sit in the small room. Jake and I sat down, while Scarborough remained standing.

"I'm not the only one who has noticed the romantic relationship budding between the two of you. Some of the other officers have voiced their concern." My eyebrows rose in surprise. What business was it of theirs? It wasn't as if we weren't exemplary employees. But, to my surprise, Jake just nodded.

"In any other circumstance, I would put one of you on a different job immediately." My eyes bulged. "But seeing as you are the only two people I can trust right now, my options are limited enough that I am going to have to take the risk of keeping you both." He took a deep breath and rubbed at his temples again. "I expect you both to be mature enough to put this little crush on hold for now and do your work. You both have responsibilities, and you will both be taking risks out in the field, risks with your lives. It's a danger to have two people in a relationship on the same team. For instance, I would never work with my wife—I couldn't trust myself to do the right thing if the options came down to doing the right thing or saving her life."

I swallowed, beginning to understand a bit. Could I be trusted to do the right thing if Jake's life were on the line? Though, if I were being honest with myself, I wasn't sure that I could do the right thing if it were Liam or Lena's lives on the line either. If it were my life on the line, I wouldn't think twice, I wouldn't hesitate. If it were someone else, someone I cared for . . . I wasn't so sure.

Jake spoke first, "With all due respect, Officer, this is far more than a little crush." Scarborough's eyebrows raised, and I tried . . . I *tried* to hold in my smile. "I can assure you that we have tried to ignore our feelings, but it hasn't been working out as well as we'd hoped. I understand the other officers' concerns about our current status, and I will talk to everyone if you think that's necessary." My head snapped up. He wanted to tell everybody? I felt adrenaline rush through my body, and I wasn't sure if it was due to excitement, shock, or horror. Jake wanted to make whatever was between us public? That made me a little giddy but also a little nauseated; I didn't want the rest of the crew all up in our business. He went on, "But I can assure you and the rest of the group that I understand the risks and I am willing to accept them. I have made a commitment to this mission, and I take that very seriously."

Scarborough nodded and turned to me. I was still a bit stunned. Jake pumped my hand, encouraging me to, what? Make my vows to the mission? Tell Scarborough about my feelings for Jake? This was weird and more than a little uncomfortable. I cleared my throat. "Officer Scarborough, I am also committed to this mission; it is my first priority."

He shook his head and closed his eyes. If I had to guess, I would have said he was thinking that he didn't get paid enough to deal with this sort of thing. "Look, you are both adults, and I'm not trying to act like your dad or your priest, but I would appreciate it if you would take a step back from anything physical until the mission is complete. I know how you feel about each other, I understand that you can't turn those feelings off, and I'm not asking you to. But I and the rest of the group need to know that you aren't going to put each other first, that you will put the mission first. I am asking you to put this on hold again and to try harder this time. Is that acceptable?"

Neither of us looked at the other before we nodded. Jake gave my hand a quick squeeze and dropped it. It felt so glaringly final.

Scarborough nodded. "Good. I just want to be perfectly clear, here; if I even smell so much as a whiff of preference between the two of you out in the field, one of you will be off the mission without so much as a goodbye." He looked to Jake, because we all knew it was Jake who would be off the mission and not me. They needed me to know the ins and outs of the AGI. But this mission needed Jake, too, and I mentally firmed my decision to put what was going on between us on pause. His belief in me was what made this whole thing possible. I didn't want to do it without him.

"Now let's talk about the actual crisis on our hands, shall we?" Scarborough didn't wait for us to nod before forging ahead. He used his fingers to tick off each item that we'd just learned, each one in need of serious attention. "We know that the AGI and NexGen Organized Solutions are connected. We know that through DNA Global, the AGI has access to hundreds of millions of people's DNA. We know that the AGI is in the business of personalized viruses and that there is a good chance that Belarus is ground zero for that particular project. We know that the AGI has access to the most incredible and dangerous computer technology to come around in ages. And now we know that we have some sort of leak within our ranks." He rubbed his temples again and looked like he had suddenly aged ten years.

Jake nodded in agreement. "Some questions have been answered, like why the AGI wants Brahim so badly." He rubbed his face. "If word got out about what Brahim is capable of, the entire world would want him." He sighed. "But for every answer, we get five new questions." He shook his head. "And let's not set aside the fact that there seems to be a connection with the AGI and the missing Barker girl." My heart sank, still sad for Brahim and all that he'd been through, as well as for the Barker family.

"A connection that involves the viruses," I added, and then asked the question that had been on my mind since the reveal. "Why her, though? Why go to such lengths to kidnap this girl? How is a seventeen-year-old from Arizona connected to the AGI?"

Scarborough strummed his hand on his knee and said, "That's the million-dollar question."

We were a silent for a few moments, pondering which item it was on our long list that needed the most urgent attention, when there was a knock on the door. Scarborough grunted, which must have been invitation enough, because the door started to open, and Megan timidly walked in, her eyes swollen, face wet with tears.

Jake stiffened. Scarborough's eyes widened a fraction, and then his expression became disappointed for a flash before he schooled his features and said, "Megan, it looks like you have something to tell us."

She nodded, her tears coming faster. "I think that I have been used. I think that I might inadvertently have been the mole."

Jake, his voice as cold as ice, said, "You think, or you know?"

Megan sniffed. "I am fairly certain."

Jake's hands were back to their fisting, and his breathing had taken a turn for the angry. His energy was rising, and I could almost feel his need to pace, to stomp, just to let some of it out.

"So . . . are you going to tell us, or do we have to guess?" My words came out sharper than I'd intended. But I was really and truly angry.

Megan flinched. "I started seeing someone within the CIA in December, just about the time that this group had been formed."

Jake looked at her, his expression dangerous. "Who?"

She swallowed. "Officer Reed."

Jake swore and my mouth gaped. Officer Reed? The recruiter? So many questions went through my mind. But the two that were the loudest were: Was Officer Reed the one who gave me the letter from the AGI in the first place? And why was Megan with Reed? He was close to twenty years her senior, and Megan was pretty, Reed was not so much. They seemed a very unlikely pairing.

I looked at Jake; reading the questions in my eyes, he said, "He was the one I suspected back when you told me about the letter from the AGI, but I could never find any proof." I was a bit dumbfounded. Reed was always so nice, and he seemed so . . . just kind of normal. Though there was that one time that he had insinuated that he'd known my dad. At the time I'd assumed that he knew him through the CIA, but I had never gone back to examine that comment.

I was a bit dumbfounded. But this was not Scarborough's first rodeo, and he plowed ahead, "How did this relationship start?"

Megan sniffed again and wiped at her eyes. "He approached me the day after the first time we all met as a group." She looked at me. "When we first attempted to take out your ICT." I nodded for her to go on. "He asked me to dinner. Reed was my recruiter and trainer, and I had always respected him. After I joined the CIA, he would stop by my office periodically to check on me and ask me how things were going. But he had never asked me to dinner. It seemed like a date, and I was flattered." Megan must have been able to read my thoughts, because she shrugged and said, "He's powerful within the CIA, and everyone is somewhat attached to their recruiter and trainer." She gave a knowing glance between Jake and me that had me bristling. She didn't know me, and that wasn't the reason I was attracted to Jake. It was grating, to say the least, to be placed in that category. I was not so simple. But also, everyone was attached to their trainer? How many women did Jake have pining for him within the CIA? I looked over at the gorgeous ginger and figured that the number was likely far higher than I was comfortable with.

Megan went on, "At dinner he made his intentions clear. He told me that he wanted to explore this thing between us and see where it might go. He came home with me that night." I reared back; that was a visual I could have lived without. "We were together every night, for the first few weeks. On the second night, he started asking me questions about my work. He knew things, like that I was on a project with Lyon." She swallowed. "I confirmed that. I thought that he must have been in the know, if he knew that much."

Jake was livid; his nostrils were flaring, and his breaths were long and hard. He'd told everyone in the group the day that we'd met that first time how top secret this was. I'd heard him say the words, *"You know how top secret this is. Every one of us works with someone who also works for the AGI. If anyone outside of this group gets wind of this information, it will mean the end of hundreds of innocent lives, including every single one in this very room."* Megan had heard it, too, and within a day she was talking about it? Either she was a complete idiot or Reed was incredibly convincing.

Jake must have been thinking about that same day and the words he'd said, too. "Did you not hear what I said about things being top secret? About each of us working with someone who also worked with the AGI? Were you even listening that day?" His words were coated in venom, each one sinking deeper, killing Megan's career with the CIA.

Scarborough motioned for her to go on. She nodded, her eyes downcast. "He brought up the AGI." She wrung her hands. "Again, I thought that he must have already known; it didn't even cross my mind that he could be a part of it. I had trusted him completely. Until one day, I was walking back to my office and he was at my desk, and I could hear him typing on my computer. By the time that I'd walked fully inside, he had backed away from my computer and acted like he was just there patiently waiting for me to come back from my meeting. I accused him of being on my computer, and he said that he was browsing the internet while he was waiting for me, but if that were true, he wouldn't have felt the need to stop and try to hide it from me."

Scarborough said, "How did he access your computer?"

She shook her head. "That night, I'd asked him the same thing. He shrugged and said that he had a master code, that he could get on to anyone's computer."

Jake's face contorted in disbelief. "And you believed that?"

She flinched again. "It seemed plausible that the higher-ups at the CIA could get into any of our computers. What if one of us was a double agent? Surely there are checks and balances."

Jake threw his hands up. "Yes! From your direct line of superiors—not from your trainer. Did you ever contemplate, even for a second, whether his security ranked high enough for that kind of activity?"

Scarborough was stone faced. "What else?"

Megan shook her head. "Nothing else. After that night he never mentioned the group or the AGI again."

Jake asked, "You always met at your house?" She nodded.

I closed my eyes briefly. "I guarantee that her place is bugged and that he downloaded everything off her personal computers as well as her work laptop and phone. That is typical AGI behavior. He also likely granted himself remote access to her devices."

Still wearing that mask of stone, Scarborough said, "You're a psychoanalyst for the Central Intelligence Agency, and you never thought we might find that information useful? You never though that Officer Reed's actions might have serious consequences?"

"I did, but I didn't come forward for a couple of reasons. First, I am ashamed to say that I didn't tell either of you"—she motioned toward Jake and Scarborough—"out of fear that I would lose my job. I love my job and I'm good at it." She cleared her throat. "Second, I think I was holding out false hope that Reed wasn't that kind of guy. That he was still the person I'd idolized for so many years." She shrugged, her countenance dimmed. "That what we had was real."

Apparently it was a combo. Megan was an idiot, and Reed was *that* good. I was angry at her stupidity, but I would have had to have been heartless to not feel for Megan at least a little. She knew what she had lost. Not just her job but her credibility. And not even just that, but also a mentor, a man who she had thought had turned into something more.

I could see a gamut of expressions cross Scarborough's face; sadness was the last. "Megan, you know how this ends."

Fresh tears escaped her eyes, and she nodded her head. "I do."

"We need some time to discuss, but in the meantime, pack up your things. You will be going into a safe house until this is all over." She continued to cry silently but nodded her understanding. And then she turned and walked back through the door, closing it behind her.

I sighed. "Well, at least we have answers."

"Answers that leave us with more questions," Jake replied. "How much does Reed know? How long has he had access to her devices? Does he still?"

Scarborough rubbed his face. "I really don't want to lose Megan. She is an excellent agent. I can't believe she allowed this to happen." He looked to Jake. "Lyon, do you think she's telling us the whole truth?"

Jake thought through the confession. "I think she's telling her version of the truth. But she knows that there is a lot that she doesn't know, that she can't be sure of, for instance how deep Reed's infiltration went. She gave us the simplest version of the truth, but yes, she was telling the truth as she knows it. She didn't embellish, though I think we could get her musings out of her if we pushed. She may know more than she thinks she does."

Scarborough sighed. "We're going to need Fin to go through her computer to see if he can figure out what information was up for grabs when Reed broke into it. Her phone as well. Also, I would like to know if we can find out whether or not Reed has continued to have access."

I cleared my throat. "No offense to Fin, but he is an engineer, and an amazing one, but computers are not his area of expertise.

Lena and Brahim are straight up computer geniuses. Have them work on it. If they can't find it, it will never be found."

Scarborough scratched his head. "I do want to find out how deep their skills go, but I don't trust them yet, Brahim the least. I know that he has had some traumatic experiences with the AGI recently. But he has been loyal to them for a long time. Making the switch to believing that they are what they truly are is not an easy thing, and it doesn't happen overnight. His constitution may waffle." He pursed his lips in thought. "Lena, though, I might be okay with her doing the research."

He looked to Jake for his assessment of Lena. Jake nodded. "She's angry and wants retribution. I think that she would be more than happy to search Megan's computers."

"Okay. Kate, why don't you and I go talk to Lena." I nodded. "Lyon, while I am fairly certain that the threat to our secrecy has been found, I want to be as sure as possible. I'm assigning you to speak with each officer alone and give them the Lyon special."

My eyebrows rose, and Jake turned to me and said, "He wants me to interrogate them."

Scarborough ghosted a smile. "Lyon has a unique skill set when it comes to interrogation, and every officer here knows it. As soon as they see him come in their rooms, they'll know that they may as well just spill their guts outright. They'll never be able to fool him."

My eyebrows inched even higher. And as soon as Scarborough looked the other way, Jake winked at me. I rolled my lips between my teeth to hold in my smile. Gah—why did he have to be so attractive? Putting this thing between us on hold was going to be even harder than I thought.

I did have one thought, though. It might not work, but it might be worth a try. I'd schooled my features by the time Scarborough looked back, and I cleared my throat, indicating that I had one more thing to say. Scarborough nodded for me to go ahead. "I have an idea."

CHAPTER 27

Palo Alto, CA
Vinny

Tracy was doubled over in laughter. Vinny took one look at her and felt his own laughter bubble up, and soon they were both laughing so hard that his cheeks hurt and Tracy had tears streaming down her face. Tracy attempted to take deep breaths to calm herself down. Just when she had a hold on herself, she looked at Vinny and said, "Brazilian . . . ," and the laughing fit started all over again. She was hiccuping so profusely, and so deeply, that she finally put her hand up. "Stop. It hurts . . ."

Vinny followed her lead and took deep breaths to try to stop laughing, but it was just so funny. They had been on the Oliver Strands job for weeks now, and even though Tracy hated it and thought that it was absolutely wrong to push a politician the way that they were, she had decided to stay at Search, for now. But Vinny knew that she was walking a fine line and just one more push in the wrong direction and Tracy would bolt. The Oliver Strands gaffe could not have come at a better time. They needed some comic relief.

Tracy leaned back in her office chair, head against the headrest, her arms flopping over the armrests, as if all of that laughing had zapped her energy. She sighed. "Oh, it's just so good. I know that we're going to have to bury this, but even with our best work, it'll be out there. All of the news stations are playing it on repeat." To prove her point, she went to CNN.com, and the pundits were laughing at the clip.

Vinny gave a small cringe. "I feel a little bad for him. He's not the first presidential candidate to make a gaffe, not even in this cycle."

"I know, but this is the best one by far." She giggled again. "This totally made my week." Tracy tucked some of her blonde hair behind her ear and sat up, straightening her T-shirt. The shirt du jour had a picture of a bowl of lettuce on it, and the caption read: "Lettuce, the taste of sadness."

"Do you personally have it out for Oliver Strands, or is it just all of our optimization that has you so angry?"

"'Optimization' is playing it down quite nicely." She rolled her eyes and then thought for a minute. "It's several things. He seems like a nice enough guy, but he's too slick; he says all the right things, all the time. Which is why this gaffe is so funny." She pointed to her monitor at the picture of a frozen Strands. She looked at his picture a beat too long. "Honestly, we shouldn't be trying to cover up the gaffe—we should be using his strategy. He's pretty darn good at charming his way around people." She looked at Oliver Strands's face on her screen. "I mean, look at that guy—there isn't a woman in the world who doesn't want to forgive that face." The gleam in her eye indicated that Tracy knew just how attractive the political candidate was. In that moment Vinny started to like Oliver Strands a whole lot less.

Tracy's smile faded. "Ultimately, I don't want the American public to be marketed into picking a president. It should be a sacred process. One that requires thought and principles. It shouldn't be dictated by who has the most money." Her face scrunched up. "Also, remember last year, the shady things we had to do to get him his seat in Congress?"

Vinny swallowed. He did remember, all too well. At first, Search Directed Personalized Marketing was a game, something fun to see if they could bend the human mind to their will by knowing an individual, through their online footprint, and feeding them well-placed ads, some subtle, others outright. As a research and behavioral scientist, this type of experiment was right up his alley, and he found it so fascinating to watch people buy the item that Search was strategically pushing on them. Vinny's boss had first called the process personalized manipulation marketing but then thought better of it and changed it to Search Directed Personalized Marketing, or SDPM. "Yeah, I remember."

Tracy looked down. "We used SDPM on the governor of New Hampshire to push her to appoint Oliver Strands to take Barbara Randall's place in Congress. And it worked." She shivered. "I still feel guilty about that. And now here we are pushing the same guy for president, but to the *entire* American public. We have our whole team out there"—she swung her arm in the direction of the door, where the team they managed had their cubicles—"working on that exact thing right now; that's over one hundred and fifty Search employees." She shook her head. "It seems like the ultimate deceit."

Vinny scratched his neck, trying to rid his skin of the itch that SDPM brought. He hated SDPM—it made him feel more like a con artist than a behavioral scientist. He gave Tracy the same explanation that he gave himself on a regular basis. "Yeah, but people don't have to buy what we sell them—they still make their own choices. People don't sway our way every time. It's not a perfect science." He shrugged, trying to lighten the whole thing.

Tracy leaned forward in her chair and pointed a finger at him. "Eight out of ten times—that's how often we're able to successfully manipulate people. Eight out of ten."

Vinny sighed. "Those numbers are skewed. We don't know how many of those people would have gone that direction anyway. We say that it was our marketing that got New Hampshire's governor to appoint Oliver Strands, but she may have been planning on doing just that regardless. We can't account for changing minds when we don't know what direction those minds started at in the first place."

Tracy harrumphed. He had her there. That was the truth, too. Did Search's marketing sway individuals? Most definitely, but to what extent, they really didn't know. They had used test groups and knew that some people's minds were easier to sway than others, but it was impossible to get any real numbers on what it took to manipulate a mind. Everyone was different, and inevitably there were some minds that could not be swayed. She looked up at him. "For the record, I hate SDPM, which is the large bulk of what we do now. I hate that I had a part in its creation. Regardless, it's one thing to manipulate a person to buy a different brand of toaster and another thing entirely to manipulate a person into who they choose to vote for for president." Vinny agreed, but he didn't want to admit it out loud. He didn't want to strengthen Tracy's resolve against Search.

He was quiet for a minute, and then he got up from his chair. "I think you might be right about Strands being charismatic enough to work this gaffe out on his own. I'm going to go talk to Ezra about it."

He walked through the gleaming Search hallway to his boss's office suite. He stopped short of the door when he heard voices coming from inside the office. The door was cracked, and Vinny peeked in and saw Ezra and Mr. Franks, Ezra's boss, one of the *big* bosses at Search, facing a dark-haired man, whom Vinny could only see the back of. Vinny thought better of interrupting, so he stepped away from the office door and took a seat in the suite just outside of it. Despite the distance, he couldn't help but overhear the conversation.

He heard the man say, "I am expecting this to be completely buried."

Mr. Franks replied with, "We are on it and will do all that we can, of course."

"Good. We don't ask nearly as much of you as we could, but when we do, we expect it to be the top priority."

Ezra, his voice more intimidated than Vinny had ever heard it, said, "I assure you it is. I will have the best of my team on this project." He and Tracy were the best of Ezra's team, and Vinny wondered what sort of job they would be getting next. He also wondered who could intimidate Ezra and Mr. Franks like that. Not to mention why the man had the right to ask anything of Search that he wanted. There was a stiltedness to the conversation that furrowed Vinny's brow.

Vinny watched as the visiting man left the office. His suit was impeccable, his shoes expensive. Then the man looked at him, and it was all he could do not to recoil. The man had two of the thickest, ugliest scars Vinny had ever seen running down both sides of his face, from the corners of his eyes to the sides of his mouth. The man narrowed his eyes at Vinny, assessing him momentarily, and then, gauging that Vinny was no threat, continued his walk out the door.

Vinny heard relief in the voices of Ezra and Mr. Franks when the man left. Vinny felt relief, too; it almost was like the air had lost some if its charge. He heard his boss say, "I don't think that man has a clue what he's asking of us."

His boss's boss replied, "He doesn't care. He gets what he wants."

Vinny didn't want to appear as if he were snooping, so he got up from his seat and softly knocked on Ezra's door. Ezra called him in, and Vinny popped his head through the door. "Hey, boss, Mr. Franks,"—he nodded his head toward Ezra and then toward the big man who practically ran Search—"I had a quick question about Oliver Strands."

Ezra cut him off. "Forget Strands. We have something more important at the moment." Vinny arched his eyebrows. For the past month, nothing had been more important than Oliver Strands. "There's been a situation at DNA Global. We need to head it off at the pass." As his boss continued to talk, Vinny's heart sank. This was the thing that was going to make Tracy quit for good.

CHAPTER 28

Cambridge, MA
Kate

It took us two weeks to come up with a plan to get past the Zimmermann lock. Two weeks of brainstorming and debating and arguments. The CIA-style brainstorming was one of the things I disliked most about being a CIA officer. But this time it didn't bother me so much. We all felt the same about this job: it needed to be top priority, and we needed all brains on board. We couldn't let the AGI have any more time to study Brahim's computer breakthrough.

I hated that we always seemed to be one step behind. That instead of heading the AGI off at the pass, we were just trying to minimize potential damage. But this could minimize an enormous amount of potential damage. It had to be done, and this was a one-time deal. As soon as they knew that we had moved in on the technology, we wouldn't get another chance. They would move it or protect it in some way that would likely make another crack at it impossible. Brahim's discovery had to be destroyed.

We were staying at a hotel just a few doors down from the DNA Global headquarters. Only a handful of us were on the break-in job. The rest of the crew stayed at the house in Richmond, our latest location. Most of them would be helping us behind the scenes and over our comms—it was all hands on deck. Brahim was on the job with us, and he was as nervous as one could get. He kept telling us that he wasn't a spy for a reason and that we would be better off if he just told us what to do over our comms. We debated it for a long time, but Brahim was the only one who had been inside the facility before, and we needed that kind of familiarity for this job. Also, we needed to know how far the AGI had gotten in breaching his work. We needed it airtight, and that was a job only Brahim could do. When it was decided that he would come with us, he looked like he might be sick. Since we had gotten here, he *had* been sick, several times.

I looked over at him and smiled. "You got this, Brahim. It's going to be in and out." He looked like he wanted to thank me for the encouragement, but instead he started to gag, running for the bathroom. He knew as well as I did that my words were just that: words. Truth was, Fin had been correct when he'd said that no one had ever broken into a Zimmermann before. The officers in our group had searched all of their contacts trying to find someone who could help us. Scarborough even had several who were "off the books"—basically criminals. Most everyone laughed when we told them that we were attempting it. We got a lot of "Good luck" and "If you get in, I'd sure like to know how you did it."

We'd purchased a few Zimmermann locks so that we could study them and try to disassemble them, but we triggered them every time. It was easy to tell why they were the brand to buy. We tried every avenue we could think of to make the job fast and easy. Even knowing that Zimmermann, as part of their sales pitch, refused to give anyone, including government officials, access to their locks, we called them anyway. Scarborough, with his massive credentials, being the one talking, they'd politely refused.

Eventually we had come up with a plan, and I hoped it would work, because after endless hours of brainstorming, it was the best that we could do.

Jake attached the final fastener on his bulletproof vest and looked up. "Ready?" He was looking at Brahim but talking to all of us. We all nodded, even Brahim. He had been given a pep talk from Candace that seemed to work, at least somewhat. He was ready to go but still looked a little pukey.

I took one last deep breath and mentally went through the plan for the hundredth time, then followed Jake out the door. We split up; some of us used the back entrance to our hotel, some the front, and others the side entrances.

It was fairly early on a Friday, earlier than most people went to work. Our research told us that it was the perfect time and day to deal with the fewest DNA Global employees. Jake and I were playing the same role, and so we left the hotel together. Brahim had stayed with us up until that point, but he needed to be on his way. I gave his arm a squeeze, reminding him that we were all in this together and that he could do this. He walked away without so much as a look back.

Liam's job was first, and he was already in place when Jake and I started walking up to the DNA Global office building. I couldn't help the smile that ghosted my face when I saw Liam in action.

He was in a gigantic chicken costume, head and all. It had been no small feat to find one big enough for him, and he was twirling and flipping a sign for a new fried chicken fast food joint that was opening in the area soon. His sign flipping was impressive. He was throwing it in the air more than fifteen feet; sometimes the sign would flip end over end, sometimes arching, and sometimes it went up so fast and so high that it was hard to follow, but Liam always caught it. He was gaining a crowd, who were all cheering him on. I looked at Jake. His brow lifted in surprise; Liam had been practicing since we'd come up with our plan, but he had never seemed this good. His head was in the game.

We watched from just far enough away as the doorman/security guard for DNA Global—we'd learned from Brahim that his name was Don—came out of the door. According to Brahim, Don was a no-nonsense kind of guy who took his job a little too seriously. He never let anyone into DNA Global without them either being an employee or having their name on the list with proper identification. Even Brahim, who had worked there every day for six weeks, had to show his ID every time. Don was yelling for Liam to stop. We watched as Don gestured with his hands for Liam to go somewhere else. Some of the crowd dispersed at the drama, but many stayed, especially the young college students, wanting to see how it all played out. A few of them started recording with their phones.

Liam completely ignored Don and kept on flipping his sign. Don, with his arms flailing, told Liam that he'd better cut it out or he was calling the cops. Liam didn't give him the time of day, and Don's patience had lost its very thin tether. He unhooked his phone from off his belt, where all self-respecting doormen and security guards kept them, and called the Cambridge Police. That's where Jake and I came in. Fin intercepted the call and sent it to Jake, a.k.a. officer Leopold. By the time Jake and I were on the scene, Liam had taken off his chicken head and was using his hands, encased in feathered wings, to point and yell at Don—something about it being a free country and that he still had his right to freedom of speech. I had to bite my lip to contain my smile when Liam told Don that if he tried to make him leave, he would start a protest of DNA Global right outside their doors, because the last time he'd checked, he still had that right, too.

Don was clearly taken aback by Liam's size, as any smart man should be, and he started to tell Liam to calm down. That was the wrong tactic. Liam yelled, wings flailing, "You want me to calm down? Calm down? Did I hear that right? Why don't you take your own advice, little guy! You come out here all aggressive, wanting a fight. Well, I'll give you a fight." The collegiate crowed oohed and snickered.

Liam leaned toward Don, and Don backed away a step and pointed down the street. "I never said that I wanted a fight; I want you to move this crowd down the block, away from my building."

"Oh, it's your building? Is this your sidewalk? Your city? I don't think so. In fact, last time I checked, doormen got paid less than sign flippers." Don bristled, and Liam leaned in, "What, you think you own this place?" Liam exaggeratedly rolled his eyes. "Please, you probably can't even afford your own apartment."

Don's face turned a bright shade of red, and Liam pushed even harder. He used one of his wings to point to the building. "You making what the CEO is making? I didn't think so." Don growled, and Liam lifted his chin and said, "Come on, buddy, bring it." Liam punched his fist into his hand, a kind of come-get-me gesture, but from the outside, it looked like he was flapping his wings. Jake lost it, having a coughing fit to disguise his laughter. I was biting the inside of my cheeks so hard that I tasted blood, trying to keep it together.

Don had had enough. He pushed Liam hard, but Liam didn't budge. He just laughed and said, "That all you got, doorman?"

As soon as Don went to give Liam another shove, Jake and I started to push through the growing crowd. "All right, all right, that's enough," I shouted. I flipped my police officer badge, just because I could. If I was going to play the part of a police officer, I was going to be an obnoxious one. I turned to Don and said, "Sir, I suggest you back away."

Liam piped up, his wings in the air, "He shoved me twice, Officer; I haven't laid a hand on him."

Don scoffed, but the crowed indicated that what Liam said was true. Jake held up his hand. "We saw enough." He looked to Don. "You, sir, are under arrest."

Don sputtered, "Are you kidding me? This guy stands in front of my door, a working establishment, and builds a crowd so that none of my employees can get in or out of the building? If anyone should be arrested here, it should be him!"

Jake frowned. "Assault is a crime, sir."

"He provoked me!" Don continued to sputter in disbelief.

I sidled up next to Don and said, "I can cover the desk for you until you get this straightened out."

He looked at me like I had two heads. "I have a backup in there. We don't leave our building unguarded." That was Candace's cue. I watched as she waltzed up to the door in a white dress that revealed quite a bit of cleavage and clung to her hard body like it had been painted on. Her makeup was flawless, her posture indicating that she was too good, and too beautiful, for everyone around her; she didn't so much as look at the growing crowd before waltzing into the building.

I put my hands up in mock surrender to block Candace from Don's view. "Just trying to be of assistance."

"Why don't you *assist* me in getting your partner's hands off me." He scowled at Jake. "This is insanity!"

I folded my arms and looked down my nose and said slowly, "No can do, sir."

Jake hit the radio communicator that was attached to his vest at his shoulder and spoke into the receiver, "We have a ten-ninety-six and possibly a five-one-five-zero. We are going to require assistance." Jake looked at Don and drawled, "The more you resist, the bigger this problem gets for you."

Brahim, somewhere in the crowd, shouted, "Resist!" And people started laughing, and then shouting together, "Resist, Resist, Resist." Brahim left the crowd then, following Candace into the building.

Being mocked was not a thing that Don enjoyed; his face turned an even deeper shade of red, and he shouted, "I want to speak to your boss, Officer Leopold!"

Jake snort coughed. "You can do that down at the station."

Just at that exact moment, Charlie pulled up in a Cambridge PD cruiser. He got out of the car in a uniform that matched mine and Jake's and said, "I hear we got a problem?"

Don spat, "Yes, we do! Are you his boss?"

Charlie smiled and said, "No, sir. He's my boss. And it appears that you are coming with me." Charlie came over, took Don by the handcuffs, and guided the irate man inside the car, "Watch your head." When Don was in the car, his door shut, the crowd cheered the win for the little guy against the big corporation. Liam preened.

As soon as they drove away, Jake turned to Liam and said, loud enough for the crowd to hear, "Why don't you move this ten feet that way?"

Liam said, "Yes, sir. No problem." He motioned for his entourage to follow him, and they moved to his new location just on the other side of the door, high-fiving his new fans the whole way.

Jake and I walked into the building. The backup doorman was watching Candace walk away with a gleam in his eye. I spotted a card in his hand that had Candace's phone number on it, and he was on cloud nine. We had learned from Brahim that the backup doorman had a weakness for pretty women, and Candace was as pretty as they came. But in that white dress, she was stunning; it looked like it hadn't taken much for him to fall under her spell.

He was so entranced with the backside of Candace's body that I think we could have said that we were there to burn the place down and he would have waved us in. Instead I said, "Sir?" He looked over at us, momentarily confused as to why two cops were standing at his front desk. "We just want to do a quick, complementary sweep of the building, in light of the commotion outside."

The backup doorman didn't so much as look at the badges we had open to him before he shrugged, allowing us access to the building. Backup doorman was no Don. We took the stairs down to the basement. "We're in, going to the basement now," I said for the sake of Fin and Scarborough and whoever else was listening over the comms. In the stairwell we took off our police attire to reveal the catsuits we wore underneath. Jake's wasn't as much a catsuit as mine—his wasn't a one-piece. But I liked to call it a catsuit because on occasion I enjoyed flirting that was of the annoying variety.

The police costumes were so uncomfortable and impossible to really move in. I felt bad for police everywhere, with those non-stretch pants and button-down shirts, not to mention the thick leather belts. They were an atrocity, being both unflattering and uncomfortable. It felt like my body had been freed from prison when I took those pants off.

I adjusted my bobbed brown wig farther down on my scalp and took off the glasses—both were annoying, but I could work with the wig. Jake looked at his watch and said, "Thirty more seconds." We waited silently.

After the seconds had passed, Jake slowly peeked out the door. He saw Brahim jogging down the hall ahead of us. Brahim was late. We hoped that Candace had gotten to the door on time—otherwise we were going to have to cut our losses and come back a different day. As soon as we stepped into the hall, our comms went silent. Jake looked at me and pointed at his ear; I shook my head to let him know that I couldn't hear anything either. He nodded once—we were on our own.

We jogged on silent feet, coming up on Brahim's heels just as we heard voices. No one was supposed to be down here but us. Jake swore under his breath, and Brahim's head whipped around to find us right behind him. He was so startled that I had to cover his mouth before he made a noise. He calmed and nodded, silently letting me know that he had it together and I could move my hand. I did, even though he was still shaking like a leaf.

Jake motioned for us to wait there, and he silently crept around the corner to see what he could see. He came back a few seconds later with Candace. She mouthed, *"Arthur Whitehall."* Our eyes went wide at the mention of the CEO of DNA Global. What was he doing down here?

Brahim shook his head, his eyes wide, reminding us that Arthur and he had met when he was working in the building, more than once. He'd described Arthur as a "nervous man." Brahim mouthed, *"He will know me."*

Jake gave a quick nod acknowledging Brahim's concern and held up his finger, indicating that he needed a moment to think. But just then, the voices down the hall came closer, and there was nowhere to hide. Jake grabbed Brahim by the arm and started pointing down the hall toward Whitehall. Brahim went white as a sheet, panic written all over his face. He was shaking his head and tugging back from Jake's grip. Jake turned back to Candace and motioned for her to go back out of the building; she left without question.

Jake motioned for me to take Brahim's other arm, and I nodded. It appeared that we were going with plan B. We took the Nex-Gen Organized Solutions patches from our pockets and slapped them on our catsuits.

I swallowed down my fear as we walked toward Arthur Whitehall and whoever he was with.

It appeared that he was with a security guard and they were having an intense conversation. Jake started talking to warn them of our approach and also let them think that we weren't a threat. "Mr. Awan, please stop struggling." Arthur's head snapped up, as did the guard's.

Arthur looked different than his pictures—older, more tired. He was in his late fifties and had mostly salt in his salt-and-pepper hair. When he saw Brahim, his eyes widened. Then he took in Jake and me, our NexGen badges, practically dragging Brahim along, and he furrowed his brow. "Where have you been?" he practically spat at Brahim. "We have been looking for you for weeks."

I looked at Brahim. "Cat got your tongue, Awan?" Brahim swallowed, his apparent terror very real.

Jake looked at Arthur. "We found him; it appears that he hasn't been able to access any of the secure information, but we're here to make sure that's true. He's going to open his program, and we're going to replace him so that everything remains secure."

Arthur looked relieved. "And then what are you going to do with him?" His nostrils flared, indicating that he didn't like NexGen's practices but also wouldn't fight against them.

Jake said, "Let us deal with that."

Arthur motioned for the door and said, "There's already a NexGen employee in there." My heart stuttered. "Go ahead and do what you need to do. Apparently we are having a NexGen party down here." His smile was forced and tight. Arthur did not like NexGen Organized Solutions.

Jake dragged Brahim up to the door and told him to unlock it. Brahim looked at me, his eyes panicked; I nodded, and he lifted his shaking hand to the pad, and as soon as he touched it, an alarm blared. Everyone covered their ears, and the security guard said, "I told you, sir." My heart hammered. They knew now; the AGI knew that Brahim was here.

Arthur motioned for him to take care of it, and in a hurry. The security guard put his hand on the pad, and the alarm stopped. The retina scanner popped out and scanned his eyes while he said, "Something's wrong with the door—the alarm went off earlier when the other NexGen employee was trying to get in."

Arthur frowned. "That's why I'm down here; apparently I have nothing more important to do than to be a babysitter for NexGen employees."

I said, "Sorry to inconvenience you, Mr. Whitehall. I assumed that you would be happy to see Mr. Awan."

"Oh, I assure you, I am." That tight smile again. "Next time, don't lose your charge."

"NexGen isn't a prison, Mr. Whitehall."

He huffed, "Could have fooled me." With that, he was on his way back down the hall.

The security guard punched in the second code, and there was a sucking sound as the door opened.

I could see her red, curly hair before she turned around. "There y'all are. Took you long enough." We'd assumed that the AGI had been sending agents in to work on opening Brahim's program regularly. So we sent Lena to go down first, disguised as a NexGen employee, to try to get in the door. We knew the alarm would go off. She was to act like the lock was faulty and inform security that someone needed to let her in so that she could work. Then she was supposed to listen for us and let us in when we arrived.

The tightness in my chest eased when I saw her unharmed. The security guard smiled at her and said to the group, "Let me know if you all need anything else." Lena winked at him, and he blushed, backing out of the office, shutting the door behind him.

Jake looked at Lena, incredulous, his hands in his hair. "Why didn't you let us in?"

She shook her head, eyes wide. "I came out looking for you guys minutes ago, when you were supposed to arrive, but it was just Whitehall and the security guard out there. And I couldn't just keep popping my head out—it looked weird. I was waiting until I heard y'all knock, but it's silent as a tomb in here. I had no idea y'all were trying to access the lock." She looked mildly panicked.

Brahim sank to the floor, his head in his hands, breathing heavily; it seemed like he was having a serious panic attack. But his job was just beginning. Jake looked at him. "Brahim, either tell Lena what to do or get up and do it yourself. We are on borrowed time. The AGI knows that you're here."

His head shot up. "The alarm?"

Jake nodded. "The handprint. Zimmermann accesses a government fingerprint database whenever anyone tries to access their locks, though yours was probably already alarmed to let them know immediately if you tried to get in. The AGI knows. We need to get out of here. Now."

That was the understatement of the year. We couldn't hear anything outside that door, not even the alarm, and that was terrifying. The unknown was so much scarier than the known.

That got Brahim into action. He jumped up and sat in front of the computer. The dilution refrigerator looked like a chandelier made of steel, copper, and gold. Real gold. It looked to me like some sort of conductor circuit. Jake, Lena, and I all stared at it in awe. It was a pretty amazing sight, especially now that I knew what quantum computing was capable of. Which was both terrifying and mind-blowing.

Brahim took a deep breath and started tapping at lightning speed at the keyboard that was connected to the quantum computer. He seemed to relax somewhat in front of the computer. I could tell that it was like coming home to him; it was something he knew, something safe. I wondered if Jake knew that and it was part of why he had pushed Brahim so hard just then. The other part being imminent danger, of course.

We all waited, not so patiently, for Brahim to finish. Jake and I made eye contact, and his growing concern was clearly written on his face, his fingers tapping his pants. I realized, then, that he and I had not done many jobs together. He had always been the person in my ear, helping me and guiding me. This was the third one, if I counted the time that he got the CIA to jump on the Grup job, the one where I was playing the role of Viktoriya for the second time. But while we were in on that together, it wasn't the two of us from start to finish.

Jake was a good officer, very good; his mind was as sharp as a steel blade. I found a comfort in working with him, a trust. I wasn't sure if that was a good thing or not. I didn't want to feel a false sense of safety. I needed all of my wits about me—I needed to make sure that my head was in the game as much as his was. This was not his burden alone to carry. I counted on him too much; he may have been my superior within the CIA, but my ideas were valuable, and I knew that he valued them. It occurred to me in that moment that I had been in a bit of a fog the last few months, chasing the AGI. I had lost an important part of my self-confidence. I could now see that it was because I was embarrassed that I was working with these very talented CIA officers, who all knew that I was dumb enough to take a job with the AGI. Dumb enough to think that they were real. It made me feel so stupid and had been a cloud over my head, effectively making me second-guess myself and turn to the others for guidance.

But none of them were there the day that I was hired. They had no idea how convincing the AGI was. Also, the AGI had been growing in power right under their noses, for hundreds of years. Who was stupid now? Not to mention that without me, they would still be clueless, thinking everything was fine while the AGI took over the world. I had done something for the country that no one else had successfully done: I had brought the Alternate Government Initiative to light. They were known now, and there was no going back to the way things used to be for them. I had done that. I was valuable. And I would start to act like it.

I noticed then that Jake was looking at me. At first his brow was furrowed, and then his eyes got brighter and he started to smile. He knew that I was coming back to myself, and he liked it.

Brahim hit the last key, and the computer started to make weird noises. I heard a pop, and I could feel the heat coming off the machine. The noise it was making grew until I heard a sizzle, and then smoke started to come out of the wires, then out of the quantum computer's metal connectors, the smell of burning metal and plastic wafting into the air. Lena whimpered, "Is it wrong that I'm so sad to see this beautiful machine destroyed?"

Brahim nodded his understanding, but he didn't look sad—he looked relieved. He rolled his chair back and looked at each of us. "There was a breach." I took in a sharp breath. "But it was shallow. I'm confident that they have nothing of too great a value." Lena nodded; she must have seen as much before we got there. He stood up and smiled. I hadn't seen Brahim smile in far too long. I could tell that a weight had been lifted from his shoulders.

I pointed to the computer and looked at Brahim. "Is that thing going to catch on fire?" It may not have been such a bad thing, but I wanted to get us out of there in a hurry if it was a possibility.

He looked at the machine as it continued to smoke and crackle and shook his head. "The hardware is loaded with fail-safes; it's unusable, but it won't blow up or anything."

Jake nodded and moved on. "I don't have to tell you guys that our comms don't work in here." We shook our heads. He didn't have to tell us—we could all hear the absolute radio silence in our ears. "It's been"—he looked at his watch—"thirty-one minutes since Brahim put his hand on the scanner, alerting the AGI that we're here." He turned to me. "What should we expect when we open that door?"

When we were prepping for this job, Brahim had informed us that the AGI had a facility in Boston that he'd stayed in while he did his work.

"How many agents were there at any given time? And where is the building located, exactly?" I asked, trying to do some quick mental calculations.

"I can't remember the address, but the building is a block off Newbury, adjacent to the Boston Public Garden. I didn't see a lot of other agents at the local facility, just a few, but I worked very long hours when I was there, so it's possible that they were sleeping when I came and went."

I pulled up a map of Boston in my memory and zoomed in. "That's only about four miles from the DNA Global building. It could take a while during rush hour, but likely fewer than thirty minutes."

Jake said, "Surely that facility is filled with all types." He gestured to Brahim to make his point. "Not everyone there is a field agent."

I shook my head. "Boston has been a point of interest for them since losing Brahim; they know that he's with us and has likely told us what he did. I'm sure they stacked the facility, waiting for us to make our move."

Our plan was, first, not to alert them that we were there, and if we did alert them, then we would be fast.

Unfortunately, we'd alerted them, and we weren't that fast. Jake looked at his watch. "Thirty-four minutes, now." He blew out a breath. "Let's not give them any more time."

I shrugged. "The hallway will probably be full of agents who are prepared to take us. The AGI won't want us dead, particularly Brahim. They'll want to question us, using their own particular methods." Lena paled.

Jake said, "Only one way to find out."

Brahim looked like he was going to be sick again, and Lena was white as a ghost. Jake looked at both of them. "Kate and I are going in front; we know that espionage and combat are not either of your top skill sets. Just stay behind us, and if things go to hell out there, take the first opportunity to run. Do not worry about us, do not look back."

He looked back at me. "You ready?"

I took my gun out, removed the safety, and nodded. I pulled the door latch—the sucking sound that would bring us back to the outside world was like a siren in my ears.

CHAPTER 29

Cambridge, MA
Arthur

Arthur sat at the desk in his office. His leg was bouncing at the speed of light, one hand tapping voraciously on his desk, the other was at his mouth, nails in between his teeth, shredding what was left of the tough keratin. He hadn't bitten his nails in years, and he knew that meant his anxiety was through the roof.

He opened his drawer, pulled out his bottle of Xanax, and poured one pill into his palm. He popped it in his mouth and swallowed it down without water. He stood up and then sat back down. Then he stood up, took a deep breath, and sat back down again.

He'd received a phone call informing him that the people in his records room weren't with NexGen. That Brahim Awan had been taken by them and that they were accessing DNA Global's records for their own nefarious reasons. Arthur said that he was calling the police, but NexGen had said that they were prepared for this and to let them handle it.

But Arthur had let them handle things before, and they had been ready to throw him under the bus.

He spit out the piece of nail that he'd managed to rip from his thumb. Then with shaking hands, he picked up the phone.

"This is nine-one-one, what's your emergency?"

Arthur cleared his throat and began to talk.

CHAPTER 30

Cambridge, MA
Kate

We used the door for cover as we opened it, the four of us crouched behind it. Jake and I heard the telltale click of a bullet entering a gun chamber. Though the sound made my hair stand on end, I internally calmed myself. I looked to Jake and reminded him, and possibly myself, "They'll want us alive." He nodded back to me.

In a sing-song voice I heard, "Edison . . . Come out, come out, wherever you are . . ."

Time stood still. I knew that voice. Lena spat his name, a name I'd hoped I'd never hear again, like the ugliest of curse words: "Richter."

I could hear my blood pound in my ears, my heart rate skyrocketing. My nerves, which I'd mastered mere seconds ago, catapulted and united with crippling fear, while my brain ran through all of the possible outcomes. Richter was the one who had tortured Claire. I could hear what Westwood had told me about Richter while he'd had me chained up in the Montana facility—my mind played it on repeat: *"I hear he has a thing for you . . . if he got you alone, who knows what he might do to you. He's a sadist, that one."* Richter had always made me uneasy, in the rawest sense of the word. He did a good job of playing off his true nature. While he had always seemed like a creep, I wouldn't have pegged him for a sadistic torturer. My fear had become a burn in my throat, a twisting in my gut.

I felt Jake's hand on my back, and he whispered, "I take it you know him?"

Lena answered, "We all do, and he's a monster. He always held a flame for Kate that verged on fiendish." Jake's hand on my back stiffened at that little piece of information. She whispered to me, "Keep far away from him, Kate." She pumped my hand, and then to my utter surprise and terror she said, "Good thing he's never scared me" and shot around the door and walked out.

I couldn't grab her back fast enough, and before I knew it, she was out in front of the firing squad.

Richter laughed, "Johnson?" He laughed again. "Wait, let me get this straight: I have found Lena Johnson, Kate Edison, and Brahim Awan all at the same time? This is too good." He laughed again. "I'm going to be a hero!"

I didn't have a long time to think, but a couple of things were apparent: Richter didn't know that Jake was there, and there was no way I was leaving Lena to fend for herself with Jeremy Richter. I whispered to Jake, "I don't think he knows about you; let's keep it a surprise."

Jake nodded, and I grabbed Brahim and stepped around the door. Richter's steel-gray eyes, filled with mirth, hit me first. It had been a few months since I'd seen him, but he still looked the same, still had that darkness in his light eyes, still had that blond hair, styled just right, that attractive but twisted air about him. He smirked at me. "I sure hope your long blonde hair is hidden under that wig, Kate. I've thought a lot about that hair wrapped around my wrist." I heard Jake take in a sharp breath behind me. There were several ways to interpret that comment, so I wasn't entirely sure what he was alluding to, but I was absolutely positive that I never wanted to find out.

"Keep dreaming, Richter." That was from Lena. I let the two of them spit insults at each other while I assessed our odds of getting out of there.

There were fifteen agents in total, at least from what I could see from my vantage point. There may have been more around the corner or upstairs at the entrance as backup. Regardless, I needed to deal with this group before we could see what lay beyond. Fifteen was a lot but not impossible. They were all dressed in suits—I imagined that the AGI didn't want to make a scene, and the building swarming with people wearing catsuits and wielding guns would have done just that. I didn't know any of the agents aside from Richter, so I couldn't assess their level of field expertise. But I knew that Richter was good, very good. During training, I'd had the hardest time beating him in the ring, mainly because he wasn't above dirty moves. And if he wasn't above dirty moves in the training ring, when it wasn't allowed, I could only imagine the things he would do here.

I was coming up blank about where to start, when Richter said, "Awan, why don't you come over here and show these two idiots whose side you're really on."

I rolled my eyes, but to my outright shock, Brahim shook himself free of my hold, and under his breath he said, "Everything I said was true—the program is dead and they may kill me for it, but they have something on me, and I've been acting to them like I've been playing both sides." Then he started walking away from me. It was like being sucker punched. No way was this happening. But then the past few weeks started to resonate. I had thought that Brahim wasn't acting like himself because of all of the things he'd learned about the AGI and him having given them access to the world's most dangerous computer technology. Also because he'd had the wounds from his sister's brutal murder reopened.

I was wrong. He wasn't acting like himself because he was a traitor. Whether he wanted to be or not, he was a traitor.

Lena gasped out a "No!" as Brahim walked toward Jeremy Richter. I thought I should shoot him in the back. He was too valuable to go back into the hands of the AGI. I debated whether to kill him on the spot. My finger grazed the trigger, every logical part of my brain telling me to pull it. As my finger started to pull back, before it pushed enough to force the round out of the chamber, I slid my finger down, away from the trigger. I couldn't do it. I may have been the most naive person alive, but too much of me believed that Brahim was not the traitor he appeared to be at the moment. I stood there, gun up, while I let the chance to kill him slip through my fingers like water.

Jeremy grabbed Brahim by the arm and spun him around to face us. But Brahim's eyes were downcast; he refused to look at us, the shame written all over his body, he throbbed with it. But Lena, she throbbed with anger. It radiated from her and was so acute that I felt as if it might be a living, breathing thing. She took a shaky breath and quietly, so quietly, said, "Brahim, I will hunt you down and I will find you. I will find you when this is all over, and I will Rip. Your. Throat. Out." I saw a tear from Brahim's face hit the ground, and then he shook Richter's hand off and bolted to the back of the group of agents, hiding like the coward he was.

"Edison and Johnson, you will be coming with us, too; whether you walk or get dragged is up to you. And, for the record, I'll be dragging you, Edison." Richter smiled his smug smile and held out his hand, beckoning me with his fingers.

Feigning resignation, I put my hand out for his, and his smile became even more smarmy, with a touch of victory, when he reached for me.

As soon as my hand was in his, I tightened my grip and pulled him toward me, forcing him off-balance. Caught off guard, he started to fall forward, which is when I gave him the Kate Edison special and kneed him in the groin, hard. He doubled over, moaning. That's when I heard several bullets enter their chambers. Richter groan-shouted, from his bent-over position, "Don't shoot, we need her alive." I was sure he had some expletives that he would have liked to have added about me, but he was in so much pain that the basics were all he was able to get out. That made me smile.

There was one thing I was sure of: I was either getting out of there alive with the CIA or in a body bag. I wouldn't ever go back to the AGI. I had felt that way for a long time, but seeing Richter solid- ified that fact for me. I didn't want to be anywhere near him ever again. I knew that if I were, the things he would do to me weren't things I could come back from. I was less afraid of death.

I yelled, "Now!" and pulled my gun up and started firing. Jake came out from behind the door and started firing alongside me. We got three down, out of sheer surprise, before bullets started to fly in our direction.

Lena, who had never been all that great of a shot, had her gun blazing. Even if she wasn't taking anyone out, she was helping to cause confusion and fear among the AGI agents who had bullets coming at them from the three of us.

With eleven trained AGI agents shooting at us from such a close distance, the odds started to weigh heavily out of our favor, but if I went down, I would go down fighting. Lena got hit first—I heard her yelp and then saw her fling herself behind the door.

Then I felt a sharp pain in my calf, and my knee buckled involuntarily. The man who'd shot me smiled, and in his split second of celebration I shot him in the head. Ten left. But I had been injured and I couldn't stand on my left leg, so I continued to aim from the position I was in on my knee.

From the corner of my eye, I saw Richter slink away with Brahim. I fired at them, but the bulled didn't hit, and I watched them get away unscathed. How could Brahim do this?

Without being able to move, I was a sitting duck. Another bullet hit me in the bicep, and I yelped in pain. But they didn't get me in my shooting arm, so I kept firing. I heard Jake's gun run out of ammunition. He grunted as he was hit. He grabbed me by the arm, my bad arm, and dragged me back into the office and behind the door. It was all I could do not to cry out in pain. The pain reverberated through my entire arm, and I clenched my teeth together as hard as I could to stop the tears and rising panic. I had to get myself to think. I needed the full capacity of my brain, and I needed it fast.

While bullets rained on the door, Jake yelled, "Switch out your magazine!" The door, along with the room, was a Faraday cage encased in thick steel: it was bulletproof, soundproof, even EMP proof. Never had I been more grateful for the AGI's security measures.

I dropped the almost-empty magazine out of my gun and went to get the other from my belt. My injured arm screamed in agony. I dropped the magazine and swore, struggling to pick it back up. I started to shake and sweat, my adrenal glands working overtime. Lena looked over. "I was grazed in the leg; I'm okay." She grabbed my gun and the full magazine and snapped it into place. She looked at me, her eyebrows raised in question. It was an offer. She was in good enough shape to keep going. I knew that even though she wasn't nearly as trained as she should be for this level of combat, she was telling me that she would go out there shooting that gun like only her crazy Texan self could.

I almost let her, almost. But I was afraid that she would get hurt, or worse, that they may have wanted us alive but they would shoot to kill if it came down to it. I was also worried that she would damn the consequences and go after Brahim. She was angry enough and crazy enough to do just that. But Brahim was long gone; going after him now would just lead to a world of trouble, perhaps more trouble than we were already in.

I shook my head and put my hand out for the gun. She handed it to me and said, "Wise choice." I huffed; she could always make me laugh. She smiled briefly, and then loud enough to be heard over the gunfire, said, "What if I hold you up, would that help?"

"I could definitely use help to stand." I put my arm out, and she helped me up so I stood on my good leg. I tried to put some weight on the other leg and was surprised to find that it could withstand a tiny amount. Thank goodness for bulletproof catsuits.

I looked over to Jake, who was shooting from behind the door. I could tell that he was struggling. I didn't know where he had been hit, but I could see the sweat forming on his brow and upper lip, the slight tremor in his stance. Even still, he was a masterpiece of pain management and concentration—in comparison I looked like an injured little bird.

I took a deep breath, settled more weight on my injured leg, and got behind Jake, shooting around him. One more down. Jake took another bullet, this time to his shooting arm. His gun dropped and he swore. I pulled him back around the door, his breathing heavy. He looked at me, his eyes somber. He knew as well as I did that getting out of this mess was going to be near-impossible.

I looked above his head, having a hard time thinking clearly while looking at him in pain, and worked through my muddled brain in attempt to assemble my thoughts into a plan to get the three of us out of there alive. My thoughts were interrupted, though, and I reared back slightly, my mouth dropping open in surprise. I started to hear the grunts and toppling of men going down outside the office. They were falling one after another, each one down with a single bullet.

I looked back at Jake, and he was smiling. It was a wince-smile but a smile nonetheless. "William David, to the rescue."

I smiled and sagged in relief, allowing the breath I'd been holding to release from my lungs.

As soon as the gunfire had ceased, Liam's head popped around the door. "Someone call the Cambridge PD?" He came fully around the door. He was dressed in Jake's discarded police costume, and it was far too small. The buttons were straining for their lives. "What are you all doing back here hiding like little girls?" He smiled to let us know that he was kidding. But we all knew that having ten-to-one odds, even when the opposition was well trained, was nothing to Liam.

"'Bout time you got down here, you big old woolly mammoth," Lena said from her huddled position, crouched in the corner.

Liam smiled and winked at Lena. "Nothing woolly about this mammoth . . ."

Lena rolled her eyes. "I guess I walked right into that one."

Liam waggled his eyebrows. "If you ever want to see just how smooth this body is for yourself—"

Lena cut him off, "Do not finish that sentence." Liam helped Lena up from her position of cowering in the corner. Then he looked around the office and said, "Where's Brahim?"

Lena was instantly angry again. "Don't you ever say that lying, cheating, weak, despicable excuse for a man's name in my presence again."

Liam's eyebrows rose in both surprise and question. I turned toward him. "Brahim left with Richter; turns out he's still a part of the AGI."

Liam's eyebrows shot down in anger. "Hold up. *Jeremy Richter* was here?"

I nodded. "Yep. He and Brahim snuck out during the shootout."

Liam was momentarily lost in his thoughts. "I hate that guy. I once heard him brag about basically raping Claire Neman. That agent who'd gotten fired?" He didn't have to specify; I knew exactly who Claire Neman was, and it didn't surprise me one bit that Richter had violated her that way when he was torturing her for information. He was a coward who preyed on the weak. It did make me sad all over again for Claire, though. Too much. She went through too much at the hands of the AGI. I could tell from the look on Liam's face that it upset him a great deal. "Claire was quiet but nice." He looked back out the door and down the hall, as if he might be able to see Brahim and Richter. He looked back at us, his brow furrowed. "I would have liked the pleasure of putting a bullet in his head."

Lena nodded. "Richter is a disgusting excuse for a human being." She frowned. "Why aren't you reacting about Brahim?"

Liam shrugged. "Of course I'm concerned about Brahim. They just walked away with the brain that made the discovery that we almost died to keep out of the AGI's hands." His expression was determined when he said, "We'll get him back."

Lena's expression hardened. "He wasn't *taken*; he left *voluntarily*."

Liam shook his head. "No way is Brahim on their side. I've worked in special ops my entire career, and I've seen enough to know that Brahim hated the AGI, of that I'm sure. They must have something serious on him to make him go back."

I nodded. "That's what he said to me under his breath before he went to Richter's side. He said that the AGI has something on him but everything he'd done and said was true. He said that he acted to the AGI like he was playing both sides."

Liam nodded. "I'm far more concerned about what they're going to try to make him do and how long he can hold off before he's forced to do their bidding."

"No." Lena was shaking her head adamantly. "No, no, nope, no way. Did I just fall into the twilight zone?" She was flailing her arms, using them to make her opinion louder. "If that were true, he would have told us. Why would he keep it a secret from *us* that he was playing *them*? He would have known that we could have used and exploited that kind of information. He never said one word to me about the AGI having anything on him, not a word about his having to go back to them. I'll never trust him again, and neither should any of you." Her face was red as flame, eyes misty, but she didn't shed one tear. I knew that she wanted to but wouldn't in front of us. She had been betrayed by someone she trusted—it was a pain that would last a long time.

Jake had been lost in thought about Brahim, and I wanted to pick his brain as soon as possible. He could have shot Brahim while he was walking back to the AGI as easily as I could have. He didn't, and I wanted to know why. He looked up and said, "I think Brahim is still with us. He'll know how to get in touch with us." Lena threw up her hands in disbelief. "I could be wrong. Either way, we will have plenty of time to discuss this with the whole group. Right now, we need to get out of here." He turned to Liam. "Where is everyone else? And why are you in the police costume?"

"We've all been trying to take care of the other AGI agents that had stormed the building. They were all dressed as professionals, so it was hard to tell who they were. As for the costume, Whitehall called the cops a few minutes ago. Fin intercepted it and sent me." Liam motioned with his arm. "Follow me, there's a back entrance that's been cleared."

I started walking and my knee buckled. I had almost forgotten that I had been hit. There was no blood, thanks to the catsuit, but that didn't mean that there weren't broken bones. Lena hefted my good arm over her shoulder and helped me forward. I looked back at Jake, who was also limping. What a disaster. We killed the quantum computer program, only to lose the creator. We were going back to the CIA with our tails between our legs.

CHAPTER 31

Richmond, VA
Kate

We were all seated in the large living room of the house we were renting, staring at each other. All twenty-four of us: the original twenty-two CIA agents that made up our task force as well as Liam and Lena, who seemed, for now, to be accepted as part of the group. Even Candace seemed inclined to keep them on the team; on the return trip from Boston, she told them how impressed she was with their performance during the DNA Global job. She was really impressed, and perhaps a little concerned, with how well the AGI trained their agents. We'd returned from Cambridge just minutes before the whole crew was brought together so that we could debrief. We had gotten to the part in our story where Brahim had left us to go back with the AGI, and everyone was speechless. They already knew that he hadn't come back with us, obviously, but they didn't know why until just now. Only Scarborough had known before we'd arrived, and it was clear that he hadn't told anyone else. I wondered if he wanted to watch the reactions on the others' faces. He would probably be on edge about moles for the rest of this mission.

I looked at Lena. Her head was in her hands, with so many emotions rolling across her face. I wanted to take her to my room so that we could talk, like two girls who weren't trying to save the world from the greatest threat it had ever known. Like we were just two girls whose friend had betrayed them. Lena had been more than friends with Brahim—I didn't know how deep that relationship went, but it was clear before and clear now that she had feelings for him that extended beyond friendship. Lena needed time to just be a girl who had lost someone she cared about for a few minutes. Unfortunately, that kind of free time wasn't going to be available to us anytime soon. I vowed to make it happen eventually.

The shocked silence at Brahim's alliance didn't last long—the room exploded with noise. "What?" "How could he go back to them after all he knows?" "You just handed the quantum computing breakthrough right back to them!" "After all that work and loss of life?" Several AGI agents had died that morning, and we took that seriously. They likely weren't guilty people—they didn't know that they worked for a corrupt organization, and they had lost their lives. The weight of that was heavy. But the one comment that was the loudest in my ears, the one that stung the most was, "Why is he still alive?" Why was he still alive? Because when push came to shove, I was too weak to do what I should have done. I just couldn't do it.

Jake shouted, "Everyone stop." The room quieted down instantly. "We aren't going to get anywhere if you all keep shouting out questions." He blew out a breath. "Yes, Brahim is back with the AGI. We don't know what they have on him, but it's clearly significant."

Mark threw his hands up and said, "Who cares how significant it is? He left the team in the middle of a shoot-out. He walked away and left you all to the wolves? He is the brains behind quantum computing! I don't care what they have on him. He should be dead. End of story."

Jake nodded. "I understand that, and in part I feel the same way. But I have no doubt that he was on our side when he was with us. The intel he gave us about the AGI was true. He did kill the program. I don't know why he went back, but I'm hoping that we can get to him and still use him."

Someone from the back said, "After destroying the computer, he told you that no one was able to crack the program entirely. How can we trust him?"

L.A. CLAYTON

Lena spoke then, "I was there several minutes before Brahim, Edison, and Lyon arrived. The first thing I did was check for breaches. There hadn't been any, and it wasn't for lack of trying. Whoever the AGI sent in there to crack Brahim's signature left time stamps all over. Their work wasn't messy, but they never had success. I am one hundred percent sure of that."

Fin stood up, as if it were impossible to sit through his tirade. "It doesn't matter that he killed the program—he can just make it again! What the hell is wrong with all of you? Did I not explain what that kind of technology can do?"

Lena cleared her throat before Jake could defend himself. "I wasn't finished, Fin. I was going to add that it will take Brahim weeks to recreate that program again. It's no joke; it's layers upon layers of code, and he's going to have to start from scratch. It will take time, even knowing what he knows."

Fin, incredulous, said, "But it can still be done! And the person who was the first to do it is still alive and with the enemy!"

Jake sighed and rubbed his forehead. "Fin, you have never been in the field. You have no idea what it feels like to make difficult decisions in a split second. Sometimes you have to follow your gut, and my gut was screaming at me to let him live."

Fin threw his arms up wide, wearing his sarcastic face. "Oh, now it all makes sense; it's your gut you have to follow out in the field. I guess when you're making split-second decisions, it never occurs to you to USE YOUR BRAIN?"

I stood then, putting the bulk of my weight on my good leg, not being able to take one more second of Jake shouldering the blame for what I didn't do. "It was my fault. I should have killed Brahim. I knew that I should have pulled the trigger, and I didn't." I took a short breath through my nose. "I couldn't."

Jake shook his head. "I could have done it as easily as you, Edison."

"No, you couldn't have. If you had, we would have lost the element of surprise. Without that, we all would have been dead."

His head cocked ever so slightly to the side, as if he were seeing something in my expression that clicked things into place for him.

"Is that what you think? Edison, anytime I came out from behind that door, it would have been a surprise. We both would have started firing immediately." I took a breath to counter, but he cut me off, "This mission isn't on you alone anymore. Just because you brought the AGI to the attention of the CIA, it doesn't mean that you are at fault for everything that goes wrong. You have a vendetta against the AGI, and rightfully so. But, Kate, you didn't lose your way today; you didn't lose the footing that you fought so hard to gain." He paused, and his eyes bored into mine. "You didn't betray your father with the decision not to kill Brahim." I felt my breath catch and my eyes prick. "You are on a team. The things that happen in the field aren't always in our control. Sometimes we're faced with surprises and we have to make split-second decisions that have huge consequences. Sometimes we choose right, and sometimes we choose wrong." He looked intensely sad for a moment, and I remembered him telling me, back when I found Nick's body, that he knew, firsthand, how difficult it was to lose someone you worked with, someone you cared about. I had never gotten the story from him, but I could tell that whatever it was, he was thinking of it now. "Going with your gut is a good thing, despite what Fin thinks; it's a combination of using your intellect and your emotions, and you are always better off with both."

I nodded and sat back down, drained. I needed time to think about what Jake had said. With one look at me, he'd hit the nail on the head. He'd been able to make connections that I hadn't yet made, and there wasn't much left for me to say.

Fin, who was still seeing red, sneered. "If you're done trying to make your girlfriend feel better, maybe we could get back to the crisis of the moment."

Jake, to his credit, kept his cool. "That is something I would like to speak about briefly. I have feelings for Kate—that is apparently no secret—and her judgment is poor enough that she returns those feelings." A few chuckles. "We have decided to keep all of that at bay while we work together. The mission comes first, and we have made a commitment to the job and to each of you that we are going to see to the end. Edison and I are both all in on this."

I saw a few eyebrows raise and a few nods. Fin, for his part, just rolled his eyes and said, "Fine. Let's get back on topic." That was the equivalent of Fin giving us a rousing speech of acceptance. I was kind of shocked.

I looked at Jake, and he responded with the smallest trace of a smile. He knew how to win Fin over—blatant honesty—and he'd used that knowledge to his advantage. One day when this was all over, and it would be over someday, Jake was going to find out just how much I reciprocated his feelings.

Scarborough finally entered the conversation, from his comfortable chair across the room. "Johnson, is Brahim most likely to make contact through you?"

Lena sighed. "Probably. Though I did tell him that I was going to find him and rip his throat out for what he'd done, so maybe not. The honest truth is that I don't trust him. He and I were close, more than friends for some time now. If he were telling the truth, he would have told us, me at the very least, that he was playing the AGI. He didn't so much as hint at it. He only said what he did to Kate to make sure she didn't put a bullet in his back when he walked away."

Fin huffed. "Finally, some with their head on straight."

Lena was so listless that she merely shrugged. "But if he does make contact, it will still probably be through me. We've been messaging for months—he'll be able to get through to me the easiest."

Scarborough nodded. "I don't need to tell you that *all* contact with him needs to be immediately brought to my attention." Lena nodded her understanding.

Mark gestured that he would like the floor, and Scarborough dipped his head in response. "How can we be sure that Awan is telling the truth when he does make contact? How can we possibly trust him after this? I trust Lyon's assessment and all, but even if Awan is, in his heart, on our side, the AGI can use whatever they have on him to get him to play ball. They may very well make him get in contact with us, if for no other reason than for him to get us off their tail."

Scarborough looked to the back of the room and said, "I think we might have a solution for that."

Megan stood up, her once vibrantly pink hair now faded, much like her countenance. "I'll exploit my contact within the AGI to corroborate the things that Brahim is telling us." Everyone looked confused—they didn't know about Megan and Officer Reed. "I was unknowingly in a relationship with a CIA/AGI double agent. He manipulated me to find out information about our task force. I was the mole." There were several gasps, followed by absolute silence. Megan cleared her throat. "I've gotten back in touch with that officer via Sekur, and we have been messaging, under Scarborough's watch. We are going to manipulate him back."

After Megan's confession, I had told Jake and Scarborough that I thought, if Megan agreed to it, that instead of sending her to a safe house, we could use their relationship to our advantage. We could feed Reed half-truths and lead him just enough in the wrong direction that he would have no reason to suspect that Megan wasn't being genuine. But now we could also use the connection to make sure that Brahim was telling the truth.

Amy from legal said, "Why not try to get the double agent on our side?"

Megan shook her head. "It's not just any officer." She swallowed. "It's Officer Reed." That got quite the reaction: several people in the room had been recruited and trained by Reed, and they were having a hard time believing he could be a double agent. Once things calmed down enough, Megan spoke again, "Obviously he's not some newbie who doesn't know better." She gave me a somewhat apologetic look for the cut. "Even if he doesn't know what the AGI is exactly, which I think he might, he has been loyal to them for years. I'm not sure he would believe the things we told him. Regardless, I believe that he knows what the AGI really is and works for them willingly. He can't be trusted."

I nodded. "I discovered in my time at the Montana facility that the AGI requires information and fundraising from their top tier. If Reed wants in with the top tier—which his stealing from Megan's computer and handing the information over to the AGI would suggest he does—then he'll be more than happy to exploit her further."

Megan nodded. "He's trying already."

Fin sat back in his chair. "He was my trainer; I would have trusted him with my life." He looked at Megan, who was trying hard to look confident but whose inability to make eye contact gave her away, and said with sincerity, "I get it. Reed could have probably gotten any information he wanted out of me." He let out a breath and shook his head, his eyes glazed over. "Reed is part of the AGI? How could we all have been so blind?"

Jake looked at Fin. "There's a lot of trust between a trainer and their trainee in the CIA. Angela Reed, the other Reed,"—a few smiles; that must have been an inside joke—"who trained me, is also part of the AGI. I found out when Edison found her file. She's been with them for over twenty-five years."

While everyone was trying to process that information, I asked, "Why didn't she refer you to the AGI?"

He shrugged. "I've thought about that. I think that my particular skill set would have been a threat to them."

"Ah, that makes sense." I frowned. "Too bad. This could have been uncovered much sooner."

He gave me a small but sincere smile. "It's a miracle we found out about the AGI at all."

Scarborough stood. "Okay, we'll keep a close watch on both the Brahim and Reed situations. Some other matters worth discussing are that Search is still pushing Oliver Strands, but his momentum seems to have stalled out somewhat, due to his gaffe." Scarborough smiled, and there were a few chuckles in the room; if you didn't find Strand's gaffe funny, you didn't have a sense of humor. "But that will blow over, and he will be the front-runner again. Search is also trying to bury the DNA Global story. Two weeks ago, the tip that we'd anonymously reported about DNA Global's records being breached played once on CNN, but they have since retracted their story, and no other network picked it up. Not only that, but you can't find so much as a whiff of it on the internet. Which makes me think that the AGI is working with Search on this." We'd tried to get the information out to the public that DNA Global had had a breach and that millions of DNA files had been stolen. Our hope was to, at the very least, stop any new members of the public from getting their DNA tested. At best, we hoped that the public would be outraged and demand DNA Global be shut down for not properly securing their files. I wasn't totally surprised that nothing came of it. No one liked anonymous whistleblowers. The only way that kind of thing could grow any real teeth was for there to be a person with real proof behind the accusation. "Not completely unexpected but still disheartening. I was hoping it would garner a little more attention."

"In further news, I was informed that Lena made a discovery while at DNA Global." He turned his attention to Lena.

She nodded. "I can confirm that the information transfer from DNA Global is going to Belarus. Specifically, Minsk. I couldn't get an exact address,"—she shrugged—"but it's a place to start."

John Richardson, who worked in foreign affairs for the CIA, stood up. "I have a contact in Minsk; I'll see what I can find." With a nod of Scarborough's head, Richardson was on his way to find a quiet place to work in the house.

Scarborough stood. "I've spoken with an expert in the quantum computing industry. He was astounded, to say the least, to find out that an individual had been able to take quantum interference to the level that Brahim has. After begging me to let Brahim come work for him, he confirmed that if the system he was working on wasn't saved to the cloud, then Brahim would have to start all over. So like Johnson said, it's going to take some time. And if we have to break in to the AGI building to get him before that happens, we will."

I think that went a long way to soothe everyone's concerns—I know it did mine. But as Scarborough continued, my concerns found brand-new heights. "Finding ground zero for the virus has been moved up to our top priority. It has come to my attention that Easter Island has been hit with a virus; it appears that it is the same virus that Nigel Brown had. But instead of the virus being formulated for just one person, it looks like it was formulated for the indigenous Rapa Nui population, about thirty-six hundred people. That's roughly half of the population on the island. Not one tourist nor the remaining forty percent of locals, made up of mostly Chileans, have been affected. Everyone who is Rapa Nui is horrifically sick or already dead. The few that are showing signs of recovery are those who are of mixed heritage. But most of those individuals will die too. Right now, there are just a handful of individuals who look to be recovering. There are doctors and scientists and World Health Organization members, along with other CIA officers, who are flying there now. We hope to have a better scope of things when they arrive."

"They're testing." The words tumbled out of my mouth, even as bile coated my throat. "They're going to do more." I shook my head. "We have to find where this virus is being made. Now."

CHAPTER 32

Minsk, Belarus
Liv

Liv Barker watched her door crack open. She could barely see—everything was blurry. She wasn't sure if the man in the suit was coming to take notes on her current condition, bring her food, or finally give her the medicine that would make this all go away. But all she wanted in that moment was to die. She wanted this to be over.

He spoke to her, asked her how she was feeling. She didn't respond. She didn't have enough energy. He lifted her arm to look at her skin, and it was covered in red spots. He brought her up into a seated position, and she started coughing, bright-red blood spraying out of her lungs, down her chin. His eyes, the only part of him that she could see, looked sad, and he apologized for taking so long this time. Said that things had been busy, as if he had been golfing while her life drained away. He brought water to her lips and made her drink. Her throat was on fire, and she tried to push away the cup but couldn't manage to call her arms to action. He said soothing words and shushed her, making her drink more of the liquid in the cup. He pulled a needle out of the pocket of his hazmat suit, and Liv worked harder to push him away. She didn't want it, the medicine. It was a constant roller coaster: the woman would make her sick, and the man would make her better. She couldn't take anymore testing. She just wanted to die like the other lucky people whose souls got to leave this hell.

Her protests were too weak, and the man stuck her arm with the needle and pressed down on the syringe to give her the one thing she didn't want—life. He gave her a few more shots and more water. He left momentarily and came back, his arms full of food, more than usual. He hid the food along with gallons of water under her cot, like he always did when he gave her the antidote, and then he left.

She had no appetite; she didn't want the food, didn't want the medicine. Didn't want to live.

CHAPTER 33

Richmond, VA
Kate

"There has been another hit," were the first words that Scarborough said to us the following morning. "The Trobriand people of the Trobriand Islands. Twelve thousand people live on the islands, and though there are people from other parts of the world living on and visiting the islands, only the Trobriand people are getting the virus. One thousand deaths and climbing."

The next two weeks went on like this. Every few days we learned of new remote places with indigenous peoples catching the virus. Places in Africa, Asia, and remote islands all over the world. It never spread beyond the people that it was created for, and the only people who got the virus and lived to tell the story were of mixed heritage—the less of the affected heritage you had, the better you fared. News organizations around the world were going crazy. Our news agencies were going crazy. The virus was on every news station every day, featured more than our upcoming presidential election.

Every day Officer Richardson and his contacts in Belarus would work harder to find ground zero, always coming up empty. It was incredibly frustrating and dominated both our waking and sleeping hours.

We worked all day using Search World to locate places in Minsk that might house a lab, but to no avail. There was always the chance that perhaps the actual location wasn't in Minsk but that the IP address was just a stopping point on the road of traveling information. It could be bouncing from Belarus to anywhere in the world. But the one thing that kept us tethered to the idea that Minsk was the right place was the Barker girl.

We'd heard nothing from Brahim, and very little communication was happening between Megan and Reed either. All in all, we were frustrated, restless, and angry.

Jake and I walked upstairs together to our rooms that night, both still limping slightly from our brush with the AGI at DNA Global. Fortunately, neither of us had any fractures, but we did have deep bruising that pretty much felt like fractures. We were exhausted and disheartened after another day of fruitless searching. My eyes were seeing double from having spent so much time on my computer that day; it felt like they might be damaged beyond repair.

We got to my room first and both stopped at my door. He gave me a small smile and leaned against my doorframe. "We're going to get a break in this case soon, I can feel it."

I smirked. "Is that your other gift at the CIA? Your spidey senses?"

He chuckled. "My spidey senses should have their own paycheck. They've saved me multiple times. And right now, they're telling me that we're going to get a break in this case." He smiled. "I'm just going to say, 'I told you so' in advance because I won't want to waste my breath later."

"Ha!" I smacked him playfully on the arm, and my smile faded. "I hate sitting around. I hate feeling like there's something I should be doing but doing nothing. How do we get in front the AGI? We're always five steps behind."

He nodded. "It's frustrating; Scarborough's losing his mind always playing catch-up. I've done a lot of information jobs with the CIA. I've found terrorists and infiltrated groups of them, blowing them up from the inside. But I have never, in all my time, worked on anything of this scale, and certainly not with a group this small. I wish there were more people we knew we could trust. We can barely trust the people in this group as it is." He was referring to Megan—he was less hopeful than I was about Megan being able to use Reed properly. He did believe that she was earnest in her desire to make things right, but he also thought that her feelings for Reed ran deeper than she would like to admit. I thought he was just still mad at her.

"I guess we'd better get to bed"—I blew out a breath—"and hope that big break comes tomorrow."

Jake looked both directions down the hall. When he saw that we were alone, he leaned in and kissed my temple. Breathed in my scent. "Why did we agree to Scarborough's terms?"

I smiled. "Because we want to save the world."

"Is that all? I'm starting to wonder if it's worth the cost . . ."

I laughed. "I'm not going anywhere, Lyon. I'll be here, ready for this thing between us to really begin when this is all over."

"You better be." He tucked a strand of hair behind my ear and rubbed his thumb along my jaw, close enough for me to breathe in his woodsy, all-male scent. I took a nice deep breath, not knowing when I'd get my next hit. "And just to be clear, Edison, what's going on between us is more than a *thing*." He kissed my temple one more time and then walked farther down the hall to his door. I watched him until he looked back at me and winked. I smiled myself to sleep.

I fell asleep fast and hard, my nightmare vivid.

I was back in the AGI torture room. My arms chained to the wall, my body shivering from the cold. Pain reverberated from the wound in my head, and bile burned up my throat from the intensity of it.

The tools the AGI used for torture were laid out on the table in front of me, filthy and rusted.

Westwood walked in, said a few words, and used his fingers to press down on the fracture in my skull. The pain was blinding. I almost passed out. Westwood laughed.

He got close to me, his hands pulling roughly on my hips to draw me closer, his body flush with mine. His wandering hands made my eyes water. I could feel his breath on my face as he pressed his cheek to mine to whisper something in my ear. Just a tactic, it was a tactic to make me panic and talk. I kept repeating that to myself in an attempt to stay calm.

He stepped away, and knowing that my life was forfeit, I made a bargain with him that if he answered my questions, I would answer his. His response was said with a smile: "If it will give you more peace in your coffin, I'll trade questions."

I asked my first question: "What is the mission of the AGI?"

Westwood smiled again; it was slimy. "Novus ordo seclorum."

I gasped awake and shot up to a seated position. My eyes wide, breathing heavy. I sat for a minute and stared into the darkness of my room, the crescent moon offering very little light through my window. I blinked a few times as my brain registered that I'd finally figured it out.

I closed my eyes briefly, trying to catch my breath and calm my racing heart. My attempt failed, and, body trembling, I got out of bed and went down the hall to Jake's door. I knocked, and when he didn't answer I knocked louder. My foot tapped the floor. I had to get this out, I had to tell someone.

I finally heard a scuffling in Jake's room, the door opened, and Jake stood in front of me, shirtless, his muscled chest and stomach on display. It was proof of my distress that my eyes didn't linger for even an instant. His sleepy expression instantly turned to alarm when he saw me. He could see that this was important. He looked into my eyes and said, "In here?" He pointed back to his room. "Or out there?" His head indicated the hallway.

I thought about it for half a second before saying, "In there." He stepped back and to the side to make space for me to get by him, into his room. It registered that it smelled like Jake, and even though we were in ever-changing rentals and this hadn't and wouldn't be his room for long, it felt like him. I liked that feeling.

Jake drew close to me and put his hands on my shoulders, his concern for me etched in his face. "Are you okay? What happened?"

I wasn't okay, and Jake knew it—he just didn't know the extent of it. "I had a nightmare about being in the torture room at the AGI." He let out a relieved breath, thinking that that was the only reason I'd come in here. His expression turned into one of sorrow and understanding. I knew that he hated that experience as much as I did—maybe he had the occasional nightmare about it, too. "I have them from time to time." He nodded. "But that's not exactly why I'm here." He went back on alert in an instant. "I think I might have been having them because my subconscious was trying to tell me something. Something that has been frustrating me for months." I stepped away from him and paced, biting my lips for a second while I tried to figure out how to explain it.

"When we found Nigel Brown, when we saw the things he wrote on the wall, I knew there was a connection regarding NOS that I wasn't making. It drove me nuts. I remember everything, but for some reason this slipped my grasp. Every time we looked at pictures of Nigel's writings, I would get frustrated all over again. There was something there and I knew it, but my brain just couldn't make the connection. Then when we found the connection to NexGen Organized Solutions and the AGI, I still wasn't satisfied. It wasn't the connection my brain kept telling me was there, but I tried to push it aside because concentrating on it never seemed to glean any real answers."

Jake's head cocked to the side, his expression a mask of concentration. He nodded for me to go on.

"When I was chained up in the torture room,"—Jake winced—"Westwood and I had a conversation. He let me trade questions with him."

He nodded once. "I remember that."

"The first question I asked him was, 'What is the mission of the AGI?' His answer was 'Novus ordo seclorum.'" I let that sink in for a minute. "New order of the ages. The mission of the AGI was to bring about a New World Order, a one-world order. They've been in place since seventeen eighty-two; they were the ones who helped design the dollar bill, with their insignia on it and *their name*. Novus ordo seclorum. It's the name of the worldwide AGI. *NOS*." I huffed out a humorless laugh. "It's so obvious, I can't believe I didn't see it before."

Jake was gaping at me, his breaths coming fast. It looked like his mind was running right to where mine had gone, but I voiced my thoughts just to be sure we were on the same page. "The Alternate Government Initiative was a real thing put into place at the time of the creation of the atom bomb. They weren't official for very long, but they kept the name here in the United States—they didn't go back to their original name, Novus Ordo Seclorum. NOS is the AGI."

I could almost see the wheels in Jake's head turning. I pressed ahead, "NexGen Organized Solutions is owned by the NOS, and I think that the companies owned by the NOS all have NOS acronyms."

Jake, still gaping, said one word: "Search."

I closed my eyes and nodded, the depth of the NOS's reach almost causing me physical pain. "Yes. Search's full company name is Nanotech Optimized Search. And they own all of the social media giants."

Jake sat down on the bed without a word. He looked as if his legs could no longer carry him. His phone was next to him, and after a few minutes of silence, he picked it up. "I'm going to call Scarborough. We'll go to his room, or he can come up here; either way, he needs to hear this right now."

I nodded and waited for him to make the call. Scarborough picked up on the first ring. They spoke for just a few seconds and then hung up. Jake put on a shirt and said, "He's on his way."

When Scarborough arrived, he knocked once and walked right in. He was wearing old man pajamas, the matching kind with a button-down shirt. His gray hair was mussed from sleep, his eyes tired. He'd never looked so old. I felt bad, momentarily, for dragging him out of bed, but my guilt didn't last long because there were things he needed to know. Scarborough sat on the edge of the bed. "I'm not even going to say, 'This better be good,' because if it's not, I will fillet you both alive. I was finally sleeping."

Jake and I nodded our understanding—good sleep was hard to find these days. Jake gestured toward me, and I told my story, start to finish. When I got to the part about Search being owned by the NOS, I was worried that Scarborough might have a heart attack. He put his hand over his chest and rubbed while he stared blankly back at us, his mouth slackened.

He finally spoke, "I guess we can quit trying to find the virus lab in Minsk on Search World." Huh, I hadn't even thought of that. Search would never render results for what we were looking for. It was so natural to Search up everything, we were going to have to research differently . . . think differently. "That also explains why our campaign against Search on social media never took off. Sound the alarm—let's wake everyone up and get this ball rolling in a new direction; maybe we can actually make some headway."

We all met in the living room, keeping the blinds down and the lights dim. It was four a.m. and we didn't want to look suspicious to the neighbors. I explained my discovery for the third time that night. There were gasps and shocked noises at all the right moments. Then the silence as everyone took time to absorb the facts as we now knew them.

There was no arguing against it, shocking as that seemed. I was waiting for someone, possibly Fin, to counter my theory. But, with the exception of Lena and Liam, they had all heard the recording of me with Westwood that fateful night. They had all heard his words. It made perfect sense.

Fin spoke first, "So, I guess we're going to Minsk?"

CHAPTER 34

Palo Alto, CA
Vinny

Vinny looked over at Tracy's boxes. It was her last day, and she was all packed up. She was sitting in her chair, in her silly T-shirt and short cutoff shorts, her long tanned legs on blatant display, looking melancholy. "Vinny, are you still going to be my friend?"

He smiled, kind of surprised that she wanted to stay friends; their relationship had always been about work. "Of course." Vinny called up all of his courage and said, "Maybe we could get lunch this weekend?"

Her smile widened, and she bit her bottom lip. "I'd like that."

Vinny's smile grew, and he said, "It's a date." Then, mortified, he tried to retract his last comment, "I mean not a date, exactly, just two friends . . . two friends getting lunch." He felt his cheeks heat.

Tracy laughed. "I kind of liked the idea of it being a date better."

Vinny's head snapped up in surprise and shock. Tracy was way out of his league; he was smart enough to know that. "Y-you want to go on a date? W-with me?" He hated his stutter; it hardly ever made an appearance these days, but when he was nervous, it sometimes reared its ugly head.

Tracy laughed again, and then soberly, in no uncertain terms, said, "Yes, Cousin Vinny, I want to go on a date. With you. More than one."

Vinny huffed out a laugh. "If we're going to go on a date, you need to stop calling me your cousin."

She tipped her head back and laughed heartily, her bleached blonde hair swaying across her back. "But it's a term of endearment!"

He put his hand up. "Nope, no cousin talk on our date."

She pointed at him. "Dates. Plural."

He smiled like a kid. "Okay, no cousin talk on our dates."

She nodded. "Deal."

They looked at each other shyly, neither quite knowing what to say after their admission of attraction. Eventually, Tracy sighed and said, "Are you sure you want to stay here? There are other places to work, you know."

Vinny took a deep breath and then coughed and sneezed. It was Bring Your Dog to Work Day, and Vinny was allergic to dogs. He usually took a personal day every year when it came around, but with it being Tracy's last day, he'd decided to put up with the watery eyes and near-constant sneezing. There were many things to hate about Search—Bring Your Dog to Work Day was pretty close to the top of the list for Vinny. But there were also some things to love about working for Search, and Tracy had been at the top of that list. He wasn't sure what working at Search would be like without her; he wished he didn't have to find out. "I need to stay for now, but that could change at any moment."

Tracy gave him a sad smile. "I liked working with you, Cousin Vinny." He gave her a stony look, and her smile brightened when she shrugged and said, "Hey, we're not on our datessss yet."

Tracy had given her two weeks' notice when they were asked to cover up a breach at DNA Global. She said that covering up information wasn't what she'd signed on for at Search; she'd joined Search because information should be shared. Vinny thought that she'd just had enough of compromising her values for a paycheck, and he understood that. But he'd miss her just the same.

As for himself, there were things that he did at Search that had bothered him for years, but he usually let it slide, always reminding himself that no job was perfect. But Search had become less and less perfect ever since instituting Search Directed Personalized Marketing, what Vinny and Tracy did most of the time. He'd considered quitting when Tracy did, but Mr. Franks called him into his office and offered him a great deal more money and his own office. Vinny decided that he could take a little more time there, get his student loans paid off and put away some money, and then he'd find something that didn't disrupt his moral compass so thoroughly.

Tracy stood, straightening her T-shirt—today's said "MOIST" in huge letters, and underneath, in much smaller print, it said "because someone hates this word." It was a toss-up what Vinny would miss most: Tracy's T-shirts or her legs.

She went to pick up her boxes of things, and Vinny jumped up to help her. "Here, let me take those to your car."

She looked at him, quizzically. "These boxes are pretty small; I can handle them myself."

"Humor me."

She smirked and motioned at her boxes. "By all means . . ."

Vinny and Tracy walked to her car in companionable silence. He loaded the trunk of her car with her things, and then he walked Tracy to her door and said, "So, lunch Saturday?" She nodded. "Can you text me your address?"

"You don't have to pick me up; we can meet somewhere if you'd rather."

"Tracy, I'm a gentleman. I'll be picking you up for this date and every one after."

She smiled and bit her lip. "I'm looking forward to it." Then she surprised him completely when she stood on her toes and kissed him on the mouth. It was much shorter and far more chaste than he would have liked, but he wasn't complaining. She smiled shyly—well, shyly for Tracy—and cleared her throat. "Just, you know, a preview."

Vinny smiled. "I'm dying to see the feature film."

Tracy laughed and tucked a stray hair behind her ear. Vinny decided to take a chance, the second one on the same day—a rarity for him, but the first one had worked out very well. He lifted her chin with his fingers and licked his lips. "Maybe one more preview?" Her eyes brightened, and she tipped her chin up toward his—he didn't wait for further permission. He dipped his head, and his mouth met hers, this time in a kiss that was soft and lingering, with feeling behind it, feelings he'd been carrying quietly for a while now. She smelled like the ocean, just like he'd imagined she would. They stood that way in the parking lot for a few minutes, and when Vinny pulled his face away, he looked into her eyes for another few seconds and then pulled fully away. "I'll see you Saturday."

As Vinny walked back, he mused that maybe Tracy quitting wasn't so bad after all; it gave him the courage to finally do what he'd wanted to do for the past three years.

CHAPTER 35

Dulles International Airport
Kate

"Come on, slowpoke." Liam jabbed me in the ribs.

I jabbed him back. "Shut your face, Liam, I'm still bruised."

He snickered. "Oh geez, how long are we going to have to hear about the bullet wound that never was?"

I laughed. "It really hurts, you jerk. My arm does, too." I rubbed my bicep that was still smarting from the DNA Global shoot-out.

"I know, that's why I'm carrying your bag. Now suck it up, I want to get some food before we take off." Of course the Hulk wanted some food. Liam sped up, and it was all I could do to keep on his heels.

Last night after our meeting, Scarborough had split us up into two groups: one that would stay in the States to continue the work here and one that would go to Minsk. We'd purchased tickets so last minute that our group had to split up. We had to fly commercial because we didn't want a whiff of our location sniffed out by the CIA. The CIA officers who were loyal to the AGI could out us and ruin the entire mission. Liam and I were the only two on this particular flight to Munich and would meet some of our group there and travel to Minsk together. Others would be going a different route entirely. By this time tomorrow we would all be on the ground and looking for the virus lab the old-fashioned way.

We were passing a bookstore, and I yelled up to Liam, "Hey, I'm going to grab something to read; I'll meet you at the gate."

He gave me a thumbs-up. I strolled into the bookstore and started perusing the shelves. I wanted something that would offer me an escape from reality. So, no political thrillers, no mysteries, and no romance. I already had too much pent-up frustration from my nonromantic romantic relationship for the latter. I was browsing the fantasy section when it happened.

"Katherine Elaine Edison?" I stiffened. I was traveling as Kaylee Edwards. Kate Edison's passport was still traipsing around the world. Whoever it was, they knew it was me. I knew this was going to be bad, but I didn't know how bad until I turned around and saw four federal agents approaching me.

"You are under arrest." I think my heart stopped beating. I could hear my breath loud in my ears while I contemplated my options. I couldn't believe that in all the craziness, I had forgotten that the AGI could turn me over to the Feds on charges of child sex trafficking at any time. I had no wig, no colored contacts, nothing. I looked for all the world like Kate Edison. We were all so busy trying to find ground zero for the virus that my possible impending arrest took a back seat.

I looked around me for Liam, but I was surrounded by strangers. Scarborough had ordered that I always be with someone in public. I had forgotten, and my mistake would cost me and my team precious time. If we didn't find out where that virus was being made, countless lives would be lost.

I couldn't tell the federal agents that, though. I couldn't tell them that I worked for the CIA. I was a non-official cover; if they looked me up in the system, I wouldn't be there.

I looked at the four agents, affronted. "I'm being arrested? On what charges?" I stalled. I knew the charges.

"We'll do you the favor of not announcing them in public." The federal agent who spoke was stone faced. Another quick look around me revealed that everyone in the store had stopped to stare. It wasn't every day that you saw a person arrest by the Feds. There was a crowd growing outside the bookstore as well.

As embarrassing as this was going to be, I had to stall, and I had very few tactics that I could think of. "I'd like to know what I'm being charged with before you take me . . ."

The stone-faced agent shrugged and said, "Have it your way." Loudly enough for the growing crowd to hear, he said, "You are being charged with ten counts of child sex trafficking, kidnapping, and one count of first-degree murder." There were gasps and looks of horror on the faces around me. Murder? They couldn't be serious. The AGI must have made it look like I, rather than Cave, had killed Jay Conner. I shot him in the wrists, but he'd been alive and still talking when I left. I started to internally panic. I looked around at the crowd again, hoping that one of those faces would be Liam, but no luck. What I did see were a lot of cell phone cameras taking video.

I looked at the agent like he was insane. "What! Are you kidding me?" Stall, stall, stall.

Stone Face looked around him at his fellow agents and then back to me. "Does this look like a joke to you, Ms. Edison?"

"Yes, actually, it does. It seems like an elaborate prank, honestly. I must be being punk'd, or on *Candid Camera*, because I have *never*, nor would I *ever*, sell children. I have never kidnapped, and I have certainly never murdered anyone."

The man barely even blinked. "We have evidence that says otherwise." The crowd gasped again. "Regardless, that is for a court of law to decide. Please put your hands behind your back."

I had to find a way to stall long enough for Liam to come looking for me. At this point there probably wasn't much that he could do to keep me from being arrested, but at least the team would know where I was and they could start working on getting me out. If they didn't see me with the Feds, they would think that the AGI had got me and look in all the wrong places. Too many innocent people were going to die in the meantime. This called for an all-out battle. I had to find a way to let the team know where I was. An idea was forming, but it wasn't pretty.

"No. I did not do that, and I am not coming with you. I have a flight to catch." In order to play this right, I schooled my haughty features into something fearful. "For all I know, you all are dressed up as federal agents and you are going to sell *me*." My eyebrows shot down. "Do the Feds really arrest women from airports? Is this common practice?" I looked around to see if I could garner any support. Maybe someone would stand up for me. Not a soul so much as nodded their affirmation that the situation seemed weird. Turns out that nobody wants to help a child sex trafficker. Can't say I was very surprised. But, honestly, didn't people know that innocents were arrested every day?

"Are you asking if it's common practice to arrest a serious criminal before they fly out of the country?" He had me there. But just to appease me, Stone Face pulled out his badge, holding it up so that I could see it clearly. His name was Stonewall, which would have been funny in any other circumstance. "Let's not make this more difficult than it already is." He pulled out his handcuffs. "You're coming with us, Ms. Edison."

Where was Liam? I had been gone awhile now—why hadn't he come looking for me? He was probably completely clueless, eating several pounds of food to fuel that gigantic body. I inwardly groaned at my very poor options. Stonewall approached me and, backed into a corner, I did the only thing I could think of. I threw a punch. Hard. In the federal agent's face. I felt the crack and crunch of bone as his nose broke under my fist. The crowd went wild. Stonewall let out a string of expletives, but I couldn't hear him over the noise of the crowd paired with my heartbeat pounding in my ears. Now they could add resisting arrest along with assaulting a federal agent to my charges. That last one was a class C felony, since I'd caused bodily injury.

That had done it. All four agents were on me in half a second. Two grabbed my arms and held fast. I flailed like my life depended on it. I used the leverage of the two agents holding my arms and lifted my legs and kicked the other two agents in the groin. One of them was Stonewall, and between his broken nose and what I could only imagine was excruciating pain from his neither regions—he was hunched over groaning—the threat from him, at least, was neutralized.

The two agents holding me were momentarily stunned, but in a flash, guns were out, trained on my face, and they yelled at me to get my hands up in the air. Out of options, I did as they asked. The crowd was so thick now that even if Liam had come looking for me, I wouldn't have been able to see him. The agents approached and threw me on the floor, my cheek colliding hard with the tile—my teeth sang from the impact.

My abdomen was pushed into the unforgiving floor by the knee on my back, making it hard to breathe. My arms were roughly pulled back, my wrists cuffed. I couldn't think of a more vulnerable position. Having your hands tied behind your back felt so violating; you couldn't defend yourself. It reminded me momentarily of being chained up with Westwood. Having to withstand his assault. I pushed it from my mind. I couldn't go there—it would be debilitating.

They hauled me up, and whichever officer was at my back gave me a callous shove, and I tripped over my feet, causing me to almost go down again. He pulled me back up by the handcuffs just before my face met the floor for the second time. Then he pushed and pulled again, just to show me who was boss. The cuffs cut into my wrists with the coarse treatment.

My mind whirled. Where were they going to take me? Could I escape? Were any of these federal agents also AGI agents? They pushed me forward, and we were walking, with no way for me to stop the progression. I tried to look around one more time for Liam, but the officer forced my head forward roughly with his palm. I had never wanted to see Liam so badly in my life. If I could just make eye contact with him, then I would know that I was going to get out of this mess. But Liam was nowhere to be found as the agents walked me toward a fate I couldn't control.

CHAPTER 36

Washington, D.C.
Oliver

Oliver Strands took the stage at the benefit for the International Child Recovery Operation. His hands shook, and he did his best to keep it from showing. He wasn't acting tonight. Tonight felt like the first time in a long time that he was allowed to be himself. And he wished that he could be anywhere but here. His heart and soul hurt here.

He had a great appreciation for this organization. More than that, he loved this organization. They helped families find their missing children when the local authorities had given up. The ICRO had been started by a husband and wife, the Radfords, who had a child who had been abducted while on vacation abroad. After several months of searching, she was never found, and the local authorities gave up, telling the Radfords it was time to assume the worst.

The Radfords refused to believe that their precious daughter was dead. They felt in their hearts that she was alive, and they would stop at nothing to find her. Mr. Radford had had a successful career as an investment banker, and they used their own wealth to take over the search. They hired the best former CIA and FBI agents to work the case, as well as bounty hunters and private detectives. Their daughter was found alive within two months. After some much-needed therapy and medical help, she was now twenty-two years old and the face of the organization. Year to date they had found and rescued over two hundred abducted children.

These benefits served to help them raise the money to keep their work moving forward, and Oliver was more than happy to help their mission. Truly, he was desperate to help their mission.

When Oliver got to the podium, he cleared his throat, giving himself a moment to gather his thoughts. This topic made him emotional, and rightfully so, but he wanted to give a rousing speech, one that would keep money flowing into ICRO for a long time to come. "I am honored to have been asked to give the keynote address for the International Child Recovery Operation tonight. Some of you may know that the ICRO holds a place near and dear to my heart." He paused, took a deep breath, and pressed forward, "Some of you may know that my beautiful goddaughter"—Oliver paused again, his throat constricting, eyes filling—"My beautiful goddaughter, Liv Barker, was abducted over six months ago while on vacation with her family in Spain." He sniffed and blinked rapidly, trying to quell the impending onslaught of tears. Oliver had never spoken publicly about Liv's abduction. He'd never had the opportunity to. When she had been taken, he was a state senator for New Hampshire, virtually unknown. While Liv's parents, Luke and Jill, had done interview after interview, no one asked to hear from the godparent. He'd had to sit on the sidelines and watch things unfold. Watch things go nowhere.

Well, he was no longer a nobody; he was a member of the United States Congress, and he was running for president—he had a voice, a big one. He was more than proud to use it if there was any chance that it might help find Liv. "Liv was about to start her senior year of high school, and she was a smart and vivacious student. She made friends quickly and always had a smile for everyone she came in contact with. Liv was and still is loved fiercely by her parents and two sisters." He motioned to the weeping family at a table in the front of the room. Oliver motioned for them to stand, and his voice cracked when he said, "Luke Barker, my oldest and dearest friend; his wife, Jill; and their two daughters, Brenna and Sarah." No one clapped—instead many held their hands to their hearts in silent acknowledgment of their shared sorrow.

His friends sat back down. "Only two months into the investigation, the police stopped searching for our dear Liv. We believe with our whole hearts that Liv is alive, and we will stop at nothing until we find her." There was a round of applause. Tears were running down Oliver's face, and he let them roll freely, powerless to stop them. "We turned to the ICRO for help, and they accepted us with open arms and open hearts. We knew that their promise to do everything in their considerable power to find Liv was a promise made with integrity. They have promised us that they will not stop, they will not quit. They will help us to find Liv whether she is alive or otherwise." His voice cracked again at that last word. Never, he could never say "dead" where Liv was concerned. He loved her like she was his own child.

Oliver took his job as a godparent very seriously. He was there for her baptism, never missed a birthday, even after Luke moved his family to Arizona for work. Oliver was there for every important event. Sometimes he would even stop by for a few days just to help Liv with a project for school. The AGI had given him a month off to grieve and help when Liv was abducted, but that month of searching had yielded nothing useful, and eventually Oliver had to return to his work as a state senator.

"The Barkers and I are eternally grateful for the work that the International Child Recovery Operation does. It's impossible to know how desperately necessary an organization such as this one is," he choked on the words, "until you need them." With his hands grasping both sides of the podium, he bowed his head while his body silently shook with sobs. There wasn't a dry eye in the entire ballroom by the time Oliver had gathered himself together enough to keep going. "Please consider donating to this incredible cause. The ICRO can't do this lifesaving work without you. We need you. The Barker family needs you. Liv and children like her all over the world need you. Thank you."

There was rousing applause at the end of Oliver's speech, but he only wanted to go somewhere to be alone and cry. This had reopened his wound, and the pain was almost intolerable. Instead he took his seat on the stage next to his wife, who looked at him through wet eyelashes. When he sat down, she grabbed his hand and squeezed it, then leaned in and whispered, "I'm so sorry, Oliver."

CHAPTER 37

Washington, D.C. Federal Courthouse
Arthur

"That's her." Arthur Whitehall looked at the blonde woman with disdain. He never forgot a face. Especially a pretty one. He knew without a doubt that he was looking at one of *them*. One of the people who had broken into his building and, among other things, ruined his practically priceless quantum computer.

"Are you certain?" the bald FBI agent asked.

"One hundred percent certain. She was wearing a wig before, but the face is the same." He tapped the window in front of him, and she looked up. He knew that she couldn't see him, but he wished that she could. He wished that he could see the surprise on her face when she recognized who he was. The guilt—he wanted her to feel guilty for what she had done. That was likely a pipe dream; Arthur surmised that most criminals were sociopaths.

In order to breach DNA Global's security measures, she wasn't your average criminal. No, she was a criminal mastermind. Those blue eyes looked at him through the glass; if he didn't know better, he would have thought that she could see him. They were the same ones he had thought about every day since the break-in. He made sure to commit those faces to memory because if they were ever found, he wanted to be the one to help convict them in court.

He had already picked her face from a picture lineup, but seeing her in person made him seethe all over again. He was in a heap of trouble because of her and her cohorts—the chances of him losing the job he'd worked so hard for were higher than he wanted to admit. He had a family to think about, a reputation. He had no reason to feel bad for her, even as he looked at her deceptively innocent and pretty face. He reminded himself that she was nothing more than a con artist.

The federal agent cleared his throat, and Arthur spun around. "We have one more photo lineup we would like you to look at."

Arthur nodded his head, and the Fed motioned down toward the table in front of him. There were pictures of ten different men with red hair and short beards. But only one with gray eyes. Arthur pointed him out, almost instantly. "This one."

The agent nodded. "Okay, thank you very much, Mr. Whitehall. That's all the information we need right now. We appreciate you coming all the way from Boston; having you here in person makes your witness more credible to the prosecutor, judge, and eventually the jury."

"I'd like to talk to her." The words tumbled out of Arthur's mouth. But as soon as he said them, he felt his desire to get some answers strengthen. Why had they destroyed DNA Global's quantum computer? What did they want with DNA Global?

The federal agent's brow furrowed. "I'm sorry, sir. That's not possible."

"Well, make it possible."

The agent shook his head. "She is currently a suspect here on several different charges. She has yet to be officially charged"—he put a hand up to stave off Arthur's impending argument—"though I assure you she *will* be charged. But there is a process for these things, and the only place the defendant and the star witness meet is in the courtroom."

Arthur nodded once. He was smart enough to know when he'd lost. "I'd like to watch for a bit, then. Is that possible?"

The agent thought for a minute and said, "We can probably make that happen. But understand that I may have to ask you to leave at any moment. As a witness, there are things that you can't be privy to—it would invalidate your testimony."

Arthur nodded and took a seat.

CHAPTER 38

Washington, D.C. Federal Courthouse
Kate

I was in an interrogation room somewhere within the federal courthouse. It was a bleak space with a cement floor, plain white walls, and a stainless steel table with just two plastic chairs. The lighting was fluorescent and unforgiving. I was facing the large two-way mirror, and I wondered how many Feds were staring at me like a zoo animal from the other side. I had been in the room for hours. They had plenty of incriminating evidence on me—they could have just thrown me in a cell and made me wait for my arraignment. I didn't know why they didn't do just that. Until they officially arrested me and locked me up, I wouldn't go into the system. So, if my team was wondering where the Feds had me, they wouldn't know until the arrest was officially logged, which they were certainly taking their sweet time doing. Law school had taught me enough to know that state and city police will arrest first and ask questions later; in contrast, the Feds didn't arrest until their questions were already answered. There was a reason only two percent of federal cases went to trial and that the rate of conviction for those cases was astronomically high. But that didn't mean they got it right all the time—certainly not in my case. I was innocent, and yet, considering the evidence the AGI had given them, if I were stupid enough to let twelve random people choose my fate, I would lose.

Not that it mattered. As soon as the AGI was aware that I was here, they would send someone to kill me. They *would* find out that I was here—I'd made a big enough fool of myself at the airport to ensure it. I'd done that to ensure that my CIA team would find me as well. With all of those people taking video, I knew it would go viral quickly and would probably be picked up by major news organizations within the hour. The only question was who would get to me first, my team, or the AGI.

I sat and sat, not knowing what time it was. I was thirsty, hungry, had to go to the bathroom, and my wrists were still cuffed behind my back—the latter I think was payback from the agents who had brought me here, due to my being a total psycho at the airport. Perhaps some punishment was deserved, but my wrists ached, and my chest and back did as well. It was an awkward position to be in for so long. I couldn't sit back against the chair, but the seat sloped downward, and holding myself up was making my back cramp, and it was starting to spasm. I wanted to crawl up on the table and lie down on my stomach—maybe I could sleep until they decided what they were going to do with me.

What a mess. I couldn't say definitively that I wouldn't have been arrested if I had worn a wig and taken all of the proper precautions. Our government employed facial recognition software, so it may not have mattered either way. I just wished I'd stayed with Liam; at least he would have known where I was and I wouldn't have had to resort to assaulting a federal agent.

The doorknob started to turn, and my stomach dropped; anyone could be on the other side of that door. And regardless of who it was, I was at their mercy. I hated these handcuffs. I vowed from then on to carry a handcuff key on me at all times.

I sighed in relief as one of the agents who had arrested me walked in. It wasn't Stonewall, it was one of the two that I hadn't managed to assault. He gave me a tight smile. "Ms. Edison, I'm Federal Agent Winslow."

"Agent Winslow, can you remove these cuffs, please? My back is spasming."

He huffed, "Oh, your back is hurting?" Condescension dripped from his tone. "That's too bad; I bet Agent Stonewall feels really bad for you, too. He is currently getting his nose reset." Well, he did make a good point, but still, this seemed cruel and unusual. "I won't be taking your cuffs off, as I am particularly fond of my nose as it is." Cute.

He sat down, threw his folder on the table, and shot me that tight, mirthless smile again. "Let's see, Ms. Edison, or should I call you Ms. Edwards?" He lifted an eyebrow—at least I would be getting rid of that pseudonym. When I didn't respond, he continued, "Ten counts of child endangerment, ten counts of child trafficking, ten counts of kidnapping, one count of first-degree murder, one count of resisting arrest, two counts of aggravated assault of a federal agent, one count of breaking and entering, and one count of first-degree burglary." He took a breath, like stating all of my charges had made him run out of air. I internally rolled my eyes. "That's as it stands now. I have a feeling that more charges will be added to that list eventually."

I was sure he was right—additional charges were almost a guarantee. Those last two charges were new, though. Too curious to let it go, I said, "Burglary is a state crime."

"Not when the property you stole were DNA files that belong to citizens all over the country."

The DNA Global job. I didn't steal any files, but I was sure that the AGI could, and apparently did, make it look like I had. I shrugged. "I want a lawyer."

He smiled, little more than a baring of teeth. "I bet you do. But first, I have a couple of questions for you."

I bared my teeth right back. "I won't be answering any of your questions until I have a lawyer present. Let's not forget that it's illegal for you to question me without one once I've put in the request."

Agent Marshall's eyes crinkled in delight, as if he knew he'd get to me one way or another. "That's only true if we've charged you. We haven't."

"False." Please, if he knew anything about me, he would have known that I was a law school graduate. I knew my rights. One did not have to be charged to have the right to a lawyer. I also knew that cops, state and federal, could say *anything* they wanted to get you to talk. They are legally allowed to lie through their teeth. Of all of the flaws in the justice system, that one was particularly heinous to me.

"Ms. Edison." He scrubbed a hand over his face and looked at me sincerely. "I know it seems like I am the enemy, but, in all actuality, I may be the only one who can help you." He played the good cop well. "When I turn you over to the prosecutor, they are going to eat you alive. Talk now, and we can make some early deals for you, possibly grant you immunity on some of these charges."

I rolled my eyes, unable to help myself. "False." This guy must have taken me for a complete idiot. Only prosecutors could grant deals, including—and especially—immunity.

He shifted in his seat. "Listen, Ms. Edison, I really am trying to help you. We know that you weren't working alone. You tell us who you were working for, and I'll get a federal prosecutor in here right now to work a deal with you."

Grrrr. "False." Criminal Procedure 101: never talk before a deal is made and signed. It's called a proffer, and if the informant's intel is deemed good, then the deal is honored. If the information is false or unusable, then the contract is null and void.

Agent Marshall leaned forward, his voice quieter. "How about this? We know that you have been working with Officer Jacob Lyon of the CIA." My heart stuttered in my chest. "We believe that there is a possibility that all of these crimes you've committed may not be crimes at all. Tell us who you're working for, and this can all disappear, just like that." He snapped his fingers.

If they thought that I was connected to the CIA, they would have looked me up, and I wouldn't have been in the CIA records. Agent Marshall may have suspected that I was a non-official cover—an NOC—or an informant, but if he suspected that I was an NOC, then he would know that I would never give myself up. If I were an NOC, the CIA would use their power to come and get me, covertly, so that I could continue with my work. If someone confesses to being an NOC, it's a sure thing that they're not. If he thought I was an informant for the CIA, me being on missions wouldn't have made sense. He was looking for a confession. It was ironic that the only thing that came out of my mouth that he would believe was a false confession. I took a deep breath and repeated to myself over and over: I will not fall for his tricks, I will not fall for his tricks. "False. I want an attorney."

His smile turned predatory, his good cop act over. "You want to know what I think, Kate? I think you're a criminal, a hardened one, and I have it on good authority that it's a family trait. According to the file we have on your dear ol' dad, you learned everything you know from him. I was looking at his crimes today, and let me tell you, they are atrocious." My anger was a palpable thing, a burning in my lungs and a fire in my veins. It wasn't enough for the AGI to kill my dad, but they had to drag his name through the mud as well? "He was a blight on society, just like you. I bet he's watching from wherever he is, so very proud of what you have become." It's a good thing that Agent Marshall hadn't uncuffed me, because if he had, I would've jumped over that table and beaten the ever-loving life out of him. He stood up, kicking back his chair. "You want a lawyer?" He leaned down, smiled, and whispered, "We have an appointed one all lined up for you."

I knew, I knew that he was trying to get me mad, to evoke enough emotion in me that I would lose it. I would not let him win. "False," I said. "Judges appoint attorneys, not glorified cops." I hadn't been in front of a judge yet, so there was no attorney appointed to me. Agent Marshall walked out the door; the only indication that my insult hit its mark was his fisted, white-knuckled hands. On his way out, he held the door open for my so-called lawyer. I waited to see who would carry out the next of their deceits.

My blood ran cold when Jeremy Richter walked in the door.

CHAPTER 39

Washington, D.C. Federal Courthouse
Kate

"Hello, Ms. Edison." Richter walked in wearing a light-gray suit and carrying a black briefcase. From the outside, he looked like the consummate professional. He turned to face me, so that his back was to the two-way mirror. His air of professionalism went out the window as soon as he was facing me and the Feds in the next room could no longer see his face. He smiled like a snake with its next meal coiled up tightly in its long body. "I am the appointed attorney working on your defense." He winked.

My blood pumped through my body, high on adrenaline, my guard up in Richter's presence. "First of all, it's a felony to impersonate an attorney. Second, *you* are *not* my attorney. I haven't been arraigned, haven't been in front of a judge, and therefore, could not have been appointed an attorney."

He smiled again. "I can assure you that I am a member of the bar, both state and federal." I supposed that could be true—the only thing I knew about who Richter was prior to the AGI was that he was with the Department of Justice, and they employed attorneys there. "As for your second matter of business—turns out that I am friends," he elongated the word just slightly, enough so that I caught his meaning, "with Judge Hudd, the judge on your case, and he confirmed when I saw him this morning that I would be appointed to your case as soon as it was brought before him." He paused. "I assume you know that you cannot request a change of judge in a federal case?"

That was another flaw in the justice system: a defendant should always be able to request a change of judge. Case in point, my judge, Judge Hudd, was clearly an employee of the AGI. And because I couldn't request a change of judge, they might as well just string me up now. "You can tell the *honorable* Judge Hudd that I have no need for an attorney; I am going to defend myself."

Richter laughed, and the chill of it slithered down my spine. "Don't be an idiot. No one defends themselves in federal court. Ms. Edison, your charges are serious." When he said "serious," that snake smile slithered back into place, letting me know that he had helped trump up those "serious" charges. "As it now stands, you are facing several lifetimes in prison. I am here to help you."

I smiled at him, too sweetly. "If you are here to help me, then why don't you help me with these handcuffs? They're hurting me."

He bit his lip. "Being in handcuffs for so long can be painful." He mouthed, *Sometimes pain is pleasurable,* and he smiled, his gaze going hazy. "I'll be happy to help you out of those cuffs when we meet in private." He mouthed, *I'll help you out of more than that.* "The Feds refuse to meet with you unless you are cuffed. I hear you have a mean right hook."

I willed myself to stay calm; Richter could probably smell fear like the wild animal he was. He could not hurt me here—we were constantly being watched. He could scare me, but he couldn't touch me. In this room, I was safe, relatively anyway. My back spasms and raw wrists suddenly felt a lot less like pain and a lot more like safety. I leaned in closer to the table. "I don't want an attorney. Leave."

He leaned in, his gaze still hazy, and said, "How about if I take those cuffs off for a few minutes? Would that give you incentive to talk to me?"

"Nothing would give me incentive to talk to you."

He chuckled. "Let's give it a try, shall we?"

He stood and came around the table. My eyes widened, and if he couldn't smell my fear before, I was sure that he could now. "Leave the cuffs. Just leave them and get out."

"It'll feel good to get a break from them for a minute. If after that, you still don't want to talk to me, I'll cuff you back up and leave." He walked behind my chair and lifted me to a standing position. His fingers touching my skin made me feel like I had spiders crawling all over me. I fought against him, but he held fast to my handcuffs, and the raw skin was so painful that I yelped. Richter turned me around so that we were both facing away from the window. With one hand pulling tightly on my handcuffs, he placed his other hand on my hip bone and clamped down, digging in painfully. He whispered in my ear, "There is no point in fighting me, Kate. I will win, and I rather enjoy the struggle." That had me holding still. I had no intention of giving Richter anything that would further his enjoyment. "That's a good girl," he purred into my ear.

I thought I might vomit—I wouldn't have made such an effort of holding the contents of my stomach at bay had I been facing him. Richter let go of my handcuffs, and the lack of pain made my body flood with relief. The hand on my hip remained, however.

Loudly, for the sake of those watching, Richter said, "I just need to find my key, hang on." While he rummaged through his pocket, he moved me forward ever so slowly, toward the wall, until I was pressed up against it. Richter pressed to me. The deep bruising on my leg and arm from the DNA Global job ached from the pressure. How could this possibly look legit to the people watching behind the mirror? Would no one come in here? I supposed that if none of the Feds from the other room had come to help me by this point, they never would. They must have all either been AGI, dirty enough to accept a pay off, or perhaps they thought that I was a bad enough criminal that I deserved this kind of treatment.

He had me so tight against the wall that I had to turn my head to the side. It was the wrong choice; Richter pulled my earlobe into his teeth, his tongue caressing it. I whimpered. At the same time, he used his head to push my head against the unforgiving wall so hard that I yelped again.

"Oh, sorry!" He chuckled. "I didn't mean to pull on your cuffs like that. I still can't find the key; I could have sworn I put it in my pocket." I'd bet my life he hadn't.

"Cut the act, Richter. What do you want?"

As one hand rummaged in his pocket, the other began to roam freely, and a sob escaped my lips. He said, "You want me to stop? Then you better answer my questions. Why were you flying to Germany today?" I had never been more relieved that the CIA took such precautions. I was flying to Germany as Kaylee Edwards, and from Germany to Minsk under a different identity altogether. With the AGI knowing the identity of most of our group, we couldn't be too careful. "Where is the rest of your CIA team?"

His roaming hand became bolder when I didn't respond. "Answer me." His voice was little more than a growl. "Let me toss you a little bread crumb, in good faith." He whispered the next three words, his mouth on my ear as he spoke, "We have Liam." No. I closed my eyes, heartsick. "He's in the next room over. We'll break one of you. So let me make another deal with you. Whichever one of you breaks first gets to live."

I couldn't think—panic seized my body, my lungs, my vocal cords. How were Liam and I going to get out of this? Richter's hand continued its roaming, and it was easy to see why the AGI used this as a dirty tactic to get information. It wasn't the first time it had been used on me. Westwood had tried it when I was chained up. In retrospect, it was less terrifying then because I knew that Westwood was purely using a tactic—there were no feelings behind it. Richter wasn't the same; he'd had a twisted thing for me since we'd met, and he'd seen me soar above most of the other new recruits. I got more missions than he did, more praise. And Richter was vindictive and a sadist. In a split second my mind cleared—all I needed was to get out of my panic.

I decided to give the sadist a bread crumb of my own. "Please, Richter. Please stop." There was nothing that Jeremy Richter wanted more than to have me in a place of weakness and him in a place of power. Not my body—he already had that. *My mind.* He wanted power over me, and that was his weakness.

"I've always wanted to hear you beg, Kate." He pushed me harder against the wall. "Now answer my questions."

"Just give me a little room, Richter. I can't breathe. Give me some room and I'll answer your questions." I made sure my voice came off sounding panicked, afraid, and resigned.

As soon as Richter pulled back enough, I used all of the strength I could gather in my current position and reared back my head, crunching a nose for the second time in the same day. Hearing and feeling Richter's bones break against my head felt much better than it should have. I never wanted to delight in someone else's pain; I never wanted to become one of them. But it felt good nonetheless—a thing I would have to ruminate over another time.

Richter let go of me and backed away, cursing. I turned around and saw blood running like a river down his lips and chin. The door slammed open and federal officers filed into the room, ready to finally take me out of there. But as they pulled me from the room, I couldn't look away from Richter and the look of determination on his bloody face, mixed with attraction. He was disgusting. Even in the commotion all around the room and my handcuffs being painfully tugged on, Richter and I watched each other, and then he started to smile.

I'd just become an even greater prize than I had already been.

CHAPTER 40

Minsk, Belarus
Liv

Liv woke up for the first time in a considerable length of time. She didn't remember much—the illness had been more brutal than ever before. And she wondered, again, what exactly she was testing. When the testing was over, what would be left of her? She imagined, not for the first time, that they were making her into something superhuman. In Liv's wildest dreams she would sprout wings and fly out of there, having the power to unlock doors with her mind, and she would free all of the people who were imprisoned around her, and together with all of their new capabilities they would kill their captors and be free.

But in reality, she was lying on a dirty cot, in a locked room, in a foreign country, covered in dried blood. She was so sore, and so stiff, but she was improving, no doubt about that. She remembered that in her fits of coughing up blood, she'd wished for death. Truly wished for it, ready to die. And yet, now that she was improving, her will to live had swelled considerably. She was young and still had so much life to live, if she could just get out of there. She missed her family. Her parents, who had always shown her so much love. Her sisters, who may have borrowed her things without asking, but looked up to her with the kind of hero worship that only little sisters could. She missed her uncle Oliver, who was not really her uncle but her godfather. She'd always called him "uncle" because "godfather" sounded weird. Uncle Oliver, who had never missed a birthday or any other significant event in her life. She bet that he was missing her, too. She didn't know what day it was, having no window and no sense of time, but from her calculations based on the comings and goings of the people in hazmat suits, she believed that it was somewhere around her eighteenth birthday.

She was eighteen, possibly had been for a few days, or would be in a few days—either way, this was not how she had pictured turning eighteen. She imagined being home in Phoenix, surrounded by her friends and family. She could almost smell the desert and citrus. Could feel the heat coming up from the ground, smell the chlorine from the pool in her backyard. Because she would definitely be having a pool party, with barbecue on the grill and bowls of juicy fresh fruit set out on the patio table. There would be balloons, at her mother's insistence, because, in the words of her mother, "it wasn't a party without balloons." She could see Oliver keeping Sarah and Brenna busy in one corner of the pool so that Liv could enjoy the time with her friends. Liv could hear her parents' laughter and see them with their arms circling each other, watching the scene around them and reminiscing about how grown up their little girl had become.

Liv rolled over on her side and cried.

CHAPTER 41

Washington, D.C.
Kate

I was in a cell. Solitary confinement, because they didn't know whose nose I would break next. Their words, not mine. That suited me just fine; I didn't want to be around anyone at the moment. I needed peace and quiet so that I could think.

Escape on my own was unlikely, though many people successfully escaped from prison, so it wasn't impossible. The jail they took me to was about twenty minutes from the federal courthouse. But we were stopped often, which made me think that traffic was what made the drive take so long. It was Saturday, so I would be stuck in this cell until Monday, when they would take me to see Judge Hudd, who would surely deny bond and throw me right back in here.

It was possible that the AGI had no intention of killing me now that I was facing several life sentences. As long as I wasn't actively fighting against them, they would probably be happy to just let me rot. But even if I were stuck here, unable to do anything but feel sorry for myself, the team was out there.

I both hoped that they were and were not looking for me. Of course I wanted them to value my life and be worried about where I was and working night and day on finding a way to get me back. And a part of me that I was mildly ashamed of, but that also made me human, was hoping that Jake was absolutely losing his mind with worry. I wanted it to consume him, keep him up at night. But the bigger part of me, the better part of me, hoped that they were doing the job we'd set out to do. I hoped that they had success finding the virus lab and that they blew the pace to smithereens. The lives of thousands were at stake, millions if the AGI/NOS decided to release that virus into portions of the general population, snuffing out innumerable lives. And when that was done, then I wanted them to get me out of here.

That day and the next were much of the same: with me sitting in the corner of my cell, because the bed was that uncomfortable, waiting to see the judge. The monotony was starting to get to me. The cell was the kind of silent that reminded me of walking through the halls at the Montana AGI facility. The cell was dirty; the dust bunnies that scattered the floor were acutely apparent from my vantage point. They consisted of dust buildup mixed with tangled pieces of other women's hair.

The small locked metal food slot on my cell door opened, and a tray with two pieces of nutraloaf shot through the opening, the food tumbling onto the filthy floor. Nutraloaf was something I'd only heard of, a thing I thought was rumor. Unfortunately, it was a real thing, and even more unfortunately, at this facility, they served it to those of us in solitary for all three meals. From what I understood, nutraloaf was a mixture of different foods: meats, vegetables, fruits, and grains, all mushed together, thrown in a loaf pan, and baked. That was true enough, and sounded gruesome enough, but what I knew of nutraloaf had nothing on the real thing. It seemed that the prison cooks took the leftovers from whatever they fed the inmates—Italian and American cuisines were most common, and for the record, those original meals were not cooked well—and then threw the leftovers together, adding things to make it more disgusting, like dried fruit, rancid nuts, and mushy vegetables. Supposedly, it had all the nutrients one needed to sustain life, but that was only true if one could keep it down. If a person had never had subpar chicken à la king mixed with overcooked spaghetti and Spam and then spotted with pieces of dried cranberries and pineapple, baked together and cut into slices, they could not understand nutraloaf. I made a vow that when I got out of here and the threat from the AGI was all over, I would use my law degree to fight against nutraloaf.

When my "meal" fell to the floor, a normal person would have picked it up and thrown it in the trash. The floor was disgusting, the food was disgusting, and quite frankly, even the trash can deserved better. But I knew that this was the only food I would be getting, and if and when the CIA sprung me from this awful place, I would need my strength. So, like a wild animal, which was exactly how I was treated, I crawled over to the food and picked out the edible pieces from the tops of the slices of loaf, making sure not to eat anything that had touched the floor. I gagged on what I had thought was cheese but was actually something else entirely, something I couldn't place. I choked down all that I possibly could and then picked up the rest and threw it away. The food left my stomach in knots—it was all that I could do to keep it from coming back up.

My cell door opened bright and early on Monday morning. "Get up. You're going to court today." The kindness of my guards never ceased to impress me.

I crawled off the bed, my muscles protesting. The bed was as hard as a rock, and it made my bruises ache, the old ones and the new ones alike. I was thrilled to get out of there, though; being alone had gotten old quickly. The guard cuffed me, this time with my hands in front, for which I was grateful, and then I was shackled. Another guard took me outside to a waiting van filled with other inmates. There was just one spot left. I got in and they buckled me, like I was a toddler. The buckles locked with a key. I supposed that at some point in time the inmates had unbuckled themselves and wreaked havoc. So now I got to be strapped down with a five-point harness. None of the other prisoners spoke. We drove in silence. I couldn't complain too much—I did score a window seat, and through it the sun was shining on my face.

When we got to the courthouse, they unbuckled us one at a time, and guards were there to escort us inside. I had three, while everyone else got one. It was hard to believe that they thought that I was that much of a threat. I figured it was for show: if they treated me like a dangerous criminal, then the perception of others would follow suit.

They put me in a holding room while I waited for my arraignment. I sat there by myself for hours, sick and tired of being alone. Finally, there was a knock on the door, and when it opened, Jeremy Richter stood at the threshold. I decided on the spot that there were worse things than being alone. My only solace was Richter's swollen and bandaged nose—I could see purple bruising on the edge of the bandage.

I stood, shackled as I was, and said, "You are not my lawyer. Get out."

He looked at the guard and rolled his eyes, sighing, "I have the most thankless job."

The guard grunted. "Tell me about it."

I got louder; I wanted everyone to hear this time. "You are NOT my lawyer. Don't you dare step foot in this room." There were few times I could point to in my life as truly and horrifically mortifying—not embarrassing, like making you blush or stammer—but mortifying, like making you cry tears of humiliation. Standing in front of Jeremy Richter shackled, in an orange jumpsuit, not having had a shower in days, was perhaps the most humiliating experience of my life. Tears burned the backs of my eyes, but I refused to let them out; my cheeks flamed, and my body started to tremble.

Richter looked at me. His eyes lit and the corners of his mouth turned up at my clear embarrassment, he said, "I'm not coming in there, Edison; you're coming with me. It's time for your arraignment."

"You. Are. Not. My. Attorney."

The guard pulled me roughly out of the holding room and said, "Take it up with the judge."

Richter's smile grew. "Yes, Ms. Edison, you are welcome to take it up with the judge. Because, until he says otherwise, I am the attorney on file." He knew that I would be powerless in front of Judge Hudd, but that didn't mean that I wouldn't try.

We walked in silence to the courtroom. When we walked in, I managed to feel even worse about myself and my circumstances.

The courtroom was opulent, beautiful, with the high-beamed ceiling, marble floors, and dark wood benches that matched the judge's bench. Some of the windows were made of beautifully stained glass, and the sunlight that filtered through them cast a golden glow over the room. My hair had never felt greasier, the cheap fabric of my jumpsuit scratched against my skin, and the shackles somehow seemed even more confining.

The one thing that caught me off guard was that the courtroom was mostly empty. There were a handful of attorneys with their clients waiting for their turn on the docket as well as various court employees, but that was about it. I was mildly surprised that there were no reporters there to record my shameful moment. I had made such a scene at the airport that I expected a little more fanfare. It made me concerned.

Richter looked over at me and smiled. "Did you expect more people here, Kate?" I stiffened, hating that my thoughts were so apparent. "Did you really think that we would let that little stunt you pulled at the airport make you famous? As much as I would have loved to humiliate the great Kate Edison in the deepest way possible, we couldn't allow your friends in the CIA to know where you were, now could we?" I tried not to react. But I momentarily panicked enough that Richter noticed and quietly chuckled. How could they have known that was my goal in breaking Agent Stonewall's nose? Furthermore, how could they keep something like that under wraps? I knew that they had the power of Search, but with all of those people taking video, I was sure that the news would have gone places other than Search alone—social media, for one.

He sneered at me, "You underestimate who you're up against." I did, I continually did. And it angered me more than I let on. Always behind, I was always playing catch-up. "We had our people there at the airport, ready for you to pull a stunt." He shook his head at me in mock disappointment. "So predictable, Kate." If I weren't shackled, I'd have broken another bone in his smug face. "We had FBI agents there to collect every phone that had a recording on it and erase it. Your precious CIA agents have no idea where you are, and by the time they find you, you are going to need a pardon by the president to get out of the mess you've made."

I scoffed, "The mess I've made? Don't you mean the mess the AGI has made for me?"

His eyes slid to mine, the corners of his mouth tilted upward. "Potato, po-tah-to."

I'd have to think about the fact that the CIA didn't know where I was later. It would have consumed me just then, so I switched topics. "What about Liam? Where is he?"

"Aww, worried about your new boyfriend? He went crazy when he'd realized what had happened to you." *Oh, Liam, I'm so sorry I was so stupid and got us both in trouble.* "Is he your replacement for Nick?" He taunted me, "Maybe you were using them both at the same time back in training? Haven't you ever wondered what happened to your dear old Nick?"

It shouldn't have surprised me that Richter could be so callous about Nick, but for some inexplicable reason it did. Who spoke ill of the dead? Particularly the murdered? Well, at least in one regard I wasn't playing catch-up. I couldn't decide if I should feign shock about Nick or let him in on the fact that I already knew, just to have the upper hand for a moment. I waited too long, and Richter spoke first, "Huh, looks like you were just using him. I guess we all have a little evil in us."

There was no response for that. Nothing that I could say that would have hurt him in the way that his comments hurt me. In some ways Nick's death felt like a lifetime ago, but in others it felt like I'd found his cold, lifeless body only yesterday. Time was speeding by, and I was having a hard time keeping up. So much had happened in such a short period. I felt like we were making discoveries about the AGI almost every day, and the plan of our counterattack was always changing. Maybe that was their plan? To keep their enemies on the move for their smaller crimes while they did the bigger work right under our noses?

The court personnel stood, and the judge came out from his chambers. The clerk began to speak, "The Honorable Judge Hudd. Hear ye, hear ye, the United States District Court for the District of

Columbia is now in session. God save the United States and this honorable court."

Judge Hudd called me first. "United States verses Katherine Elaine Edison, please approach."

Richter and I walked through the low gate at the head of the courtroom and stood behind the defendant desk. The federal prosecutor was standing behind the desk to the side of ours. She looked over at me with disdain. She should have looked at me with appreciation—this was an open-and-shut case, and a large one at that. It would make her look good with very little effort. Of course, my charges were lengthy, and prosecutors hated criminals, so . . . there was that.

Judge Hudd was a heavyset man, perhaps in his early sixties, with slicked-back black hair. There was a bit of white regrowth at his scalp, making his hair appear to be almost floating. He probably colored it to look younger, but the black was so harsh against his skin that it aged him instead. He looked at Richter. "Counsel?"

"Go ahead with the reading, Your Honor." What a jerk. Richter could have waived the reading and entered a plea of not guilty. He just wanted to embarrass me further.

His eyebrows lifted in surprise. "Very well. Ms. Edison, here are your charges as they now stand: ten counts of child endangerment, ten counts of child trafficking, ten counts of kidnapping, one count of first-degree murder, one count of resisting arrest, two counts of aggravated assault of a federal agent, one count of breaking and entering, and one count of first-degree burglary." He took a deep breath and looked at me from over the top of his reading glasses. "What say you?"

"Ms. Edison enters a plea of not guilty. And requests a bond hearing." Well, at least Richter did that right.

Judge Hudd nodded. "The bond hearing will be set for Monday at nine a.m." He banged his gavel, and we walked out.

I turned to Richter. "Monday? I thought that I had to have a bond hearing within three days."

He flippantly said, "I told the judge that you would wait. His docket is busy, and he will be out of town for a long weekend."

I gaped at him. "I never agreed to that."

"Um . . . did you *hear* the reading of your charges? You're never getting out on bond, so it really doesn't matter."

"It matters to me." He may have been right that I was never getting out on bond, but I still had my right to that hearing, and I wanted to at least try.

"Kate, don't be naive; the hearing is just a formality."

As soon as we were out of the courtroom doors, Richter turned to me. "I thought that you were going to request a change of counsel."

I looked over at him. "It's not as if the judge gave me time to ask questions—the last thing I needed was to add contempt to my list of charges." Truth was that I was second-guessing asking for a change of lawyer; in the five minutes that we were walking to the courtroom, Richter managed to tell me that the stunt I'd pulled at the airport had been covered up, and even more importantly, he let me know that they didn't have Liam. Liam was a professional; he would never have "gone crazy" when he found out what had happened to me. He would have kept his mouth shut and worked on scheming a way to find me.

Richter did have the acumen to look suspicious—I had all but lost it when he walked in to get me just an hour earlier, after all. But he should have been more than suspicious; he should have been worried. He was prideful, and pride made you stupid. He couldn't help but rub my nose in the AGI's wins. I was going to eke out every ounce of information I could from him, and he would be too caught up in himself to notice.

CHAPTER 42

Cambridge, MA
Arthur

Arthur Whitehall was home with his family. His wife and daughters gathered around the table, chatting about school and boys and teachers. His wife was doing most of the talking but would look at him every once in a while, her eyebrows raised, a silent question of whether he was okay. He would just give her a nod and a small smile and then tune out his family again.

That wasn't his normal way. He loved his children and his wife dearly. Which was precisely why he'd been so relieved three days ago when the perpetrators who had broken into his company building had been caught. He was informed by NexGen that Brahim Awan had been kidnapped for his discoveries in quantum computing and that he had been recovered from his captors that fateful day. Everything had been on the right track until he watched Kate Edison's interrogation.

The first agent who had gone in had done a good job, and at the time, Arthur was sure that she would cave soon and admit her crimes. He had been shocked by the crimes the woman had committed. Selling children? Disgusting. In that moment he'd been proud to witness against her and separate her from the rest of society. Hopefully until her dying day.

But then the man who was appointed her attorney came in. Arthur recognized him immediately. He had been with the NexGen crew who had come to take care of Ms. Edison and her cronies. He worked for NexGen and he was her defense attorney? It didn't take a genius to figure out that something wasn't right here. Arthur had every intention to figure out what was really going on.

CHAPTER 43

Palo Alto, CA
Tracy

Tracy sat in her desk chair in the office portion of her studio apartment and debated her next move. She looked out the window; if she looked at just the right spot, on the far-left side of the window, and squinted, she could just barely see the Bay, a view she paid handsomely for. That little tiny strip of sparkling blue salt water might have actually been worth it, though—she loved the ocean.

Tracy hemmed and hawed over pushing the publish button on what she hoped would be the first of many blog posts that would shed some light on the dark side of Search. Her new anonymous blog was titled *The Truth about Search*, and she planned on telling the world exactly what they had been up to.

Her first blog post dealt with the fact that Search knew everything about everyone. With the click of a few keys they could have a list of everything a person had purchased online, every social media advertisement link they'd clicked, every social media post they'd made, forums they'd joined, recipes they'd downloaded, their current location, religion, level of education, job, spouse, children, parents, siblings—and that was just the tip of the iceberg. There were rumors that they were always listening, through the microphone on your phone. People didn't know how true that was. They listened to *everything*. They knew what a person talked about with their friends over the weekend; if and how their children had misbehaved; and if a person's spouse had cheated on them, often long before it became known to the offended spouse.

At first the information was used for effective advertising. With that kind of knowledge, the advertising capabilities were beyond compare. Why pay to advertise your family law firm to the whole city when you could pay to have those advertisements sent directly through social media and every other online avenue to those who were already leaving their spouses? Why advertise a historical romance novel to someone who only read thrillers? If a company could pinpoint its advertising to those who were actually in need of its services, those ads would be worth a lot more money. And one could argue that, in return, the rest of us wouldn't have to endure ads about getting rid of our migraines when we didn't suffer from migraines.

Personalized marketing made a lot of sense. But it also breached a lot of privacy. When Tracy started out at Search, she found it fascinating. As a behavioral scientist, the study of why people made the choices they did was irresistibly compelling. She got to look at what someone bought and then feed them ads accordingly, seeing if they would bite. But people weren't fish, and baiting them eventually felt slimy.

The problem was that once companies had a taste of personalized marketing, they offered top dollar. It was so incredibly effective that it changed the marketing world forever—there was no going back. In the name of money, Search partnered with social media giants and doubled down on their efforts to know the people they marketed to and in so doing went way too far.

Once you knew that much about a person, where did you draw the line? If someone committed a crime, did you turn them in? If a man was catfishing underage girls, did you alert the authorities? If a girl admitted to her friends that she was going to accuse the teacher she hated of touching her inappropriately, did you tell the school principal? What about a nine-year-old who was viewing horrifically inappropriate things on the internet? At what point did you alert the parent?

Many times it seemed like the answer was yes. Of course you should alert the authorities if you knew someone was planning on hurting someone else, right? Maybe so. But what about the mechanic who purposefully and continually overcharged for his work? What if that mechanic was doing that to pay for his daughter's chemo treatments? What if the boy who went into his school's records and changed his grades so that he could graduate did it because he would do just about anything to escape his abusive home? Lines blurred, and very little was black and white.

Tracy did the one thing she could do. She tried to help people through well-placed ads. To the overcharging mechanic, she would send ads for hospitals that treated childhood cancer for free. To the parents of the young child who was wholly addicted to internet pornography, she sent articles to their social media feeds about how that happens and what signs to look for. It was why she hadn't left her job sooner—she wanted to help people with the information they gathered. And she did, for as long as she could stomach the rest of the work.

But Tracy had been pushed to the edge, and she'd finally quit. It was so freeing. She had a new mission now. She wanted to out Search to the world. She would have to find a way to get paid for it, because her Bay view apartment didn't pay for itself, after all. But she had some time before push came to shove.

The only person she would miss was Vinny. She shook her head, smiling. Vinny, with his stupid-adorable suits. He was such a rule follower. She had never told him how she'd spent her extra time at Search, but she knew that, though he would have outwardly disapproved, he would have ultimately helped her. Vinny was a good guy, someone Tracy could trust; she couldn't wait for their date. She was going to tell him everything.

CHAPTER 44

Washington, D.C.
Kate

The door to my cell closed with a clank. I slumped to my spot on the grimy floor. Clearly no one had cleaned it in my absence. I supposed it wasn't a hotel, but did it have to be so filthy? I would have been happy to scrub the place down myself—maybe I would ask for some cleaning supplies the next time someone came around. Of course, I had already spent almost three days in here before my arraignment hearing, and no one had talked to me, much less checked to see how I was faring in my cell. And now I had an entire week until my bond hearing. Seven more long days in this filth, and how many after that? Who knew—especially if what Richter said about the video not getting out was true. I wish I were like Jake and was able to tell if someone was telling the truth just by looking at their face. To be a human lie detector would be far more useful than my photographic memory at the moment.

Seven more days of silence. How many people had died of the virus in the last three days? How many places would be hit in the next week? Which remote place in the world would be hit next? What happened after they'd hit enough of the remote places? Who would be hit after that? I had endless questions running through my mind and absolutely no way to get answers. So I sat.

When my food shot through the slot in the door, I tried to catch it before it hit the floor. No luck. It was especially upsetting because it was a bologna sandwich, which was practically a delicacy compared to the nutraloaf. I hadn't eaten since the dinner I'd picked at the night before, and I whimpered at the wasted food. Half of the sandwich was salvageable, and the applesauce had a lid, so that at least was okay. Every bite of the sandwich was heaven. You knew that your life had taken a wrong turn when bologna tasted like filet mignon. I vowed to sit in front of the slot in the door to catch my meals from then on.

My nightmares came back with a vengeance and had taken a turn for the worse. Instead of being back with Westwood, I was with Richter. Instead of being chained to a wall, I was handcuffed and powerless against his advances. I woke up sweating, panting, and in tears. It wasn't the first time I'd dreamed about being powerless with Richter, but it was the first time that the dream had so much clarity, the first time I could smell him and feel his spider-crawl touch. It felt so real. I hated being afraid of a person, hated the feeling of being powerless. Being handcuffed around Richter was so terrifying that it made my bowels loose. I sat up on my bed, done with sleep. It was still black as pitch in my cell, but I didn't care. I was up for good.

I questioned my sanity in regard to keeping Richter for my attorney. I was handcuffed in front now and was therefore less powerless than when I was cuffed behind my back. There are a lot of effective maneuvers that can be done with your hands cuffed in front, but far fewer in the back. Also, if we were ever alone together, I didn't have to be cuffed. He could request it, and he would be an idiot if he didn't, but he couldn't request how they cuffed me. In any case, I wanted information about the AGI or the NOS, as it were. I wondered if Richter even knew about the NOS—that the AGI was worldwide and that they had been around for centuries. Regardless, he knew plenty, and I wanted to glean everything that I could. We needed any footing we could get. I was tired of being behind—the next time we would surprise them.

The lights started to come on, which meant breakfast would be served soon, and I went to the door and waited for my food like a dog. It would not fall on the floor this time. Within minutes the tray came thorough, I caught it, and I thanked my lucky stars that it was another bologna sandwich. I ate it like I'd never had a meal before, which was pretty much what it felt like. And then I worked out. I did push-ups, sit-ups, and burpees until my limbs shook with exertion. I couldn't sit around for days on end; I needed the movement.

I was elated the next day when a female guard opened my cell door and said, "Shower day." I had never felt so dirty in my life. The guard handed me a fresh jumpsuit, sports bra, and underwear, along with a travel-size bottle of hair and body soap. She turned on the water and said, "You have five minutes before the water turns off."

I jumped in and went as fast as I could, scrubbing my body and washing my hair as many times as the five minutes would allow. When the water turned off, I got dressed, and the guard handed me the tiniest black comb I had ever seen for my long, thick hair. On the way back I asked the guard for cleaning supplies so that I could clean my cell. She said, "Sure, I'll get those right to you, princess." And then laughed in my face. I tried one more request—the one I wanted more than any other, more than food. I asked to make a phone call, and she said that only some of the prisoners in solitary were permitted phone calls, and I wasn't one of them.

Defeated, I was quiet the rest of the way back to my cell. The guard slammed the door shut, and in seconds I heard her yell, "Shower day" to the woman in the next cell over.

I sat on my bed, taking a break from the floor since my jumpsuit was freshly clean. I mourned that phone call. How could I let someone know that I was here? I had been arraigned, so I should have shown up in the system, but who knew how far the reach of the AGI was? They'd probably managed to keep my name out of the system somehow.

Solitary confinement was awful. It's not as if that came as a surprise, but I was surprised at exactly how awful it was. And with no prospects of getting out anytime soon, the bleakness got bleaker. The days seemed longer, and I found I had no energy to bother to do anything, much less work out. By Thursday I barely got out of bed. The food was back to the nutraloaf, and I couldn't be bothered to wait by the door for nutraloaf. I wasn't even feeling hungry, anyway. I lay in bed and let myself imagine how my life would be here.

What if no one ever found me? What if the worst-case scenario had happened? What if the mission had gone badly and Jake was dead, the rest of the team with him, and I was just left here to rot my years away? What if I never heard from anyone again? Never saw my mother or my sister? My brother and sister-in-law and my nephew? How much had he grown in the past several months? Would I even recognize him? I just lay in bed all day Thursday, and then again Friday, Saturday, and Sunday. When the nights came, I allowed the tears of fear and depression to flow out of the corners of my eyes and soak the pillow.

CHAPTER 45

Madison, WI
Oliver

It was the first Tuesday in April, and Oliver Strands had just, more or less, been declared the winner of his primary, and he was easily the front-runner in every general election poll. The video of his speech at the International Child Recovery Operation had gone insanely viral. His gaffe long since forgotten. The public swarmed to him like flies. He hated it. He hadn't spoken at the event to gain political traction—he'd spoken at the event because the cause was very near and dear to his heart. But that very heartfelt speech had become so politicized, it was all anyone talked about when he was interviewing these days. Didn't the reporters see what giving that speech had done to him? What remembering Liv did to him? He knew they did; they were vultures, and his pain was fresh flesh.

Valentina loved the speech, and she smiled every time it was played. She didn't smile for the cameras—oh no, for the cameras she cried and spoke of how she'd met Liv at their wedding. That much was true, but Valentina had barely said two words to Liv that day. Valentina only smiled watching the speech when no one else was looking. She tried to hide her giddiness over it from Oliver, but it was impossible—they were together all the time and she was too happy about it. Oliver knew why she liked it so much. It was his ticket to the heart of America. His first-class ticket to the White House and hers to being First Lady. Every time Oliver caught her watching it with glee, he started to dislike her more. He felt like he had sold his goddaughter for that first-class seat, and he didn't want it anymore. He didn't want any of it anymore.

Oliver sat with a stiff drink in their dark hotel room, watching the news on the day of the Wisconsin primary. He'd won. By a landslide. It was over; he was the nominee. Though a few hadn't dropped out yet, it was impossible for anyone within his party to beat him now—his numbers were too high. He knocked back the rest of his drink, angry. He didn't want to give an acceptance speech, didn't want to win, didn't care about his paycheck, didn't care about the fame or the accolades. He wished he could go back to being an out-of-work actor.

The hotel door opened, and Valentina came waltzing in, all dressed up, the skirt of her silver dress swishing with every step. She turned on the lights and Oliver moaned. She saw him, and her eyes grew ten sizes. "Are you drinking?"

He looked at her and then the empty cut crystal tumbler in his hand. "I was. If you could bring me the scotch, that'd be great; I'd like to start up again." Her face twisted in anger. Why had he never noticed how ugly she was when she was mad? He didn't mean in looks—Valentina could never *look* ugly—she looked ugly beneath her perfect veneer, in her soul.

"How dare you?" She walked over and grabbed for the glass in his palm, but he pulled it back fast enough that she couldn't grab it. Her face twisted further and turned a deep shade of red. "Oliver, you will give me that glass right now. Staying sober is part of your contract; you are allowed one drink at an event. But never, never at home."

"I remember the contract, Valentina." He met her stare, "And *I don't care.*"

Her eyes went wild. "So what? You think you're going to quit?" She threw her arm in the direction of the television. "You are up to your neck in this, Oliver!"

"I'm tired of being used. I'm tired of my goddaughter's memory being used. I'm tired of you and this whole charade." He was calm while he spoke; he wasn't even giving Valentina the courtesy of looking at her. Instead he was looking at the tumbler, wishing that there were more amber-colored liquid in it.

She knelt down beside him and blew out a breath. "Oliver, I'm sorry. This is a lot to handle for anyone, less yet someone who never had the lifelong dream of becoming president. I know that you have been pushed into this." She timidly touched his arm so that he would look at her. "For what it's worth, I think you will make an amazing president. You are humble and kind. Everyone has had a chance to see the real you, and they love you."

He ripped his arm away. "That video of my heart breaking on-stage is the only reason I have come this far. If there is one thing in my life that I wish I could take back, it's that."

Valentina nodded, and her voice became a whisper, "Oliver, can't you see? That speech shows so much more than your heart breaking; it shows your humanity, your weakness, *and* your strength. It is so powerful to the American people because it resonates with them, it speaks to their souls." She took a chance and touched his arm again. "Oliver, with you as president of the United States, Liv will be found—how could she not be?"

Oliver had thought about that, too, but lamented, "I could be extorted as well." He shook his head slowly and turned to finally look at Valentina. "If they offered me Liv in exchange, I would do whatever they asked." He said it with no shame, only finality. He wanted her to know that the presidency meant nothing to him when it was compared to his family.

Valentina smiled softly. "I know you would, Oliver."

He stood up from the chair, walked out of the hotel room, took the elevator down to the ballroom, and gave a rousing acceptance speech. All with Valentina on his heels. He wanted her to know that she was not the only conductor on this train. By the murderous look on her face when they got back to their hotel room, the door safely shut behind them, it was apparent that his intent had been crystal clear. He didn't give her a second to speak. He bid her good night and walked into the second bedroom, locking the door behind him.

CHAPTER 46

Washington, D.C.
Kate

I had been up most of the night, only falling asleep when absolutely necessary because my nightmares were messing with my mind. Most of the time that I had been awake in bed had been spent crying, and I hoped that I'd run out of tears—I was sick of crying. In the light of day, the food I'd allowed to pile up on the floor over the past few days had started to stink, and the smell made my stomach turn uncomfortably. I got up and used the napkins that came with my meals to scoop up the rotting pile of nutraloaf. It squished under my hands, making me gag, and I wondered how I had managed to eat it when I'd first gotten there.

It was clear enough to me that the person I was when I'd first arrived in my cell was not the same person I was now. That person had known that she would be rescued, had believed that she was only a few days for this place. But now I knew better. Jake didn't know where I was, I was never going to be allowed to make a phone call, and the list of crimes the AGI had so scrupulously set me up with was long—all of them atrocious and all "provable." My chances of escaping this place had shrunk so thoroughly that the very real possibility of me having to stay here for the long haul had sunk in.

That reality was horrifying. My will to live had dwindled considerably in just a week and a half of being there. I'd never imagined what solitary confinement could do to a person. What normal, law-abiding citizen did? It wasn't so much the confinement itself, though not being able to talk to another living soul was more painful than I'd ever imagined. It was the unknown. How long would I be in here? Days, weeks, months? There were people who had spent forty years in solitary confinement. That was absolutely unthinkable. I couldn't imagine how anyone could last that long. They would have to have had better guards than I did—guards that didn't throw their food on the floor, for starters.

The experience was soul sucking. I couldn't believe how quickly I could go from a mentally healthy person to one that contemplated starvation as a means of permanent escape. But in the past couple of days, I had done just that.

The door to my cell opened, and the guard came in with the shackles. I sighed, annoyed with myself because my eyes filled up with tears as he locked me in them. Tears helped nothing. The next guard appeared, and in silence they both walked me to the transportation van.

I got in without looking at any of the other prisoners. The guards buckled me in and shut the door and banged on the top of the van twice, signaling that everyone was inside and the transport could leave. The driver looked back at me, and out of the corner of my eye, I saw him wink.

I did a double take, and when we made eye contact, my breath caught, and *Charlie* smiled back at me. Tears spilled over. They had found me. Charlie started to drive off, and the person next to me put their hand on mine. My head jerked over to look at them, and when my eyes settled on Jake's face, I crumpled. I tried to cover my face with my hands but couldn't because they were shackled to my sides, so I just bowed my head as my body silently shook with sobs. I cried for the part of me that had thought that I would rot in that cell, for the part of me that gave up hope so easily. I cried for all of the people locked up by themselves for years with no one to talk to but the walls and nothing to eat but rancid leftovers. I cried for the way that Richter had touched me, for the way I had been violated by his hands. I cried because my team was still alive and hadn't forgotten about me.

I heard Jake's seat belt unbuckle, and through my blurry eyes, I saw him, in an orange jumpsuit that matched mine, unlock my shackles. Slowly, so slowly, he carefully took them all off me. When the cuffs came off my wrists, he took in a jagged breath at the sight of the raw, cut-up skin. Then he gathered me in his arms and pulled me onto his lap. He tucked my face where his shoulder and neck met and softly ran his hand down the back of my head, over and over, while I soaked him in my tears. He didn't shush me or try to take my mind off it—he held me until I stopped crying and looked up at him.

His face was wet, and the sight made more tears leak out of my eyes. He pressed his forehead to mine and fiercely whispered, "I'm so sorry, Kate. I'm so sorry it took us so long." I closed my eyes and nodded against his forehead, nodded that I understood and that it was okay. I was so grateful that they were there, that he was there. That I was being held so carefully and closely by a person who knew me, and came for me—a person who'd fought for me.

He wiped my tears and hugged me close one more time. Then he blew out a breath and said, "There are five of us that came back to get you. The rest of the team is working in Minsk, and they believe that they've found the next place the NOS is going to hit with the virus. If our intel is right, then Tahiti is next. Our plan is to head there." He took my face into both of his hands and looked into my eyes. "We were going to take you with us, but not if you aren't ready. We can find a safe house for you if you'd rather."

I shook my head. "I'm coming. I'm not leaving your side again."

He let out the breath he'd been holding in one big whoosh. "Charlie is taking us to the airport now." He hugged me to him again. Then louder he said, "She's coming, guys!" And the van filled up with cheers.

I looked over Jake's shoulder and saw Liam, Mark, and Candace, all of them dressed in orange jumpsuits. I laughed, and it felt so good. I don't think I'd laughed, or smiled for that matter, since I was last with Liam at the airport.

I looked at Liam, and his smile disappeared. His eyes bored into mine, and he said, "I'm so, so sorry, Kate. I should never have left your side." I felt Jake stiffen at the sound of Liam's voice. Jake was angry with Liam—he shouldn't have been; it was as much my fault as it was his. I said as much, but Liam shook his head. "I knew better, I wasn't thinking. I've been sick with worry about you. We all have."

I didn't quite know how to respond. I wanted to say that I was okay, but I wasn't. Not yet. I felt a little bit broken, but I knew that I could be put back together. It would just take some time. "I'll be okay."

Liam said, "We know you will. But I was a POW for a few weeks, years ago, and if you ever want to talk, I'm here for you."

Liam had been a prisoner of war? I wondered if I would always be learning new things about him. I was positive that being a prisoner of war was far worse than solitary confinement. I wasn't sure that I really wanted to know what he'd endured. "Thanks, Liam."

Jake handed me a comm. "There is one person who really wants to talk to you." He smiled.

I put it in my ear and said, "Hi, Lena."

She squealed, and everyone winced from the screechy noise—apparently they all would be in on our conversation. "Kaaaaaate! We have been worried sick!" That made two of us. "Are you okay? Did those other women in the pokey hurt you? Did you have to show them who was boss by beating up the baddest and meanest chick there? Too bad you didn't have a chance to buy any cigarettes on your way in; I hear those are a valued currency in the stony lonesome." I laughed out loud—who said "stony lonesome"? I missed her.

"I wasn't with the other prisoners; they had me in solitary." There was a group intake of air, suggesting that they all knew at least some of what that entailed. But unless they'd spent time there, they were sure to be missing a few details.

Jake rubbed my back and said, "We're going to need you to debrief." I looked at him and he cringed. I knew he didn't want to ask, but I also knew that he didn't have a choice. It was how it was done in the CIA. Also, I knew that he wanted every detail. He wanted to know what I'd been through.

I nodded. "I can do that now, if you want."

Jake's mouth twisted in apology, but he said, "I think that would be best, if you're up for it." He tapped his comm. "Lena, is Scarborough around?"

"Yeah, I'll patch him in for the debrief."

Within a few seconds, Scarborough sounded in our ears. "Kate, it's good to have you back."

"It's good to be back, sir."

Then he said, "Whenever you're ready."

I wasn't ready, not really, but it had to be done. I made to move back to my seat, so that Jake wouldn't have me in his lap like a wounded animal the entire story. He tightened his hold, hit his comm as well as mine off, and said in my ear, "Please don't move. Charlie is a safe driver, and I'm not ready for you to be that far away from me just yet."

I gave the barest hint of a smile and said, "Okay." We tapped our comms back on, and I began.

But as I was telling my story I realized that I should have moved; it was too much for Jake, what I'd been through. He was more and more tense with every turn of events. I told them about hitting the federal agents out of desperation. "I was hoping that Liam would come looking for me,"—Jake tensed, still angry at Liam—"but the crowd was growing, and even if Liam were there, I couldn't see him, so I broke the Fed's nose and then kicked him and another in the groin." The guys groaned; Lena laughed. "There were all of these people recording, and I figured that it would make the news faster, and you guys would know what had happened to me, if I resisted the arrest."

Liam said, "I wasn't there, but the news spread through the airport quickly, and I knew that it was you when I heard people talk about the blonde who could throw a punch like Mike Tyson. I ran to the bookstore and you were already gone, but I saw the agents— some of them I recognized as AGI—collecting phones and erasing the video from them."

I nodded. "Richter told me they had done that." As soon as I said the name Richter, Jake tensed again, and his arms tightened around me.

Liam's eyes bulged, and he and Lena shouted, "Richter?" at the same time.

"Hold on, I'll back up." I told them everything—about sitting in the interrogation room at the federal courthouse, cuffed for hours. About the first federal agent who questioned me and then Richter being appointed as my attorney. Everyone started yelling that that was illegal, and I rolled my eyes. "I know that was illegal, I'm an attorney. The judge was AGI." That quieted them all down. That's right, a federal judge was AGI, along with how many others?

I continued with my story, and when I got to Richter cornering me while I was cuffed in the interrogation room, Jake had stopped breathing entirely. His hands were fisted, his knuckles white. There was no way to sugarcoat it—I had to just get it out there. I tried to stay all business when I told them about Richter's wandering hands, but my choked voice gave me away. I could still feel his hands on me, his hot breath, still hear his foul words. "He was trying to get me to talk, told me that they had Liam in the next room over and that only whichever one of us broke first would get to live. I broke his nose with my head."

Everyone cheered at that except Jake, who was still simmering in silent rage. He looked at me. "Did he pay you back for that?"

It was a fair question. I could tell that he didn't approve of my poking the bear. "No, after that I only saw him one other time, at my arraignment, and we were in public the entire time." Jake nodded, far from okay but ready for the rest of the story.

I told them about solitary, how dirty the cell was, how I got one shower in ten days, and the nutraloaf. Jake kept getting quieter and quieter—he stared straight ahead, no longer looking at me. I briefly told them about my listlessness over the last couple of days, but I figured that my state of mind wasn't necessary for a debrief—they just needed the facts. I could tell that Jake wanted every piece of information, including and especially my feelings, but I could tell him that sort of information at a later date.

When I finished, Liam handed me a protein bar. "You need this more than I do."

I took it to make him feel better; I still didn't have an appetite. "Thanks, Liam."

Charlie pulled up to the executive airport, thank goodness. I think I had a little PTSD from Dulles International. While they were still in the car, everyone zipped off their jumpsuits to reveal the normal clothes they were wearing underneath. Jake handed me some clothes. "We bought these for you. Candace helped. I hope they're okay. We'll leave so that you can change." They all filed out of the car, and I made quick work of changing my clothes. I really wished that I could have taken a shower, but clean clothes would have to do. I found myself tearing up at the feel of the normal clothes—I'd spent a lot of time wondering if I'd get to wear anything aside from that scratchy jumpsuit. The pants were a little big on me; I knew I had lost some weight in the last ten days but wasn't sure how much. I hadn't seen myself in a mirror in so long that I really had no idea how I looked. Jake waited by the car until I came out and then walked with me to the plane ramp. He didn't leave my side one time. Normally I would have found that suffocating, but not now. Now it was comforting, and I hoped he never stopped.

I stopped walking for a second and turned to Jake, my brow furrowed. "Why haven't the police been chasing us?"

He smiled. "We have yet to tell you the story of what happened while you were away." He motioned for the plane bound for Tahiti. "We've got a long flight—hop on, and we'll fill you in."

CHAPTER 47

Minsk, Belarus
Johan

Johan heard Aksana cursing in Belarusian all the way from the lab. She was down the hall, and he knew that she had seen that 1017 was recovering. She came into the lab like a raging bull and pointed at him. "You." Her gaze was piercing. "You are doing this. You are giving her the antidote."

Johan looked up from his work and said, calm as ever, "No, Aksana, I'm not. Your science is faulty."

She huffed, her eyes wild. "*My science is faulty?* Aside from that girl, my science has a one hundred percent track record. My viruses are flawless."

Johan shrugged and kept working while he spoke, not even giving her the consideration of eye contact. "Not completely flawless, obviously."

She roared, "They are flawless! All of them! You are doing something—you are undermining my work." She threw up her hands. "Why? Are you trying to look better than me to the NOS? Do you have a soft spot for that pretty girl? Why are you doing this?"

He looked at her then, through his face mask, over the top of his glasses. "Your failure is making you paranoid. If I wanted to look better than you, I would simply turn on the camera in her room so that our superiors could see that you have yet to kill the subject. I have kept your secret, but it won't keep itself much longer."

Aksana was seething. She was angry and frustrated, and Johan knew better than to pull the dragon's tail too hard. He went back to his work.

She stalked over to him, and Johan looked at her, his eyes wary, while she said, "I don't trust you. I know you are up to something, and when I figure it out, the NOS will have your head. Here's what I'm going to do: I am going to reformulate the virus and give it to her again. And this time, I am not leaving this lab until she is dead." She got as close to Johan as their hazmat suits would allow. "I will watch her every second to make sure that you don't intervene."

Johan merely shrugged and got back to work.

CHAPTER 48

Papeete, Tahiti
Kate

I looked down over the bluest water I'd ever seen as our plane made its descent. So much had happened in such a short period of time. The team had filled me in on as much of it as they could between D.C. and Tahiti, but I was so tired and my mind was still so jumbled that it was hard to concentrate. They had made discoveries regarding the Easter Island epidemic, thanks to tourists. Oliver Strands had won the Wisconsin primary, making him the effective winner of his party. And Brahim had finally gotten in touch. Every new revelation seemed to bring on a discussion, and I was barely able to muster an appropriate response. Jake sensed my exhaustion and told everyone else to get some sleep, that we could finish this discussion later. He warmed me some canned soup, as it was apparent that I had eaten very little over the last ten days. He sat with me while I ate, and then he leaned my seat back and gave me a blanket. I didn't remember falling asleep, but I woke to Charlie's voice announcing our descent.

Charlie landed the plane, and immediately a ground crew greeted us at the door. They were in hazmat suits. The one closest to us shouted to be heard over the other planes taking off and landing, "Are you medical?" The man looked tired. Liam was closest to him and shook his head, no. He frowned and said, "Then we can't let you off. The virus has spread here, and we are at ground zero protocol."

Jake jumped in front of Liam with his badge out and shouted, "We're CIA, we're here about the virus."

The man was momentarily confused. "We haven't been informed that CIA were coming. Due to our protocol, if you get off that plane, we can't let you leave the island. What we need are medical professionals. We're up to thirty-three deaths, most of those in the last few hours. Unless you can help these people, we have no use for you here. There is nothing the CIA can do. All you need to know is that sickness is spreading with no way to stop it. We have been in compliance with the World Health Organization and have been updating regularly."

Jake nodded, deflated; we were too late. If the symptoms had progressed this far already, then we were at least two days too late. "Has it spread to anyone that isn't of Tahitian descent?"

The man looked behind him for confirmation, then turned back to us. "None reported yet, but it's still early days here."

Jake nodded. "What if we wear class A hazmat suits? Will we be permitted to leave the island?"

The man again conferred with the person behind him, then turned back and said, "Class A?"

Jake nodded, and the man said, "That would be permitted, but you would have to go through our bleach spray before getting back on your plane."

"Will do. Thank you—we only need a couple of hours."

Jake closed the door and went to the closet in the back of the plane, and said, "Let's do what it takes to check things out." We all knew that we didn't need the protective suits, but I did appreciate the way that the situation was being handled. They certainly were taking things seriously. "We have five suits; someone is going to have to stay behind."

Charlie immediately piped up, "I'll stay here in case we need a quick getaway."

The rest of us donned the protective gear. We looked like we were ready to travel to outer space. Jake gestured to the door. "Let's go." We filed out of the aircraft into the beautifully sunny Tahitian day. The juxtaposition of the beautiful weather and the virus that was taking over the island felt strange. Like it was wrong for a place so beautiful to experience something so ugly.

We walked through the empty Faa'a International Airport out into the streets, and nothing could have prepared us for what we saw. I thought that since I had seen Nigel Brown dead from the virus, I was aware of what I was getting into. I wasn't.

People were outside of their houses, sick with fever, sweating and shaking, calling for help. When they coughed, their hands came away bloody. Crying mothers were holding and rocking their dying children while they both vomited blood and more.

I couldn't take it. I turned away from the sight, sick with horror. Mere hours ago, I had escaped the most harrowing experience of my life, only to be shown how much worse things could be. My heart ached, utterly *ached* for these people and all of the other people who had died in the same way. Jake grabbed my hand, and I knew that it wasn't just for my own benefit. We walked through the streets for an hour, bereft, every single one of us in tears.

The one bright spot was watching those who weren't Tahitian help the sick. They held the sick babies of their dying friends and of strangers alike. They held bowls for the physically ill and set cold compresses on the foreheads of the fevered. They spoon-fed broth and cleaned up bloody vomit and other waste with no care at all as to whether they, too, would get sick.

The people who weren't sick weren't barricaded in their houses or hotels, trying to avoid contamination—they were out helping, feeding, and holding. The grocery stores had signs on them that said, "Everything for free," "Take anything you need," and "No charge." The non-native clergy from various religions went from house to house praying over the people who dwelt there. Non-native restaurant owners delivered soups and broths.

The sight made my tears course down my cheeks at an even faster rate. The dichotomy of the sick and the outpouring of love from those who remained healthy was something I'd never forget as long as I lived.

This, this humanity—this love—it could not be killed out of the population. The NOS could do their worst, as they had to the

Tahitian people, and still love won. Humanity won. The NOS might be able to win a fight against governments and world leaders, but they could never win a fight against those who loved others more than they loved themselves. When it came to the kind of love that transcended mortality, they would lose every time.

Jake squeezed my hand and said, "It's time to go back; the ground crew was right, there's nothing for us to do here. The NOS is long gone."

I looked back at our crew of five and their wet, tear-stained faces and felt a kind of bond with them that only something of this magnitude could forge. As one, we all turned and walked back to the airport, through the decontamination process, and back onto our plane.

Charlie saw our faces and soberly said, "Wow. You guys okay? I mean, obviously you aren't okay, okay. But is anyone hurt?" We shook our heads. "All right then." He tilted his head toward the cabin. "Scarborough is waiting for you all to call. We're heading to Minsk. I'm sure he will fill you all in." Charlie walked to the cockpit and started firing up the plane.

We walked back and stripped out of our hazmat suits, then sat in our seats and made the phone call, Scarborough's face appearing on the screen. His expression was grim when he saw our splotchy faces and swollen eyes. "I guess I don't need to ask how it went. Was anyone from the NOS still there?"

Mark shook his head. "If they were, they weren't wearing the packs. It appeared that the virus was spread approximately three days ago. They're all dying." He choked on the last words. We knew how they operated now—that was one thing that had been discovered while I was in prison. The virus could be spread in several ways, but we had reports from the tourists on Easter Island, the first place hit, that they saw people who were dressed as local bug exterminators come into churches, schools, grocery stores, and other public places with packs on their backs. Thanks to the tourists, some of them were caught on camera, and none of the local extermination companies recognized the people from the pictures as employees. The packs had long tubes attached, and they pumped what was in their packs onto surfaces and into the air. Within two days, the Rapa Nui people started getting sick. The virus spread so far and wide, so quickly, that hospitals were immediately overwhelmed. The numbers of casualties grew so rapidly that for most people, no medical help could be given. The death toll reached 3,540 in just days from the onset of symptoms.

Our plan had been to beat the virus here and catch the NOS employees tasked with spreading it. We wanted to take at least one of them alive, with their pack, so that our scientists could study the virus and hopefully make an antidote or at least fashion a vaccine that gave people a fighting chance. The United States had an Ebola vaccine, and they were giving it out like crazy in case the Ebola-like virus started to spread beyond these remote islands. Our group knew better. The vaccine didn't stand a chance against this. It wasn't the same as a normal virus—it was man-made and programmed for a person's, or ethnic group's, DNA. It was personalized in a way that the vaccine wasn't.

The thing about the world today is that it is a melting pot. There weren't many places in the world where there was an abundance of indigenous people who had very little mixed blood with other races. And so far, the virus was not hitting the people of mixed heritage nearly as hard as those who were full-blooded. I wasn't sure what the NOS was playing at. When or if they let the virus loose in the US, they had to know that with generation upon generation of mixed DNA, it would be almost impossible to have near the impact that we were seeing in these more remote populations of the world.

I said as much to the team. Candace nodded. "I've thought the same thing. It seems to me that they're testing out the effectiveness of the virus on these remote islands. The only idea that I can come up with is that we're just seeing the beginning of what they can do. Perhaps they can formulate the virus for other components in addition to DNA."

"Exactly." I bit my lip as my thoughts formed. "Their plan can't be to kill everyone off—what's a New World Order without any subjects?"

"Right," Liam agreed, "a New World Order is all about control. My two cents is that they're going to use the virus as a means of control, either by showing us what it can do—like they are now—or by using it as a means of getting rid of the people who aren't, and will never be, loyal to their cause."

I snapped my fingers. "Yes! I think that there must be a way to connect the virus to DNA combined with other things, like lifestyle and hobbies."

Scarborough's brow furrowed. "Can you explain that further?"

I bit my lip again, giving myself a second to think. "I'm not a scientist, and I have no idea how this would work, but surely there are ways to group people together by category—political parties, for example—and find common links within their DNA that you could use to formulate a virus that would kill off a particular part of the population that wouldn't support your agenda."

Jake's brows rose, and then dropped again, while he thought.

Mark shook his head. "But what about the virus spreading once it started through whichever demographic they chose? How do they stop it from spreading outside their desired demographic to other people who have that same DNA characteristic?"

"I don't know. I don't even know if it's possible. But they can't have created the virus just to kill off remote areas of people. Knowing their agenda, it also doesn't make sense that they would want to kill off large sects of the population. But if they could use it strategically, if they could kill off people with certain beliefs, then it makes sense. What if large sects of people who believed in different political parties had something in their DNA that the NOS could isolate?"

Scarborough hummed. "Something to think about. I agree that it doesn't make sense that they would make a virus with the plan to kill everyone off. That can't be their intention." He rubbed his chin. "I really don't want to find out what they plan to use the virus for. I want to cut it off at the knees."

That much we could all agree on. Jake said, "I guess that's why we're on our way to Minsk?"

Scarborough nodded. "We've found a box located at the central post office in Minsk that is related to the address that Brahim gave us." The AGI hadn't noticed that he had a comm when he went with them in Boston. They were so small they were practically invisible, thanks to Fin's genius. "We have someone watching it at all hours that the post office is open; so far they haven't come in to pick up their mail. Mail has been added to the box daily, and we expect that anytime we will get a hit. Hopefully by the time you all get here. We won't be going in without you, so expect to hit the ground running when you all arrive." We nodded, and he said, "Get some sleep. It may be your last chance for a while." Then he was gone.

Liam roughly ran his hands through his hair. "I don't know if I can sleep; I think I'll be up with nightmares about Tahiti."

Everyone but me nodded their heads. I, on the other hand, felt like I had cried myself out over the last few days. "I'm exhausted, I could definitely sleep." Liam sent me a sad smile. "I'm really okay, Liam. After witnessing what we did today, I have a new lease on life. I feel like I have completely moved on from solitary confinement, and I'm fully invested in finding where that virus is coming from. I can't think about anything aside from those sick people."

Liam pursed his lips. "I get that, but just know the things you went through can still haunt you, and it can come when you least expect it. The offer to talk is always on the table." I thanked him, and then he said, "There is a bed in the back. You should take it. I'm sure you haven't slept well in days."

I looked around to see if anyone else wanted to claim the bed, and when they all nodded that I should take it, I wasn't dumb enough to ask again. Jake stood. "I'll show you where it is."

There was really only one place it could be—it wasn't like I could get lost. Candace, Mark, and Liam were suddenly busy on their phones, acting like they were ignoring Jake and me completely. I got up and motioned for him to lead the way.

It was all of ten feet away. The door opened outward, and the only thing in the room was the queen-size bed. It filled the entire room—I had to crawl onto the bed from the door. Once I was on, Jake cleared his throat and asked, "Can I lie with you for a bit?"

I was absolutely not going to say no to that request, but I hadn't showered in days, many of those spent in a filthy prison. I told him my concerns.

"Kate, I couldn't care less."

I patted the bed beside me, and he crawled on, shutting the door behind him. He lay right next to me and pulled me into his side, his arm under my neck, my head in the crook where his shoulder met his chest. It was a perfect fit and almost too good to be true to be next to Jake and no longer alone on the rock-hard bed of solitary confinement.

He ran his hand up and down my arm and softly asked, "What are you thinking?"

I smiled and lightly huffed, "Where do I start?" He continued to softly stroke my arm while he waited for me to answer. "I'm thinking how I'm afraid I'll wake up back in prison." His hold on me tightened. "I had a lot of nightmares there, hardly ever getting more than a couple hours of sleep a night. But this would be the cruelest nightmare of them all—the one that gave me false hope."

He moved the arm that was under me and adjusted himself so that his head was resting on his hand. From his new vantage point he could look at my face. He smiled softly and stroked my face with his free hand. "Do you want me to pinch you? Pull your hair?" I laughed lightly, and he bent to kiss my temple; I think it was a favorite spot of his. "Kate, I told you a lot of what happened while you were in prison, but I didn't tell you everything." I cocked my head to the side slightly, and he said, "I lost my mind when I found out that you were gone."

"Back when Scarborough talked to us about putting our relationship on hold, I thought that I could do that. I'd tried already, and failed miserably, but what Scarborough had said about the dangers of having real feelings for another person on a mission causing problems was true. I've seen it myself. Also, I knew what this mission meant to you, and I wanted to make your priorities mine, so for you, I decided that I could put my feelings on hold again. And that I would try harder this time. But when you were taken by the Feds, and ultimately the AGI, I knew that that had all been a lie. I couldn't put my feelings for you aside any more than I could stop breathing. I knew the moment that I heard you were gone that I didn't care about this mission anywhere near the amount that I cared about you." He swallowed and then let out a humorless laugh. "I'm really bad at this."

I shook my head. "No, no—this is good stuff. Please go on."

Jake moved his face closer to mine and moved his hand to the side of my face, gently cradling it so that he was looking into my eyes, and said, "I'm in love with you, Kate." Time stood still. "I've known it for a while now, but I had never wished I'd told you more than when I no longer could. I wanted you to know that I would fight to get you back, that I would never give up, never stop. I would have gone to the ends of the earth to find you." Even though I'd thought that I had cried all that I possibly could, tears leaked out of the corners of my eyes. "I barely slept while you were gone; I was plagued with nightmares of my own. Nightmares that someone was hurting you." His voice caught on that last sentence, and his eyes misted. "Then to find out that Richter was hurting you. I've never been so angry, I was trembling with it. It was everything I could do not to have Charlie turn that van around so that I could hunt him down." He sniffed and roughly wiped his face with his hand. "And the truth is, I knew that every single officer in that van would have been on board. They all love you, too, Kate."

"Do they love me the same way that you love me?"

He chuckled. "No. They love you, but I am *in* love with you." I laughed lightly. I had been teasing, but also, there was a part of me that wanted to make sure that I was hearing what I thought that I was hearing. A little clarification never hurt anyone. "Kate,"—Jake's hand that cradled my face became more firm, holding my head in place, making me look him in the eye so that I knew the words he spoke were true—"none of us would have left you there. Not one of us, but especially not me. As soon as Liam told us what had happened to you, that you had been picked up by the Feds and that the AGI was involved, we jumped into action. Every single person on the team. Scarborough included. We were all one hundred percent on board with finding you, above everything else." The tears came faster, and I knew this was turning into an ugly cry and I had no way of stopping it. Jake knew my fears. He must have been able to read them on my face when he was unbuckling my shackles.

I felt so many things: shame for how easily I had given up on him and the rest of the team, and also how awful it was to feel I'd been forgotten. There was no use denying it. "I'm sorry, Jake. I didn't want to give up on you, but I felt like I had to—for my sanity." He tried to shush me, to tell me that I didn't have to explain, but I did—I wanted to. "I didn't know how long I would end up in there, and I couldn't keep thinking that any minute you all would find me. The list of crimes that the AGI had set me up with was so long and so awful, I think I physically shrank every time they were read." I wiped at my eyes, but it was useless because the tears kept on coming. "The treatment there was so awful. No one cares about you, the guards purposely throw your food on the floor, if one can really call that food, so that you have to eat it like a dog, which is how they see you." I shook my head thinking about the hair and grime all over the floor of my cell, but I didn't want to go there. I wanted to put it all behind me. Never more so than when I saw those people dying today. It put things into perspective for me in an instant.

"Kate, what we witnessed today was awful; it was one of the worst things I've ever seen." I didn't know if I'd ever get used to him reading my mind like that. "But it doesn't make what you suffered through disappear. What you went through, the trauma that you experienced, that doesn't stop existing just because there are worse things that happen in the world." He swallowed. "Kate, when you were crying while I was removing your shackles, when you were crying while I held you on my lap? That was up there with my worst moments. I had failed you, the woman I love." His tears mixed with mine as they dropped on my face. "I hadn't told you how I felt and that you came first for me. And you thought I'd forgotten about you. I could *never* forget about you. You are it for me. You are everything. I am sorrier than I can express that you didn't know that before."

He put his arm under me and pulled me back into the crook of his shoulder and held me while we both cried. Right before I finally started to drift off, I said, "I love you too, Jake."

I heard him quietly say, "I know." And I smiled my way into a blessedly, dreamless sleep.

CHAPTER 49

Palo Alto, CA
Tracy

Tracy hit Enter on her latest blog post on *The Truth about Search*. She had been getting a lot of hits, mostly because she had worked at Search for so long that she knew how to market it. The people at the top of her marketing list were those who already distrusted Search. Many of them had blogs dedicated to educating the public about what Search was really about. Those bloggers salivated at getting information, firsthand, that validated what they had been preaching. From a former Search employee, no less. Even though her blog was anonymous, it was clear that she had insider information. They shared her blog posts on their sites, and in no time Tracy had a slew of followers.

Her phone rang, the caller unknown. "Hello?"

"Tracy Sinclair?" a male voice asked.

"This is she."

"Hi, Tracy. This is Officer Matt Sanders. I'm with the CIA, and I'd like to ask you a few questions regarding your time at Search."

Tracy's brows shot to her hairline. The CIA? "No offense, Mr. Sanders, but I'd have to see some identification before I answer any questions."

"I'd be happy to show you some identification. I'm outside your apartment building. If you like, you can meet me out here in public."

Whoa. "Am I in trouble?"

"No, not at all. We've been keeping up with your blog and just have a few questions. I won't take up much of your time."

She supposed that her blog being anonymous meant nothing to the CIA—they could probably find out who was behind anything, so there was no use denying it. His voice sounded nice enough, and if he really was with the CIA, then she wasn't likely getting out of his questions. Also, if he was CIA and she wasn't in trouble, then maybe Search was in trouble. Perhaps the government was looking into some of their practices, hopefully the invasion of privacy, which as far as she was concerned, they should be. "Okay, I'll meet you downstairs at the coffee shop across the street in five minutes."

"Thank you, Ms. Sinclair."

Tracy Searched up what a CIA badge looked like and then headed downstairs.

As soon as she saw the guy in the suit standing outside the coffee shop, she could tell it was him. He was tall, middle-aged, and very clean cut. He looked like he could have been the poster boy for the Central Intelligence Agency. She gave him her easy smile and put her hand out for him to shake. "Officer Sanders?"

He smiled without showing any teeth and put his hand in hers. "Ms. Sinclair. Thank you for meeting with me." He handed her a coffee and took his badge out of his pocket; it matched what she had seen online.

She nodded and took the offered cream and sugar packets. "I didn't know how you took your coffee."

She looked at him funny. "Why would you?"

He smiled then, fully. "It was just something to say." She laughed, and he continued, "I was hoping we could talk outside of the coffee shop, maybe a bench somewhere?"

With her hands full, she nodded her head to the left. "There's one down the block a little way."

They began walking, and Officer Sanders started right up. "How long did you work for Search?"

"I was there for five years. I got my master's while working there."

He nodded. "Why did you quit?"

"That's a short question with a very long answer. Let's just say that their practices didn't mesh well with my morals."

"That answer says quite a bit."

They arrived at the bench and sat, facing the sun. Squinting, Tracy wished that she'd brought her sunglasses. Officer Sanders looked over at her and continued his line of questioning. "Tracy, I've seen some of the things that bothered you when you worked there from your blog posts. What exactly was it that bothered you most in regard to privacy?"

She huffed. "What didn't bother me would be a much shorter answer." She chewed on her cheek and tried to think of what answer to give him. "They listened to people's conversations and then used those topics to market to them."

His eyebrows lifted slightly. "Sounds effective."

She rolled her eyes. "Sounds disturbing."

He nodded. "Quite. I've had it happen to me a time or two. But disturbing doesn't equal illegal."

"Right, it's in the privacy policy that no one reads. When you sign up for social media, they can utilize the microphone on your phone to their advantage. Search bought all of the social media giants so that they have the monopoly in the information business. They have access to what you do in your apps as well, *all of your apps*. They use that information to feed you information in just the right way to sway you in whichever direction they want. It's not illegal, but it should be." She angled her body toward his. "At the very least, the fact that they're spying on you should be more well known. I don't think that the public fully understands that if you don't pay to use a service then *you* are the product. *You* are what's being sold." She was on a roll now. "And just what of you is being sold? Your privacy, your autonomy. The price you pay is steep, far steeper than people realize. There are memes out there making light of this, but it's no joke. If they really knew what was being done with the information Search gathered, they would be outraged."

"Care to expound on that?"

"Is your phone on?" Hers wasn't, and she always kept a signal-blocking device plugged in it.

"Our work phones are built with blockers, but if it would make you more comfortable, I'll turn it off." She nodded that it would, so he pulled out his phone and turned it off and showed it to her. "Now care to expound on what you just shared?"

"They're using the intel to shape people's opinions, their thoughts and choices. And I'm not just talking about products, I'm talking about politics and the future of our country."

He nodded. "That's what we thought." He was quiet for a moment, and she so wished that he would share his thoughts with her. Instead he said, "Do you have anyone who is actively employed at Search that you are still close with, who might be willing to talk to us?"

She was quiet for a minute as she thought about Vinny—she didn't want to jeopardize his job or their budding relationship. But the idea that the CIA might step in and do something about Search's practices was too much for Tracy to pass up. "Vinny Rossi."

Officer Sanders thanked her for her time and handed her a phone. "This is a burner phone. It's untraceable. We, the CIA, are the only people who have the number. Please answer it when it rings. We will be in touch." With that, he got up from the bench and walked away without looking back.

CHAPTER 50

Minsk, Belarus
Kate

We landed in Minsk in the middle of the night. The flight had taken us almost twenty-two hours, including the stop we made for gas. A car was at the airport ready to take us to a hotel so that we could join the rest of our group that had already been in the city for the past eleven days. Scarborough was up, in the lobby, waiting for us when we got there. He gave us keys to our rooms—I was sharing with Lena. If I had to share with someone besides Jake, she was my top choice. "You all can go up to your rooms; we'll meet in my room at seven a.m. for you all to debrief and get assignments over breakfast." He looked down at his watch. "That's in just three hours, so go get some sleep." He smiled at us sincerely. "It's good to have you all back." We beamed back at him—that was as warm a welcome as I'd ever heard Scarborough give; he might as well have given us each a hug.

Jake walked me to my room and hugged me and kissed my temple; in my ear he whispered, "Love you." My eyes grew two sizes, and chills ran the length of my arms and legs, my smile wide. He'd said it so casually, like this is just how we talked to each other now. He pulled back and smiled at me. "It's true."

My smile turned mischievous. "I know."

"Touché." He laughed and turned to walk to his room. I watched him the entire way, my gigantic smile likely bordering on psychotic.

I opened the door as quietly as I could so I wouldn't wake Lena. But my efforts were wasted, because as soon as I walked in, Lena sat up, scaring me half to death, and said, "Kate! You're back!" She jumped out of bed and onto me like a spider monkey. Then she coughed and jumped off me as fast as she'd jumped on. "And you stink."

I laughed. "I know. I haven't been able to shower since I was in jail, and that was a pathetic excuse for a shower."

She sniffed the air again. "Ugh, it's permeating our whole room. You get some clean clothes from your suitcase—" My head whipped to where she was pointing.

"My suitcase is here?" I ran over and gave it a hug. "I'm so happy! I had no idea what I was going to do for clothes!"

Lena laughed. "It was already on your flight to Munich when you got picked up by the Feds. By the time my group got there, we had already heard from Liam about what had happened. I picked it up for you and brought it with me." I put the suitcase down and walked a few steps toward her. She held up her hand to halt my progress. "Please spare me the hug." Her nose scrunched up to remind me that I stank. "Get your clothes; I'll go turn on the shower for you. It takes a minute for the water to get hot here." Her fiery curls bounced while she walked into the bathroom. I put my stuff down and started taking off some of my layers of clothing.

Lena came out and literally pushed me toward the bathroom. As soon as I was inside, she said, "You've got one minute to get in that shower, and then I'm coming back in here to talk to you. So make it quick." She shut the door and I hurried—I knew that she was counting down the seconds until she came back in. I'd just hopped in and pulled the curtain closed when the door opened.

"Okay, girl, spill it. Tell me everything."

I poked my head out from behind the curtain. "You tell me everything. I hear that Brahim got back in touch?"

"Ugh, yes, and so far his intel has amounted to a big ol' fat nothing. Not a soul has come to pick up the mail." She could try to act tough, but I could hear the sadness in her voice.

"Lena, it's okay to be hurt by what happened."

"Well, that's good, because I am hurt. But I'm angrier than I am hurt, so that emotion wins out at the moment." I could almost hear her brain turning, so I waited for her to continue when she was ready. It didn't take long. "You know what really gets me? I could tell that something was wrong with him after we'd been rescued by the team in Montana, but no matter how many times I asked, he never so much as hinted at it. Why? What could they possibly have on him? Scarborough has asked him since, and he is so tight lipped about it. Brahim actually told Scarborough that there was nothing he could do to help the situation and that if Scarborough continued to ask, he would stop the communication. How could that be true? The CIA could help him. Why won't he even let us try? He knows this group is on his side—Scarborough has told him that he will do everything in his power to fix whatever it is they have on him. But the only thing Brahim says is that it's not something that can be fixed."

I poked my head out again so that I could see Lena when I talked to her. "It seems like you're feeling differently about Brahim than you were after the DNA Global debacle." When she'd told him that she would rip his throat out.

She pursed her lips while she thought. "Yeah, well I can be pretty hot headed." She cleared her throat. "Thanks for not killing him that day. It seems pretty clear that he is actually on our side. But for how long? How long until the AGI forces him to do their work?"

I frowned. "I don't know how long he can hold out. Hopefully, we can get him back before it's too late." I went back to my shower. "We are going to get him back—we're going to need his gifts if we want to bring down the AGI for good."

"The AGI or the NOS? Everyone keeps using them interchangeably, and I feel like we need to pick one and stick with it."

I laughed while I scrubbed my scalp with the shampoo. "I kind of use them interchangeably, too, but mostly I use the AGI when I'm referring to domestic things and NOS for the rest of the world."

"All right. We have a lot more to discuss, so hurry up in there, and come get in bed. I don't know if you saw, but there's only one. We get to snuggle."

I laughed as she headed for the door. I had noticed that there was only one bed, which didn't bother me. But I felt a little badly for the other agents that were sharing rooms—there were few that were as close of friends as Lena and me. I bet that there were a lot of agents sleeping on the floor. I finished my desperately needed shower and threw on sweats from my suitcase. They were too big—I had to cinch them tightly. I did eat some food on the plane ride, but having been so long since I'd eaten anything substantial, I intentionally didn't overdo it, worried that I might not keep it all down otherwise.

I came out of the bathroom and got into bed. We only had a couple of hours until we were supposed to meet up in Scarborough's room. I wasn't particularly tired, having slept for the bulk of the plane ride, and even if I were, it wouldn't have mattered—Lena had no intention of letting me sleep. "Okay, let's trade stories—one for one—and see how far we get. Deal?"

I laughed lightly; I didn't really want to tell any more of my stories, but Lena was a force to be reckoned with. "Deal."

She smiled. "I'll go first. When we got the news that you had been taken into custody, Lyon lost it." Maybe this trading stories thing hadn't been such a bad idea after all. "Girl, he lost it. I think that if Liam had been there in that moment, Jake would have killed the Hulk with his bare hands." Lena, Jake, and Mark had all been traveling together in the same small group. Scarborough, Candace, and Charlie in another. Liam and I were supposed to meet up with both of those groups in Munich and travel to Minsk together. The rest of the team were taking a different route. "Before Scarborough could get a word in, Jake told him in no uncertain terms that he was leaving to get you immediately, with or without permission and with or without a crew."

"Whoa." That was so unlike him—not that he wanted to find me but that he would put his job on the line like that.

"Scarborough stopped his tirade, though. He told him that he had no intention of leaving you there and that he was already planning to send a team to extract you. That calmed Lyon down somewhat, but I think he really needed someone to fight, to get out some of that manly aggression." I laughed at the very "Lena" retelling of the story. She loved a good drama. "Kate, I am not exaggerating; the man was on fire. Mad as hell. Anyway, it was decided that I would stay with Scarborough and help via computer, and Jake, along with Charlie, Candace, and Mark would travel back to meet Liam in D.C. Liam had never left, saying that he wasn't leaving until you were with him. He felt awful, Kate."

I shook my head. "I don't blame Liam. It was as much my fault as it was his. Also, if he were with me, we both would have been taken, and who knows how much longer it would have taken you all to find us. The whole thing was a mess, but it probably turned out as good as it could have." That made me stop to think for a minute. "Why wasn't Liam taken, I wonder? Richter knew that he was there. He tried to make me believe that they already had him."

"It was the surveillance feed from the airport. Liam was in the footage just minutes after you were taken. The AGI must have seen him, but it was too late, you were long gone. They had the person they wanted most anyway." She gave me a sad smile. "I'm sorry you had to go through what you did." She blinked slowly. "And for the record, I will kill Richter if I ever see him again." I swallowed, definitely not wanting to talk about Richter. "How are you doing with the aftermath of all that, really?" Lena was on the comm when I'd told them all what happened, but she hadn't talked to me about it face-to-face. She wanted my feelings, not the facts.

I blew out a breath, knowing I was going to have to talk about it with Lena eventually anyway; she wouldn't just let me off the hook. "Honestly, I think I'm as okay as I can be. I expect to have nightmares about it for years to come. But the worst never occurred—it could have definitely been worse." Those were the nightmares that plagued me the most, the ones in which Richter did his worst.

"Thank goodness it wasn't, but him touching you like that is so violating, and vile. Getting some therapy after this probably wouldn't be such a bad thing."

"You might be right. Honestly, being violated by Richter isn't what haunts me the most—it was being at his mercy. Being hand-cuffed and having no way to defend myself."

She smiled. "You did manage to break his nose, though." She threw her hands in the air. "Triumph!"

I laughed. "That did feel pretty good. But it also terrified me that there might be a punishment for that." Lena's smile faded and she nodded. "That was the worst part of the whole experience, not knowing what was going to happen next, having no control in the outcome of any situation. Prison is a violation of the senses, solitary even more so. I had to just sit there and wait; hope that you all would be able to get to me. I'm ashamed to say that I eventually lost that hope."

"Don't be ashamed of that, of being human."

I nodded. "I've always been a fighter, but I just gave up those last few days. I didn't get out of bed, didn't eat. I only got up to use the bathroom, since I didn't want to lie in my own filth—that, at least, was going too far. But I felt hopeless and scared of the future in a way that I never had before, not when my dad died, not when I found out that I had been implanted with the ICT. Never—I had never felt like that before."

Lena grabbed my hand and squeezed gently. "I'm so sorry, Kate. I'm sorry that happened to you. You got out, though; you're out, and that's the important thing."

"How did I get out, exactly? Jake filled me in on what happened while I was locked up, but between the update on the mission and what happened in Tahiti, he never got around to telling me the story."

Lena's smile widened, and she said, "I can do one better. I have it on video." She jumped out of bed and grabbed her laptop. We sat up against the headboard, and Lena found the file she was looking for and pressed Play.

I gasped. The clip was surveillance footage that was taken via camera that must have been worn by Jake—I could hear his voice, but I couldn't see him. When I heard him introduce himself to the president of the United States, my eyes felt like they were bulging out of their sockets. The feed showed his point of view, with Liam, Candace, Charlie, and Mark in the White House with the president. "What?"

Lena paused the footage and smiled at me like the Cheshire Cat. "Scarborough and President Connell worked together in the past. They have a good relationship. We have no reason to believe that the president is AGI, because Strands is running against him. Why would they replace a president that is already on their side?" I nodded. "Anyway, Scarborough called President Connell and told him that he had something top secret and of utmost importance to tell him. That he was sending a team of officers, as well as *William David*—you would not believe how much clout Liam gives us—to fill him in. He asked if they could meet privately. President Connell agreed, with the condition of one Secret Service member being present. Scarborough and I were present at the meeting over our comms, and Jake wore a video feed so that we could see what was happening." She smiled again. "I wasn't supposed to record the exchange, but since when have I followed rules?" She winked. "Okay, enough back story. Watch." She pressed Play again.

I watched as Jake told the president all about the AGI/NOS. Jake laid out the details beautifully—he was clear and concise and layered each fact in such a way that the truth of his story was evident. He used video clips to show the inside of the Montana AGI facility; he showed video of my ICT extraction surgery—I didn't know that video even existed. He played audio of me being tortured by Westwood, including the things Westwood told me about what the AGI really was. He brought the AGI employee files that I had scanned and uploaded to him back when this was all getting started. He told the president about them owning DNA Global and the connection to the recent epidemics. He told him about Search and Oliver Strands, Barbara Randall and Jay Conner. Everything. He laid it all out on the table. And as if all of that weren't enough, Liam threw the final punch. He told the story of his recruitment and how he had become an agent of the AGI, and how he eventually got out. The president, bewildered, asked Scarborough over the comm if this was all true. Scarborough confirmed that it indeed was. The president slumped back in his seat, his eyes wide. "What can I do?"

Jake spoke, "That's one of the reasons we're here, Mr. President. We're fighting with everything we have to rid the world of the AGI, but they have taken Kate Edison, the woman responsible for bringing this all to light." His voice was rough. "She is being held here in D.C. on charges that the AGI trumped up, and in order for this work to continue, we need to get her back." The ends of the earth, that's how far Jake said he would go to find me. He got a meeting with the president of the United States—he was true to his word. My eyes started to tear, unable to keep my emotions tethered.

President Connell responded, "I'll call the DOJ right now, get the charges dropped."

But before he could do just that, Jake spoke again, "We have to have this done covertly. For a few reasons. The first is that we know that there are employees within the Department of Justice that are AGI, but we don't know who." The president sighed and rubbed his forehead. "We also don't want the AGI to know you're involved or that you know anything about them. But the biggest reason this needs to be kept under the radar is because we believe that if the AGI gets wind of Kate having any possibility of escape, they will kill her." He paused. "We *need* her."

The president nodded. "What's your plan, then?"

Mark and Candace laid out the plan they had come up with. It started with Lena adding them all as employees within the D.C. Department of Corrections and ended with the president making a visit to the Department of Corrections on the same day requesting that as many employees of the DOC and of the local correctional facilities as possible be present. It would keep the DOC and the big guys at the local correctional facilities busy while they were infiltrated by the team of CIA agents. Lena would erase any evidence that Kate had ever been held or committed any crimes. She wouldn't simply have the charges dropped but would erase Kate's existence there entirely. None of the authorities would even know to go looking for her. The AGI would understand they had been bested and, not willing to do anything to garner public attention, would be forced to let it go or refile the charges at another time. The federal prosecutor would be the only person who would be informed—by Scarborough—that Kate was a non-official cover officer for the CIA and would no longer be held or prosecuted.

The president nodded and made the call to the DOC himself, setting the plan into motion. When the group got up to leave, the president shook each person's hand, and when he got to Charlie, he said, "I heard about the bullet train. Impressive."

Charlie preened. "Thank you, Mr. President, sir." And the feed cut out.

Lena shut her laptop and turned to me and said, "Tell me we don't work with the most awesome people on the planet."

I was speechless. What could I possibly say? They had met with the president of the United States for *me*. And it wasn't just Jake, who had feelings for me; it was everyone—including Scarborough. They thought I was important enough to go to the president for. I wish that I could go back to the Kate who was in that hard prison bed, depressed and hopeless, and tell her this. Tell her what she meant to her team.

Lena grabbed my hand again. "We love you, Kate. Not a single one of us was willing to leave you in there longer than it took to form and execute a working plan."

I nodded while a tear fell from my chin and hit my lap. Jake hadn't told me any of this. I wondered why. I turned to Lena and said, "Thank you for this. For showing me this, for helping me get out, and for being such a good friend."

She looked at me, her eyes shining with unshed tears. "I'm alive because of you, Kate. You have saved so many of us." She smiled. "And thanks to you, we are gonna save the world."

An hour later we walked into Scarborough's room. I went directly to Jake, who was standing next to the food table by himself. I put my finger in the pocket of his pants and tugged. He looked over at me, surprised. I got on my tiptoes, and in his ear I whispered, "I am completely and utterly in love with you, Jake Lyon."

CHAPTER 51

Minsk, Belarus
Kate

"Okay, we need four officers watching the post office today, one for every entrance," Scarborough, frustrated, announced that morning. We were meeting in Scarborough's suite for breakfast as had been the pattern since arriving in Minsk. It had been two days since my team had been back from Tahiti, and no one had been to the central post office to collect mail from the box yet. They had been monitoring daily for almost a week, and no one was saying what we all were thinking.

I finally did; I couldn't take it anymore: "Why are we not entertaining the idea that Brahim has given us misinformation?"

Scarborough sighed. "I've been the one communicating with him; he's sincere."

"Perhaps that's true, but maybe he has been fed misinformation, for the very fact that the AGI are worried that he'll pass it along." No one in the room wanted to believe that we had been sent on a wild-goose chase, but this constant monitoring of the post office was getting ridiculous. We didn't have this kind of time to waste.

"He was right about Tahiti being the next place hit," Fin piped up.

"That's true, but we got there way too late. According to Brahim's information, we should have arrived before they were hit, and we were at least three to four days too late. The symptoms were rampant already." Couldn't they see that things weren't adding up here?

Lena stepped forward. "Let me talk to him when he reaches out next. If things stay like they have been, we should hear from him at some point today between eleven and noon." Minsk was nine hours ahead of Mountain Daylight Time. Brahim usually got in contact when it was the middle of the night in Montana.

Everyone turned toward Lena—she had wanted nothing to do with Brahim since he'd left. But our conversation from the night that I'd arrived suggested that she was softening toward him at least somewhat. "Let me talk to him," she said again, this time with more confidence.

Scarborough nodded. "Fine, Lena will be here when he makes contact, but until we know anything different, we'll watch that post office box." I stifled a groan as he gave out assignments. Jake and I weren't put on post office duty that day, thank goodness. Yesterday had been a lesson in patience. I stood in the same spot, alone, hidden from the public, for nine hours watching the central post office's back door. I got one food delivery, courtesy of Lena. Today Jake and I would be acting like tourists and looking for any clues that might lead us to the lab.

Scarborough held up his hand. "Before you all go, Sanders has made contact with the blogger who started *The Truth about Search*. She is credible and sharp. He's trying to find any legal angle possible to stop Search. He has the name of a current employee and is going to attempt contact today. Hopefully, by the time you all get back, we'll have more information on that front." There were so many different entities in this AGI/NOS mess, it was hard to keep them all straight.

We all went our separate ways for our prospective assignments. Jake and I left the hotel and began to walk around in the early spring morning. It was the middle of April now, and the weather was mild, the city beautiful. It was incredibly clean. The sidewalks were so clean, I mused that they must have swept them several times a day. As the morning progressed, the sidewalks filled and the streets got busier, with people heading to work, kids to school, and people living their day-to-day lives. There were tourists from all over the world, but mostly the Baltic region of Europe. I heard a lot of Lithuanian and Latvian. I knew that Russian was the most common language spoken in Belarus, but I heard a fair amount of what I could only presume was Belarusian as well. There had been a revival of the Belarusian language in the 1990s, but Russian was still the most common language spoken in the republic.

Jake and I held hands as we strolled. We ate lunch at a café, saw some incredible sites, and basically got to act like two people in love for the day. We got to be normal, instead of officers of the CIA on a mission to save the world. The break was a balm to my run-down spirit. This work was hard and most often disappointing, so having an entire day to act like normal people was a gift that I soaked up every minute of. We kept our eyes peeled but never came across any suspicious activity.

It was late evening, the streets and sidewalks pretty empty, and we were on our way back to the hotel when Jake finally broached the subject. We were passing the Red Church when Jake squeezed my hand and said, "So, you are completely and utterly in love with me?"

"Yes." I didn't hesitate, didn't tease. It was the truth, and I wasn't going to deny it, not to myself nor him.

He stopped and looked at me. "You heard about our meeting with the president, didn't you?"

My brows lifted. "Were you trying to hide it from me? You had to know news like that was going to get out." He chuckled and looked somewhat sheepish. I play gasped. "You *were* trying to hide it from me!"

"Not hide it, exactly." He stopped, and his smile grew. "Yeah, I was trying to hide it."

I laughed. "Why?"

He kicked at the ground, his cheeks heating slightly. "I didn't want that to play a role in your feelings for me."

"Jake! Of course it's going to play a role in how I feel about you."

He looked at me then, the concern etched on his face. "I don't want you to love me because of what I do for you—I want you to love me because you just do. I want you to love me for the person that I am."

I took his other hand, facing him entirely. "Jake, don't you see that you are your actions? You have shown me who you are. And not just by your meeting with the president to get me out of prison." I tugged on his arms to bring him a little closer to me. "Jake, you have shown me who you are from the beginning. When I ran into you outside that coffee shop when I worked for the AGI, after the Jay Conner job? You were livid with me. You had every right to be. But even after I had seemingly stomped on your recruitment and left you with virtually no answers, you gave me your number and were willing to help me. You knew that something was wrong, and you were willing to look past what I had done to you, and your reputation, to help me. And months later, when I called you on your offer, you met with me immediately. And you believed my insane story about the AGI. *You believed me.* You helped me. You helped me in the middle of the night to uncover secrets about the AGI, and you helped me when I found out that I had been implanted with the ICT. You helped me mentally," I started to choke up, "when I thought that I was going to die any moment. And then you created this team and ultimately saved my life and thousands of others in the process." A tear coursed down my cheek. "So, yes and no, Jake. Yes, I love that you met with the president of the United States on my behalf. But no, that is not why I love you. I love you for the selfless person you are, for the man of action that you are. I love you for *who* you are, every single piece of you."

Jake cradled my face and used his thumbs to wipe away my tears. He opened his mouth to speak, but before he could say a word, I saw a movement out of the corner of my eye that had me screaming his name and pushing him out of the way. "JAKE! Behind you!"

After a split second of confusion, he turned, and there was a man to his left with a full syringe, the needle going right for Jake's arm. Jake grabbed the man by the arm that was holding the needle and kept it upright so that he couldn't get close enough to Jake to inject him. Jake used his other arm to punch him in the stomach and then again in the face.

The man went down at the very same time that I felt a needle pierce my skin. The world around me suddenly moved in slow motion. Everything became clearer—the sounds of the people eating in restaurants around us, the clinking of their glasses and silverware. I could hear cars go by and the water splash as the tires rolled through puddles; I heard kids calling for their parents and the sound of my own breathing that was like a freight train in my ears.

Time sped back up as I immediately pulled my arm away, but the attacker was prepared for that, and his hand clamped down on my arm like a vise. I screamed for Jake, but it was too late. I felt the needle go all the way in, felt the cold liquid of the virus as it was plunged into my body. The man whispered in my ear, his accent Russian, "This one is just for you, Kate Edison. Long live Novus Ordo Seclorum."

Jake looked over and saw the needle poking out of my bicep, the syringe plunged all the way down. His eyes went wild, and in a split second, faster than I'd ever seen a person move, he grabbed my attacker from behind, his arm around the man's throat, and yelled into his ear, "Where is the virus being made?" The man didn't answer. Jake bellowed, "WHERE?"

The man laughed and said, "It doesn't matter; you're too late."

Jake snapped his neck.

He then went back to the other man, his assailant, who was trying to get up, and Jake grabbed his neck and pointed it toward the dead man. "You're going to be next if you don't tell me right now where the virus is being made."

The man held up his hands and, in Russian, said, "I know nothing. That man paid me and gave me the needle, telling me to stick you with it. I am a street thug. I know nothing about any of this." He was telling the truth, even I could see that. Hasty, Jake had been too hasty in killing the first guy.

Jake cursed, then knelt down, gave him a card, and in Russian said, "There will be far more money in it for you if you can find any information at all about who that guy worked for"—he picked the syringe, full of virus that had been meant for him, up from off the ground—"and even more money than that if you can find out where this is being made." The man nodded twice quickly and scampered to his feet, running away as fast as his legs could carry him.

Jake came over and frantically searched the dead man. He had nothing on him but some cash. No wallet, no ID. He took a picture of him with his phone, to get an ID on him later, I surmised.

Jake looked over at me, his eyes still wild, a mixture of anger and fear. I hadn't moved, frozen to the spot where I had been injected. "Kate?"

I swallowed, took a deep breath, and closed my eyes for a moment. Jake pulled me into his arms, his breath racing in my ear. "Kate," his voice strained with emotion. "Please talk to me."

"Two days. I have two days before the symptoms begin."

CHAPTER 52

Minsk, Belarus
Liv

The woman in the hazmat suit waited by the door and watched. She had stuck Liv again, yesterday. She was always the one who made her sick, so Liv knew it was just a matter of time before her tired body was trembling with chills and fever. She knew it was only a matter of time before she wished for death.

But she didn't wish for death now. Her body had fully healed from the illness, thanks to time and the food stashed under her cot. She'd had enough food for days. Real food: dried fruit and nuts, foil pouches of meats, canned vegetables with pull-back lids, bread, and among other things, her favorite—peanut butter. She didn't know why he had left her so much food this time, but because of the abundance and the directions that the man had written on the food labels, she was smarter about how she consumed it.

She'd had classes about the Holocaust and remembered the story of the prisoners who were freed and ended up dying from eating. After that kind of starvation, people are prone to refeeding syndrome, which can cause sudden shifts in the balance of electrolytes and fluids. It could be fatal. There were gallons of electrolyte-infused water placed out of view of the window, at the end of her cot. And under her cot on top of the food was a small bag of vitamins and instructions on how to take them.

The woman watched her, like she was a zoo animal rather than a human being. Liv felt a renewed strength in her desire to get out, to get away and be with her family again. While the sickness brought on pain and hopelessness, the healing brought Liv's will to live to the forefront.

The woman came again the next day and watched from the window. Liv was surprised that she was still feeling normal—healthy, even. The woman came in her room and asked her, in heavily accented English, "Why aren't you sick yet?"

Liv didn't respond; she hadn't used her voice in so long, she wasn't even sure it would work. But the woman was right—she wasn't sick yet, not even a little.

The woman charged at her, grasped her by the shoulders, and screamed, "How are you still alive?"

CHAPTER 53

Minsk, Belarus
Kate

Jake had called Scarborough while we were on our way back to let him know about the dead body as well as me getting the virus. When Jake and I walked into Scarborough's suite, everyone was silent. They looked at me with pity, and fear. I hated both. The shock had worn off somewhat but not entirely. I still felt like I was living in a virtual reality, that this couldn't be my life.

I needed to rip off the Band-Aid and decided the best way to do it was to address everyone at once. "When he stuck me, he told me that the virus was made just for me, so I'm probably not contagious. If that's what you all are worried about."

Jake's head whipped from me to the group; his voice sounded like it was cut from ice. "Is that what you're all worried about?" he snapped at everyone. He'd barely spoken two words the rest of the way back to the hotel. He was stuck in his head, and I was, too. I thought we were both in shock, but Jake wasn't in shock, he was angry. So, so angry. The group's eyes grew at his tone and question.

Fin was the only one brave enough to answer. "Of course that's a concern, Jake. But she won't be contagious until the first symptoms hit anyway."

Jake lost it. "She's standing right here, Fin! You can talk directly to her!"

Fin nodded, acknowledging that he had been rude. "I'm sorry, Kate. I wasn't trying to act like you were already dead."

Jake went still, utterly still. "Say that one more time, Fin."

Fin recognized his mistake right away, and instead of trying to backtrack, he wisely kept his mouth shut for once. Jake was primed for a fight, and I think at the moment he hoped that Fin would say one more stupid thing and he would have an excuse to pummel him. In Jake's current mood, I was afraid he would lose himself and kill Fin; it wouldn't take much. Fin was lanky and untrained—Jake was an expert at hand-to-hand combat and corded with muscle.

I took Jake's hand and squeezed it. We would get nowhere like this. He looked over at me, and I tried to write that in my expression. He seemed to understand and nodded.

At that moment, Lena ran into the room and wrapped me in a giant hug, pulling my hand from Jake's. I hadn't even noticed that she wasn't with the group. "Kate!" She pulled me back so that she could look at me. "Are you feeling okay? Are you sore yet? Weak?"

I smiled. "Not yet. It will probably take a little time to set in."

She hugged me again and said, "We are going to find those scientists and get the antidote."

Jake's head whipped to Lena, and at the same time as me, he said, "There's an antidote?"

She nodded emphatically. "I was just on the comm with Brahim. He normally can't talk during the day, but I told him that it was an emergency. I told him that you had been given the virus and that if he ever loved me a day in his rotten, good-for-nothing life, he'd better find a way to fix this. He told me that there was an antidote. The scientists had created it early on in case either of them were somehow infected through their work, but also for the AGI to use on people they wanted to scare and not necessarily kill. If we find the scientists, we find the antidote." An antidote. There was an antidote. I let that word soak in, not sure if I wanted to hope but no longer having a choice. Hope had been born.

"Did you tell him that they haven't been by to pick up their mail?" Jake asked. He was wearing his high-ranking CIA officer expression now, the one that was pragmatic and smart. I liked it—it made me feel secure. Nothing stopped Jake when he was in this mode.

Lena nodded. "I did, and he told me that he would look into finding their address. He is going to get back to me as soon as possible. He did confirm earlier today that the lab is in a basement. He'd overheard it, and he believes it to be true."

Jake nodded and then looked at the group. "I have the syringe of the virus that was supposed to be given to me." He pulled it out of his jacket pocket. "Also, before I killed Kate's attacker, I asked him where the lab was. He said that it didn't matter because we were too late."

Scarborough said, "Too late?" Jake nodded. "I haven't heard any news of the virus being spread. We'll tell the president to hold a press conference in regard to the virus. It's time the world found out that it's man-made and how it's spread. It just might give the next place being hit a fighting chance."

Jake took his phone out of his pocket and sent everyone the attacker's picture. "This is Kate's attacker; let's see if we can get an ID on him, maybe find some information that way." Fin nodded and went directly to his computer. Jake turned to Scarborough. "I'm going out to look now. That lab is in this city, and I will scour every building until I find it." He looked at Scarborough, not for permission, I realized, because he was going with or without it. He looked to him for a plan.

Scarborough nodded. "Get me a map of this city."

A map was produced in minutes, and it was pinned to the wall. Scarborough scanned it for a few minutes and then started drawing up a plan of action. In just seconds, he, Jake, and Mark had the map split into sections, and everyone was paired off with a section of the city to search.

I noticed that I hadn't been assigned to an area. I cleared my throat. "Why am I not being sent out?"

The three of them looked over at me. Scarborough spoke first, "We don't know when you are going to start having symptoms; I'm not sure it's wise for you to be out in the city in the middle of the night."

I set my jaw. "I'm not having any symptoms yet, and *no one* is going to look for that lab as hard as I am. I want to go." Jake's eyebrows shot up. He may have disagreed that I would look harder than he would, but it was my life we were talking about.

Scarborough looked to Jake, as if he needed Jake's permission. I may have been in love with Jake, but he did not make my decisions for me. Jake was smart enough to say, "If Kate wants to go, I support it." He turned to me. "But I would ask that you go with me and Liam, just in case."

Just in case I got sick while we were out. I guess that was as good as I was going to get. I nodded.

With the city split into sections, each team got their assignment. Scarborough said, "Be thorough; I'd rather you get less of your area done, but be certain, than for you to go too quickly and have to search the entire area again. I probably don't need to say this, but by whatever means, the NOS know that Jake and Kate are here, so that means that we all could be compromised. Be careful out there, watch out for each other." Everyone left to search their assigned area. The entire team was out looking, except Fin and Lena. Fin so that he could research and Lena because she was waiting to hear back from Brahim.

Jake held my hand while we walked out of the hotel, the other officers around us trying to deduce how they knew we were here. There were many ideas thrown out, one of which was that we had another mole or that Megan had given too much away when trying to get information from Officer Reed. The most plausible answer, though, was that there were still NOS agents on the ground in Tahiti and they'd seen us. They could have easily gotten our flight plans from the air traffic control. We didn't conceal our destination. None of that mattered, though; I had been given the virus, what had been done was done. And finding out how they'd found me was moot.

When we got out of the hotel, each team went its own way. Liam gave my arm a squeeze, and I turned to look at him. "I'd ask how you're holding up, but that's a stupid question. So instead, I'm not going to ask you how you're doing. I expect you to tell us if you need to go back. I'll keep my opinions to myself." He gave me a tight smile. "If the tables were turned, nothing could stop me from trying to find that lab."

"Thanks, Liam." I appreciated his understanding. I think that some of the other officers expected me to stay back and wait for them to find help. They were the ones who didn't know me very well.

We walked our portion of the city. The only places still open were bars and some late-night restaurants. We scoured every basement window, getting down on our knees and rubbing the dirt off the hopper windows and using flashlights to see anything that we could. After hours of searching, we came up empty, and judging from the lack of noise on our comms, so did everyone else.

When dawn started to light the darkness, I became extra tired. I dragged on our way back to the hotel. I'd been up for twenty-four hours, which was reason enough to be tired, but I knew full well that the exhaustion was due to the virus infesting my body. I was a different kind of tired. To their credit, neither Liam nor Jake said anything when I slowed down slightly on the way back.

After congregating in Scarborough's room, we made a plan to get a few hours of sleep and go back out, seeing what we could see in the daylight, with the exception of a couple of officers staying up to watch the box in the central post office. I turned to walk to my room, but Jake stopped me. "Come with me?" I nodded and followed him to his room.

Whomever he had been sharing with had been kicked out. The room only had his suitcase in it. As soon as we got inside with the door closed, he pulled me to him, hugging me tightly. "We will find them, Kate." I nodded, hoping that he truly believed that and knowing that if it came down to sheer will, Jake would come out the victor.

He lifted my chin and looked at me. I could see oceans of pain in his eyes, deep and dark, a sadness so acute, it threatened to bring me to my knees. It was the first time since I'd been stuck with the virus that he showed me how he was feeling, and I almost wished that he hadn't. My own pain and sadness, I could handle. His would break me.

His eyes filled with tears. "I'm so sorry, Kate. I'm so, so sorry. I should have known that if they were coming for me, they were coming for you. I was so concentrated on taking out my attacker that I wasn't thinking straight. I wasn't thinking at all." His glassy eyes closed but not before a tear escaped, and I watched it while it ran down his cheek. "I didn't think, and it could cost me *everything*."

I wiped his tear. "Jake, this is *not* your fault. Using that logic, I'm as much to blame as you are. I wasn't thinking either. I stood there, panicked, my eyes tracking the syringe that your attacker was trying to put in your arm the entire time. I was ready to jump in if he got too close." I blew out a breath. "I didn't think about the very obvious conclusion—that someone was likely coming for me—either." He started to shake his head, but I cut off whatever he was going to say next. "Jake, look at me." I grabbed his face and held his eyes with mine. "None of that matters. It wasn't either of our faults. We didn't create the virus. The fault belongs squarely on the shoulders of the NOS. Directing our anger inward will get us nowhere. Let's let the blame and anger fall where it belongs, let it strengthen our resolve against them."

He took a deep breath and nodded. "You're right, as usual." I smiled. "I'm just so furious. The anger is so consuming, I can't get a handle on it."

I looked deeper into his eyes and pleaded, "Stop trying to get a handle on it. Channel it."

That seemed to resonate with him, and he hugged me close again. He pulled back just enough to lean in to kiss me, but I jerked my head back. The hurt and surprise were written clearly on his face. "Jake, we can't be positive that I'm not contagious. This virus is like Ebola, and if it transmits like Ebola, then it does so through bodily fluids. I'm not willing to take that chance. Not with you. I love you too much."

He deflated but nodded, knowing that there was nothing he could say that would change my mind. "Will you sleep in here with me?"

I nodded. "There is nothing I want to do more." He sighed in gratitude. "But as soon as I start having symptoms, I should sleep in a room by myself. Everyone should be careful about their interaction with me at that point."

He kissed my temple and said, "It's not going to get to that point." I wished that I were as confident as he was. He walked me to the bed and tucked us both in, me snuggling into him, enveloped in his woodsy scent. It was the happiest I'd been in days. If I had to die, dying in Jake's arms would have been the best way to go.

CHAPTER 54

Washington, D.C.
Oliver

Oliver Strands watched the president's address, his eyes threatening to bug out of his head.

"Through our Central Intelligence Agency, it has come to light that the virus that has been spreading in remote places around the world is man-made. So far the virus has been formulated for certain ethnicities, and we are saddened beyond measure to lose these unique and special cultures throughout the world. This virus can be formulated for individuals through DNA and can also be formulated for entire nationalities. The CIA is homing in on finding where this virus is being made, but until then we feel that it would behoove the world to tell all people how it is being spread. The more aware we are, the more vigilant we can be in eradicating this threat. The people who spread the virus carry backpacks with thin tubing coming from the pack." Pictures of people dressed as exterminators from various companies, though all with the same black backpacks, walking by themselves, flashed on the screen. "These are pictures of individuals we believe spread the virus on Easter Island. We have similar pictures from the Trobriand Islands; Motuo County, China; Tristan Da Cunha; and Tahiti. If you see anyone who is carrying a backpack like these, say something. Call the authorities; do not approach. We have reason to believe that they are now targeting larger and less remote parts of the world. We will have a federally mandated curfew, of nine p.m., beginning immediately. The local authorities, along with the military, will be scouring the streets looking for these terrorists. We encourage the rest of the world to follow suit. I repeat that we all must be vigilant to eradicate this threat. If you see something, say something. Please work with us to protect our great nation, as well as all the citizens of the world."

The television station flashed back to its regularly scheduled programming. Oliver turned off the TV. He could hear his racing heartbeat. He turned to Valentina, whose expression could only be defined as calculating. The day before flashed through his mind. He had been in the Capitol for a meeting with Congress. When he walked out, Valentina had been waiting for him. She was talking to an exterminator who had a black backpack on. In his hand, the man was holding tubing that came from the pack.

"The man that you were talking to yesterday, the one with the backpack. He was one of them; they're already here."

She didn't so much as look his way. "He very well might have been," she dismissed him, going back to her thoughts.

"We need to call the authorities."

Her head snapped in his direction. "We will do no such thing."

He thought that he was going to vomit—there was only one reason that she wouldn't want to call the authorities. "Is this the AGI's doing?"

She didn't answer, just sighed deeply.

The room started to spin. The AGI was killing people, innocent people, and now they were spreading the virus in America. "How? How could you be involved in this?"

She rolled her eyes. "Grow up, Oliver. Changing the world requires extreme measures." Bile burned up his throat. His shock and disgust were too much to contain. "Oh, stop with your innocent act. You knew who you were in bed with. You wanted fame and notoriety, and you got it. We gave that to you. You were nothing before the AGI, and you would have stayed nothing without us. You wanted this, and your hands are as bloody as ours. So no, you will not call the authorities; you will keep your mouth shut like a good lackey. We are taking out your competition—this is for you."

He ran for the bathroom and vomited. He'd seen the footage of the sick on those remote islands. He was part of that, he worked for the people who did that, and he was powerless to stop it. He vomited again.

CHAPTER 55

Cambridge, MA
Arthur

Arthur watched the press conference with the president from his home office. He turned off the TV and stared at the black screen. NexGen had been taking the DNA results from his company for this. To use it against people. They had encouraged him to buy up all of the smaller DNA companies around the world. Offering far more than they were worth, NexGen always there to convince him that it would ultimately be for DNA Global's good. That it would make DNA Global the most powerful name in DNA testing in the world. NexGen had encouraged Arthur to collect DNA samples from the world's most remote people, including, among others, every single area hit with the virus, so that the individuals who paid for their DNA to be tested got the most accurate results possible.

NexGen was behind this virus, but it would look to the world like DNA Global had sold individuals' test results to the highest bidder. Arthur sat in his study for an indiscriminate amount of time. He just sat there and waited.

There was a knock at his front door. His oldest daughter answered it. He heard a male voice, heard her say that she'd be right back. Timidly, she entered his study. "Dad? There are some FBI agents here to see you."

CHAPTER 56

Palo Alto, CA
Vinny

Vinny was slowly making his was to Tracy's apartment for their date. Earlier when the president had made his announcement, Search had gone crazy. Some people were calling for the news to be put above the sponsored ads so that everyone had a chance to see it as quickly as possible. Others wanted to bury it, concerned that every citizen with a backpack would be targeted as a terrorist. Others still thought that it wasn't Search's responsibility to spread the government's news and that there was no evidence that this was hitting the States yet. The powers that be decided to sit on it and work as usual. That the cable news would have it on their websites and it would be easy to find via Search or any other outlet. They wouldn't bury it, nor would they promote it.

Vinny thought anyone who wanted to do anything aside from spread the word was insane. Disgusted, he walked out, and he wouldn't be coming back.

He was chomping at the bit to see Tracy. He wanted to help her with her blog about outing Search. Vinny had finally had enough. She'd told him what she was up to during their last couple of dates. She was excited and proud about outing Search to the world. And she was making money, which she certainly hadn't expected. There was a bit of buzz about Tracy's new blog at work, but most people shrugged it off. One ex-employee against the gigantic company would amount to less than nothing. He wondered if anyone there suspected it was Tracy behind the blog, because Tracy wasn't just any ex-employee—she was a force to be reckoned with. She was a research and behavioral scientist of the best kind. Her ideas, when they'd worked together, blew his out of the water. Even when she played volleyball half the day, she still got as much work done as he did.

Their dates had been even better than Vinny had anticipated. They hardly talked about work. They talked about themselves, their families, and what they wanted out of the future. They had gotten to know each other on a whole new level. And Vinny liked everything about Tracy. Her legs were no longer his favorite thing about her—not that he liked them any less, they just took a back burner when compared to the rest of her. She was a good person, an honest one. She loved her family and always put the greater good above herself. Vinny had a lot of work to do to be worthy of Tracy, but he was more than willing to make the effort.

When he pulled up to her building and saw a car pull out of a spot right in front, he breathed a sigh of relief. The last couple of times he'd been to her apartment, he'd had to circle the block several times before he found a spot to park. The six-mile drive had already taken a lifetime. He hated California traffic. Not enough to move back to the Bronx, but there was certainly something to be said about the subway system. Vinny walked up to Tracy's apartment and found her door cracked. He knocked lightly. Tracy didn't answer, so Vinny opened the door slightly and called out to her. She had a studio apartment, and you could see the entire place from the front door. Tracy could have been changing her clothes or something, and as much as Vinny would've liked to have seen that, he didn't want to appear like some weird creeper. "Tracy?" he called out. No answer.

Vinny's brow creased in concern. "Tracy? I'm coming in," he called to give her fair warning. He opened the door all the way and saw blood pooling on the floor on the far side of her bed. "Tracy!" he yelled and ran to her side. What he saw had him stumbling to his knees, pulling out his phone, and dialing 911. His pants soaking in her warm blood.

"This is nine-one-one, what's your emergency?"

"My girlfriend's been shot." His voice echoed in his ears, sounding hollow. She looked so small, so fragile, the ends of her blonde hair soaked red.

"Where are you located?"

Vinny gave the emergency operator Tracy's address.

"The emergency vehicles are on their way."

Vinny was hyperventilating. "W-w-what c-c-can I do to help her?" He could hardly force the words off his tongue. He'd never been angrier at his stutter than at that moment.

"Where was she shot? Is she still bleeding?"

It was hard to tell, there was so much blood everywhere. He looked around her body and saw that blood seemed to be pumping from her shoulder. "Um, it l-l-looks like she w-was shot in the sh-sh-shoulder. St-still bleeding."

"Okay, stay calm. You will be no help to her if you are panicked." Vinny tried to calm his breathing. "Use a towel, shirt, anything you can find to stop the bleeding. You need to put pressure on it, a lot of pressure. Use both hands."

He didn't hesitate to pull off his shirt and scrunch it into a ball and press down hard. She twitched in discomfort, and he yelled into the phone, "She moved!" More quietly and almost on a sob, he said again, "She moved."

"Okay, that's a good sign. Keep the pressure on—the loss of blood is the most dangerous thing right now. The ambulance is just a few minutes away. I'll stay on the phone with you until they get there."

True to her word, the operator stayed on the phone with Vinny, telling him that people survived gunshot wounds every day. After what felt like hours but was probably minutes, the paramedics arrived. They moved him out of the way, and one expertly applied pressure while the other two checked her vitals and declared that her heart was still beating, then lifted Tracy onto a stretcher. Vinny's shoulders slumped with relief. He started to follow them out the door, and the paramedics asked if he was family. He said no, that he was her boyfriend, stretching the truth for the second time that day.

They said that only family could ride in the ambulance but gave him the name of the hospital so that he could meet them there.

They could hear sirens coming down the road—police officers, most likely. The paramedic who was putting pressure on Tracy's shoulder said, "That's the police; they're going to want to question you. If you ask, they may do it at the hospital so you can continue to receive updates on her care." The paramedic looked at Vinny's crumpling face and said, "We'll take good care of her." Vinny watched as they rolled her down the hall to the stairs.

It was only then, in the silence, that he noticed a ringing phone. He went in search of it, thinking that it was Tracy's. He found a phone that wasn't hers, one he didn't recognize. Could the phone belong to the person who had shot her? The phone stopped ringing and then started up again almost immediately. With no small amount of trepidation, he answered, "Hello?"

There was a pause on the line. "Vinny Rossi?" Vinny pulled the phone away from his ear and looked at it. Was he on camera? How could this person possibly know it was him? "Is that you?"

"This is Vinny," he said slowly.

"Vinny, this is CIA Officer Matt Sanders. Are you with Tracy? Is she there? I need to talk to her—it's an emergency."

The CIA? What had Tracy gotten herself into? "Tracy's been shot. She's on her way to the hospital."

The officer cursed. "Vinny, keep this phone. I'll be in touch." Then he hung up.

He put the phone in his pocket just seconds before the police appeared at the door.

CHAPTER 57

Minsk, Belarus
Kate

I woke up after our allotted three hours of sleep more tired than I had been to begin with. "Kate? It's time for us to go back out." Jake softly caressed my face. For a minute I almost forgot that I was dying. But it all came crashing back when I could feel a tenderness in my muscles that hadn't been there before. I decided to ignore it. I opened my eyes to Jake's face hovering over me, and I smiled. "Are you up for going back out? You can stay sleeping if you want to."

I really did want to, but I refused to give in to the virus. I forced myself up to a seated position and rubbed my eyes. My muscles felt so tired, my legs in particular, but I threw them over the bed and let Jake help me to standing. "Are your muscles sore?"

I nodded, figuring that I might as well tell him the truth. He deserved that much, but also, he could probably read it on my face anyway. "Yeah, I'm a bit sore; I think I'll feel better after I get moving."

He smiled sadly and kissed my cheek. "I'm not sure it works like that."

Before leaving, we gathered in Scarborough's room to get our instructions. "Several things have transpired in the last few hours. President Connell had a press conference at one a.m. this morning, six p.m. Eastern Daylight Time—since then several pictures with exterminators carrying black backpacks with tubing attached have been turned in to the local authorities. All pictures were taken in Washington, D.C., yesterday, around the Capitol Building. They were there while Congress was in session. No reports of any illness yet, but we expect them to start coming in shortly. Congress, as well as everyone else who was in the Capitol Building yesterday, is under strict quarantine." He gave us a minute to let that sink in, then continued, "Arthur Whitehall, the CEO of DNA Global, is under arrest for giving out the DNA results of their customers and breaking their privacy policy. And last but not least, Tracy Sinclair, the former Search employee and owner of *The Truth about Search* blog, has been shot and remains in critical condition. Megan found out through Reed that the AGI was going after the blogger. She told Matt Sanders, but he got ahold of her minutes too late. Vinny Rossi, Tracy's former coworker and boyfriend, has agreed to talk to Matt; he will keep us posted." I wanted to growl—how could we always be so behind?

Scarborough wasn't done, though. "We haven't heard from Brahim since yesterday. We hope to hear from him at our usual time"—he looked at his watch and said—"in about an hour. Lena will let us know if and when he calls and pass on any updates." He blew out a breath and said, "Let's get back to looking for that lab."

Jake, Liam, and I headed out. We walked a mile, and my legs felt like they might buckle under my weight. Both Jake and Liam could see that I was struggling, but Liam, true to his word, didn't say a thing—he didn't so much as give me a questioning look. He was letting me decide how far I was going to push myself. Jake, on the other hand, had made no such agreement. "I'm calling a ride share; we don't need to walk the whole way." I was so grateful that I didn't even act like I didn't need it.

After arriving at our assigned area, we started where we'd left off the night before. We were in a seedier part of town, and being there in the day felt a little safer. We searched and searched for the lab, with me forcing my exhausted legs to just go a little farther, and then a little farther after that. By the time we reached the end of our territory, I was at the point of collapse. The ache in my legs was merciless.

Jake held me up, with my arm around his shoulder, while Liam got us a car. I wanted to cry, and not because I was in pain, though that was worthy of tears in and of itself. But the pain meant that the virus was infecting my body and I was that much closer to death. I felt like I was having symptoms much faster than I should have. I said as much, and Jake nodded. "I wonder if because the virus was made specifically for you, the reaction time has sped up."

That made sense. It seemed that in the places where the virus had hit, it took on average a couple of days for the symptoms to start. Perhaps when it was formulated for one person, it was stronger and the reaction was faster. In addition to the symptoms starting quickly, I also felt that they were evolving faster as well. I knew from my research that the muscle weakness came on first. I'd had muscle weakness before, but never like this. Nothing had ever felt like this. My legs weren't merely sore—it didn't feel like muscle soreness; the pain felt like it was in my bones. It was a deep and resonating pain that clanged and reverberated throughout my body with every movement. The rest of me felt okay, though, so I dealt with it. But I knew it was only a matter of time before the fever set in.

Jake helped me into the car. Sitting at first felt like a relief, but then my legs became restless, and they moved of their own accord— small movements, but it hurt all the same. The pain wouldn't quit. It was frustrating and disheartening. I didn't want the virus to win, I didn't want the enemy to win, but I had only so much control. And what little I had was running out. We got back to the hotel, and Jake carried me up to his room. He laid me on the bed and looked me over with that deep sadness in his eyes again. He touched my brow. "I'm going back out. I can't sit, or rest, I have to work, I have to keep looking. Is that okay? Are you okay here without me?"

I smiled as much as I could and nodded. "I love you, Jake."

"I love you, too." His voice choked, and he had to look away. I wanted to ease his pain, to tell him that it would be okay, that I would be okay, but lying had no place here. I was not okay, and odds were that I wouldn't be. He held my hand for a moment and then walked out, wiping his beautiful face as he went.

Not long after Jake left, my phone rang. It was a video call from Dr. Bakshi. I answered, "Hi, Doc."

He smiled sadly. "How are you, Kate? Tell me everything you're feeling."

"I'm not great. I'm really tired and sore. So sore. The ache in my legs is intense."

He nodded. "Fever?"

"Maybe just starting. I don't have a thermometer, but I'm feeling a little warm." I could also tell from the forward-facing camera on my phone that I was flushed.

"We have a few members of Congress that are fighting it as well; they were hit just before you were. I've examined them, and we are fighting it the best we can. I've ordered you some medications that have worked well with other viruses in hopes that it will give you all more time. Scarborough is doing everything he can to find the lab. Hang in there. We're all rooting for you."

I smiled as much as I could. "Thanks, Dr. Bakshi."

It didn't take long until I started to feel truly feverish; then the chills began. They racked my sore body, and I shook violently. So violently that I began to whimper, and I wished for anything to help my body to calm down. I was so hot and the chills so strong that I lay there, wondering how long this process was going to take. How much time did I really have?

I allowed myself a moment to just feel sorry for myself. For the situation I was in. I was sick, and unless something changed really fast, I was going to die. I felt sorry for those people in the world who had already died of this awful disease. It was one thing to see it happen to someone else but another to feel it happen to you. Both were awful—the first caused me intense sadness; the latter made me realize how very much I wanted to live and how terrible it was when life was cut short.

I remembered my mom always saying "Life's not fair." And it certainly wasn't. Me dying wasn't only unfair to me but also to my family. Who would tell them? I hoped it would be Jake. I wanted him to meet them, and them to meet him. They would love him, and I think he would get a kick out of Lizzy. Maybe those two would end up together. That thought caused me an intolerable amount of anguish. I wasn't sure why. I loved them both and wanted their happiness, but I just didn't want their happiness to be found together. I let myself wonder what my sweet nephew would grow up to be like. If he was anything like my brother, then the world was lucky.

I let myself think briefly of my mom. She had already been through so much at the hands of the AGI. When she learned that they had taken me, too, I hoped that it wouldn't be too much for her. I hoped that it wouldn't dim the light in her eyes. She deserved more—a better, happier life. But life wasn't fair.

Before long, I was feeling a new symptom: my head began to hurt like I was having a migraine. I picked my phone up off my bedside table and called Lena. She answered on the first ring, "Kate?"

My teeth were chattering, and I had a hard time getting words out. "Jake's . . . room . . . painkiller."

"I'm on it. I'll be right there."

She let herself in a few minutes later. "We're still waiting on the meds Dr. Bakshi called in. I've only got Midol, but it's a pretty awesome pain re—" Her words cut off when she laid eyes on me. "Oh, Kate." She looked me up and down, and her eyes filled with tears. "Kate," she said my name like it was causing her physical pain. I must have looked as bad as I felt. "I'm so sorry, Jake left me his key and asked me to check up on you while he was gone. So many things have happened that I haven't gotten in here yet, and you have been suffering. I'm so sorry." She closed her eyes for a moment and took a deep breath and then opened them again. Her eyes had cleared of their tears, and she sat down by me. "Come on, let's get you up so that you can take this. It will help."

She put her arms under my shoulders and lifted me up, stacking pillows behind my back. She set me gently back against the cushions and gave me four pills with a glass of water. "It says that you're only supposed to take two, but I think this situation calls for extra." My hand was shaking so hard that the water kept sloshing over the top of the glass. Lena took it back. "Here, let me hold that for you." I put the pills in my mouth, and she held the water up so that I could drink them down. Then she came around to Jake's side of the bed and sat next to me.

"I don't want you to get sick."

"You aren't contagious. Brahim confirmed it. It would spread like wildfire, and that's not the intent of the NOS." I nodded that that made sense, and for a moment I really regretted not kissing Jake when I'd the chance the night before.

"Brahim?"

She nodded. "I talked to him earlier today; he didn't have too much information, though he says he has been trying as hard as he can to find out where the lab is. The good news is that we finally had a hit on the mailbox." I sat up straighter. "It was a woman, in her thirties-ish. Pretty, to boot. Candace was on post office duty today, and she followed her home to an apartment that she apparently shares with an older man. Candace had been up for thirty-six hours when she called it in on her comm. She got pictures of them both and neither of them can be found in our database, or any database for that matter, which makes us all believe that they are indeed the scientists that we're looking for. Jake, Liam, and Mark left right away to relieve her. Candace is back now, and she said it looked like the woman was coming home from work. The hope is that they're going back to work tonight; they want to catch them at the lab, if at all possible. We want to burn that place to the ground, after we get the antidote, of course. If they aren't going back to work tonight, then they'll take them from their apartment and do what they have to do to get the information we need."

I had a chance. I had a possible fighting chance. It was almost too much to take. The hope consumed me in seconds.

Lena grabbed my hand. "That's why I hadn't been in to check on you. It's not a good enough excuse. Lyon certainly won't think so." She cringed.

Lena's exaggerated fear of Jake's wrath was enough to make me smile. Through my chattering teeth, I said, "We won't tell him."

Lena laughed, and it made me happy. I loved the tinkling sound of her laugh. I had good friends here—people I loved and a man that I was in love with. I grabbed Lena's hand. "Call Jake. I want to go with them tonight."

I thought she would look at me like I was crazy, like there was no way she was letting me out of this bed. Instead, she smiled widely—"That's my girl"—and made the call.

Jake was there within the hour to get me. And even the sight of me, sick as I was, couldn't dampen his mood. He was smiling from ear to ear. "We found it, Kate. We found the lab. It's really close to our search area of the city, in the seedy part of town. It's in the basement of an abandoned building. The hopper windows have all been covered over so that no one could see anything when they tried to look inside. Liam and Jake are waiting for us to go in." He let out a small sigh. "You're going to be okay."

I smiled back, not only because I was happy that they'd found the lab but also because seeing Jake with a smile that took over his face was contagious. He helped me sit up and gave me some pills. "These are from Dr. Bakshi—he says that they're helping infected members of Congress. It's not a cure, but it's making a difference." I winced as I swallowed them down with water; my throat was on fire.

He looked at me in the bed. "Can you walk?"

"I think so." I focused my effort on getting my legs over the side of the bed. And then with Jake's help, I got to a standing position. My body felt like it weighed a thousand pounds, and my legs felt like little sticks expected to carry that weight across the world. Jake looked down at the rash growing on my arms and pulled one of them closer to his face so that he could examine it.

The abrupt change in balance made me sway, and Jake caught me. "Whoa. Are you sure you want to go?"

I bit my lip. "I think I need to go. The virus is progressing much faster than I expected, and I think I need that antidote as soon as possible in order for it to work. If the virus progresses too far, the antidote won't be able to save me."

Those were the magic words, because Jake picked me up, one arm beneath my knees and one behind my head. "I'm going to carry you so you can conserve your strength." I nodded, humiliated, but not enough to make me change my mind.

Jake had a car waiting for us outside the hotel. He helped me in, and Charlie turned from the driver's seat and smiled at me—he always had one at the ready. Charlie was great like that. "Let's get you that antidote, Edison." We were off racing for the lab. We took alleys and roads that I didn't think were actually roads, but with Charlie at the wheel, I knew that we were perfectly safe.

Jake used one of his hands to hold mine and the other to drum on his thigh, his excitement and adrenaline spiking. I loved that feeling, the blood rushing through your body, the high before and especially after a mission. I wasn't exactly feeling that now, not with my body in its current state, but I was no longer feeling hopeless. And that hope was worth more than any mission high. If this didn't work, if there was no antidote, then that hope would black out, but I was grateful for it in that moment, anyway. I turned to Jake. "Excited?"

He laughed. "Just a little. I'm more than excited, though; I'm anxious. I don't like to celebrate until a job is over, but the thought of you getting better makes me happier than words can adequately express."

I chuckled, but it turned into a cough. My hand came away bloody, and Jake, no longer smiling, looked at my hand and then my face, and while still looking at me, he said, "Faster, Charlie."

CHAPTER 58

Minsk, Belarus
Liv

The man who had kept Liv alive came to check on her. Liv hadn't realized that she was supposed to be dead, not until the woman told her as much. He was doing it behind the woman's back. Why? She looked at him this time; she usually didn't bother. Why was he doing this? Why keep her alive against the woman's orders? Why keep her alive at all?

He checked Liv's vitals and smiled and lifted his hazmat mask off his face. It was the first smile she'd seen in a long time. It was the first face she'd seen without a mask in a long time. He spoke to her in his heavily German-accented English, "I gave you my vaccine this time, after giving you the antidote. Aksana used different variations of the virus so that each time she gave it to you, you were susceptible." He patted her shoulder. "But the vaccine worked against the mutated virus. I am a genius, and you are going to be just fine."

Liv almost smiled, but she wasn't sure she knew how to anymore. She did, however, say the first word she'd said in months: "Why?" Her voice was scratchy, barely understandable from the disuse.

If he was surprised that she spoke, he didn't act like it. "Because it's too dangerous. This virus could mutate on its own and kill ninety percent of the population. It was a stupid idea, a dangerous way to gain power, and I decided when they brought you in that I

302

would no longer be a part of it." He smiled again, but it was a sad smile. "Aksana would never get on the right side of things—she enjoys the science too much and has lost her humanity in the process."

It was as much as anyone had talked to Liv in months. It was strange, almost jarring, to have someone in real life talk to her like she was a normal person.

She wanted to say one more thing, she wanted to thank him. But before she could get the words out, there was a commotion.

Foreign sounds coming from down the hall. Liv heard voices, voices that weren't screaming for help. She heard voices of action. They were Americans.

The man who'd saved her jumped up from his seated position and bolted out the door.

He'd left it open.

CHAPTER 59

Minsk, Belarus
Kate

Liam picked the lock on the door to the lab and silently swung the door open. Jake, who had been holding me, put me down and handed me a gun. My legs were shaking like the last leaf hanging on a tree in the fall, but I used every ounce of strength I had left to keep myself upright.

I took the first steps on my very uncertain legs. One of my knees threatened to buckle, and Jake put his arm around me to hold me up.

The door led to a vestibule made of cloudy plastic sheets. There were street clothes on hooks and stacks of scrubs encased in plastic, like they were brand new, in a large container. There wasn't much else. Liam's gigantic feet were utterly silent as he led us through the draped plastic sheeting. The first vestibule led to a second—this one had two shower heads for decontamination. Which meant that beyond this vestibule would be the lab. I shrugged off Jake's arm, knowing that he needed his whole body in order to do his job from here on out. He looked back at me, and I nodded, letting him know that I was okay to stand on my own. I had received a much-needed shot of adrenaline from my body—even in its sick state, it had finally caught up with what I was doing.

Liam hit his comm on and opened the next plastic sheet and shouted, "CIA, put your hands up." We all filed into the room after him, no longer concerned about silence. A dark-haired woman was there, in a class A hazmat suit. She was holding up a silicone pouch, much like an IV bag, but thicker, full of liquid. The bag had skinny black tubing hanging from it, and she was pointing the tubing at us.

Liam shouted, "Put the virus down, and put your hands in the air."

Mark repeated the phrase in Russian, and the woman scoffed and replied in very good English, "You think I don't understand you? Can you understand this? Stay back or I will poison all of you." Her voice came out slightly muffled from behind the mask.

She had already made the decision to use the virus, though. The bag must have been filled with a type of the virus that infected all humanity. The liquid started to spray, and the woman received four bullets. Two in her head and two in her chest right over her heart. She dropped dead, but it was too late. The virus was in the air, and we were all too close not to get infected. For me it didn't matter, but I was livid for Liam, Mark, and Jake. I didn't want them to suffer like I was. I didn't want them to die. I was more determined than ever to find that antidote. I would rip that place apart if I had to.

There was a door with a window at the back of the lab, and I saw a flash of movement through the window. I shouted, "The door!" and everyone looked just in time to see it open. An older man, the woman's partner, was standing there.

We all had our guns trained on the man's face in a flash. He had a hazmat suit on but no mask. Jake shouted, "Hands up!"

Then a girl, a teenaged girl, came up beside him. She was little more than skin and bones—her face was gaunt, her eyes huge in comparison to her sunken face. She had long, dark hair that was stringy and dirty and thinner than it looked like it would normally be. She said, "Don't shoot." It came out somewhat garbled, but I could detect her American accent.

I gasped, "Liv Barker?"

Her face crumpled. She nodded, and sobbed, and nodded some more. I used all of my energy to limp over to her, tears instantly welling in my eyes. I pulled her into me. She weighed next to nothing. I put my arms around her bony frame, holding her close while she shook with sobs.

I looked over at Jake, in shock, my face wet with tears. Liv Barker was still alive. This was an outcome that I had never thought possible, had never even imagined. Jake's and Liam's eyes shone with unshed tears, and Mark, who had daughters of his own, had tears streaming down his face while he filled in Scarborough and Fin over his comm.

The man looked at me and said, "You need the antidote." It was a statement, not a question. It was clear enough to him that I was sick with the virus.

Liam's and Jake's guns were still trained on him, and Jake said, "Where is it?"

Liv put her skinny arm out in front of the man and said, "He"—she cleared her throat; she seemed to have to concentrate in order to speak—"saved me."

I pointed to the scientist. "He saved you?" She didn't look very "saved" to me. She had been starved and sickened, and who knew what else.

She tried to talk some more but got upset that the words weren't coming out right. The scientist spoke instead, "I gave her the antidote, regularly, after she was given the virus by Aksana." He motioned to the dead woman on the floor. "I gave her the vaccine that I'd made most recently, and her body hasn't succumbed to the virus since."

Liam spoke then, "There's a vaccine? Does the antidote not work like a vaccine?"

The scientist shook his head. "Not in this instance. The antidote kills the virus; once the virus is gone, then your body heals itself. The vaccine is made the traditional way, and I was able to formulate it for variations. It won't work for the actual Ebola virus, only the one made by Aksana and me. My name is Johan."

"Why make a vaccine in the first place?"

"I was never supposed to; it was something I've been working on in secret. Something to help, if the virus led to pandemic."

"Where is the antidote?" Jake asked, getting down to business.

Johan pointed to the corner of the lab. "It's in the refrigerator. I'd be happy to administer it."

Liam stepped forward. "We'll administer it ourselves."

Johan nodded once. "The antidote are the syringes with the blue caps. The needles are in the drawer over there." He pointed to a set of plastic drawers.

Jake holstered his gun and went to the fridge, got the antidote, and held it up to look at it. The virus had been yellow, and this one was clear. Mark said, "How can we trust him?"

I coughed, and blood splattered my hand and ran down my chin. Johan pointed to me and said, "It appears you have no other choice."

Liv Barker squeezed my arm and said, "It's the . . . it's the right one."

That was enough for me. I nodded to Jake, and he grabbed a needle, screwed it on, and walked over to me. He looked me in the eye and said, "You sure?"

I nodded, and he stuck me in the arm with it, emptying the syringe completely. It was somewhat anticlimactic. I felt no change, not that I expected to, but I had certainly hoped that my pain would magically disappear. I prayed that it would go to work fast. I told Jake, "Each of you need to take that—there was virus in the air."

Jake nodded, and he administered the antidote to himself, Mark, and Liam. He then turned to Johan. "How long until we can take the vaccine? Where is the vaccine?"

Johan cleared his throat. "You can take the vaccine when you are fully healed. I will give you everything, all the vaccine and the antidote that I have as well as the formula. I only ask that you deal with me the same way you dealt with Aksana." He wanted us to kill him?

Mark shook his head. "We can't do that. That isn't how we operate. We will have to take you into custody. Besides, we will need your help mitigating the spread of the virus and making the vaccine and antidote correctly. The virus has been spread to several within Congress already."

Johan slumped his shoulders and shook his head. "They will find me and take me back and force me to remake the virus. I can't be left alive."

I turned to him. "I used to work for a sect of the NOS too. They're looking for me as well, and so far this group of CIA officers has managed to keep me safe."

Liam said, "Me, too, and we aren't the only ones—there are others, and we all fight against them now."

Johan's brow furrowed. "Impossible. Whoever you worked for must be keeping it a secret from the board."

My brow raised in question. "The board?"

"Yes, the leaders of the NOS. There are six of them, representing the seven continents minus Antarctica. They have changed over the years, but there are always six. If they knew about you, you would be dead. No one leaves and lives to tell the story."

Johan had just sealed his fate—he was coming with us. He knew more about the inner workings of the NOS than any of us did. And that was knowledge that we could use.

Jake said, "We need to take you with us. If they come for you, we promise to kill you rather than let them have you back. Is that fair?"

Johan shrugged; he wasn't pleased, but he seemed to understand that it was the best he was going to get, and it spurred him into action. "We need to go, then, they could be here anytime." He pointed to the fridge. "Get the remaining antidote, and the vaccines—they are the red-capped syringes—and put them in the cooler. They must stay cold to be effective. The formulas are here." He handed Mark a notebook.

Jake, Liam, and Mark packed up what we needed from the lab, and then Johan said, "There is one more thing." We looked over at him in question. "There may be people still alive in the testing rooms. They will need the antidote." We looked at each other in horror, and Jake grabbed a few of the syringes and needles.

We went back into the hall. I hobbled along with Liv, the guys well ahead of us, and looked in the windows—the rooms were empty. That was when we heard the gunshot. Johan was dead.

CHAPTER 60

Minsk, Belarus
Kate

Our team walked into the hotel, along with Liv; my legs still hurt, but I felt stronger. I wasn't sure whether that was due more to the medicine that Dr. Bakshi had prescribed, the antidote, that we'd destroyed the lab, or the fact that we'd found Liv Barker. It seemed like all of us were walking on air. We went directly to Scarborough's room, where the rest of the team who had come with us to Belarus was waiting. When we walked in, the team was smiling—every single one, even Scarborough.

They began to clap, and Liv's face started to crumple again. I put my arm around her and whispered to her that it would be okay and that she was safe now. A thing I'd repeated to her several times already. Lena came up and gave her a hug. She said, "How would you feel about making a call to your parents and a shower with some clean clothes?" Liv nodded her head but continued to cry.

Lena helped Liv to her computer and used a secure line to video chat with Liv's parents. They had already been contacted by Scarborough, letting them know that their daughter had been found. They answered on the first ring, likely having been waiting by their computer for the communication to come through. Their wet faces lit up the screen, and when they saw their daughter's face, Liv's mom said, "Liv?" When Liv nodded her head, all of them—Liv, her sisters and mother and father—all broke down. Liv's mom touched the screen as if she could touch her daughter's face, the longing to hold her child so apparent and acute that it made me ache.

When the call was ended, there wasn't a dry eye in the room, many of us were holding each other and openly weeping. Lena helped Liv up and to her room to shower. I wanted to go with them—I had this kind of visceral need to stay by Liv and keep her safe until she got to her parents—but I had to stay to debrief. I was still incredibly tired and weak, though I was beginning to feel improvements already. The fact that I was walking on my own, though feebly, was a testament to the effectiveness of the antidote.

We told everyone what had happened at the lab. They'd heard much of it over our comms, but they weren't there to see it, and it was pretty sensational. We told them about when we'd walked back into the lab and seen that Johan had shot himself in the head with a gun that he'd had stashed in a drawer. Liv had sucked in a breath at the sight, but she didn't cry for Johan. No one did.

Johan may have had some redeeming moments, mainly in keeping Liv alive, but he had still held her there, in filth, with only enough food to survive. He took part in killing thousands with the virus— test subjects and remote peoples alike. He would find no fan in me. And as much as I wanted to know what he knew about the NOS, I did worry that taking him with us would have put an even bigger target on our backs.

The last thing we told the team was that we'd torched the place when we left. We made sure the fire was started deep within the lab so that by the time the fire station was alerted, there would be nothing left of the place. We didn't tell them that we let Liv light the first match. We'd finally caught the NOS by surprise. I wished I could see their faces when they found out that all of their work had been destroyed and that their prized scientists were dead.

After our debrief, I went to the room that I shared with Lena and said good night to Liv. She was in Lena's nightclothes, and I don't think that she cared one bit that they were several sizes too big. She was clean, and she was in clean clothes. Liv watched me limp to my suitcase. "How are you feeling?"

It was such a normal question that it caught me off guard. "I'm okay, I guess. Still in pain, my legs ache like crazy."

She nodded. "It will take a few days, and a lot of rest, to get fully better." Huh, I guess I'd forgotten that she had been through what I was going through several times over. This poor girl—I wanted to coddle her and make up for all of her suffering for the past seven months. She had spent *seven months* in a dirty basement office, and she was still here. Not only to tell her story but to offer me help. Finding Liv had been, and would forever be, a highlight of my life. I thought in that moment that knowing her might even be better. She had come through something not many others could have, and I couldn't wait to see what she would become.

She was staying with Lena tonight, which meant that I had been kicked out. I didn't mind, there was somewhere else I wanted to be anyway. I told them good night and walked a few doors down.

I knocked on Jake's door, and he smiled when he saw me. "I got kicked out of my room."

"Oh good, so Lena got the payment I sent?"

I laughed, and it made me cough—this time the blood was minimal. I knew that without the antidote I would have been on my deathbed, but thanks to Johan, I was improving. My health was improving slowly, but mentally I had traveled by leaps and bounds. Jake took my hand and tugged me through the doorway. "I ordered you some soup. I hoped you might want to eat."

Jake sighed in relief when I said, "That sounds good, actually." He was concerned about my recent weight loss, but I knew that I'd put it all back on. I was healing.

CHAPTER 61

Washington, D.C.
Oliver

Oliver hung up the phone, his mouth gaping. He stared off into the distance, trying to comprehend what he'd just heard from his lifelong friend Luke Barker.

Liv had been found by undercover CIA agents, and she was coming home tomorrow. He wiped at his face.

Valentina peeked around the corner. "Are you ready for your press conference?" Oliver had just officially become the nominee for his party. The convention was a few months off yet, but the last person in his primary had dropped out that morning. He had already been the presumptive nominee, but this was the final nail in the competition's coffin. He would be in the final running for president of the United States. Whether he wanted to or not.

He looked at Valentina, and her eyebrows rose in question. "Are you okay?"

He shook his head and, his voice reverent, said, "Liv has been found." He wiped another stray tear.

Valentina's brows shot downward. "What?" She shook her head. "That's not possible."

He cocked his head—she didn't sound surprised, she sounded like she knew otherwise. "What do you mean, that's not possible?"

Valentina picked up her phone and started typing frantically. "No. No, no, no. That. Is. Not. Possible." She was lost in her own thoughts, saying things that Oliver was sure she wasn't meaning to say aloud. Her face turned a deeper shade of red every moment. Then with fear in her voice, she said, "They're going to find out."

Oliver stood and turned slowly, taking the phone from his wife's hands. "Valentina, what do you mean *that's not possible*?"

She looked at him then, really looked at him, and for the first time she said to him what she was really thinking: "She was supposed to be dead."

She was supposed to be dead. Oliver heard his blood rush through his body, heard his every breath. Just weeks ago, she was telling Oliver that Liv would be found if he became the president. She'd been lying to him, stringing him along, about everything. About Liv. "You've known where she was this entire time." It was a statement, not a question.

"Yes. I knew where she was." She stepped closer to him, her eyes frantic; she was on the verge of panic. "I knew that she was rotting somewhere, because she was supposed to be dead!"

Oliver fisted his hands. Never before had he so much as considered hitting a woman, but he wanted to hit Valentina, he wanted to make her bleed. He held himself back, not because he was a gentleman but because he was afraid that if he got started, he would kill her. "She was at our wedding. You met her, and you let her suffer like that? She is little more than a child."

Valentina lowered her voice. "Yes, I met her. Who do you think told them about her in the first place?" He thought he might pass out; his breathing became labored, his vision blurry. He had married the person who was behind Liv's abduction. This whole time, he'd been the reason that Liv had been taken. Accepting this cursed job had been the catalyst. "Oliver, none of that matters. She was your collateral. She was to keep you on the path to the presidency—the NOS always hedges its bets."

"Who the hell is the NOS?" he roared. He would not be quiet for her, would not give her what she wanted.

"Oliver!" she whisper yelled. "They will kill us both." She swallowed; her fear was glaring. "The NOS is the worldwide AGI. And they will know that we haven't been being honest with them. They will know that mistakes have been made and loose ends have not been tied up." She was almost speaking to herself now. "They are going to find out."

Oliver was still completely lost, but he knew a few things. The first was that his niece had been taken for his ultimate compliance. Thus far he had complied for a paycheck, and nothing he'd had to do had been against his beliefs. He could only assume that they meant to control him when he was in the White House. He said his next thought aloud: "How would you control me if Liv was already dead?"

She shook her head, deep in thought, and said, "We were planning to use her sisters. Threaten you that they would have the same ending if you didn't comply."

His blood ran cold. His best friend had suffered, and could still suffer, in ways that were incomprehensible, just because of their friendship. What had he been thinking, taking this job? He was in so deep, with no way out. When it first started, the stakes were so low—he was just a state senator. But now he was a national figure. He worked for an organization that made and spread viruses, that kidnapped children and manipulated political outcomes. He had been complicit in the latter, but no more.

He was a national figure. He had a clear path to the White House; it was his for the taking. He was on the verge of having massive amounts of control, and he could use it all to fight against the AGI, or the NOS, as it were. They might kill him for it, but before they did, he would fight.

He turned on his heel for the door. Valentina looked at him. "Where are you going?"

He smiled; it was cold and calculated. "I have a speech to give and a presidency to win."

CHAPTER 62

Palo Alto, CA
Vinny

Vinny walked along the beach, still in shock. After Tracy's surgery, the doctors who spoke to Tracy's parents said that she should make a full recovery. But she died in her hospital room only hours later, and as far as he knew, they still weren't sure what the cause of death was.

With Tracy gone, California didn't feel the same. Vinny felt lost, and for the first time he yearned for the Bronx, anything but this loneliness. He kicked at the sand. He could go—there was nothing holding him there anymore. He'd left his job, and the girl he had fallen hard for was gone.

He looked out over the Bay, and it cemented his decision to leave. It all held too many memories. With his heart still heavy, he started the trek back to his car. When he got there, there were a man and a woman, both wearing suits, waiting for him. He was irritated. He'd spent enough time with detectives already.

When they'd found him, after Tracy had been wheeled away with the paramedics, Vinny had been shirtless and covered in Tracy's blood. He'd had a lot to answer for and spent many grueling hours in an interrogation room, when all he wanted was to be at the hospital. Eventually the detectives absolved him of the crime. Though, last he'd heard, they still had no suspects. He hoped that these two weren't here to question him further.

"Vinny Rossi?"

Great. Vinny sighed and nodded his head.

"My name is Matt Sanders." Vinny's head snapped to attention. That was the man who'd called Tracy from the burner phone the day that she'd been shot. He'd kept the phone in his pocket since that day, but he'd never heard from him again. Mr. Sanders motioned to the woman next to him and said, "This is Amy Richards. We are officers of the CIA, and we'd like to ask you a few questions."

Good. Vinny had some questions for him as well. They held out their badges for his inspection. He had no idea what a CIA badge looked like, but he nodded his head in acceptance that they were legit anyway. "Do we need to go somewhere private?"

Officer Sanders smiled tightly and said, "Why don't you come with us. We can talk in our car." He motioned to a black SUV that was a few spots down from his own. Vinny nodded and followed them into the vehicle.

Once they got in, Officer Sanders said, "If you wouldn't mind putting any phones or electronic devices in here." He lifted the console, which appeared to be a built-in Faraday cage. Vinny wouldn't mind having one of those.

Once all of the electronics were stored away in the console that blocked all electromagnetic signal from entering or exiting, Officer Sanders began. "We have reason to believe that Tracy Sinclair was murdered for the things she was ready to tell the world about Search." Vinny blanched; he had been worried that it might have to do with her blog, but he'd worked hard to convince himself that it was a random act of violence. "Tracy was using her blog as an outlet to let the world know what they were really agreeing to when they accepted Search's various privacy policies."

Vinny nodded. "She quit because she disagreed with their practices. Search isn't doing anything illegal. Reprehensible, but not illegal. Why would they feel the need to kill over the information?"

"Because people would leave social media in droves. We believe that Search is run by a worldwide organization that is intent on a New World Order." Vinny's head reared back. "We believe that this is a pivotal time for them, where much of what they have been working on is coming to a head. They do not want their practices looked into, do not want to be in the spotlight. Tracy's blog was gaining followers at an alarming rate. Most anti-Search bloggers are small town. But Tracy had worked there in an upper-level position; she was credible, and it showed in her posts."

Vinny chewed on that for a minute. "So what does this have to do with me?"

"Tracy gave us your name as someone to contact who is still working for Search."

That kind of surprised him, but at the same time, he knew that if they were going to help Tracy with her mission, she would have done just about anything. He missed her tenacity. And he knew that she would love for him to help her cause. He had been ready to do just that the day that he found her bleeding out in her apartment. But things had changed now. Tracy was dead, and Vinny wanted to go home; he had no desire to end up in a casket as well. "I'm not sure that I can help you. I've quit my job at Search, and I've planned to move back home to New York."

Officer Richards tucked a piece of her auburn hair behind her ear and spoke for the first time. "We know that this is a lot to take in. But, Vinny, if we allow this organization to finish their work, you may not have a home to go back to. Everything that you have become accustomed to will change. Everything in your life will change, and not for the better. These people will stop at nothing to accomplish their work. We need all hands on deck to fight them. We need your hands, your brain, as an informant for the CIA. This will only be for a few months, and then you can go home and start your life fresh, knowing that the world is a safer place and you were part of making that happen."

That was quite the speech, but Vinny still wanted no part of it. He'd never wanted to be a hero—he'd leave that to the CIA.

Before he could tell them as much, Officer Richards spoke again, "We can see that you aren't convinced, so let me tell you one more thing, and then you can be on your way. In the autopsy, they found cyanide in Tracy's bloodstream. Whoever shot her came into her hospital room and made sure the job was done right the second time." Vinny thought he might throw up. "She deserves vindication. She can get it from you. Keep the burner phone; Officer Sanders's number is the only one programmed into it. Think about it."

She opened up the protective console and gave Vinny back his things, including the burner phone, and he got out of the car.

CHAPTER 63

Phoenix, AZ
Kate

The plane was descending, and it was bittersweet. I would miss Liv. I never knew her prior to two days ago, yet I felt a kinship with her. I had such a desire to know her and give her everything she'd missed out on over the past months. I wanted to stay in touch, but I knew this was the end of the road. Her knowing me would do her no good. I wasn't even allowed off the plane. None of us were. The airport would be a zoo of press. Much of America had followed Liv's story, even before everyone found out that she was Oliver Strand's goddaughter. But now the story was an absolute sensation. The whole country was excited that she'd been found, and they were anxiously waiting to see her.

We couldn't risk being seen, and so the team would stay on the plane. The world knew that a group of undercover CIA officers had found her, and that's all they would ever know. A quote from one of the books I'd read during my CIA interviews came to mind: "Ultimately, your failures are known, and your successes are not." Rescuing Liv was one success that I was proud of, one that I wouldn't mind being known for, but that was part of the job. It was funny how life turned out—we hadn't gone looking for Liv Barker, and I never considered for one minute that she could still be alive, but when we found her, I felt like I had been searching for her forever.

Like something in the universe clicked into place that fateful night, something good.

When the plane landed, Liv's eyes were filled with tears, as were several of the agents'. Liv was strong and sweet, and though she was dealing with a huge amount of inner turmoil, her spirit shone though. We gave her hugs and said our goodbyes. When she got to Lena and me, she said, "Are you sure we can't keep in touch?"

I said, "When this is all over, we'll find you."

Liv nodded and whispered, "Thank you, thank you so much," in my ear when she gave me a hug. I held her tightly for one moment, and then we all watched her go down the stairs into the waiting arms of her parents and sisters. A reunion so beautiful, it was almost blinding.

The stairs were rolled away, and I watched Liv with her family as the plane pulled forward, and continued to watch for as long as they were still within my view.

Jake came over and sat next to me, handing me a tissue. "How are you feeling?"

I smiled through my tears. "Really good." And I was; I was feeling good about Liv being with her family. And my body was feeling better. I wasn't one hundred percent yet, but I was on my way, and I knew that I would get there. I had a man that I loved who loved me in return. At the moment, life was really good.

Jake grinned at me sheepishly. "Well, hold on to that feeling for the next few minutes, because I have some news. Scarborough spoke with Brahim. The NOS is days away from having quantum computing figured out. We have months at most until they will have it up and running to the point that they can break any encryption."

I whimpered, "Can't I just have one moment of happiness?"

"I gave you your moment. I told you to hold on to it."

I slumped back. "So what now?"

"Now, we go back to work. Our first task is to get Brahim back." I nodded, and Jake said, "Have I told you that you are the most beautiful woman I've ever laid eyes on and that I'm crazy about you?"

I smiled. "Not nearly enough."

My thoughts briefly traveled back to when Scarborough had told Jake and me that being in love with your coworker was a danger and could lead to the wrong kind of priorities out in the field. At the time I'd agreed, but I wondered now if that were actually true. Maybe instead, love made you stronger, made you work harder than you otherwise would have. Perhaps love was the driving force of all of the good in the world, and if there was more of it from one person to another, we would all have different priorities—the right ones.

THE END

SNEAK PEEK

TEN SECONDS TO FREEFALL

Glacier National Park, Montana

The note was rolled and encased in a small plastic tube, and the note writer dropped the tube into the floor air vent on the right side of the hallway, just outside the entrance to Building Five, better known as the barracks. At the allotted time, the note was picked up by a man in the maintenance department, who dropped it into an empty drawer in the cafeteria and it was then picked up by a cook. She dropped the note in with the white linens heading for laundry, then added one black napkin to the top of the pile.

One of the workers in laundry saw the basket of white linens with the one black napkin on top and put the linens into the washer one by one so as not to miss the note. When it rolled out of a napkin, she discretely tucked it into her pocket to deposit later. When the time came, she took the tube from her pocket and put it inside a bath towel. When one of her co-workers came to pick up the towels for delivery, without looking at him, she cleared her throat and patted the stack of the towels in the far left corner of the bin three times. He cleared his throat and left with the bin, and she went back to her work.

He took the towels and delivered them to the apartments in Building Three. At his first stop, room 311, he picked up the top three towels from the far left corner, and put them in the linen closet of the apartment, then went on to finish his job.

There were several ways that notes were passed within the Alternate Government Initiative Montana complex. All of them were through the least monitored departments, all of them making a stop at the same apartment in Building Three. Sometimes the note's journey ended there, other times, a response was given and then a different colored cap was put on the tubing and through the secure network, it was sent on.

When the resident of room 311 got back to his apartment, he went directly to the bathroom, shut the door, and opened the linen closet. He picked the bottom towel out of the stack and opened it up. He caught the note as it rolled out of the towel, before it hit the floor.

He pulled off the cap and upended the tube, letting the note fall into his palm. Then, he rolled it out and read the script twice.

Getting there. Estimation: 8-12 weeks -C

He huffed out a breath, closed his eyes for a second, and swallowed. It wasn't nearly enough time. When he opened his eyes, he looked at himself in the mirror. He couldn't help but notice how ragged he looked. If he weren't careful, others would start to notice as well. He needed more sleep, but there was no time for sleep, or any other luxury for that matter. He ran his hands through his thick dark hair, while deciding how, or if, he should respond. Notes were only passed when absolutely necessary. If any of the note passers were caught, it would mean instant death—if they were lucky. Torture, if they weren't.

Brahim turned on the faucet and splashed his face with cold water. He dried his face with the towel and then rubbed his forehead while he decided what his next steps should be. He was telling the CIA one thing, the AGI another, but he wasn't telling either of them the whole truth. No, the whole truth was reserved only for his group of trusted renegades. The people who were fighting for their freedom, the ones in the trenches. He would give everything he had, including his own life, to secure their safety.

He was walking the edge of a blade with all of his lies and half-truths. So much to keep up with, so little time left. In mere months, quantum computing would be up and running for the AGI at a capacity never before seen. Until just months ago, quantum computers could only work with thousands of quantum bits, more commonly referred to as qubits. But with the new algorithm, the computers would be working with *millions* of qubits. With that kind of capability, the possibilities were endless. And not endless in the way that meant "we don't know where they end," but endless in the literal sense, capable of things seen and unforeseen, with no limit to the possibilities.

With this discovery, the AGI could and would rule the world.

And Brahim, as the leader of the resistance within the AGI, was the only one who could stop it from happening. So he walked that blade's edge, and tried his best to stay balanced.

COMING FALL 2020

ABOUT THE AUTHOR

L.A. Clayton has been an avid reader her entire life, devouring books at an alarming rate. Her husband often jokes that if she didn't buy so many books they could retire. She went to bed one night a reader and woke up with a fresh memory of a dream she'd had the night before, sat down and became a writer.

L.A. Clayton lives in St. Louis, MO with her husband and their four young children. She makes time for writing in between wiping noses and packing lunches.